COPPER
CHAIN

ALSO BY JAMES MAXWELL

THE SHIFTING TIDES

Golden Age
Silver Road

EVERMEN SAGA

Enchantress
The Hidden Relic
The Path of the Storm
The Lore of the Evermen
Seven Words of Power

COPPER CHAIN

THE SHIFTING TIDES, BOOK III

JAMES MAXWELL

Published by 47North, Seattle

www.apub.com

Amazon, the Amazon logo, and 47North are trademarks of Amazon.com, Inc., or its affiliates.

ISBN-13: 9781612185767
ISBN-10: 1612185762

Cover illustration by Fred Gambino
Cover design by Richard Augustus
Map illustration by David Woodroffe

Printed in the United States of America

For my wife, Alicia, with all my love

1

Agathon didn't want to die.

Of course, he wasn't a fool. He knew his time would come at some point. But despite being a man who prayed regularly and believed that when death knocked at his door his soul would be welcomed in paradise, he wanted his end to be as far off as possible. Ideally, he would be in bed, tended by his favorite wife, who would wail and weep, kissing his wrinkled cheeks, as he closed his eyes and finally slept forever. He'd always imagined it would be that way, decades in the future. Not like this.

Not death in battle.

He was well aware that he wasn't a skilled swordsman; his talents had always served him in other areas. He was a bureaucrat, the viceroy of the city of Malakai, governor of a restive populace. Malakai's wealth of gold, furs, slaves, and spices flowed to Agathon's cousin, Kargan, ruler of the Ilean Empire. It was Agathon's job to keep the shipments coming.

His task was far from easy. Malakai was ostensibly the capital of Imakale, but in truth the Ilean garrison rarely patrolled the dry, inhospitable terrain south of the port city. Traders acted as intermediaries between the fierce desert clans and the merchants from Lamara. Even within Malakai's strong walls the locals resented Agathon and the soldiers who served him.

But until recently he had taken pride in his achievements: pacifying unrest, pitting the desert traders against each other, sending fat-bellied ships back home with their holds full of manacled slaves and ingots of gleaming gold.

Then the situation changed.

It began with a rumor. The tribesmen of the south were massing under a new leader, a man who promised to liberate Malakai and unshackle the city's population from the Ilean yoke. The rumor made its way into the city and soon the locals were chanting his name: Palemon.

All through winter the sense of anticipation grew. There were riots in the streets, quickly stamped down by the garrison but becoming more and more unmanageable. Palemon was always spoken of but never seen. They said he was pale-skinned and that he commanded more than a hundred tall warriors, men who wore strange armor of steel links and carried huge swords and axes. A dozen mysterious foreigners in robes traveled with them, carrying staffs that could banish darkness with a spoken word. These people came from across the sea. They were from the lost nation of Aleuthea, destined to reclaim Malakai, for it was the Aleutheans who built the city long ago and now they wanted it back.

Then, when spring came, Agathon's scouts raced back to tell him that there was a large force advancing on the city.

The force wasn't as big as he'd originally feared: less than a thousand strong. A decade ago, before Agathon's time, the clans had rallied and four thousand tribesmen with wooden spears and tall bows had assaulted Malakai and been soundly defeated. The desert men were fierce, but their weapons, not to mention their discipline, made them no match for Ilea's trained soldiers. Wrapped in cloth to ward off the sun's rays, they would face trained swordsmen wearing leather armor and holding triangular shields linked closely together. The city's garrison was far larger than it had been ten years ago; they now had twice their enemy's numbers, as well as the strength of the city walls.

Nonetheless, Agathon was afraid.

The foreigners were an unknown element. The city was primed for revolt. And in battle, someone always died. Agathon was smart enough to know that the first casualties would be those most fearful, the fighters with little experience. People like him.

Standing on the city walls, Agathon clasped his shaking hands together, casting a swift glance at General Dhuma to see if the veteran soldier had noticed. But everyone, including Dhuma, was gazing at the flat, yellow horizon, where the enemy had gathered like a thin line of distant trees. It was just before dawn, and the sun was steadily rising, washing the sky with purple and gold. The air was utterly still, filled only with the occasional cough of a soldier, creak of leather armor, or whisper of men talking in hushed tones.

Agathon scanned along the line of defenders gathered on the battlements, trying to take comfort in their numbers. Nearly two thousand men prepared to defend the city. Standing four or five deep, bows, spears, and swords at the ready, they were all staring in the same direction. Drawing in a deep breath, incredibly conscious of his heartbeat, Agathon inspected the defenders in the other direction. Were they all as terrified as he was? If they were, they didn't show it.

When he turned back, he realized General Dhuma was watching him, his lips curved in a tight smile. A decade older than Agathon, with weathered skin and sharp, patrician features, Dhuma wore full leather armor, well worn, the tears and scratches reminding Agathon that the general had survived more than a few battles in the past. His helmet had a tall crest of horsehair, bleached white, yet Dhuma appeared unperturbed that a man like himself, so clearly an officer, would draw enemies like moths to a flame.

'You'll see, Viceroy,' Dhuma said, nodding in the direction of the enemy. 'We'll send these vermin back where they came from. No doubt we'll be celebrating our victory over lunch.'

Agathon and Dhuma hadn't always been on the best of terms, but now the general's presence was solid and reassuring. Whatever Dhuma had done to get assigned to this distant outpost, far from home, it didn't matter anymore. What mattered was that he was confident of victory, and he was well aware that Kargan, the King of Kings, was Agathon's cousin. Dhuma had assigned six of his best warriors to Agathon's personal protection. Things wouldn't go well for him if Agathon died.

Again Agathon found his mind turning to his own death. He tried not to, but couldn't help imagining what it would feel like to have a spear thrust into his chest, tearing at his insides, or to take an arrow in the throat, trying in vain to clasp his hands over the wound as red liquid gushed out and he drowned in his own blood. He bit his lip, knowing that Dhuma could see his face turning white.

'Perhaps I might be more useful—' he began.

Dhuma glanced to the left and right and then came in close, lowering his voice. 'Viceroy, you are honor bound to stand with the men. I've told you: I'll keep you safe. I know this isn't what you're good at, but it heartens us all to see you here.' He gazed into Agathon's eyes, fixing the nobleman with an unblinking stare. 'Remember, every one of the savages is going to face two of our soldiers. Victory is assured. If you stay, when they talk about this battle, my men will remember that you were here. But if you leave, you will carry the stain with you for the rest of your days.'

Agathon steadied himself. 'Of course, General. It's my choice to be here, and I would never have it otherwise.'

'Good man,' Dhuma said, clapping him on the back and withdrawing.

Suddenly a soldier cried out. 'Something's happening.'

Agathon squinted at the enemy on the flat desert plain. Their line still hadn't moved, but with the sun cresting the horizon a clutch of warriors in the middle had begun to sparkle as slanted rays shone off their steel armor.

He tensed, wondering what it was that had made the soldier shout. It wasn't that the enemy was approaching; the large force was still assembled at the limits of vision.

Then, peering into the distance, he realized.

4

A haze of yellow dust had begun to color the sky where before it was a pure shade of blue. It came from nothing: there was no wind. In the midst of the enemy, a fierce light suddenly flared. As the light shone brighter and brighter, the haze became a thick cloud, filled with swirling particles of grit. A sandstorm was gathering, rising higher, becoming thicker, until soon the enemy couldn't be seen at all.

Agathon and the general exchanged stunned glances.

So close to the desert, sandstorms struck the city occasionally, but Agathon had never seen anything like this. Without wind . . .

Wait. He realized there was a wind.

The still air gave way to a steady breeze, causing the orange flags carried by the standard bearers to snap and crackle. The growing wind whipped at Agathon's loose trousers and blew his long hair around his face as it became stronger. Soon it was howling with sudden ferocity.

Dust and sand billowed above the plain. There was no way to say where the enemy was or what they were doing. Squinting into the storm, Agathon felt tiny grains strike his exposed face and he jerked his head violently when sharp grit flew into his eyes. He ducked his head and shielded his eyes with his hands, blinking as tears trickled down his cheeks.

Over the sound of the wind he could hear his soldiers muttering prayers to the gods, while others called out to their companions, asking what was happening.

'Hold your posts!' General Dhuma bellowed. 'No one leaves these walls!'

As it became almost impossible to see, Agathon copied the soldiers around him and sank to one knee, burying his head into his chest. The defenders fought their own private battles with the sandstorm, and at the forefront of every man's thoughts was the notion that surely the timing was too close to be coincidence. Agathon remembered the stories about the dozen foreigners who wore robes and carried strange staffs.

No, he told himself. The wind would die down. Long-lasting sandstorms needed days to build up their strength. It would soon pass.

Yet time dragged on, and if anything the wind gained in power. Agathon occasionally heard Dhuma's voice roaring over the storm, telling the defenders to stand fast. His cries were like a beacon on a dark night, providing hope that someone else was out there.

But then the general gave a command that caused Agathon's heart to beat out of time.

'To arms! We're under attack!'

Agathon shot to his feet as he heard the sudden clang of steel striking against steel. He closed his eyes into thin slits and drew his sword. Hearing grunts of effort and screams of pain at his left, through the haze he saw the tops of ladders leaning against the battlements. Attackers in armor of steel chain were climbing the ladders, and Agathon's eyes widened as he saw that his archers' arrows were bouncing off them without striking flesh. Below the armored soldiers, clansmen were gazing up at the walls as they ascended, and Agathon's enfeebled vision took in dozens of ladders just in the section of wall he could see.

Holding his sword with both shaking hands, he was forced to face forward when, just in front of him, two ladders slapped against the stone in quick succession. A tall, pale-skinned warrior with gray-streaked hair and a braided beard threw himself onto the battlements. Defenders rushed at the warrior as he swung a two-handed sword in great sweeping arcs, cutting his opponents down one after another. Dark eyes blazing, the warrior met every defender head-on. Arrows ricocheted from his chain armor until he cannoned into the men holding the bows. While the tall warrior cleared the wall, more armored attackers surged up from below. Every one of them was met by a defender. Every defender fell under the onslaught.

Suddenly there were no more Ileans for the tall warrior to face. He turned his attention to Agathon, and Agathon raised his weapon.

Palemon's men poured into the breach he'd opened and he quickly scanned the battlements before rushing to the next melee, charging into the fray and scattering enemies with savage blows of his broadsword. A swarthy soldier raised his triangular shield to ward off Palemon's overhead strike, but the wood shattered into fragments, the blade continuing into the man's neck, cleaving his head from his body. Another opponent tried to bring his spear to bear, but Palemon knocked it away and thrust the point of his weapon into his enemy's chest. The grim-faced Ileans fought bravely, but their shorter swords couldn't touch him, their spears were too big for close combat, and their arrows couldn't pierce his chain mail.

Hundreds of defenders died from being thrown off the walls, screaming as they fell into the void. There was fighting everywhere; vicious hand-to-hand combat with every one of Palemon's men facing two or more opponents. Bodies littered the area and combined with the pools of blood to make footing treacherous.

The thick line of defenders splintered into fragments, each group vainly trying to stem the flow of Palemon's cold bloods as they climbed up from the ladders and formed knots of their own. The clansmen from the desert played their part too, launching volleys of arrows and supporting the warriors from Necropolis with their greater numbers. The Ilean archers directed their fire onto the natives, sending cloth-wrapped warriors screaming as they fell from the ladders with arrows sprouting from their bodies.

With the aid of half a dozen cold bloods Palemon cleared section after section. Looking past the next group of defenders, he saw an officer, a veteran with weathered skin and a white crest on his helm, calling on his men to hold together. Palemon fought to reach him, but Ilean soldiers kept coming at him, and then he lost the officer altogether.

He was red-faced and panting, his arms growing heavy from wielding his sword, but he knew that despite the streaks of gray in his hair he was at the peak of physical fitness, the warrior king of a people born to fight. The defenders fell like flies, swatted into oblivion by axes, hammers, and swords fashioned long ago in Aleuthea. The magical wind was dying down and the air was clearing, but Zara's work was done: grit was in the defenders' eyes and terror was forcing them to flee in droves.

His chest heaving, Palemon paused to scan the long walls for the next pocket of resistance. The officer was gone: either fled or fallen, but he saw Zara a hundred paces away. The sorceress stood at a corner tower with two of her fellow magi. She was easily distinguishable from her companions: the two men wore gray robes and clutched staffs crowned with hoops of gold, while Zara held the staff that she had used to summon the wind that brought the *Solaris* to these lands and to cast sand into the eyes of the defenders: a straight wooden pole with a warped twist of pure silver at its summit. Slender and beautiful, with high cheekbones and skin like marble, Zara's black hair flowed sleek and straight down her back and she wore a figure-hugging dress of dark blue. She was pointing out something to one of her fellows when a wiry Ilean suddenly launched himself toward her. She turned and calmly pointed her staff at him. The silver device glowed, and a pocket of air struck the center of his chest and propelled him from the walls. A moment later she was speaking with her companion again.

Smiling and shaking his head as he panted, Palemon continued to rove his eyes along the walls. The haze had cleared enough for him to see all the way to the farthest tower, and now he knew without a doubt that his plan had succeeded. A few final skirmishes were being fought here and there, but the last of the Ileans were throwing aside their arms.

The defenders were swiftly cut down anyway, dying with piercing screams. Palemon and his people were cold bloods. They had no warmth in their hearts. They were as strong as iron, as hard as ice.

The battle was over, the walls now filled with warriors clad in chain mail and a greater number of dark-skinned clansmen from the desert.

Blood-drenched and gasping, dazed but victorious, one after another broke out in smiles as they stood over the fallen.

But Palemon didn't smile with them. He had yet to achieve his true objective.

'Sire.' A rough, gravelly voice cut through the sudden quiet.

The fighters ranged along the walls stirred as a shorter figure moved through them, his broad shoulders shoving them out of the way. Kyphos finally appeared, stomping toward Palemon, a half-moon axe in his hand and congealed blood coating his forearms.

He was moving quickly, urgently. His shaggy black eyebrows were close together, narrowed over his deep-set eyes. Palemon wasn't surprised to see Kyphos covered in gore; despite the fact that his neck was hunched forward on his shoulders, he had a powerful frame, with muscular arms and a broad chest, and was nearly as skilled in battle as Palemon himself.

'Kyphos!' Palemon barked. 'Gather the men. We need to secure the harbor.'

There were ships in Malakai, at least seven of them: merchant vessels, but still seaworthy enough that they might be used to return to Necropolis for the women, children, and old men left behind. Palemon had embarked on a dangerous voyage to find these lands, but the remainder of his people wouldn't survive long: the musk ox, reindeer, white bears, and orca had all been hunted to near-extinction. Winter supplies were meager. Back in the land of ice and snow, he knew that starvation would have already begun to claim lives.

'There's a problem,' Kyphos said, meeting Palemon's eyes. 'At the end, the officer with the white crest on his helm fled with the last of the defenders.' Kyphos's face was grim. 'They were heading for the harbor.'

Palemon whirled to face the city. During the fighting he'd had little chance to take it in, but now that he was gazing at it, he wasn't thinking about the fact that Malakai was beautiful and grand, with a sizeable population and a wealth of riches – instead, every tall building and winding avenue was now an obstacle, a barrier between the walls and the distant harbor.

He roared at the men around him. 'Everyone who can hear my voice! Follow me!'

⌣‾‾⌣

Palemon and Kyphos watched together, wheezing as they regained their breath. The harbor was little more than a sandy shore, with fishing boats pulled up onto the beach and a solitary pier stretching out into the deep water so ships could dock. Aside from some baskets and coiled-up ropes, the pier was empty.

Filled with despair, Palemon fixed his gaze on the sails vanishing into the horizon.

'There was no way we could have stopped them,' Kyphos said.

'We should have seized the harbor first.'

'How? The clansmen aren't sailors. We have no boats. We had to take the walls.'

Palemon clenched his fists at his sides as he watched the sails becoming smaller and smaller. He finally turned to Kyphos.

'This isn't going to be easy,' he said.

2

Chloe was trapped.

Her prison was a large one: a long, low island with forests at one end and stretches of barren rock at the other. It was a place where she could roam and wander, with screeching sea birds for company and the crashing waves almost like distant conversation. There were parts she wasn't supposed to visit, such as the Oracle's cave set into the misshapen hill on the isle's western side, but everywhere else was hers to explore. Nonetheless, the dark-blue sea surrounding Athos on all sides was a barrier that separated her from everything she cared about. Sometimes she wondered if she would ever be able to leave.

She had no memory of her journey to Athos. But she did remember using her power to help Eiric fight Triton and reclaim the eldran homeland, and then finding herself alone in Sindara afterward. Soon after, an agonizing pain had struck her with force, deep inside her skull. The four magi appeared as if from nowhere. They said they'd been looking for her, and that she had to go with them.

Tears welled in her eyes when she thought about her father, Aristocles. When Chloe had told the magi she had to find him, the mysterious men who served the Oracle said that he was dead. She'd heard their words distantly, even as unconsciousness took her.

It was much later that she woke up on this island. And it was then that the magi told her how her father had died: murdered by four rival consuls, chief among them Nilus, her father's oldest friend.

It had taken her time to grieve, and to adjust to her new circumstances. Athos was a special place; the magi had told her. She needed to be on the island to recover. She had to learn the things they could teach her.

Chloe now sat cross-legged at the top of a cliff, with waves crashing far below. Blinking away the tears, closing her eyes as she took a slow breath, she kept her mind clear of all thought as she contemplated the power inside her.

She could feel it always, like the embers of a fire that only needed fuel to be added in order to become a raging inferno. Her objective was to keep it stilled. Meditation helped, and she hadn't had any headaches for at least a month. If she remained calm and at peace – something that came easily on Athos, a place where she had few people to talk to and little changed from one day to the next – she would remain in control.

It was early in the day and the sun's rays were warm on her skin. A gentle breeze carried the smell of salt from the sea, blowing her long, dark hair around her face. Now that winter was past, she spent as much time as possible outdoors, keeping herself fit by running up and down the hills, and she was strong and lean, glowing with health and vitality. Her back was straight as she breathed in and out, feeling time stand still, but knowing that when she opened her eyes she would look at the sun and be surprised at how much of the day had passed.

As always, thoughts tried to bubble to the surface. Dion's face came to her vision; he was smiling, regarding her with warm, brown, intelligent eyes. He wasn't as she'd last seen him, in the Wilds north of Xanthos, caught between his eldran heritage and human upbringing, torn between his feelings for her and the fact that she was destined to marry his older brother. Instead he was smiling and at ease, handsome and well fed, his strong jaw cleanly shaven and his flaxen hair neatly combed, wearing a regal, expensive tunic. This was how she always pictured him, for Dion was now the king of Xanthos. Nikolas was dead, said to have taken a bad wound during the battles with Ilea. Chloe was now free to love Dion, but in all likelihood, he thought she was dead. Bitter remorse welled up inside her. He might have already found a wife, a new queen of Xanthos, a woman to bear him an heir. Meanwhile she was far away, trapped on this remote island.

Her training came to the fore, and as the fire inside her spiked she acknowledged the painful thoughts but pushed them away. Instead she concentrated on the regular pulsing rhythm of the waves as they were drawn in and out by the breath of Silex the sea god. She focused on the smell of the air, and the sensation of the cool breeze against her skin. Regaining her inner peace, her power slowly stilled.

When she was finished, she opened her eyes and stretched before climbing to her feet. She swept her gaze over the sea, taking one last look at the ocean.

Chloe's eyes widened.

There was a distant ship, a bireme from its shape and size, approaching from the south as it gave the rocky isle and its cliffs a wide berth. It was too far away for her to make out its colors, but she could see the pale little lines that were its oars and the square sail opened up to catch the wind. For a moment she thought it was going to skirt the island completely, but then the sail shifted and the vessel began to turn, until its bow was facing Seer's Cove.

The ship was heading to Athos!

Trade on the Maltherean Sea always came to a halt during the winter storms, and with the Xanthian outpost of Fort Liberty in the sea's center now a thriving port of call, it had been months since a ship had come to Athos. In all the time that Chloe had been here, not a single ship from Xanthos or Phalesia had visited.

She gazed at the ship for a moment longer, and then she left the cliff behind and started to run.

‿‿‿‿‿

Chloe was panting, standing on a hillside that divided the island into two halves, screened by a grove of trees. She leaned against a trunk as she caught her breath, watching as the huge warship, eighty feet long, with two decks of oars and a towering mast, coasted slowly into the placid cove, running aground before the rowers leaped out the sides and hauled the vessel up onto the soft sand of the beach.

Disappointment sank into her chest.

She could already see from the ship's orange-and-yellow flag that it was Ilean, and the swarthy skin of the sailors and the whip marks on the shoulders of the grunting oarsmen confirmed it. There was little chance that she could pass a message to her sister in Phalesia or to Dion in Xanthos, letting them know she was alive.

The sailors lowered a gangway, until the stepped wooden plank stretched from the topmost deck to the shore. A gray-bearded man in a bright-yellow robe disembarked with a chest in his arms. His face solemn, he climbed up the shore until he reached the low stone wall that separated the beach from the bank above it. Two of the magi met him at the wall and they exchanged words, but no one stepped onto the path. As the Ilean emissary set down the chest, Chloe could see that it was heavy.

She jumped when a soft voice spoke beside her.

'A gift from Kargan, king of Ilea.' Turning, she saw one of the four magi standing beside her; he'd approached without a sound. 'We receive many offerings, but few are brave enough to step onto the path.'

He paused, regarding her for a moment. His eyes were dark, sunken into his cheeks, for like his three identical brothers his frame was emaciated, almost skeletal, making his white robe appear overly large on his body. He was as bald as they were, but had three brown spots on his wrinkled scalp, which allowed Chloe to know that she was talking to Zedo, the man she thought of, more than the other three, as her teacher.

Zedo cocked his head, assessing her. 'You realize that you are not yet ready to leave?'

'Will they be sailing north?'

'No.' He shook his head. 'Ilea always sends an offering at the beginning of spring. When they are finished here, they will return to Lamara.'

Chloe frowned. 'I'm going to talk to the captain anyway.' She started to move forward, but the magus called out.

'Chloe. Stop.'

She turned. 'I'm not trying to leave. I just want to give them a message. My sister—'

'Your sister is well. I have already told you. She lives and studies as a novice priestess in Phalesia.'

'She has no one. And our father's murderer is Phalesia's first consul!'

'Your sister is unaware—'

'And you think that means she's any safer? Sophia's clever. If she finds out the truth, she won't let it go.' Chloe's anger suddenly turned to frustration and sorrow. 'And she thinks I'm dead, too. Even if I can't go to her, I can at least tell her . . .'

'I promise you,' Zedo said, 'if a ship comes that can carry word to Phalesia, we will speak with the captain. But that is not the ship you want to entrust with your message. King Kargan is someone who only thinks of how he can strengthen the Ilean Empire.'

Zedo came forward and reached out to clasp her shoulder, a gesture that surprised her, for he rarely showed warmth.

'Your training is progressing . . .'

'I haven't learned anything.'

'You have learned inner control. The rest is closer to you than you may think.' He met her eyes as he spoke, his voice soft but filled with import. 'Remember. Your path to magic is an unusual one. You have a strong natural talent, but it was awakened late in your life. It is a dangerous combination, one that has brought you to your current position, for when the dam broke, what should have been a trickle of power soon became a flood.'

'But you still haven't told me why we have to stay here,' Chloe said. 'You said this place is special. How? Why can't we go to Phalesia, perhaps together? Even for a short while?'

He was silent for a moment, before he slowly nodded. 'Perhaps it is now time I told you some things. You have been to the heart of Sindara and seen the pool, where there is a green jewel resting at the bottom, deep below the surface. The eldren call it the Wellspring, and it is the origin of their power.'

'I remember,' she said. The pool had glowed fiercely as life returned to Sindara, emerald light shining throughout the glade.

'Here at Athos, we humans have our own wellspring, which we call the Source. It is said that the gods gave the jewels as gifts to the two races, that they gifted the eldren the magic of living things, and humans the magic of the elements.' Zedo gave a slight shrug. 'If the Oracle knows the truth, she has never told us.'

He touched the tips of his fingers to Chloe's temple.

'Being close to the Source restores your balance. But if you were to leave this island before you are ready, you would suffer again. The power of the Source is stronger in Athos than anywhere else.'

Chloe's brow furrowed. 'This jewel . . . the Source. It's in the Oracle's cave, isn't it?'

Zedo started. 'How did you—?'

'The fires. They cluster around the cave. And the flame the Oracle stares into is the biggest of all.'

'You have a quick mind. I have always thought so. Yes, the jewel is deep in the cave.' The magus hesitated. 'Like you, my brothers and I came to our powers late. After a raid saw our village enslaved, our captors decided that because we all look the same we were cursed and gave us as offerings to the Oracle. Those who were the Oracle's guardians before us taught us what they knew, but because we were no longer children we had to solve the same problems you must solve now. Even we cannot leave Athos for long periods . . . We are destined to live out our lives here. The Oracle cannot leave her cave; her ability to see the future is bound to the jewel.'

Zedo turned to look down from the top of the hill, gazing toward the opposite side of the island from Seer's Cove, where there was a sprawling cluster of crumbled ruins. Once it had been a series of grand temples, but now only a few of the stone structures were standing. Chloe and the brothers ate, slept, and studied in the shell of what had once been a long dormitory, with enough beds for hundreds.

'This is where fate has brought you. Once, long ago, we taught many, and the head priests and priestesses of our temples around the world were all able to call on the materia in times of need. Now we must teach again.'

'But what purpose is there to it?'

'We receive many gifts of precious goods and rare metals. Raiders are always a threat. But we are also well placed to know about the affairs of the world, and how to shape the future to the betterment of all. Sometimes the Oracle has visions, and gives us direct guidance, as with you.'

Chloe tilted her head, surprised. Zedo often spoke of things that she knew he hadn't seen with his own eyes – like her father's death. But he'd never revealed why they'd gone to such lengths to help her. 'What did the Oracle say about me?'

'The world is about to face a new threat, greater than any before,' he said. 'The Oracle believes that you may have an opportunity to end it.'

'She is the Oracle. Doesn't she know?'

'No,' he said firmly. 'It involves the eldren – and one in particular. His presence in your future interferes with the Oracle's ability to see.'

'Who is he?'

'I think you know the answer.' He spread his hands. 'If you learn, you can leave. But if you leave before you are ready, you will not live long.'

'Then teach me more,' Chloe said. She lifted her chin. 'I'm ready.'

Zedo smiled. 'I believe you may be.' He gazed into her eyes. 'You truly believe you are?'

'I do.'

'Then come. Today, you will learn how to listen to the wind.'

3

Kargan, King of Kings, ruler of the Ilean Empire, leaned forward on the high-backed ebony throne. The occasion was formal, and he was dressed for the part, wearing a flowing orange robe with a belt of woven gold. His mop of dark hair was combed and oiled, and his beard curled outward from his chin. He hated the ceremonies and customs of the court, but he knew he needed to play his part nonetheless.

He gripped the arms of the throne as he regarded his guest, trying to keep his expression pleasant, for Lord Samar, prince of Haria, was a powerful nobleman in his own right. Twice Kargan's age, Samar's face was as wrinkled as a raisin, but his eyes were intelligent and his bearing was proud. The nation of Haria, with its great port city of Efu dominating the Ilean Sea, had a special relationship with the empire, and trade between Haria and Ilea dwarfed that of the other dominions. In return for giving Kargan his allegiance, Samar expected Kargan's help when he asked for it.

'Well, Lord Samar, is it enough?'

Standing in front of the throne, flanked by priests, lords, and courtiers on both sides, the prince of Haria glanced down at the three wooden chests on the floor in front of him. The lids were open, tilted back on their hinges, revealing the shining gold coins within. Kargan disliked depleting his treasury, but if the gold was necessary to preserve his empire, it was a price he would pay gladly.

Lord Samar looked up again, meeting Kargan's eyes. 'I will speak plainly, Great King. It may be enough to put down the rebellion. The gold will buy weapons and armor, and the promise of greater pay will call many of the deserters back to my service. I can bribe some of the rebel leaders to betray their fellows, and perhaps it will even give me the head of the snake. But'—he let the word hang for a moment—'I would prefer to return to my homeland with twice this amount. It is to both of our interests that this . . . situation . . . is resolved quickly.'

Kargan tried not to scowl. He wasn't angry at the prince of Haria, who was doing his best to crush a rebellion and restore order to his realm, and had the grace to be candid. It was the fact that tribal loyalties and local independence movements were always trying to unravel the order he'd created. Since becoming king he'd brought about peace between the Galean nations and Ilea, and trade was thriving. He'd installed programs to reduce poverty, and at the insistence of the king of Xanthos he'd even regulated the treatment of slaves. His soldiers patrolled the streets of his cities night and day; crime was at its lowest level for decades, even in the smaller towns.

Rebellion led to chaos, and chaos led to death. As a military leader, he'd always looked after the safety and well-being of his men. Now that he was king, his responsibility was to every inhabitant of the Ilean Empire.

'I appreciate your candor, Lord Samar, and so I will share something with you in kind . . .'

As he spoke, Kargan's eyes drifted to Javid, standing behind the file of courtiers but so tall that he towered head and shoulders above the rest. A skilled warrior with broad features, thick lips, and his hair tied back behind his head, Javid was also his most loyal adviser, and the only man alive whom, now that he was king, Kargan would call a friend. But he was a commoner, and as such Kargan could only harvest his thoughts when they were away from prying eyes.

While the prince of Haria waited for Kargan's revelation, Kargan saw Javid give him a slight nod.

'The truth is that I'm expecting a shipment of gold to arrive any day. When I promised you gold, it was this shipment that I had in mind.' Kargan frowned. 'But unfortunately it's late. I'm trying not to think about pirates, or storms, or several other things that readily occur to me. You may wait if you wish, or you may return home with the gold in front of you. I respect you enough to know that the choice should be yours.'

Kargan raised his voice, casting his gaze over the assembled people all watching him speak. 'And I say this to everyone here today . . .'

He lifted his arm to point toward the huge tapestry covering an entire wall of the throne room. It was a decorative map of the Ilean Empire, with the seven great cities and the three seas represented in stunning detail.

'We remain united!' Kargan thundered, as everyone turned to look at the map. 'We lost Koulis, but Koulis was founded by Galeans, and their culture and ours were always different. We tried to conquer Phalesia, but Phalesia is far from here, on the other side of the Maltherean Sea. An empire of seven cities, working together, is our natural state, as decreed by the gods.' He glared at the yellow-robed priests in the crowd, who of course had no choice but to nod and bow. Still pointing at the map, he then named the cities in turn, from east to west. 'Efu. Abadihn. Serca. Lamara. Abbas. Verai. Malakai.'

His mouth twisted at the last, for it was gold from Malakai that was late. He lowered his arm and looked down at the prince of Haria from his tall throne.

'The seven great cities will always be linked in common cause, and that includes Efu. No matter what comes, Lord Samar, we will support you in your time of need.'

The prince of Haria gave a deep bow, and when he rose again he looked clearly impressed. 'I thank you, Great King. I will take the gold you offer, and make every coin count. I give my utmost gratitude to Helios for your continued support.'

———⌣———

'Your oratorical skills are improving,' Javid said when everyone else had left.

'It helps when you believe what you're saying,' Kargan grunted as he wriggled off his uncomfortable perch to stand in front of his friend. He glanced back over his shoulder and scowled. 'By the gods, I hate that throne.'

'Having responsibility is making you more truthful.' Javid nodded solemnly. 'It is good to see.'

'Truthful? Hah!' Kargan barked a laugh. 'Just yesterday I told the priests that they could have their new temple, but work wouldn't begin until the restorations on the arena were complete. Then I went to the arena and told them to stop working until the gold arrived from Malakai. We both know that if and when the shipment comes, it won't be used to restore the arena.'

Javid frowned. 'The god Helios says that all men must be truth—'

'Enough, Javid.' Kargan held up a hand. 'I do what I must, and, as I said, where the empire is concerned, I believe everything I say.' He raised an eyebrow. 'So, what do you think? Will Lord Samar put down his rebellion?'

'Your speech had an effect on him. He will do his best with the gold you gave him. Only time will tell.'

'Another problem deferred, rather than solved.' Kargan shook his head. 'Still, we could be lucky—'

'Great King!' A palace guard entered the throne room and bowed. 'A small fleet is approaching the harbor. They're flying Lord Agathon's colors!'

Kargan and Javid exchanged glances.

'They're from Malakai. The gold,' Kargan said, immediately spurred into action, taking long strides toward the exit.

'But why a fleet?' Javid muttered.

—

Lamara's riverside harbor was quiet. It was late in the day and the sun was slowly setting, casting a rosy glow on the huge wooden warships lined up side by side. Kargan paced just in front of the mess hall, a long, thatched structure with smoke trickling from its chimney. His brow furrowed as he watched the brown waters of the great watercourse that led from Lamara to the sea. He peered downstream, clenching and unclenching his fists, willing the first ship to appear. Meanwhile Javid's words stayed with him.

Why a fleet?

There should be one ship, or two at most if Agathon was sending a significant quantity of cargo. Two ships hardly constituted a fleet. He glanced at the long bank, seeing that even with dozens of biremes resting side by side, so close together they were almost touching, there was still enough space left over for twice their number.

But why a fleet?

Perhaps the message from the scouts had become muddled. It didn't happen often, for all runners were trained to recall messages word for word, including inflections and pauses. Anyone who made mistakes didn't last long at his job.

Kargan cursed under his breath, making sure he wasn't heard by his guards. He glanced at Javid, standing nearby, his fingers hooked into his trousers as he gazed downriver along with everyone else. He was irrationally angry at Javid for planting the thought in his mind that something was wrong. There was obviously no danger, for the naval patrols would never let an enemy fleet come anywhere near the empire's capital. Perhaps Agathon had simply decided to send some unneeded vessels home, or perhaps some foreign merchants had asked to travel in convoy.

A ship slowly slid into view.

It was a wide merchant galley, the same kind that always came to deliver gold and other goods from Malakai. Kargan, a man of the sea, even knew this particular vessel. Traveling on oars alone against the weak current, it gradually became larger and larger, until Kargan could see that it was indeed flying his cousin's flag. A second ship soon appeared behind it, and then a third. Galleys trailed after the lead vessels, while a bireme brought up the rear. The light was fading quickly, but there was still enough to see that from bow to stern they appeared to be filled with men.

Kargan ceased his pacing and frowned, his attention on the lead merchant vessel. He was relieved to see that of the seven ships that made up the fleet, not one appeared to be blackened by flame or crippled by combat. He couldn't see any storm damage and none of them were riding low enough in the water to be sinking.

As they made their laborious way into the harbor, the sun set completely, casting the approaching vessels into darkness. The sandy shore was still bright, lit by torches on poles, but the ships were hulking shadows as they drove up onto the bank. Kargan met Javid's eyes and then headed down toward the water's edge to greet the new arrivals. His ever-present guards fell in behind and lined up behind Kargan and Javid as they peered into the night. Waiting impatiently in front of the lead merchant galley, Kargan heard a series of splashes.

Suddenly a silhouette appeared and then a staggering man was revealed in the flickering light of the torches on the beach. He stumbled forward, climbing out of the shallows, and the first thing Kargan noticed was that he had a weeping red slash across his face. His leather armor, scarred by battle, marked him as a soldier, and he held a comrade in his arms like a child.

Two more soldiers exited the water, carrying a third between them. The man in the center's face was as white as a sheet, and rivulets of sweat trickled down his face as he groaned. Looking down, Kargan's chest became tight with horror when he saw that the wounded man's leg had been amputated below the thigh.

They kept coming. From every boat, soldiers made their way to the safety of their homeland, and almost every one of them bore crudely-bandaged wounds. Some collapsed as soon as they reached dry land; others fought grimly to help those with the worst injuries climb the shore.

Kargan was gasping. He couldn't believe how many Ilean soldiers had been crammed into these vessels; there must have been hundreds.

'Get these men some help!' he bellowed behind him and his guards leaped to follow his orders. 'And someone tell me what in the names of all the gods is going on!'

'Great King.'

Kargan whirled when he heard a voice behind him. He immediately recognized the officer in front of him. General Dhuma looked weary to the core, but he was uninjured, standing slumped, with his white-crested helm clutched under his arm.

'We lost the city,' Dhuma said. 'Two weeks ago. Malakai . . .' He shook his head, struggling to find words. 'The walls fell. We were the only ones who made it out alive.'

'What?' Kargan's eyes were wide with disbelief.

Kargan swept his gaze over the area, taking it all in. Everywhere soldiers were lying on the ground, moaning as their wounds seeped red blood onto the sand. He remembered hearing reports that the clans from the desert were massing, but they'd never posed much of a threat.

When he turned back to the general, his bewilderment had shifted to anger. 'Explain.'

'The city . . . Malakai's fallen . . . It's no longer ours.'

Kargan had a sudden thought. 'My cousin, Agathon.' He scanned the area again. 'Where is he?'

'I'm . . . I am sorry, Great King. He fought on the walls . . . fought bravely . . . but he was killed in the battle. I saw it myself, and my men will confirm it. Their . . . leader, a tall warrior with a braided beard, cut him in half with a single blow.'

Kargan looked away. He'd always liked his cousin. Agathon was never much of a warrior, but he'd given his life for Ilea.

He struggled to make sense of it. 'Take care of your men. Then, you and I, General, we need to talk.'

Once more in his throne room, Kargan sipped red wine from a goblet, barely tasting it. He stood near the map, staring up at it and frowning. His eyes roved over the tapestry, his dark glare fixated on the distant west.

Imakale was the farthest dominion from Ilea. It was a dry, dusty land, home to savage tribesmen. But despite its inhospitable terrain, the capital, Malakai, was one of Kargan's most important cities. Gold, slaves, ivory, and soft pelts from the great cats traveled to Malakai in long caravans, to be shipped to Lamara and sold to the city's traders. Malakai was the only place in the Ilean Empire to have a port on the Aleuthean Sea. The city was his gateway to the south, and the resources of the Salesian continent's inner heart.

Kargan took another mouthful of red wine as he explored land routes and checked supply lines, reminding himself where his armies were presently stationed.

Hearing footsteps, he glanced up as a palace guard entered and bowed. 'General Dhuma is here, Great King.'

'Good,' Kargan grunted. 'Send him in.'

'At once, Great King.'

Kargan turned to Javid, standing nearby. 'You think I should let him live?'

'I think you should hear his story.'

Boot heels rang on the hard stone of the palace floor and Kargan looked toward the arched entrance as General Dhuma entered. He'd washed his face and hands, but his jaw was unshaven and he still wore his armor. Reaching Kargan, he came to a halt, standing tall as he gave his king a shaky military salute.

When Kargan didn't respond, the general glanced at Javid and then back at Kargan. Javid didn't make any movement, his expression as stony as ever, but the general's face paled.

'General Dhuma,' Kargan said. 'I'd like to hear your account now, firsthand, without embellishment. Tell me the facts.'

The general nodded. 'Of course, Great King.' He took a deep breath. 'As you know, we have faced down the tribes many times, and I . . . Well, this time we thought it would be the same. It has been a long time since so many gathered, but they've never been strong warriors, no match for ours.'

Kargan stared into the general's eyes. 'How many did you defend the city with?'

'Close . . . Close to two thousand, Great King.'

'And the enemy?'

'Five or six hundred tribesmen . . . Perhaps a hundred and fifty foreigners. The strangers . . . I've never fought men like them before.'

Kargan's nostrils flared. 'Tell me, General, how many did you lead when you fled, leaving my city to the mercy of the savages?'

Dhuma spoke so quietly that Kargan strained to hear him. 'Four hundred and twelve.'

'So you were soundly defeated. You had superior numbers and the strength of the city walls. How did you lose? *Why* did you lose?' Kargan's voice became a roar. 'Malakai is one of my key cities!'

The general swallowed. 'They attacked with the dawn. But it was the wind that gave them the advantage. A strange wind . . . It rose up from nothing.' He shook his head. 'There was a sandstorm, unlike anything I've experienced before. So much grit that we couldn't see. It got into our eyes and into our armor. We still defeated the tribesmen in numbers, but the foreigners . . .'

Dhuma steadied himself, meeting Kargan's stare directly. 'King of Kings, I am telling you this truly, as someone who has fought all across the empire. I have never seen armor like theirs, nor weapons. They cut through us like a scythe through wheat, yet our arrows and spears barely scratched them.'

'And then you lost the walls and fled . . . Leaving the body of the viceroy, Agathon, behind.' Kargan's lips thinned as he paused, and the general's face turned whiter. 'This leader, the man who killed my cousin. Describe him.'

The general cleared his throat and nodded. 'They say his name is Palemon. The clan chiefs are in awe of him. Even as we waited for the attack, rumors were rife in the city. The locals have never loved us, and when the usual cries for rebellion began, they were shouting his name. They say he is the ancient King Palemon of Aleuthea, reincarnated in the flesh. All I know is that, without doubt, he and his warriors are the reason the city fell.'

'So he tells a good tale, and he knows how to use myths to recruit followers.' Kargan scratched his beard.

'The Aleutheans built Malakai,' Dhuma said. 'It's one of the world's oldest cities. This . . . Palemon . . . says that he is merely reclaiming it from usurpers, and he intends to do the same with the rest of the world.'

Kargan gave a short laugh. 'He may have the support of the desert men, and he may have a hundred and fifty warriors. By Helios, he may be able to summon sandstorms at his command, but I doubt he'll stand against our counterattack.'

When he saw the general's frown, Kargan waved a hand. 'Now, Dhuma. Who is he really? Where does he come from? Is he from the south, from lands we are unaware of?'

'That is my best theory.'

Kargan glanced at the map again. 'Until this defeat, we finally had the empire united.' He turned back to the general. 'We can't lose battles, not ever, or it inspires others to rise up against us. If you'd needed a larger garrison, you should have sent for support. You also should have had your ear to the ground and taken the measure of your enemy.'

'Yes, Great King. I accept full responsibility.'

'Now, let's say for a moment that you were still alive, still a general, and were tasked with recapturing Malakai. What strategy would you recommend?'

Dhuma blanched and spoke quickly, releasing the words in a rush. 'A swift assault with a large force, Great King. I would take four divisions from the capital to the Shadrian Passage. Cross them over to Verai on barges. Pick up some more men in Shadria. Then head directly for Malakai.'

The general finished, waiting expectantly for Kargan's response.

Kargan looked at Javid, who gave him a slight nod. Dhuma's strategy was exactly what Kargan had already determined he would do. He came to a decision.

'Then, *Captain* Dhuma'—Kargan saw him wince at the change in rank—'that is the plan you will be recommending to your new general. Lead the army to Malakai, take back my city, and then stick this Palemon's head up on the walls. Dhuma, if you and your commander succeed, you'll be a general again. If not . . .' He trailed off with a meaningful look.

'I live to serve,' Dhuma said, keeping his face blank.

'Now go. Get some rest. You have work to do.'

Kargan waited until Dhuma had left and then let out a breath as he turned to Javid. 'Right now they'll be plundering my coffers, killing my representatives, and rounding up the Ileans in the city and butchering them.'

'What of these reports of a mysterious wind?'

Kargan snorted. 'Despite what the priests say, I tend to believe what I see with my own eyes.'

Javid came forward. 'These strangers. They defeated a far larger force. Dhuma's description of their arms may be an exaggeration, or it may not be. Their origin is unclear. There could be worse to come.'

'That's what I'm worried about,' Kargan muttered. 'This may only be the beginning.'

4

Palemon walked toward Necropolis, snow crunching beneath his boots, seeing the familiar ridges of black-and-white rock and the settlement itself, nestled in the cleft of the fork they formed, sheltered from the cruel winds.

Hundreds of crude conical huts stood alongside the occasional wooden house formed from ships' timbers, yet the area appeared deserted. The ragged furs on the huts' whalebone frames blew in the chill air. Mist swirled into the valley, occasionally obscuring everything before rolling back out in the next gust.

Everything was so washed with white that the scene felt hazy and unreal. A thought sparked in his consciousness; he knew for a moment that he was dreaming. But then the idea swiftly fled, replaced with a nagging worry that churned at his stomach.

Still a distance from the settlement, Palemon wondered where all the people were. He turned around to gaze in a sweeping circle. Then, as another gust cleared a section of mist, he saw a collection of figures clad in furs. Several hundred men, women, and children were assembled outside the entrance to a cave.

With a growing sense of dread, he watched the crowd, still as statues, and realized he was witnessing a funeral service. Necropolis had no timber to make pyres, and at this time of year the ocean was frozen for miles in every direction. When one of Palemon's people journeyed to the next life, his or her body was carried deep within these frozen tombs. Snow was packed around the pale corpse, eventually to harden into ice.

Palemon started striding toward the crowd. Squinting into the mist as he approached, he could now see the cavern's wide mouth, as well as the sad faces of the people staring down at the ground. They were only a stone's throw away, but even as he lifted one foot and then the other, struggling to walk more briskly, the sinking ground underfoot kept slowing him down. He looked at his feet and found that with every step he was plummeting deep into the snow, forcing him to lift his boots ever higher. The quicker he tried to walk, the more he sank.

His heart hammered in his chest as he tried to call out, but he was robbed of breath, barely managing a choking croak. Instead he looked at the scrawny women, still and silent, the marks of tears cutting through the grime on their cheeks. He saw children standing alone, looking numb and pale. Strong men trembled, faces filled with anguish. Where there should have been people in groups, they instead stood in ones and twos: husbands without wives, parents without children, few of the elderly at all.

He clenched his fists and pushed relentlessly through the snow, but now when he looked down at his feet, the snow was melting around them, turning the frozen water into slush. Under his heavy clothing, he suddenly found himself sweating, and his forehead felt burning hot. Liquid trickled down the back of his neck, and moisture made his palms clammy. He stopped, slumped with exhaustion, and gazed at the rows of bodies laid out in front of the cave.

They were the corpses of young boys and girls, old men and women. Deprivation and exposure always took the weakest first. The bodies were frozen solid, lips blue and hair brittle. Seeing the babes was the worst, but he forced himself to look at them.

Palemon again tried to call to his people, but still no sound would come out of his mouth. The sweat now poured from his brow, streaming down his cheeks like tears. Finally, with a great effort of will, he managed to make a moaning sound, and the people standing and looking at the bodies all turned as one.

Their faces were skeletal and their cheeks were sunken. Their limbs were as thin as sticks.

Horror sank into his stomach. 'I'm coming!' he cried. 'I'm coming!'

———

'—coming!'

Palemon choked the word as he woke gasping. He was covered in sweat and tangled in the bed sheets. The dream was always the same, but experiencing it over and over didn't make it any easier. Each time, he came nearer to the corpses laid out in front of the cave. Each time, he screamed at the people he'd left behind that he was coming.

He didn't know if what he was dreaming was a vision sent by the gods, or simply his own nagging conscience.

He shoved the sheets aside, glancing out the window to see that the sun was up. Heat rolled in from outside; despite the thick stone walls he felt like he was in an oven. The fierce temperature in this land was relentless; he didn't know if he would ever get used to it.

Perhaps his years were starting to tell. He shook his head. No, he refused to allow this climate to weaken him. His people were strong, and he was their king. Compared to the faraway lands in the frozen north, this was nothing. Once, they'd ruled the world, and would do so again.

As he dressed – pulling on dark trousers, a bleached leather vest, and finally his high black boots – he tried to banish the nightmare, but the lingering sense of desperation stayed with him. He splashed water from a basin over his face and looked at himself in the polished silver mirror. Seeing his familiar features steadied him: his eyes were dark and determined; his long, graying hair and braided beard ensured no one could mistake who he was.

Palemon straightened, standing tall. He set his jaw, took a deep breath, and then left the bedchamber, which until a few weeks ago had been occupied by Malakai's viceroy, Agathon.

Striding along the palace corridors, Palemon ignored the slaves who shrank against the walls and climbed a short series of steps until he came to the palace's audience chamber. A huge, rectangular room with a high ceiling held up by evenly spaced columns, it was high enough to afford a direct view of the sea as well as most of the city's districts. The windows were all without curtains, and as Palemon began to pace, he glanced out at the circular Sky Tower, the city's tallest structure, lit up by the rays of the rising sun.

Palemon's gaze took in a city both grand and old, with marble facing on some of the oldest walls and broad avenues built at perpendicular angles. Every square had a central fountain or statue and every street was paved, with gutters on both sides. Hanging guardens draped from the balconies of the three-storied houses, built one against the other in long terraces. Sections of the city were in disrepair, and the newest architecture was ugly and functional, basalt and alabaster giving way to reddish structures made of mud brick, but it was clear that Malakai's long-dead builders possessed far more skill than today's. Palemon was looking at a city constructed by his ancestors, who had once ruled the world from the island nation of Aleuthea.

His pacing took him past the oversized wooden throne – rarely used; he wasn't a man who liked to sit still – and to the end of the chamber before he turned on his heel and strode in the opposite direction. He furrowed his brow as he thought, tugging on his beard and occasionally murmuring to himself.

Working with Kyphos, he'd determined that to make the journey to Necropolis they would need a dozen ocean-going vessels, with skilled crews and plenty of supplies. At least finding the way wouldn't be difficult, for Zara said any of the dozen sorcerers they'd brought with them could find their way back to their brethren left behind. The golden light of their sun staffs would guide them, but unlike when they'd followed the pull of the ark, there would be no chance of the path becoming lost.

From the captives taken during the conquest of Malakai he knew that the king of Ilea had more than enough ships for their purposes. The king of Xanthos also had a sizeable fleet. The vessels he needed would have to come from one or the other.

'So it must be war,' Palemon muttered. 'And despite capturing this city, we are weak.'

He was interrupted by a clatter of footsteps as Kyphos burst into the room, together with another warrior from Necropolis. The soldier was red-faced and panting, sweating in his chain mail. The armor had come from the hold of the *Solaris*, the ship that had brought them to these lands, and Palemon's cold bloods now wore it always. When combined with the skills learned fighting battles against the warlike kona, harpooning orcas, and hunting white bears, their equipment made them gods compared to the locals.

Shorter than the soldier, Kyphos's shaggy black eyebrows came together over his eyes as he looked up at his king. 'King Palemon,' he said. 'Sire . . . You need to hear what he has to say.' He nodded at his companion. 'Tell him.'

Out of breath, the soldier bowed to the king before speaking. 'Sire'—his chest heaved—'I've come from the northern tower. Facing the harbor. You need to see. There's a ship.'

'A ship?' Palemon frowned, looking from face to face. 'Who are they?'

'I'm guessing they're merchants,' Kyphos said. 'Since our conquest, the city is desperate for supplies. They'll be able to name their price.'

'Merchants?'

'It's a big ship, sire,' the red-faced soldier said.

'Have you sent word to Zara?' Palemon asked Kyphos.

'I've barely seen her since she started her search for artifacts.'

Palemon turned to the soldier. 'See if you can find her.' The soldier nodded and swiftly left. Palemon then jerked his chin. 'Kyphos. The roof.'

Taking long strides Palemon crossed the audience chamber, heading toward the stairs with Kyphos just behind him. Palemon climbed the steps two at a time before reaching the landing and exiting through the door leading onto the palace roof.

Now out in the open, Palemon immediately made his way to the edge facing the harbor and peered out to sea. Kyphos came up beside him, hands on his hips and panting: the hunchback was one of the strongest men Palemon knew, but he had little stamina. Together they stared, eyes narrowed, watching the blue horizon.

At first Palemon couldn't see anything, but then, in the far distance, a tiny square of white sail appeared, growing larger with every passing moment. Despite the fact that it was just a speck on the horizon, it was so far away that he knew it was big, bigger even than the *Solaris*.

Together the two men watched for a long time as the vessel grew larger. It had recently left behind the Lost Souls, the peaks jutting above the water that had once been the hills of Aleuthea, and was clearly headed for Malakai. Soon Palemon saw that the ship had a multitude of oars jutting out of its sides like the legs of an insect.

The vessel traveled with surprising speed under the power of so many oarsmen, and was soon close enough that tiny figures could be seen rushing about on the top deck. Fluttering multicolored pennants trailed from the top of the mast, snapping in the breeze.

'You've been learning about their vessels. What manner of ship is that?' Palemon asked.

Kyphos rubbed his chin and squinted for a time. 'A bireme. Wait'— he shielded his eyes—'no . . . It has three banks of oars. A trireme, then.' He made a sound of surprise. 'I didn't know such a thing existed.'

'Are they here for war?'

'No,' Kyphos said. 'See the multicolored pennants? It's here for trade.'

Palemon met Kyphos's eyes. 'You say we need a dozen ships? We might have found our first.'

'I suggest we lure them in,' Kyphos said. 'No soldiers to greet them. We'll summon the captain and give him a choice. Either surrender or we'll seize his ship by force.'

'Why not seize the ship immediately?'

'Despite its colors, it's a warship. There could be armed men on board. If there's fighting, we could damage the ship or lose crewmen, and we need skilled sailors.'

Palemon scratched his chin and nodded. 'All right then. We'll do it your way.'

5

Crossing the deck of his flagship, the *Liberty*, Dion, king of Xanthos, glanced apprehensively at the sharp islands that jutted out of the water, some several miles away, others flanking the trireme on both sides, almost close enough to reach out and touch.

The Lost Souls reminded him of the Shards near Xanthos, but on a much larger scale. There were fewer of them, but some dwarfed even his warship in size. At least, he hoped there were fewer of them. It was impossible to say what lurked beneath the surface of the water.

Approaching the helm, he glanced at Cob, who growled at him as he guided them through.

'Do we really have to do this, lad?' The old man scowled.

'I want to see the sunken city for myself. Just keep us away from the peaks.'

'Don't tell me how to do my job,' Cob said.

Dion smiled at his old sailing master, and behind his smile was gratitude that the short, bald, round-faced man who had been like a second father to him still never called him by his title. Now that Dion was king, he could truly appreciate how separate from everyone else it made him.

Since Nikolas's death and the peace accord with Ilea, Dion had slowly become accustomed to his new role. With his uncle's help, he'd found homes for many of the Free Men in Xanthos, and he'd built a new settlement at the isle of Fort Liberty, even larger than the one before it, for those who wanted to live free from the governance of kings. Once home to feared pirates, Fort Liberty now had a charter as a semi-autonomous trading outpost, and with light taxes and loose rules, wealth poured in. With the Maltherean Sea at peace, Dion had decided to venture to a new sea: the Aleuthean.

He lifted his gaze to inspect the largest of the Lost Souls: a tall island with a sharp precipice plummeting to the sea, the remnant of some mountain the ancient Aleutheans would have looked up at as they went about their daily business. Despite trusting Cob implicitly, he couldn't help glancing back at the helm.

'Don't worry,' Cob said, his eyes always on the sea. 'Roxana will skin me alive if I harm her pride and joy.'

'From what I hear, you've got nothing to fear from her.' Dion smiled. 'Don't think you can hide from me where those honey cakes you've been eating all voyage came from.' He shook his head. 'I can't believe she cooked for you.'

Cob reddened. 'She was returning a favor—'

'A favor, or a gift? I've seen the hand-carved sailboat she keeps in her workroom. It's fine indeed; you should be proud.'

Cob's face turned even redder, and with a grin Dion left the old man behind, walking along the rail and staring down into the sea, smooth and shining like a polished gemstone. The water was becoming paler, a lighter shade of blue as the depth became shallower. A boulder, covered in a fur of ocean growth, took form far below before the ship left it behind. More dark shapes became clear in ones and twos, contrasting with the lighter color of the sea floor. Soon there were more darker patches than anything else.

Spurred into action, Dion glanced at the sail, nodding to himself when he saw it was already lowered. He strode to the hatchway leading to the lower rowing decks.

'On my mark,' he called down to the oarsmen. He checked that they were well clear of the peaked islands before bellowing, 'Now!'

The oars suddenly went still, the three tiers of rowers all stopping as one. Leaving the hatchway to scan both flanks of the vessel, Dion nodded to himself, pleased with their precision: the sailors of Xanthos had learned their skills, and were now good enough to rival any Ilean crew.

And, he reminded himself, the Ileans didn't have triremes, which made this ship the most powerful vessel on the water.

Dion returned to Cob as the *Liberty* now glided over the still water, oars hovering above the surface, everything carefully controlled to create as few ripples as possible. It was far from a windy day, which was fortunate because there was little to disturb the sea, but it also meant that the heat radiating down from the rising sun was already searing hot. As they came closer to Malakai, he vowed to never again complain about a summer's day in Xanthos.

The ship became quiet, slipping over the surface of the sea with the smooth sound of flowing water. Along with the crew, Dion stared down into the sea, but despite discerning a maze of light and dark patches, the ocean floor was still too deep to make out what he was seeing. Then he heard a sailor shout from the other side of the vessel. 'Look!'

Dion, along with almost everyone on the top deck, crossed to the opposite side, gripping the rail and peering down into the water. The ocean was clear and still. Until now he'd been seeing little more than murky shadows, but suddenly he could make out distinct forms.

'By Silex,' Dion breathed.

Down below, resting on the ocean floor, were the long, curved walls of an immense, oval-shaped structure. Dion wondered for a moment what it was before he realized.

They were sailing over a crumbled amphitheatre.

Its shape made it clear what it was. But the sheer scale of it was baffling, almost disturbing. The *Liberty* passed over it for long minutes, each onlooker trying to imagine how many people had once been seated far below. They were all ghosts now, every one of them killed when Aleuthea sank long ago.

Unless, of course, the rumors about Malakai's conqueror were true.

Dion glanced at Cob, and then at the crewmen, seeing that they were all gazing down into the water.

'I've never seen anything like it,' Cob said.

'I thought you said you've traveled to the Aleuthean Sea before.'

'It was rough the last time, and we had to keep clear of the Lost Souls.'

The great ship continued to glide; her momentum would carry her forward for a long time before power was needed. After the amphitheatre, Dion saw hills and winding paths, broken houses and fallen towers. He looked out at the sea. The Lost Souls covered a huge area. The sunken city was immense.

'How far below do you think it is?'

'Thirty feet? Fifty? It's hard to tell.'

Cob's head snapped forward when a youth at the bow called out. The old man shoved the helm hard, and with a spike of fear Dion realized they'd been heading straight for a tower of some kind, with just a few flat stones showing above the surface. If the tide had been just a little higher, they might not have seen it at all.

'This is dangerous,' Cob said. 'I'm taking us out.'

'Understood.'

Cob set a course to steer them away from the Lost Souls and toward Malakai, the capital of Imakale. The drum sounded below as the oarsmen resumed their labors. The square sail made a sound like the crack of a whip when it climbed to the top of the mast.

Dion stayed beside Cob and continued to gaze at the jagged island peaks. There had once been a powerful civilization here, a civilization that ruled the world, even warring with the eldren and conquering their homeland, Sindara.

'They all have their names,' Cob said. 'I only remember a few.' He nodded at one of the craggy islands. 'That's the Shrine. See the small building just above the water? One of the only structures above the surface. That round peak is the Dome.'

Cob pointed at the mainland, where a narrow strait separated a promontory from the Lost Souls. Dion followed the old man's gaze to a large island, a lopsided hill with a cliff on the far side sloping down to a shore.

'Widow's Peak is the closest to the mainland,' Cob said.

'Widow?' Dion frowned.

'People dive off and search for treasure. They say that below Widow's Peak is a tower, far bigger than the one we just left behind. You can see the top from the surface. I've heard more than one story about a man finding gold down there. Not that I'd try it. Dangerous work. And you'd think any treasure would have been discovered long ago.'

'Probably true,' Dion said, 'but not very romantic.'

'Lad, as soon as you see me being romantic, you have my permission to throw me into the sea.'

'Well, now you mention it . . .' Seeing Cob's expression, Dion decided to let up on his jesting. 'The cape. Does it have a name?'

'Cape Cush.'

They both watched the distant promontory for a time, soon leaving it behind as the vessel's pace picked up and they made speed for Malakai. Cob began to look worried as a thin strip of land appeared on the horizon.

'They say Malakai was built by the Aleutheans, like Aleron, in Sarsica,' Dion said. 'But where Aleron is in ruins, Malakai was never abandoned.'

'Well, lad, against my better judgment, you won't have long to wait to see it for yourself.'

A yellow and barren coastline, flat and featureless, now stretched as far as the eye could see in both directions. Scanning ahead, waiting for something to break up the monotony, finally Dion saw the unmistakable signs of a settlement.

At first it was just a few dots of red and white, but then it grew in size, becoming a city of grand buildings and towers, with a long wall facing the pale sand. They began to see distant fishing boats, and old men and boys with poles in their hands staring with naked curiosity at the huge trireme.

Dion heard Cob murmur behind him. 'I still don't see why you had to come yourself.'

He turned to face his old friend. As their destination neared, both men were now gravely serious. 'They say he's calling himself Palemon, and claims to have returned from across the sea.' Dion met Cob's eyes. 'I need to find out the truth.'

'Why?' Cob scowled. 'What purpose does it serve?'

'Even if he's just using Aleuthea's legend to gain power, he's shown he has teeth. They say he took Malakai in the first assault. You can't tell me that doesn't disturb you. The Aleutheans defeated the eldren – at a time when the eldren were far stronger than they are now. They had magical abilities.'

'Stories.'

'Then why are you so worried?'

'Because my king and friend is putting himself in harm's way, for no other purpose than to satisfy his curiosity.'

'We're flying merchant colors. We're a trading ship. We're bringing supplies to a city that needs them, and our motive is simple: profit. However'—Dion gave a grim smile—'in addition to our goods, we have a hold full of soldiers. They'll see a trading vessel, but in truth we're equipped for war.'

Cob steered the *Liberty* toward a distant pier jutting from the shore, long enough for deep-keeled merchant vessels to dock in safety, though at present there was only a tiny rowboat tied alongside the wooden platform, bobbing in the waves.

The old man muttered and shook his head. 'This is a bad idea.'

———

Dion navigated the crowded hold, weaving around archers, armored infantry, and constantly moving oarsmen. He finally found Finn among the stores, making scratches on the sides of barrels.

Long-haired and slender, Finn was now Dion's master of trade and treasury. With his sharp mind and network of shady contacts, the former purser of the Free Men had helped bring wealth to Xanthos. Together Finn and Cob had transformed Fort Liberty, once a haven for pirates, into a successful trading outpost, a place where the Free Men enjoyed as much liberty as they had before, without the risk of reprisal that pirating had once carried.

'You didn't see the sunken city,' Dion said.

'Too busy here,' Finn replied absently, making another scratch on the side of a crate. Crammed among the stores, he looked up from his work to grin. 'This is a good idea. There's risk, but there'll be more than enough reward. Few ships cross through the Chasm to the Aleuthean Sea. We'll be able to name our price.'

Dion chuckled and shook his head. 'You're taking your role seriously.'

Finn shrugged. 'It's only a small change.' He smiled. 'And I get to wear expensive jewelry.'

In order to maintain the deception that they were a merchant vessel, Finn was presenting himself as the representative of a powerful trading consortium from Koulis. He wore a thick navy tunic and a belted sash the color of gold, along with a heavy silver necklace and calfskin boots. With his soft-spoken manner, long lashes, and delicate hands, he looked every inch the wealthy trader.

Dion fingered his own necklace, also made of silver but plainer than the one he'd left at home in Xanthos. He would be presenting himself as first mate, with Cob the *Liberty*'s ostensible captain. As such, his clothing was plain and functional. He looked anything but a king.

'Cob's worried,' Dion said.

'Cob's always worried.' Finn went back to his work, peering inside a barrel and making several more scratches on the side.

'What are you doing?'

'It's a private code: the price we paid for each barrel. I plan to double my money on each.'

'Your money?'

'Ah . . . The treasury's money.'

Dion watched him for a time. Finn was almost too eager to play his part. If they had to leave in a hurry, he wondered if he'd be able to tear him away from his negotiations with the city's traders. 'Come up when you're done. We're nearly there.'

6

As the trireme slowed to approach the pier, Dion and Cob stood up near the bow, appraising the city of Malakai and wondering what kind of greeting their arrival would provoke.

Dion was relieved to see that no soldiers were coming down to meet them, only dozens of brightly dressed merchants jockeying for position as they waited for the vessel to dock.

'What makes you think you'll get to meet this Palemon anyway?' Cob muttered.

'With a ship like this?' Dion indicated the vessel. 'He'll want to meet us.'

'And if he likes the ship so much that he wants it for himself?'

'That's what the soldiers are for.'

'I still don't like this.'

Hearing a shrill sound, Dion turned to see Finn walking the deck, theatrically craning his neck and whistling as he took in the nearing city. Finn then glanced down at himself, tugging at his tunic, before coming to join them.

'The famed city of Malakai!' Finn said, gazing at the walls and the soaring circular tower behind them, so high it appeared to brush the sky. 'Once Aleuthea's gateway to the heartland of the south. Picture it . . . Ships coming and going between Aleuthea and Malakai . . . picking up precious metals, ivory, and lion skins. There would have been a proper harbor then, with docks, shipyards, and dozens of piers, rather than just the one.'

For a moment Dion scanned the shoreline and imagined the scene, but then shook himself when he remembered his purpose.

'Cob,' he said. 'Remind the men below to come out fighting if they hear the bell—'

'Wait,' Finn interrupted. 'Who's giving the orders here? You're the captain's mate.'

Dion scowled at Finn, while Cob shook his head.

'We need to get into our roles,' Finn explained. 'The best actors at the theatre practice constantly. Then, when they're on stage, they know exactly what they're doing.'

Cob chuckled. 'He has a point.'

With a sigh, Dion turned to face the crew and called out, 'Men! From now on we are merchants. Cob is your captain, and I am his mate. Finn here represents the ship's owners.'

There was no discernible change in the crew, but they were all prepared and could answer any questions posed without giving themselves away. As the drum tempo slowed and the *Liberty's* oarsmen backed to slow their momentum, Cob issued orders and slowly brought the ship alongside the pier.

Finn's eyes studied the clamoring merchants on the platform, evidently taking note of the pecking order among them, identifying those with the richest clothing and gaudiest jewelry. Meanwhile Dion felt tension in his shoulders. When the first bireme had arrived at Phalesia, neither the Phalesian consuls nor Dion's father had known much at all about the Ileans.

Now there was a new potential danger, and he didn't intend to repeat the same mistake.

The Maltherean Sea was at peace. If there was going to be any threat, any change in the balance of power, he wanted to know what it was.

47

With the ship fastened to the pier and Finn already on the platform, thriving under the attention of so many buyers, Dion also played his role, helping the sailors carry up barrels from below decks. He continued unloading, making no change in his behavior as he watched two soldiers approach the *Liberty*, pushing through the merchants to stand at the edge of the platform and call up to the deck.

'Your captain. Where is he?'

Cob stumped forward, crossing the deck where he'd been coordinating the activity. Meanwhile Dion set down his barrel near the mast and pretended to fuss over one of the ropes, hanging back, partially hidden, where he could appraise the soldiers more carefully.

They were both pale-skinned, far more so than the local traders bargaining with Finn, whose complexions ranged from olive to ebony. The soldier calling up had a close-cropped gray beard, long hair, and drooping eyes, and gave away a strange accent, undoubtedly foreign, with a harsh barking inflection. His companion was bald, tall, and lean, with a curl to his upper lip.

But it was their armor that drew Dion's attention.

They were wearing shirts of steel links, like a multitude of necklaces woven together into a garment. The chain shirts were close-fitting and long-sleeved, so that only their heads and hands were exposed. Belted at the waist, the protective armor continued nearly to their knees before revealing leather leggings underneath. Shifting to get a better vantage, Dion saw that they wore black ankle-high boots.

Dion was a better archer than swordsman – by a long margin – but regardless of the weapon, he could see in an instant how difficult it would be to kill men so well protected. Their swords were also unusual, so large that they were worn on sheaths on their backs, with the hilts poking over their left shoulders. They both had daggers in scabbards at their hips; the long-haired soldier casually rested his hand on a steel hilt.

Dion frowned. Who were these people?

'I am the *Liberty*'s captain,' Cob called down.

'The king sends his regards for bringing much-needed supplies to the city,' the long-haired soldier called up. 'He wishes to thank you in person.'

'Of course,' Cob said. 'It would be my honor.'

Cob glanced at Dion, and, remembering his role, Dion caught up with him as he descended the gangway. When they reached the pier, the bald soldier, the taller of the two, looked at the axe hanging from Cob's hip.

'Leave any weapons with your ship,' he said.

With a brief glare at Dion, unnoticed by the soldiers, Cob handed his axe to one of the crewmen.

'My first mate comes with me,' Cob said, indicating Dion.

The bald soldier inspected Dion, saw that he was unarmed, and nodded. The leader of the pair then started to clear a path through the clamoring merchants, all desperate to talk to Finn, who appeared to be enjoying himself playing one off against the other.

Dion saw Finn return his glance. His finely dressed friend made no sign of acknowledgment, the slight narrowing of his eyes saying enough before he looked away, leveling a hand at a nearby merchant and barking out a price. Returning his attention to Cob, whose mouth had tightened, Dion fell in behind the old sailor. The two pale-skinned soldiers now led the way into the city.

As they left the pier behind, approaching the tall walls of yellow stone and the broad wooden gates set into them, Dion saw that there was a monument of some kind, erected directly in front of the gates. Following the soldiers across an expanse of square flagstones with grass poking up between, he found himself walking toward a statue.

Dion was perplexed as he neared, looking up as the statue loomed over him. Resting on a square base of granite, a stern-faced man made of polished marble gazed into the distance, wearing a shining crown of golden spikes on his head, like rays of light. In addition to the crown, the statue's fingers were clenched around another metal item: a golden discus. There could be no doubt it was a representation of Helios, except for one thing.

The god was sitting on the back of a dragon. Reins connected his hands to the dragon's neck, and the creature had been perfectly crafted: the sculptor knew what a dragon looked like in surprising detail, from the size of the flared nostrils to the sweeping protrusions behind its eye ridges. The powerful hind legs were so strong it could leap into the sky or land at speed. The outstretched wings had thin bones like a framework, all connected to a muscular back.

Dion remarked to the soldiers, 'Where I come from, Helios pulls the sun behind his chariot, with the great stallion Nagros in the lead.'

The long-haired soldier with the drooping eyes shrugged. 'Take that up with the locals.'

Cob glanced at Dion, looking more and more anxious as they passed through the gates. Feeling his stomach tighten into a knot, Dion reminded himself that they'd come here for information. They were merchants, about to be thanked for bringing supplies to the city. They would discover the truth about Malakai's new rulers, and then they would leave.

Their escort now led them down a wide, paved avenue, with well-maintained gutters on both sides and plants draping tendrils from upper balconies. Looking around him, Dion saw more solid stone than he'd encountered in any other city. Turning from the main boulevard, they passed through street markets and open plazas. Fountains in the squares bubbled with clear water. Dion had always heard that Imakale was a dry land of desert, but the shade cast by the terraced houses made the streets cool, while the hanging gardens and flowing water helped to dispel the heat.

Entering another broad avenue, Dion almost stopped and stared when he saw the soaring tower that had been visible from the *Liberty*. Broad and cylindrical, it was extremely far away, but so tall that it towered over the street, an optical illusion tilting it forward, as if it were about to fall. Up close, the Sky Tower was even taller than he'd thought it would be. He recalled Cob saying that whatever was inside, the priests kept its secrets close.

Urbane city folk walked past, dressed in loose trousers and tight vests, along with bare-footed clansmen from the desert, wrapped in cloth leaving only their dark eyes bare. Seeing young women shopping in the markets and children skipping in the streets, Dion decided the city's new rulers appeared to be leaving the citizens to their own devices. Ilea was a foreign power, after all, and seeing how many clansmen were armed, it was clear that denizens of Imakale had played a part in the fight for their capital, making it more of a liberation than a conquest.

His suspicion was confirmed when he glanced through a break between the buildings and briefly saw the city walls. Warriors in steel armor manned the battlements, but they were outnumbered by their dark-skinned companions from the dry lands in the south. At every turn he looked for signs of fighting – blood-stained streets or burned-out husks of buildings – but couldn't see any. The city had been taken swiftly.

The long-haired soldier broke the silence. 'The palace is just ahead.'

'Your king,' Dion asked. 'What is his name?'

'He is Palemon, direct descendant of Palemon the First, who ruled Aleuthea.'

Dion's stomach tightened further.

7

Remembering his place, Dion hung behind Cob as they were led through the gates of the palace and up a series of steps to an audience chamber, with evenly spaced columns holding up the ceiling and windows facing the sea. The view was captivating, but his eyes were instead drawn to the man standing in front of the ebony throne.

He was powerfully built, broad-shouldered with a narrow waist, and wore a bleached leather vest, dark trousers, and high boots. He wasn't a young man, and his pale skin was lined, but his back was straight and he was tall enough to tower over most men. He had long black hair streaked with gray and a braided beard, and his eyes were dark and brooding, with bags under them as if he'd been having difficulty sleeping.

Dion noted that he wasn't sitting on the throne; nor were there courtiers and advisers filling the room. This wasn't a king who was accustomed to ceremony. He had just the one companion, a black-haired hunchback with shoulders sitting oddly high and muscular, ropey arms.

The long-haired soldier nodded at Cob. 'King Palemon, this man is the captain.'

Cob bowed – the first time Dion had seen him do so – and gave his full name, which sounded odd on the old man's lips. 'King. My name is Cobrim, and I am captain of the *Liberty*.'

Palemon glanced at Dion. As their eyes met, Dion suddenly felt the worry gnawing at his guts grow even stronger. The stare was dismissive, arrogant. The dark eyes were cold. Nothing would stand in this man's way.

'And you are?'

'Andion. Captain's mate.' Rather than bow, Dion merely nodded. He saw Palemon scowl.

'I am Palemon, king of Malakai and the lands as far south as the red desert. This is Kyphos, one of my advisers.' Palemon inclined his head at the hunchback. 'Your ship. What manner of vessel is it?'

'A trireme, King,' Cob said. 'A hundred feet long, fourteen feet wide at the beam.'

'It is a sound vessel?'

'Aye,' Cob said.

'How does it handle rough seas, out on the open ocean?'

'Well enough.'

Palemon nodded. 'Kyphos has a proposition for you.'

As Kyphos talked, the king started to pace. He tugged on the braids of his beard and stared out to sea, as if fascinated by the ocean. Dion studied him, but then Kyphos's words struck him like a slap on the face.

'We are at war.' The hunchback's voice was gruff, his manner direct. 'Your visit is welcome, but your vessel is far too valuable to us to let you go on your way.'

Cob paled and glanced at Dion.

'The king wants your ship,' Kyphos continued. 'We will take it by force if necessary, but we want to spare your crew. We would much rather have you work for us than kill you.'

Dion swallowed. Gazing at the king and seeing the lines of concern on his forehead, he sensed that these people didn't just want the ship – they were desperate to have it. He thought about his soldiers, hidden below decks. If Palemon tried to seize the *Liberty*, he would soon get an unpleasant surprise.

'Why do you want it so badly?' Dion asked.

Palemon glared at him. 'Let your captain speak.' He strode directly to face Cob, towering over him, his expression grim. 'Well, Cobrim? Is it to be surrender or death?'

Undeterred, Dion pressed on. With every word he spoke, Cob turned a sicklier shade of gray. 'Who are you? Where did you and your people come from?'

'You are in no position to ask questions.' Palemon's eyes narrowed at Dion. 'Are you a fool? Do you want to be the first to die?'

Cob gaped, while Palemon stared down at the shorter man, waiting for a reply. The silence dragged out.

Dion could almost see the thoughts crossing Cob's face. Cob knew Dion wanted information, but he'd just been asked to surrender his ship, and an answer was expected. If he agreed to the demand, there would be fighting when they tried to seize the *Liberty*. If he said no, the outcome would be the same.

As the tension grew, Dion took a breath and unfastened his silver necklace. Cob was staring at him and shaking his head, but Dion put the necklace in a pocket.

Neither Palemon nor Kyphos realized the significance of what he'd done. Dion's experiences with the Free Men had taught him to accept who he was, and now he could change his form with almost as much ease as a full-blooded eldran.

Even so, sweat broke out on his forehead. He needed information, but if there was fighting, someone would die.

He now addressed both the king and his companion. 'You have given us a choice between life and death, but if we choose to serve you, we need to know what it is you're asking.'

Palemon hooked his thumbs in his belt. 'You're brave. I'll give you that.'

He scratched at his cheek and then came to a decision.

'The sunken city out there, Aleuthea'—he nodded in the direction of the sea—'was the homeland of my ancestors. When the eldran king Marrix destroyed Aleuthea, we fled to a frozen land, vowing one day to return. Since then, in honor of Palemon the First, who led us to safety, every ruler of my people has been given his name.' His voice became low. 'I am the direct descendant of the most powerful king the world has ever known.'

Palemon met Dion's eyes, daring him to challenge his claim.

But Dion stayed silent. The evidence was in front of him, from the sophisticated armor to these people's skin color, far too pale for these sunny lands. He now had the answer he'd sought. It remained to be seen what else he could learn before he and Cob were forced to fight their way free.

'We made it home,' Palemon continued, 'but we left most of our people starving in that faraway land, so far north that all the land is ice. We will take your ship no matter what you do, but your crew would be useful to us; you have an opportunity to spare their lives. Now'—he turned back to Cob—'make your choice.'

'How many of your people are there?' Dion asked. 'Are their numbers low enough to fit on this one ship?'

'No,' Palemon said shortly.

'Then what use is one ship when you need a fleet?'

'He speaks sense,' a new voice said.

Dion turned in surprise, seeing a woman approaching from the back of the audience chamber. She had a tall wooden staff in her hand, crowned with a hand-sized hoop of solid gold, but she was far too young to need it for support. More striking still was her appearance. She wore a supple garment the color of the deep sea, like a chiton but far more close-fitting, hugging her slim figure in a way that was almost scandalous. She had glittering blue eyes, straight, raven-black hair, and a face of sculpted beauty, with high cheekbones and lips tinged a bluish shade. Her jewelry reminded him of a priestess of Edra: shining copper bands jangled on her wrists and she wore a fanlike copper necklace at her throat. Strange symbols had been etched into the flat surface of the copper, angular shapes that reminded him of the Ark of Revelation, destroyed by Nikolas the previous year.

As he wondered how long she'd been watching and listening, Dion glanced at Cob and saw a wistful expression on his face. The old sailor's mouth had dropped open; he was almost drooling.

But where Cob appeared utterly captivated by her beauty, Dion saw a cold, calculating woman. Rather than Cob, it was Dion she was looking at, with an intelligent, penetrating stare.

'I am Zara. Think of me as the king's . . . spiritual adviser,' she said. 'My apologies, the king is under a lot of strain. We built Malakai. This city was always ours, but Kargan the false king disagrees, and we are expecting him to come by land or sea. But forgive us if we have been overzealous.' She gave a slight smile. 'We are recently returned to the Realm and we don't always know who it is we are dealing with.'

She turned to Palemon, whose face showed mingled anger and confusion.

'Sire, these men are not Ileans. They are from the northern Maltherean.' She raised an arched eyebrow at Cob. 'Do I have that correct, Captain?'

'Aye . . . from Xanthos.' Cob stumbled over the words. Dion glared at him, but Cob appeared to be under some kind of spell.

'We thank you for your visit, and you are free to go. Depart with our gratitude and blessing.' She looked pointedly at the king, before turning back to Cob and Dion. 'When you have sold your cargo, you may leave without hindrance.' She nodded at the pair of soldiers. 'Escort them back to their ship.' The soldiers glanced at the king, who gave a sharp nod.

As Palemon, Kyphos, and the strange woman looked on, Dion and Cob followed their escort out of the audience chamber.

Glancing back at the tall king, Dion saw that his jaw was clenched tightly.

As soon as they reached the harbor, Dion and Cob looked behind them, walking with quick strides, checking that the two soldiers were still standing motionless at the gates. They were watching, but letting them return to the ship alone.

'What was that about?' Cob demanded. 'So much for being the quiet captain's mate.'

'I had to find out the truth. And he gave it to me.'

'We could have been killed.'

'Give me your view,' Dion said. 'Why did they let us go?'

'The woman. Zara.'

'Yes, the woman. Who was she?'

'My ma used to tell me stories of witches—'

'I agree,' Dion said.

Cob frowned.

'I think she was a magus, or something like a magus,' Dion said. 'She put you under some kind of charm – I know you, my old friend, and you would never have revealed we were from Xanthos otherwise. I also think she knew who I was.'

They were almost at the *Liberty*, where just a few barrels remained on the wooden platform. Finn stood nearby, haggling with a last handful of shouting merchants.

'The stories say that the Aleutheans had a golden lighthouse so powerful it could be seen for a hundred miles,' Dion continued. 'To defeat the eldren, they must have had magic of their own. We need to learn more about them. If there's one thing I've learned, it's that magic is to be respected.'

'Let's just get out of here,' Cob said. 'And remind me not to sign up for a voyage like this again.'

'Finn!' Dion called. 'Are you done? We're leaving.'

'I still have goods to sell!'

'We're leaving. Right now. I want this ship sailing as fast as possible for home.'

'You're just the captain's mate. You can't tell me what to do.'

Dion leveled a stare at his richly dressed friend.

'Fine, fine,' Finn muttered.

But as Dion started up the gangway, out of the corner of his eye he saw Finn take a purse from one of the merchants and the two men clasp palms, before Finn hurried after him. Dion scowled at Finn, who gave him a look of innocence.

'I can't turn away good profit,' he protested.

'Make all haste!' Dion called to the crewmen. 'Get us moving!'

Soon the *Liberty* was drifting away from the pier. Dion stood at the vessel's stern, gazing at the city. He'd learned more than he'd ever thought he would.

And the knowledge was more than unsettling.

'What just happened?' Palemon thundered. He towered over Zara, fists bunched at his sides as he glared at her.

'There was something you were unaware of, sire,' Zara said smoothly. 'You were just speaking with Dion, the king of Xanthos.'

'What?' Kyphos spluttered. He slowly frowned. 'The first mate?'

'The very same. I was watching. When you threatened him, he was still confident. He removed his silver necklace. Why? Evidently so he could change his form. As we learned from our Ilean captives, he is half-eldran. I approached and it was confirmed. I can charm most men, but my magic had no effect on him at all.'

'The king of Xanthos? Even more reason to capture him,' Palemon said, whirling to face the direction of the harbor. 'We should summon our forces—'

'Sire,' Zara interrupted sharply. 'We were not prepared for him. Even you . . . Are you certain you could face a shapeshifter and be guaranteed of victory? He is a powerful king, which explains the vessel.

It will be full of fighting men. No, he took us by surprise. We will let him leave, and soon he will be gone.'

'What does this mean?' Kyphos asked.

'It means that the king of Xanthos is aware of our plans,' Zara said.

'He is bold,' Palemon muttered. 'To come himself.' His lip curled in distaste. 'But he is part monster. How could they make him their king?' He shook his head. 'So much has changed in the Realm. The eldren have reclaimed Sindara. A half-breed rules in Xanthos. Control of the three seas is fragmented, subject to constant war. Humanity has become primitive . . . These people think our weapons and armor are advanced!'

'That ship is advanced enough,' Kyphos said.

Zara shook her head. 'It is indeed large, and powerful for the current era. But the *Solaris* was far more sophisticated.'

'Can we expect war?' Kyphos asked, looking up at Palemon.

'Xanthos is far from Malakai,' the king said. 'No, I would think not. But we will need to make our next move swiftly. Making enemies is inevitable if we are to get the ships we need, but we will doom ourselves if we don't have the strength to defeat them.'

Palemon scowled, gazing out the window. The trireme was already making speed as it left. Tearing his eyes away, he turned to the sorceress. 'Zara, your search for artifacts . . . Please tell me you've found something.'

'I came because I have something to show you.' She nodded, and then gave a small smile. 'I arrived just in time, it seems.'

'What did you find?' Kyphos asked.

Zara shook her head. 'I'm sure you have work to do,' she said, pointing her sun staff at the hunchback. 'This is for the king alone.'

8

Palemon followed Zara out of the palace, only realizing when they were in the streets that neither of them had thought to ask for an escort. He smiled to himself. Now that he had a palace, it appeared he needed to be escorted everywhere he went. The trappings of power, he supposed. An escort was utterly unnecessary. Only a foolish enemy would challenge the sorceress.

As they walked side by side through the city streets, turning into one of the longest avenues, he saw that she was taking him to the Sky Tower.

'You have solved the tower's secret?' he asked.

Still clutching her sun staff, she glanced over at him. 'It was the first place we looked, of course, but aside from the fact that its design is odd to say the least, our initial search turned up nothing. Nonetheless, after exploring the city and talking to the priests, everything pointed here. It became obvious that during the reign of Aleuthea it was a place of importance, even if today's priests have only been using it for ceremonies.'

The tower grew ever larger as they approached until it dominated Palemon's vision. A tall, perfect cylinder, it was so large that it would take a man a reasonable amount of time to walk around the perimeter. The huge blocks it was made of were a pale stone, not as beautiful as marble, but evidently able to stand the test of time.

They came to an arched entrance, wide enough for ten men to walk abreast and easily twelve feet tall. Two of Zara's fellow sorcerers stood guard outside, both wearing gray robes and clutching tall staffs in their hands, and moved to the side to allow them past. Entering the dark interior, Zara led Palemon along a corridor that followed the curve of the wall, before coming to another archway, this one revealing light at the tower's hollow core.

Palemon walked across a floor of paved stone to the very center of the shaft and looked up. He could see a small circle of blue sky, high above.

'First, the tower,' Zara said. She lifted her staff, indicating the shaft they were standing in. Despite being at ground level, it felt to Palemon as if he were standing at the bottom of an immense well. 'As you can see, its basic shape is a cylinder, hollow from base to top.'

'For viewing the sky?'

'That is what the priests thought, although the mystery has always been: what does the circle reveal? The sun's passage? The moon? The constellations? Every one of the dozen magi we brought with us from Necropolis made his or her own assessment. We all agree. None of those things make sense.'

Despite living in Malakai for weeks, Palemon hadn't made time to see the tower, and he turned in a slow circle, gazing along the interior of the wall, seeing steps built into the inside of the tower and rising almost to the top of the shaft. The steps terminated at a stone ledge, encircling the shaft just below the tower's lip.

'What is the purpose of that ledge?' he asked. 'I doubt you could see anything from there.' He tilted his head back. 'Are those iron hoops circling the wall, just below?'

'To be truthful, I don't yet know the purpose of the stairway. But please, there is more. Come.'

Zara inclined her head, and he followed her back inside to the curved corridor. He was surprised to see that the path straightened and now the floor was sloping down, into the earth. The corridor, as wide as the main entrance, was steadily descending, the stone ceiling angling with it.

Palemon frowned, perplexed at the passage's immense size. He wondered where it led, and figured they were well below street level when the tunnel abruptly terminated in a chamber. He saw objects on a table: a stand for incense, a lamp, a statue of the god Helios. The table had been pushed to the side.

Strong force had torn a hole in the rear wall.

'It was only when I came back to the tower that I realized the stonework here was newer,' she explained. 'I used the power of wind to break the wall.'

Palemon tugged on his beard. The force it would have taken to tear down a wall of solid stone . . .

'This way,' Zara said.

She stooped to pass through the breach in the wall, but Palemon struggled, cursing as he maneuvered his frame into the gap. Finally on the other side, he noticed that the air was stiller. The ground was dusty rather than covered in grit and sand. The floor was made of the same stone as the sloping tunnel, but it had better stood the weathering effects of time.

My people built this tower. Someone, perhaps even one of my ancestors, sealed off this corridor.

It became gradually darker as they followed the tunnel, which made it difficult to see what lay ahead. Walking beside the sorceress, Palemon peered into the shadows and realized that they were approaching a huge door that perfectly filled the stone corridor. It appeared to be made of metal, perhaps even gold, matching the frame. The door was ajar. Zara had already come this way.

As they reached the door, she noticed him examining the angular symbols that followed the frame's perimeter. 'The door was magically sealed, and it took some time to open it,' she said. 'I almost died when

I stepped through; the air beyond hadn't been renewed in eons.' She smiled faintly. 'Fortunately I became unconscious before I'd entered far. I woke a few hours later. No harm was done.'

Palemon shook his head, admiring the strength of the woman. No doubt she'd been here, on her own, and after collapsing, she'd simply woken up and carried on.

'Coming, sire?'

The air was so still that he could hear his heart thudding slowly in his chest, beats sounding loud in his ears. What he'd seen so far was intriguing, but he knew Zara well enough to know that she was saving something for the end. Entering through the strange doorway, he sensed that he was now in a cavernous chamber, but the darkness was complete, and it was impossible to gauge its size. He took several long steps into the void, turning slowly, wondering if his eyes would ever adjust, trying to figure out what Zara had brought him here to see.

Then Zara lifted her sun staff, making a sharp sound. The hoop of gold at the top of her staff lit up, bathing the area in radiance.

The ceiling was high, and the underground chamber was even more immense than he'd imagined. Given the scale of the corridors and the golden door, the place was oversized, as if built for giants rather than humans. Turning to take it all in, the first thing he saw was that the floor, walls, and ceiling were all made of the same smooth, pale stone. He caught a glimpse of a series of barred iron cages along one side, each of an enormous size, but then Zara moved her staff, shifting the light to point out something on the opposite wall.

It was writing, two rows of large carved letters. Palemon strode up to it and frowned. 'What does it say?' he asked. 'It looks like it was written in haste.'

'It is Old Aleuthean. As you know, our language has changed over the years, but I believe it says: "*The dragons are fierce.*" That is the first line.'

'And the next?'

'"*The Arch of Nisos brings doom upon the world.*"'

He turned to her. 'Dragons?'

'Look around you.'

He spun round; there was nothing to see except the cages. He counted twelve of them, shrouded in darkness. Zara walked forward, bringing the light with her, and then he realized.

Some of the cages had occupants.

He strode to the nearest and stared inside, trying to understand what it was he was seeing. Zara followed him and threw the bolt, the metal creaking as she opened the cage. As Palemon entered, Zara's fingers danced around the staff and the light grew brighter.

Approaching the thing that filled the cage, Palemon finally stopped in his tracks. He swallowed.

He was looking at the skeleton of a massive beast. An iron collar was fastened around its neck, just behind the immense, wedge-shaped skull. The skull was resting on the ground, with empty eye sockets, each able to accommodate a man's head, and teeth yellowed with age. The curved spine was ridged like the trunk of a palm tree and led to wings made of countless delicate bones. A curled tail terminated in a diamond-shaped spike. Long claws at the end of its forelimbs looked sharp enough to decapitate a man with a single blow.

'It's a . . .'

'A dragon,' Zara said. 'Look.'

She touched the end of her staff to the skull, and he now saw a large hole punched through the thick bone behind one of the eye sockets. 'It was killed. They are all like this. Half of these cages contain a skeleton.'

Palemon tugged at his beard, trying to make sense of it.

'I have suspicions about the purpose of the tower, but I think I know what this place underneath was,' Zara said. Palemon glanced up when he heard her next words. 'It was their stables. Only the animals they kept here weren't horses.'

'But how . . . Why . . . ?'

'Look.' Zara tilted her staff to point out something hanging from a hook on the wall.

At first he thought it was simply a length of old chain, but then the sorceress used the tip of her staff to lift up one of the coils of metal links, and he saw that the reddish metal didn't look like iron.

'Some kind of harness?' Palemon asked.

'They appear to be reins,' Zara said. 'There are five other skeletons, and five more sets like this, six in total. The metal is copper, a little corroded but serviceable. And undeniably magical.'

Palemon looked from the reins to the dragon skeleton, still collared with a band of iron. He could only imagine how powerful the creature must have been in life.

His brow furrowed. This huge chamber was probably directly beneath the tower. The Aleutheans – it had to be them – had kept dragons here, dragons and reins.

Back in Necropolis, the magi had told fireside tales about dragons battling in the sky. Of course, they were always connected with the eldren, and their war with Palemon the First. But three hundred years had passed since the fall of Aleuthea, and history became distorted with the passage of time. Perhaps the eldren weren't the only ones to command the sky . . .

He suddenly had a thought. Whirling, he turned to face Zara. 'The statue. At the harbor.'

He and the sorceress exchanged glances.

Now Palemon was making strides so long he was almost running. Zara struggled to keep up with him as he left the strange stables behind, following the wide, high-ceilinged corridor – big enough for a dragon to navigate – and then sped out of the arched entrance, rushing away from the Sky Tower.

He barely noticed the city folk as he made a determined path directly for the harbor gates, where the statue of the god Helios barred entrance to the city from the sea. He was dimly aware that he had left Zara somewhere behind him as he strode along the broad avenue that led to the harbor. Finally the gates appeared ahead and he made all speed for the monument.

Panting, Palemon stared up at the statue. Both the dragon and the stern-faced man on its back were made of smooth marble, poised as if preparing to launch from the pedestal of dark granite.

He tilted his head back to examine the man's features. He had a noble cast to his face, with long, flowing hair, but wore a fierce expression, cold and deadly – a strange face for a god. Palemon pictured him without the spiked golden crown that rested on his head, separate from the stone of the statue, something that could easily have been added later. He looked up at the statue's hand, raised high, and mentally replaced the golden discus with a sword, a mighty blade to match the weapon he'd inherited from his namesake.

The statue was old. There was no doubt about that.

Inspecting the granite pedestal, Palemon suddenly had an idea. He knelt in front of the block, examining the stone. Grime and bird excrement covered its exterior. He climbed back to his feet, scanning the harbor until he saw some men scrubbing barnacles from a fishing boat's hull.

He stormed over to the fishermen, soon returning to the statue with a bucket of sea water and a stiff brush. He knelt once more, and with furious movements began to work at the crust of filth, scrubbing the front of the statue block clean. At first he thought the surface of the revealed stone was smooth, but as he worked until the muscles in his arms ached, ridges became clear.

Finally, as Zara arrived, he'd scrubbed enough from the granite pedestal to reveal the name carved into it. One word was written on the statue's base. It was the name of the king who had once ruled this city. It was the same name as the man who ruled it now.

Palemon.

Zara gasped, staring at him with wide eyes, before gazing at the statue once more. The two read the name silently, as if to say it out loud would somehow mean disrespect.

Palemon, direct descendant of the ancient king, looked up at the man's noble features and knew he was looking at the face of his ancestor. An ancestor riding on the back of a dragon.

'This is it,' Palemon said, to himself as much as to Zara. 'The answer we've been looking for.' His fists were clenched at his sides; he realized his eyes were burning. 'This is how we get the ships we need. This is how we conquer the world.'

9

Chloe was in the academy, one of the semi-intact structures that made up the complex of ruins, hidden from view on the eastern side of the island of Athos.

Wearing a plain white chiton, she sat with her legs folded under her on a floor of hard stone, opposite her teacher, Zedo. Though he rarely smiled, today his face was even graver than usual. She could sense that her training was heading to greater intensity. So far, she was managing to keep her power under her control, but as he always said, that could change at any time.

'Now that you have listened to the wind, it is time for you to recognize it in the power inside you.'

Chloe nodded, biting her lip. Day after day, she had sat on a cliff, listening to the sea and to the howling wind that blew against the coast. She spent so long in the same place that all her whirling thoughts about her home and the people she loved melted away, until she forgot where she was and felt free from the confines of her body. Sometimes it was as if there was a wind inside her, calling to the wind blowing her hair around her face. Days became weeks, with only mealtimes to break up the routine of constant meditation. Yet despite the lack of activity, for some reason she found herself sleeping soundly every night in the small chamber she occupied alone.

Nearly two weeks of listening to the wind passed before Zedo asked her to join him in the academy.

She now promised herself she would follow Zedo's instructions and learn to control her power. If she succeeded, she would be free to leave and return to Phalesia. If she failed, the headaches would return, and at some point she would die.

Seated across from Chloe, the magus's gaunt face appeared ghostly in the low light. 'First, Chloe,' he said, staring directly at her. 'Tell me what you know of the four materia.'

'Gold is light. Silver is wind. Copper is sound. Iron is fire.'

'Good. What else?'

'Gold makes people feel devotion, but also greed. Silver can bring clarity, but also confusion. Copper can charm. Iron inspires violence.'

'Keep going.'

Chloe hesitated. 'These feelings can be used to summon the power.'

'No,' the magus suddenly said sharply. He cut the air with his hand. 'Your first teacher, if you can call him that, was the descendant of Aleuthean sorcerers. You learned the Aleuthean way, which carries more risk of feedback.'

'Feedback?'

'Rather than projecting fire, it is the magus who burns. Rather than creating light, the magus goes blind. The Aleuthean way is not the true path.'

He sighed when he saw her expression.

'I can see that I am going to have to explain some things. About our magic and the time when, hundreds of years ago, Aleuthea came to dominate the world.'

He looked into her eyes as he spoke.

'Long ago, when Athos was at the height of its power, and the only sorcerers were those who were taught on this island, a magus named Nisos completed his training and left with our blessing. But Nisos wasn't content to be the high priest of our temple at Aleuthea. Soon after arriving at his new post, he became restless. He wanted power.'

Zedo paused to let his words sink in.

'A skilled sorcerer, Nisos offered his services to Aleuthea's newly crowned king. He revealed our secrets, and the king, a young man named Palemon, was duly impressed.'

Chloe frowned. Her first teacher, Vikram, had said that the Aleutheans were magic users, but he'd never said that they'd stolen the knowledge from somewhere else.

'With the king's support, Nisos founded his own school of magic, and trained many sorcerers, until he had far more studying his new, simpler way than the true path. Meanwhile Palemon was making stronger weapons and armor than anything seen before and training his warriors relentlessly in combat. He began to enlarge his borders, one tribe or chiefdom at a time. Every enemy he captured, warrior or civilian, was enslaved and collared, and fought for him or died. He waged war against larger nations, gambling on the fate of huge battles. But his enemies didn't have what he had. Palemon had sorcery at his disposal, and he had Nisos, the most talented and ambitious sorcerer of them all. With magic and might, they were able to conquer the world.'

As Zedo spoke, Chloe remembered the tales from her childhood. Palemon was always a wise king, the man who brought peace to the world, the hero who fought the eldren and won. But after making friends among the eldren – Liana, Zachary, and Eiric, to name a few – she had often wondered who the true villain had been.

'Palemon was a proud king, but Nisos was even more ruthless and arrogant. When the expanding Aleuthean Empire brushed up against the eldren, Nisos, who now called himself an archmagus, was astounded to discover their abilities, and immediately began to conduct experiments.'

'Experiments?'

The magus nodded. 'Nisos discovered that when collared, an eldran could not change his form. If an eldran was in his normal shape, or the shape of a giant, or a dragon, he would stay that way. Nisos then discovered something else. The collar would also prevent him turning wild.'

Chloe's eyes widened. She cast her mind back to when she'd first met Triton, the late, self-proclaimed king of the eldran, in the cells below the sun king's palace in Lamara, again seeing the collar around his neck. Eiric had also been collared when she and Liana had rescued him at the heart of Cinder Fen, now Sindara. She'd known that a collar could weaken the eldran, robbing them of their ability to change their form. But she'd never thought of the effect a metal collar might have on one already changed.

'Of all of the forms eldran could take, dragons most fascinated both Palemon and Nisos. They knew that with dragons at their disposal, the most far-flung reaches of their empire would never have the courage to break away. But although Nisos possessed collared dragons, he could not force them to do his bidding. So even as Palemon waged war against the eldran – a war of enslavement, rather than conquest – Nisos studied the problem relentlessly.'

Chloe realized that the stories had never been clear on one thing. How had the war between the Aleutheans and the eldran started? What had they been fighting over?

She now knew. Palemon didn't want the riches of the eldran homeland. He wanted the children of Sindara. Marrix and his people had been fighting for their freedom . . . For their very existence.

'Nisos finally solved the problem. He found a way to enthrall a dragon in the grip of magical chains. The strongest fighters and most powerful sorcerers became riders of dragons, each worth a thousand men on the battlefield, able to roam the length and breadth of the Aleuthean Empire, which they called their Realm. Palemon captured as many eldran as he could, warring against their entire race, driving them to either flee their homeland or fight until they turned wild. Marrix fought back, but it was only after he'd lost everything that he managed to destroy Aleuthea.'

The magus again met Chloe's eyes.

'The Oracle helped Marrix to do it.'

Chloe drew back, surprised.

Zedo continued. 'What you and I think of as solid ground is actually a thin crust with molten fire below it. Beneath Aleuthea was a dangerous seam, a place of special sensitivity. The Oracle saw the future and discovered that in a thousand years nature would take its course, the seam would fracture, and the island would topple. By giving this knowledge to Marrix, she brought that future forward, and helped bring about the end of Palemon's reign.'

His lips thinned. 'By then the Aleutheans had conquered Athos and torn down our temples. We once had a thriving settlement here; now it is as you see it. But that isn't why the Oracle acted as she did. After the fall of Sindara, the dragons in captivity eventually died, until Palemon had no more. He began to lose control of his empire. In desperation, he turned to Nisos.

'The archmagus, now an old man, studied the Wellspring in Cinder Fen, and the Source here at Athos. As the far-flung reaches of the Realm began to revolt, he found a solution to his king's problem. It took the form of a powerful artifact, but an artifact with a fatal flaw. The Oracle saw that it had the potential to destroy the world. It was then that she sought out Marrix, and told him how he could have his vengeance, consigning Aleuthea to the depths of the sea.'

The priest of Athos smiled grimly.

'So, there is the Aleuthean way, and the true path. We teach that you must be in complete control of your power; it must rise up of its own accord. You must meditate regularly in order to keep it quelled. And only when you have learned to make the fire inside you go cold, will you be able to leave this island, with a reasonable chance that it won't kill you.'

Chloe took a deep breath and then nodded. She promised herself she would learn.

'Now, listen carefully. You are first going to learn to work with silver, which means control of the wind. Why? Because it was copper that caused you so much trouble before, and because iron is the most dangerous. Gold we will save for another day. As I have already said, think of the power within you as a slow-burning fire. Can you feel it? You may close your eyes if you wish.'

She closed her eyes and there it was. It was just like the magus said: a seething fire pit, burning inside her. Her chest tightened. She tried not to think of all the pain that the fire might bring.

'Focus your attention on it, without drawing it in any way. Remain calm.'

Concentrating, Chloe tried, but suddenly she was afraid, remembering what had happened in Sindara.

'You are frowning and clenching your jaw. Find the calm. If you cannot make this first step, you will have to listen to the wind some more.'

'No,' she said.

She allowed her thoughts to settle, and finally was able to calmly appraise the fire. Like any fire, it rose and fell, surging and ebbing.

'I can feel it. It's not bringing any pain.'

'Good. You are close to the Source, so while you are at Athos, the power will come to you easily.'

Chloe nodded, surprised to feel a thrill of excitement.

'Now the fire consists of all four materia. Think of a real fire. When you hold tinder above it, the flame seeks out the tinder and catches hold of it. It is like this with your power. You can think of violence, and the power of iron will come, but the true path shows us another way.'

She swallowed. 'I'm ready.'

'First, let us think of the wind. Do it now.'

She remembered the wind she'd heard on the cliff, howling as it blew, bringing cool air from the sea. The fire inside her surged upward, seeking an exit. A slow pain grew in her head as it felt like more than she could handle.

She opened her eyes.

'What happened?' the magus asked.

'It grew, but it felt like it was too strong.'

He nodded. 'That is exactly what I expected to happen. It might feel difficult, like thinking four thoughts at the same time, but the wind in your mind can't have any temperature. It can't have any sound. It must just be the wind. Otherwise you will not get the one materia you want to use; you will bring a combination, which is one of the greatest sources of danger, and where many go wrong.'

She frowned, trying to make sense of what he was saying.

'Now try once more.'

She again closed her eyes and thought of wind that was neither warm nor cold. It was a soundless wind; it didn't howl. It could only be noticed by the feel of it on her skin.

The fire grew, but this time it felt more . . . pure. From the inferno, a single tongue of flame the color of silver was rising, and she was in control of it. This time it brought no pain, no sensation of discomfort.

She opened her eyes and smiled. 'It was silver. I think it worked.'

He returned the smile. 'Well done. That is enough for today, but now, when you experience the wind, try to imagine it without temperature, without sound. You will feel your mind stretching. It is like mental gymnastics. Heat doesn't actually require light, but we associate them so much that we think they belong together. Sound can move through metal or water as well as air, but we think of it as carried on the wind. It is about separating and identifying what makes each of the four materia unique.'

'What else can I practice?'

'You are eager, but be careful of pushing too hard. For now, sit far enough from a fire that you can look at the flames and imagine them to be cold. This gives you practice with light. The visual representation of the fire – the flames – is separate to the heat, which comes from the coals. Stare up at the moon on a cold night.' He paused. 'Then, after allowing your mind some rest, sit close to a fire, shut your eyes, and instead concentrate on the warmth, without light. Strike a copper bell and remember that sound and wind do not need to belong together. Separate. *Separate.* You understand?'

She nodded.

'Good. Remember to meditate, and to give yourself time to recover. You have a question?'

'What you said earlier. The Oracle truly played a part in the destruction of Aleuthea?'

'Yes, she did. And there may yet be more work to be done.'

10

Dion closed his eyes and inhaled deeply; the sea air in Xanthos always smelled like home. Opening his eyes, his city soon came into view as the trireme rounded a headland. He saw the lofty Royal Palace with its gardened terraces standing proud and tall, flying crimson flags that snapped in the breeze. Nearby the bronze hoplite statue outside the Temple of Balal glistened in the bright rays of the sun. The cleft of the river that divided the narrow city into two halves, residential and royal, was hard to make out with so many warships pulled up onto the shore.

As the *Liberty* approached, a crowd of people waited on the sandy beach to greet their return. His uncle was absent – no doubt busy with one thing or another – but Roxana waited along with a group of sailors, cheering and waving as the *Liberty* picked a clear patch of shore and executed a series of skillful maneuvers to slot itself neatly between a pair of two smaller biremes.

The crew plunged into the water, hauling the vessel high above the tide line and then, after the gangway slid out, Dion was the first to disembark, with Cob and Finn following after him. Roxana, Dion's master of the fleet, came forward. A stocky woman with weathered skin and short, sun-bleached hair, she opened her arms and wrapped them around him, slapping him on the back.

'Sire,' she said gruffly. 'Welcome home.' Releasing Dion, she then turned to Cob. 'So, Cobrim, it appears you brought my ship back in one piece. Or is there damage I can't see?' Her eyes narrowed as she cast a critical gaze over the vessel.

'She's in better condition than when we left,' Cob said defensively.

'Give me an hour with her, and I'll let you know if I agree.'

As she loomed over him, Cob was taken aback, until she suddenly barked a laugh and pulled him forward into a hug twice as tight as the one she'd given Dion. 'It's good to see you, little man.'

Dion glanced at Finn, who grinned. While Roxana and Cob caught up, Dion inclined his head, waiting for Finn to follow him a little way from the group.

'What is it?' Finn asked, becoming serious when he saw Dion's expression.

Dion rubbed his chin, gathering his thoughts. Finn was his master of trade. He was known everywhere in the city and also ran the spy network of the Free Men, which reached far and wide.

'I want you to do something for me,' Dion said. 'Find out anything you can about the history of Aleuthea. I'm particularly interested in anything related to their abilities . . . We're talking about magic, here. You understand?'

Finn frowned as he tucked a lock of hair behind his ear. 'There are things they left behind. Statues . . . Ceramics . . . '

'I don't know what I'm looking for, but I'll know it when I see it. Offer good silver to anyone who brings you artifacts that tell us something about Aleuthea. Talk to your people.'

'You're worried.'

'I am.'

While in Malakai, Finn had casually questioned some of the merchants he'd been trading with and had heard tales of the eerie sandstorm that struck the city's defenders precisely as Palemon attacked.

'You think it's true, about this wind?'

'I don't know yet what I believe,' Dion said. 'That's why I need you to do this for me.'

'I'll do whatever I can.'

'Thank you, my friend.' Dion clasped Finn on the shoulder. He then glanced at the palace. 'Now it's time for me to do something I haven't been looking forward to.'

———

'I still don't see why you had to go yourself. You left me with a thousand matters unattended to.'

'I'm sure you resolved them all, Uncle.'

Pacing the throne room, furnished only by the empty wooden chair on its raised dais, Glaukos scowled. 'A king has duties.'

'And many of those duties are given to people in the royal council, people I trust. My father had several advisers.'

'Yet you took your master of trade with you!'

'I needed him.'

A tall, lean man with neatly combed gray hair and patrician features, Dion's chief adviser turned on his heel to glare at his nephew. 'I hope it was worth it.'

'Uncle, there was cause to be worried, and still is. These newcomers . . . I believe they truly are the descendants of Aleuthea.'

Glaukos snorted. 'You're not serious . . .'

'I am.' Dion refused to be intimidated. 'I met their king. His name is Palemon, and he claims to be in direct lineage from the same Palemon who fought the eldren. His soldiers wear strange armor, and their weapons are unlike anything I've seen before. He conquered Malakai at the first attempt.'

'Malakai is far from here.' Glaukos shook his head. 'And the population has long resented the yoke of Ilea. Your father would have been the first to tell you that conquering a city and keeping it are two very different things. Whoever this warlord is, he'll soon be busy trying to hold on to his new kingdom. There is no way Kargan of Ilea will let it stand.'

'Palemon isn't going to stop with Malakai.'

'So his army is that powerful?' Glaukos finally stopped pacing. 'How many are they?'

'Not big in number. But they have magic . . .'

'Magic?' Glaukos raised an eyebrow. 'Bah. Listen to yourself.'

'Enough, Uncle,' Dion said through gritted teeth. 'Let me just say that it pays to be prepared. There are many more Aleutheans than I saw. Palemon left them behind, somewhere across the sea, and will fight until he has a fleet to go back for them.'

He decided to leave unsaid that Palemon had wanted the *Liberty* to be the first member of his new fleet.

'He sounds like a man with many problems, and even more delusions.'

'If you'd been there, you might understand,' Dion said. 'At any rate, I plan to double our naval patrols and post a heavy guard on the fleet at night.'

'For how long? It will cost us.'

'For as long as necessary.'

The two men glared at each other, and then Glaukos relented. 'You are the king. You must do what you think is necessary.'

With an effort of will, Dion regained his composure. 'Speaking of the kingdom. What have I missed?'

Glaukos took a deep breath. 'The Blackwell Mines.'

Dion's lips thinned. This wasn't going to be good. 'Go on.'

'As far as I know, neither Tanus nor Sindara have actually declared war, but there have been clashes, with casualties on both sides. The latest word is that the eldren have seized the mines, and now it's the Tanusians trying to drive them away and reclaim them. We could send some men . . .'

'I won't send soldiers to attack the mine,' Dion said firmly. 'That is a line I will not cross. I took Queen Zanthe's side, as you insisted—'

'Because Tanus is in the right! They've operated the mines since your father was a young man.'

'Yet the eldren believe the mines are inside Sindara's borders.'

'You are the king of Xanthos,' Glaukos growled. 'You know as well as I do that we had to take the side of our ally, a fellow Galean nation, or your . . . unusual heritage would have raised questions.'

Dion held up a hand. 'I understand. I sent soldiers.'

'But when the eldren surrounded the mine you ordered them to leave their posts and return home.'

'I won't have soldiers of Xanthos fighting eldren.' Dion looked away from his uncle. 'I know I've pleased neither of them. Zanthe thinks I abandoned her, and the eldren think I was prepared to take up arms against them.'

It made Dion sad to think that he hadn't seen or spoken to Eiric, Zachary, or Liana for so long, not since before he'd led the Free Men. He had wanted to visit Sindara personally to explain that he'd had no choice besides supporting Tanus, but his coronation got in the way. His eyes narrowed. And if Eiric had wanted to discuss the situation rather than provoke conflict, he could have sent someone to Xanthos.

Nonetheless, if the people of Tanus and the eldren of Sindara were killing each other, he had to put a stop to it.

'I'll try to get another message through to King Eiric,' Dion said. 'Perhaps we'll get a reply this time. What else?'

'The coming election in Phalesia. Word is that Nilus is about to be defeated by Philippos. Lord Philippos and his daughter Isobel are soon going to be visiting Xanthos.' Glaukos hesitated. His voice softened from a barking growl to a gentle pleading. 'Dion, you cannot keep holding on to your memory of Chloe. She has been dead for more than half a year. It is past time you moved on.'

Dion broke away from his uncle's intent stare. Even hearing her name made him think of how she'd died, far from home, searching for her exiled father, murdered by bandits, her body left at the side of the road like a discarded rag.

'A king has responsibilities to his kingdom,' Glaukos continued. 'When Philippos and Isobel are here, I want you to be welcoming to them both. Do you understand? You have no heir. I won't back down on this.'

Dion sighed, but he nodded. 'I'll give them a proper welcome.'

With so much to attend to in Xanthos, perhaps Cob had been right and he shouldn't have gone in person to Malakai.

But something told him that he hadn't seen the last of King Palemon.

11

Palemon sat on the ebony throne while Kyphos stood beside him. Gathered around them, dressed in a motley array of pelts from the great cats, were the seven clan leaders who'd helped capture Malakai. They'd all become rich men after their conquest of the city, but then the news came that they'd all been expecting.

'Word is that the king of Ilea is amassing a huge army,' Alfad said. A dark-skinned warrior with ritual scars on his face, he was the leader of Clan Matanu, and generally spoke for the group. 'How can we hold out against such a strong force?'

The other clan leaders nodded gravely.

Palemon leaned forward, sweeping his gaze over the assembled headmen. 'Have you forgotten the wind summoned by the sorceress? Since then, with access to the city's resources, we have constructed more weapons of silver, copper, and iron for the dozen sorcerers she leads. Believe me when I say that you have seen only a small part of what our magi are capable of. Not only do we have the gods on our side, but each of our warriors is worth a hundred of Ilea's.' He spoke with certainty. 'No matter how many men they have, we will defeat them.'

'King Palemon . . .' Alfad hesitated. 'We would like your permission to return to our wives, daughters, and mothers in the desert.'

Kyphos spoke up. 'You all gave your oaths to serve your king.'

'And we intend to fulfill our oaths,' Alfad said. 'Of course we do. There are a dozen more tribes who will now join us. We can return with hundreds more warriors.'

'And tell me, Alfad,' Kyphos said. 'This return. Will it take place before or after the arrival of the Ileans?'

'We will return as soon as we can,' Alfad said, spreading his hands. A chorus of assent from the other clan leaders greeted his words. 'We will remain only long enough to check on our families and organize a meeting of headmen.'

Kyphos glared at Alfad. 'You didn't answer my quest—'

'I will grant your request. You may leave,' Palemon interrupted.

Kyphos scowled, but he didn't open his mouth. Where Zara concerned herself with magic, it was his role to worry about their fighting forces.

'Thank you, King Palemon.' Alfad bowed, and the other six clan leaders all bowed, smiling and murmuring their appreciation. 'We will return as soon as we can.'

'I understand,' Palemon said. 'Go, all of you. Go with my blessing. Take your plunder with you.'

'Great King . . . Thank you.'

Palemon waved them away.

As soon as the clan leaders had left, Kyphos's eyes narrowed. 'Sire, we need them.'

'We don't. Their numbers were useful when we seized this city, but they are correct – against a disciplined army, these tribesmen aren't what will make the difference.'

'Then what will?' Kyphos's bushy eyebrows came together. 'Six sets of copper chains?'

'There may be more.'

'We've scoured the city. Even Zara agrees, there are no more to be found. And how do we know that the chains will do what the sorceress says?'

Hearing the metallic tinkle of jewelry, Palemon looked up to see Zara entering the throne room. The sorceress glanced at Kyphos and then met Palemon's eyes as she approached.

'I believe the chains are serviceable,' she said, 'although they are the work of Archmagus Nisos, and it is beyond my ability to make more.'

'Think about it, Kyphos,' Palemon said, pounding a fist into his open palm. 'Six strong warriors or skilled sorcerers on the backs of dragons. This is our destiny.'

'With only one problem that I can see,' Kyphos persisted. 'Where do we find the dragons? Do you plan on going to war with the eldren? Assaulting Sindara, as we did long ago?'

'No, you have reason to be skeptical . . . The eldren are too powerful for us as we are,' Palemon said. 'And you are correct. First we need to see if the magic functions, if a dragon can be harnessed and brought under control. We need a subject.'

'How is capturing a single eldran any easier?' Kyphos raised an eyebrow. 'They have a magical bond. An attack on one is an attack on them all. And how will you coerce it into changing its form?'

'There are ways,' Zara said softly.

'It is a shame the king of Xanthos is no longer here,' Kyphos said with a snort.

Silence filled the room after he spoke. Palemon tugged on the braids of his beard, before he and Zara exchanged glances. Kyphos's incredulous eyes grew wider and wider as he looked from face to face.

'Perhaps he could be,' Palemon mused. 'Zara? What are your thoughts?'

'It could work . . .'

Kyphos frowned. 'Sorceress, not long ago you advised us to let him leave without hindrance. You said he was too powerful for us. Now you think we can go to Xanthos and what, take him captive?'

'I said we were unprepared for him. He took us by surprise. But he lives as a man, and has a man's weaknesses. All we would have to do is find the right leverage, and for him to vanish without being traced back to Malakai.'

'He's a king!' Kyphos protested. 'You heard the clan leaders. Kargan of Ilea is sending his armies to retake this city. Don't we have enough enemies as it is?'

'Great power never comes without risk.'

'Perhaps there's another half-breed somewhere. Someone who isn't a king—'

'Silence,' Palemon growled.

He furrowed his brow as both Kyphos and Zara waited for him to come to a decision. Their position in Malakai was precarious. Back in Necropolis, people were starving. While Ilea's soldiers were no match for Palemon's cold bloods, a hundred and fifty men could only face so many. He needed a fleet, and to get it he needed power. He remembered the awe he'd felt gazing up at the statue depicting his ancestor, an ancestor who had dominated the world from the back of a dragon.

'Do it,' Palemon said. 'Make this your priority. Go to Xanthos. Find his weakness. He must have a child or a wife. Use someone he loves to bend him to your will.'

'Sire . . .' Kyphos tried again. 'We would be risking the wrath of Xanthos. Surely there is an easier target? Perhaps we could raid Sindara—'

Palemon shook his head as he interrupted. 'Kings have more weaknesses than other men. Sindara is far away, and the eldren are more dangerous than the Xanthians; it takes time for men to mobilize to wage war, whereas the eldren could be on us in moments. No, this is the path we must follow. We need a single subject, one who can be controlled. We must find out what the chains are capable of. Then, and only then, can we consider seizing any eldren from their homeland.'

Zara nodded, while Kyphos's scowl only deepened.

'There will be no more discussion. I want you both to leave for Xanthos,' Palemon ordered. 'Work together. I'm counting on you.'

12

Chloe stood on a tall cliff, facing the sea, with Zedo beside her. They both held staffs in their hands, crowned with silver spirals, the pale metal twisted into a conical shape.

She kept her mind calm and concentrated on the feel of the wind against her cheeks. She thought of wind without sound. She felt the fire inside her roar, and the tongue of silver flame rose up. This time, unlike the last, she was clutching a wind staff, clenched fingers pressed to the base of the metal.

She closed her eyes as she felt the silver flame leave the confines until it suddenly sizzled throughout her body, making her gasp. Opening her eyes again, she released it, and the whitened flame inside her now left the fire completely, directed through her hand into the matching silver twist. The device glowed brightly, fairly humming with power. She then swept her staff from left to right.

Out on the surging sea, a sudden gust of wind blew across the tops of the waves, shattering the crests into spray. The smaller waves joined to form a growing breaker that rose up as the wind pressed against the water. It became bigger and bigger, traveling in the same direction as her movement. Soon the wave was several feet high and swelling, with a crest of white foam on its summit as it threatened to tumble.

Beside her, the magus did the same thing, but in reverse. The device on his staff flared up, the color of the moon at night. Guiding it right to left, a wave twice the size of Chloe's built up in an instant, heading directly for hers. The two waves collided. Spray shot up and the magus's wave was the victor, the only one to survive the contest.

'You can do better than that.' Zedo smiled.

Setting her jaw with determination, Chloe cleared her mind of all other thought, concentrating on the raw feeling of wind. She fed it to the fire inside, feeling the silver flame grow. But rather than release it, she continued to feed it until she felt she was going to burst with the raging power in her mind. She held it, drawing more and more until she knew she couldn't hold onto it a moment longer. With a strong cry, she finally let it free, feeling it leap through her body to dart through the metal in contact with her skin, while at the same time she swept the staff in a powerful movement.

A new wave grew and grew until it was as big as the magus's last effort. As it sped along, forming a towering peak, she drew on her power and released it again. Her wave grew still further in size.

She flicked a quick glance at the magus and saw him frowning in concentration. He made his own cry, pointing his staff at the sea, and a wave to match Chloe's began to approach hers. Heading on a collision path, the two waves struck each other and then savagely burst apart, sending flurries of water in all directions. Neither wave was the victor as both were destroyed.

'Good,' the magus said. His shoulders slumped as he let the base of his staff fall back to the ground. 'That is enough for today.'

'I can do bigger,' she protested.

'Remember what I said about the wind. In some ways it is the most difficult to control of the materia. And more power always means less control. Of the four, it is also the easiest to disrupt. If you work directly against a strong natural wind, or against another magus, the result can be chaos.'

Chloe suddenly felt exhausted. Her knees buckled, but she managed to straighten them.

'Be careful,' the magus said. 'You have a deep well of power inside you, but danger is ever present. Until you learn to cool the fire completely, you must either meditate to calm it or release your power regularly, but when you release, it must be with control.'

The magus held out a hand, and she gave him the staff, feeling disappointed that she would only be able to test herself under his supervision.

'I will walk you back,' he said. 'There are some matters we must discuss.' Her teacher spoke as he led her over the rocky ground. 'Tell me, have you had any visions?'

'Visions?'

'Like flashes of memory, but things you haven't experienced yourself. Images of the future.'

'No.' She shook her head emphatically. 'Why?'

'If you do, you must tell us.'

'Visions of the future? You want to know if I can do the things the Oracle does?'

He hesitated. 'Yes. The Oracle is very old, ancient in fact. The Source gives her the ability to live for many years, provided she does not leave her cave. But eventually she will die, and we hope that before that day comes, the gods will provide us with a replacement. This is one of the reasons we came for you. The abilities of the Oracle are akin to the fire within a sorcerer.'

'I haven't seen anything.'

'If you do . . .'

'I will tell you.'

His expression was inscrutable. 'Good.'

13

The large galley bobbed in the waves as two sailors jumped into the water and hoisted Lord Philippos onto their shoulders, carrying him to the dry sand.

'King?' a soft feminine voice called from the vessel.

Dion turned to see a young woman of about his own age smiling as she gazed at him. He couldn't help returning her bright smile; she could only be Philippos's daughter, Isobel. She put her arms out imploringly.

'Allow me,' Dion murmured to the two bearers.

Leaving the shore and plunging into the shallows, he headed out into the water himself and took her offered hand, helping her glide into his arms. Easily carrying her slight weight to the shore, he set her gently down.

'Thank you, King Dion.'

'Welcome to my city, lady,' Dion said.

'I'm happy to be here.'

Isobel was slim and willowy, nearly as tall as him, with long blonde hair formed into a multitude of twists that cascaded down her back. Undeniably pretty, she had bright blue eyes, high cheekbones, and a small mouth, with a dimpled chin and a determined set to her sharp jaw. She wore a light-green chiton and a delicate gold necklace with a symbol of a dolphin.

As he drank in her features, she gave him another slight smile, lowering her gaze before moving away. Realizing he was staring, Dion tore his eyes off her and turned to greet her father.

Philippos, a wealthy Phalesian landowner, was young to be Isobel's father – barely in his forties and a striking man, with his daughter's high cheekbones, narrow face, and sharp-looking eyes. He had oiled dark hair, which suggested Isobel got her blonde hair from her mother, and wore a rich white tunic.

'Lord Philippos,' Dion said. 'We are looking forward to hosting you in Xanthos. Everyone says you are the next first consul of Phalesia.'

Philippos grinned broadly and gave a small bow. 'One can never say with elections.'

'Lord Philippos is known for his modesty and renowned for his work with the poor,' Glaukos said. He and Philippos had already exchanged greetings; the two men obviously knew each other.

'And you, lady?' Dion asked. 'Do you also work with those in need?'

'I support my father in all his endeavors,' Isobel said with a coy smile.

'Well said.' Glaukos chuckled. He glanced up at the sky. 'We will host you with a banquet tonight, but I notice the hour is still early. Lady Isobel, are you tired from your journey?'

'Not at all. I've been sitting in a boat since dawn and I'm anxious to stretch my legs. King Dion, I noticed the impressive shipyards. Perhaps you could give me a tour?'

Dion glanced at his uncle, who looked like he was struggling not to mouth the word 'Yes'.

'Of course,' Dion said. 'Please, come with me.'

'Do you know much about ships?' Dion asked as they followed the shore.

'Not really.' Isobel gave a soft smile and a shrug. 'But I'm anxious to learn.'

She asked him about the size of his fleet and the new harbor he was building at Fort Liberty as they walked side by side, the gentle crash of small waves providing a murmuring backdrop to their conversation. Her queries revealed her lack of knowledge, but the questions themselves were surprisingly astute. He found himself elaborating on his plans in more detail than he'd expected.

They set a path along the soft sand higher on the beach to pass above the rows of biremes, drawn up high enough that the rising tide wouldn't drag them away. Finally Dion led Isobel to the bow of the *Liberty*, the first in a group of larger warships, where two painted eyes under the bowsprit glared at them, the artist having drawn them so that they appeared to be embedded in the polished pine.

'It's huge,' she said.

'It's called a trireme. I doubt there's another like it anywhere on the Maltherean.'

'Trireme?' Her gaze traveled along the vessel's side, taking in the open lower decks and the oars, currently drawn in. 'Because there are three banks of oars?'

'Someone told you that.' Dion smiled.

'Untrue!' Her eyes widened with innocence. 'If a bireme has two decks, it stands to reason.' She patted his arm playfully. 'I don't need to be a mathematician to work it out.'

He grinned, a little unused to her familiar manner, but enjoying it nonetheless. 'We've built nearly six of them now. But this is my flagship, the *Liberty*. It's the biggest, and also the first trireme Roxana built.'

'Roxana?' Isobel frowned. 'Isn't that a woman's name?'

'She built everything you see here, and she runs it too. I'd be lost without her.'

'Is she attractive?'

'In her way.' He chuckled. 'But I think she has her eye on a friend of mine. Come, I'll introduce you to her.'

As Dion and Isobel continued toward the shipyards, he tried to think of something to say. He'd never struggled to find words with Chloe, and for some reason he'd thought it would be the same with Isobel, but already the silence was becoming uncomfortable; he could see that Isobel was pretending to examine every vessel they passed with interest while she waited for him to speak.

'I saw the dolphin on your necklace. Shouldn't a dolphin be on a silver necklace, for Silex?'

'I prefer gold, but I asked Father's jeweler to make me a necklace with a dolphin for this visit.' She paused for a moment as she lifted up the solid gold dolphin to show it to him. Despite himself, he found his eyes drifting to the pale skin below. 'I like the sea,' she finished.

'Can you sail?'

'No.' She laughed. 'I'm a woman! Men do the sailing. But I like being on boats.'

'What about horses?'

'I prefer not to ride. It's more comfortable aboard a ship. Whenever I ride I get sore.' She patted the curve of her hip and behind, just below her slim waist.

They now approached another trireme, this one obviously still under construction. The huge vessel rested in a deep, tiered depression, and there were hundreds of small wooden supports holding it in place, along with a sturdy timber frame.

'Ah, there she is. Roxana!'

Roxana glanced at them, but her attention immediately went back to the ship under construction. She was watching intently as workers on the top deck maneuvered an immense cut and polished log into place, tilting it up as ropes fastened to its end came tight, hauled by groups of workers at ground level.

'Sire,' Roxana said. 'I'm a bit busy here.'

Isobel looked shocked, but Dion laughed. 'Carry on.' He kept clear of the proceedings, pointing things out to Isobel. 'She's fitting the mast. It's an important stage and she needs to concentrate.'

'Keep it up or I'll use your skins for sails!' Roxana roared. The mast began to approach the vertical, but then started to tip. 'Kalaphos!' she shouted. 'Get your crew over there to help!'

A bunch of workers rushed to help the men hauling on the ropes. Some were Xanthians, but others were from Fort Liberty, people who'd made new lives in Xanthos. A dark-haired woman, dressed in sailor's clothing more commonly seen on a man, bumped into Isobel as she dashed past, muttering an apology but never looking back.

'Sorry,' Dion said. 'We shouldn't bother them. If it went wrong, we'd lose months of hard work.'

'It's fine.' Isobel gave him a smile. She nodded toward a grassy bank above the shipyards. 'Perhaps we could sit on the grass and watch?'

'Good idea.'

They left the frantic activity behind, looking for a place where the grass was soft and they could watch the harbor and the sea. Dion felt uncomfortable around Isobel, but she seemed far from uncomfortable around him. She held out a hand, and when he clasped it she began to settle herself, arranging the soft folds of her garment in her lap. When Dion sat down, she rearranged herself so that she sat close to him, their thighs touching.

'If my father wins the election, he will be first consul of Phalesia,' she said.

'I hear he's almost certain to win.'

Her face lit up. 'I hope he does. I'd like to know all the work has been worthwhile. My mother died when I was born, which means I'm hosting so many banquets that I've put on weight.'

Glancing at the slender young woman, Dion raised an eyebrow.

'Tell me about yourself,' Isobel said.

'You probably know all about me already.'

She frowned. 'I know some things, but I'm old enough to know that what I know is far from everything. Your mother was an eldran.'

'Yes, she was.' Dion waited.

'And you have their abilities.'

'Some of them. It's something I still struggle with.'

'Your family was killed when the Ileans seized Xanthos, all except your brother.'

'Yes.'

'I'm sorry,' Isobel said, meeting his eyes. 'I can't imagine what that must have felt like. And then to have your brother finally make peace with Ilea, only to lose his life at the end. You have no one.'

'Not true,' he said. 'I have my uncle. I have my friends, Cob, Finn, and Roxana.'

'Do you have friends among your mother's people?'

'Among the eldren? I do . . . I did. We haven't spoken in a long time. I'm sure you know about the Blackwell Mines.'

'The eldren captured them from Tanus and won't give them back.'

Dion nodded, and then there was silence as they watched the work at the shipyards.

'People say you were in love with Chloe, daughter of Aristocles,' Isobel said, looking up at him a little fearfully, waiting to see what his reaction would be. 'I spoke to her once. I always thought she was beautiful. I was a little frightened of her, to tell you the truth.'

Dion looked away from the shipyards and out to sea. 'I was. We went through a lot together.'

'You went all the way to Lamara to rescue her.'

He smiled. 'I did. But I didn't even know her then. It was on the way home that I learned how strong she was. We survived Cinder Fen together and faced the Ileans at the battle of Phalesia. But then . . .'

'Then your brother banished you to the Wilds, and married her himself. You must have hated him.'

'Hated Nikolas? No. I never did. He was always kind to me. It was only when they killed his wife and child that he changed. I never blamed him for it.'

There was silence for a time, before Isobel spoke again.

'Dion . . . May I call you that?'

'Of course.'

'I'll understand. If you . . . If you need time.'

Dion watched the waves tumble onto the sandy shore, and then sighed. 'She would want me to be happy. My uncle's right. I need to move on.'

He was pensive, before turning toward Isobel, staring into her intelligent eyes. 'You know, you're the only person I've ever spoken to like this. And I only just met you.'

Isobel chuckled. 'Well, we both know what your uncle and my father are trying to do.' She became serious. 'But let's just start with getting to know each other. For now, my verdict is that this first meeting has gone very well.'

'I would agree,' Dion said with a smile.

'And you're as handsome as they said you were,' she said, climbing to her feet. 'Now, I'm only here for a few days. We should both make the best of our time. I hear there's a waterfall in the hills, not far from the city. Would you like to show it to me?'

'I would.' Dion laughed.

She took him by the hand, pulling him up.

14

Chloe's eyes shot open. Her heart was hammering in her chest. She was lying on her pallet, in the dormitory at Athos. Her gaze flickered to the open window, seeing from the faintest beginnings of light that it was sometime before dawn.

Wondering what had woken her, she sat up when she heard shouts, fierce male voices, distant, but growing louder by the moment.

Something was happening.

She rolled out of bed and threw on clothing. Leaving her room, she immediately ran down the long corridor leading to the dormitory's exit, passing empty room after empty room. She cried out, even though the four brothers generally woke long before her. 'Wake up! Something's wrong!'

Out in the open, surrounded by the ancient ruins, she cocked her head, listening. She finally gazed up at the hillside, toward the western side of the island. The shouts were coming from the direction of Seer's Cove.

For a moment she hesitated. But when she heard another bellow, sounding closer than any before it, her gaze alighted on the grove of trees near the hill's crest. Rather than climb the slope directly, she began to sprint toward the thin strip of evergreens, where she could see from the screen of trees in the way she had before.

Chloe was breathless by the time she reached the crest. She weaved through the trees, and as soon as she had a vantage of the opposite side of the island and the hillside descending to Seer's Cove, she stopped in shock.

She could see half a dozen running men: swarthy, bare-chested warriors with curved swords. Her heart was already racing. But the sight of the raiders, with their weapons raised and kohl painted under their eyes, sent a chill along her spine.

One of them pointed in the direction of the path of blue stone that led to the Oracle's cave. He and two companions immediately started running toward the entrance, searching for the bounty of offerings made to the Oracle from far and wide. Another, slighter warrior, with pale eyes and streaks of gray in his hair despite the fact that he was still a young man, ran to the nearest of the ruins scattered around the cave and began searching for plunder near the strange glowing fires.

Two more raiders were calling out to each other as they climbed the hill. Reaching the crest, they stopped when they saw the ruins of what had once been a great complex. The older of the two, a stocky, bearded man with a strong jaw, barked something at his younger companion, who was red-faced and panting, eyes wild with battle lust. They were evidently arguing about which building to approach first, with the wild-eyed younger man pointing in the direction of the academy, which, though small, was the grandest of the buildings still standing, while the bearded warrior was trying to pull him in the direction of the dormitory.

Chloe scanned the carpet of dried foliage and twigs. She spied a stout piece of wood, closer to the edge of the small grove, and hurried to pick it up. Looking out from the trees again, she felt her heart beat out of time. The younger of the two raiders was gripping his companion's arm. They were both staring directly at her.

Her chest was heaving. They were just a stone's throw away. The bearded man's gaze flickered to the cudgel in her hand and he smiled. The red-faced younger man chuckled. The two raiders began to approach, spreading out.

Blood roaring in her ears, Chloe couldn't take her eyes off the swords in their hands. They walked toward her slowly, like two hunters cornering a wounded deer.

Backing away, wondering if she could outrun them, she spied movement out of the corner of her eye and saw the gray-haired raider approaching from the other side of the grove. The three men were working together to pin her in the stand of trees, with only one direction remaining for escape. She was forced to leave the trees completely, but realized she was being herded back down the hillside toward the dormitory. The raiders were taking their time, eyes directly on her, ready to start running when she did.

Chloe heard a twig snap directly behind her.

She whirled, immediately realizing there was someone standing close enough to grab her. But she gasped with relief when she saw that it was Zedo. He held two staffs. Both were tipped with silver spirals.

'Here,' he said, handing one to Chloe. 'Athos needs you.'

'I can't . . .'

'You can.'

Without another word, the magus narrowed his eyes and turned toward the nearest of the two raiders, the red-faced youth. The three men continued their approach, but now Chloe and Zedo had come to a halt. The youth laughed. He lifted his sword and charged at the whipcord-lean priest in the white robe.

Zedo pointed his staff. The silver cone lit up in a flash of white light, a split second before a conical blast of wind lifted the raider up and sent him flying. His back struck the solid trunk of a tree, making an audible crack before he crumpled.

The bearded raider roared. He waved his sword wildly over his head as he ran at Chloe.

Fighting the urge to freeze, she tried to remember what she'd been taught. She leveled her staff at him. Her constant meditation helped to cloak her in calm. She fed the fire inside her with thoughts of the wind.

The silver flame grew and sizzled through her skin, making her right arm tingle as the power traveled to the device on the tip of the staff.

In an instant, she released it.

The wind struck the warrior in the center of his chest. But although it was strong, he pushed against the powerful gust and snarled. She stared grimly and drew on still more of the silver fire until her entire body was quivering. Finally she made a sudden cry and a second wind slammed against him, picking him up like a leaf in a storm. Sailing through the air, he screamed as he flew backward and then fell, smashing his skull on the rock.

But her victory was short-lived. The gray-haired warrior barreled into her, and she felt the staff go out of her hands as she tumbled. Her head struck the ground hard and a burst of pain sent starbursts sparkling across her vision.

Suddenly everything was black.

———

'Chloe? Chloe!'

Zedo's voice sounded distant but gradually came closer until she realized he was leaning over her. A hand shook her shoulder as she groaned, blinking in the bright sunlight.

She sat up and put a hand to her head, relieved when there was no blood. From the position of the sun she could see that some time had passed. The raiders had come at dawn; it was now mid-morning.

'Are you hurt?' Zedo asked.

Beside Zedo stood one of his brothers, a staff in his hand with a copper fork on its summit. Both were watching her anxiously.

'I'm fine,' Chloe said, though her head was still spinning.

Scanning the hillside, she counted three bodies. One was the youth, killed by Zedo. Another was the gray-haired warrior, just a dozen paces away, his eyes gazing sightlessly and blood streaming from his ears. The third was farther away: the bearded warrior Chloe had killed.

For the first time, she had killed a man with magic.

She looked up at Zedo's brother. 'Thank you. You saved my life.' She had a sudden thought. 'The Oracle?'

'She is safe. Zeda and Zedi took care of the other three,' said Zedo. 'Are you sure you aren't hurt?'

Chloe swallowed and then climbed to her feet. She weaved for a moment, putting a hand to her temple.

'Here,' Zedo said, handing her the wind staff she'd used to kill the raider. 'Take this.'

Chloe nodded her thanks and steadied herself with the staff. 'Who were they?'

'Raiders,' her teacher's brother, who had to be Zedu, said with a shrug. 'It is not the first time.'

'Why didn't the Oracle see them?'

The two brothers exchanged glances, neither replying. Chloe began to get angry. 'Do you even know? Or do you just accept everything she chooses to tell you?'

In all her time on Athos, Chloe hadn't seen the Oracle once. She had been told to stay away from the cave and only received whatever information the brothers chose to share with her. Her close call with danger had made her starkly aware of how far away she was from the people she cared about.

Chloe made a decision. 'I want to see her,' she said.

Zedo hesitated and glanced at his brother. There was silence for a time as the two men communicated something without speaking. Zedo finally nodded. 'You have earned the right.'

Chloe's mouth tightened; she was suddenly fearful. But she lifted her chin. Zedo had only given her vague hints and premonitions. She wanted answers.

Leaving the two brothers behind, she felt the eyes of her teacher on her as she climbed the hill, passing the raiders killed by the wind. When she reached the crest and descended the other side, the terrain ahead changed and was now devoid of trees, instead dotted by the colorful fires burning without tinder on the rocky slopes. Weaving around the fires, she stepped onto the path paved with blue stone. Grateful for the support of the staff, she drew in a slow breath of fresh, salty air.

Approaching the Oracle's cave, Chloe saw the second pair of brothers. One held a sun staff – a tall wooden pole crowned with a circle of gold – the other a fire staff with an iron claw. The two men, identical aside from their chosen weapons, were standing on the path, conferring in low tones. Chloe looked for the raiders' bodies, but couldn't see them.

She opened her mouth, but it was the magus with the sun staff who spoke first. 'The Oracle is waiting for you inside,' he said, nodding at the cave.

Frowning, Chloe entered the shadowy interior and walked down the winding passage, biting her lip as she remembered the last time she'd come this way and received a prophecy in three parts. Everything the Oracle said had come true, no matter how hard she'd tried to fight it.

Following the passage, still carrying her staff, she finally saw light ahead, and after another bend she arrived at the cavern with the pale fire in the center.

The white flames were low, barely a few inches high. The Oracle sat with her back to Chloe, facing the flickering spears of light. The woman wore a black shawl and her head was lowered, her straight, perfectly white hair falling like a curtain to obscure her face.

'Welcome, Chloe.' Her voice was old and rasping.

'Why didn't you see the raiders coming?'

'One of them had eldran blood. Am I not correct?'

Chloe remembered the slim man with the gray-streaked hair and pale eyes.

'They interfere with my ability to see the future. For this reason, although I know that your fate is tied to that of the king of Xanthos, I cannot say for certain what the future will bring. I have had a vision that you will have an opportunity to destroy our ancient enemy and end a great threat. This is why we made a special effort to bring you here.'

Chloe circled the fire and crouched in front of the Oracle, with the low fire between them, trying to see her eyes. But the woman's head remained bowed.

'What ancient enemy?'

'The descendants of Aleuthea have returned. If unchallenged, they will gain the power of artifacts better left at the bottom of the sea,' she said in a low voice, barely loud enough for Chloe to hear her. 'Tell me, Chloe. Have you had any visions?'

'Visions? No, I have not.' Chloe felt a surge of anger. 'I'm nothing like you. When can I leave this place?' She straightened and reached forward, over the fire, to grip the Oracle's chin and tilt her head up.

The hair parted and Chloe was staring into a grinning skull without flesh.

Chloe recoiled, crying out in horror. Tumbling to the ground, she fell into the flames. The fire surged, suddenly as tall as the roof of the cavern. For an instant there was nothing but white in her vision.

⌣

She was inside a huge temple, a familiar place, a place she knew she'd been to before. Seeing the colonnades on both sides and the pale ceiling high overhead, the lattice screens and the oil burners, Chloe realized she was standing in the Temple of Aeris in Phalesia. She was approaching the inner sanctum, a temple within a temple, a place she had only been to a handful of times.

She wondered how she'd come to be here. Was she dreaming?

She was being drawn to the inner sanctum, where the high priestess performed the holiest of all rites. Reaching the screen that shielded it from the rest of the temple, she felt a sinking dread in her chest that grew stronger as she neared. She took one hesitant step after another, knowing she was going to find something terrible inside. She didn't want to be here. But she had to keep walking, to find out what awaited within.

She took three more steps, entering the domain of the high priestess. The urge to flee became stronger. She pressed her fingernails into her palms. Flickering candlelight revealed the interior.

The walls were covered in blood.

Chloe looked down. There was a man at her feet. She didn't know him; she was certain she'd never seen him before. A handsome man with dark, oiled hair, a narrow face, and sharp cheekbones. He was clad in a white tunic and his hands were clutched over a wound in the center of his chest. His eyes were open. He was dead.

Chloe did recognize High Priestess Marina, a tall, olive-skinned woman with a topknot. The high priestess was sprawled out at the base of the rear wall, her pale-blue robe in disarray. At first Chloe thought she was unconscious, but then she saw the red smear on the wall where her head had struck the stone after she was thrown hard against it.

Horror squeezed at her heart as she turned, and when her eyes moved still farther she saw her sister.

Sophia had grown, but she was still small, with impish features and Chloe's dark hair and wide mouth. She was curled in the fetal position, lying on her side not far from the high priestess. Her eyes were closed.

Her face had been battered.

Her cheek was bruised and swollen, and one of her eyes could hardly be seen. Her lip was torn and crusted with blood. There was a savage crimson mark on her chin. She lay motionless on the ground, utterly still.

Rushing over to her, Chloe gave a sob as she knelt down to touch her sister, but when her fingers reached Sophia's arm they passed directly through. Looking at her hands, Chloe saw that she was transparent, ethereal. She crouched and stared at Sophia's chest, praying for it to move, willing it with every fiber of her being so that she would know her sister was still breathing.

Fire suddenly seared her skull and she cried out. She felt herself fading.

———

Chloe tumbled away from the fire. Wide-eyed, she stared at the Oracle. The woman's shoulders were straight, her hair parted to reveal her smooth features. Her face was youthful and beautiful, noble like that of a goddess, with startlingly green eyes.

'You have had a vision?' The Oracle spoke in a sibilant hiss. Despite her beauty, her eyes were frightening, as if they were staring deep into Chloe's soul. 'What did you see?' She raised her voice. 'Tell me!'

Chloe shook her head, horrified by her vision.

'Remember, nothing you do can change what will happen.'

Finally Chloe managed to take a slow, steadying breath and gather herself. Placing a hand on the wall of the cave, she climbed to her feet.

'What did you see?' The Oracle's question was powerful, insistent.

'A friend once gave me some advice,' Chloe said. 'She said to act as if there is no destiny. I intend to do just that.'

Turning her back on the Oracle, Chloe rushed out of the cave.

———

It was later that Chloe explored the shoreline, staff in hand, walking along the rocky coves, until finally she found it.

The raider's galley would be difficult to manage, but it had a sail, and Dion had taught her something about how to handle a boat. And with her staff, she would always have the wind on her side.

Chloe tossed the staff into the vessel and then entered. She untied the rope holding the boat fastened around a knob of rock and pushed off, letting the current take her away from the island while she hoisted the sail.

She hadn't been given permission to leave. The magic might kill her. But this was her choice.

15

Dion didn't know if he was in love, but he did know that the world had taken on a shine that it hadn't had before. Colors were brighter; music sounded sweeter. Laughter came more easily. Time passed more swiftly.

Lord Philippos agreed to extend his daughter's visit by another two days, and Dion and Isobel spent every spare moment together. They walked the hills near Xanthos and saw the waterfall at Krastonias. He took her sailing on the *Liberty*, which she loved, and horse riding, which she hated. He tried to teach her archery, and although she failed miserably, she did it with such grace that soon they were both laughing until tears streamed down their cheeks.

But after this final evening, celebrated with a farewell banquet for Isobel and her father, she would be leaving. Dion was already sad to think that he might not see her for a month or more, and Isobel said she felt the same way. For their last day together, they decided to revisit the waterfall.

It was high on the hillside, in a forested glade, with the tumbling river surrounded by evergreens on all sides. They sat side by side on a ledge of rock with their clothing hoisted up and bare legs dangling over the void, feeling the rays of the sun on their cheeks and the waterfall's fine spray coating their bodies. Together they watched the powerful torrent above them, pounding relentlessly at the pool they were sitting above. Though it was only spring and the water in the pool was undoubtedly cold, the day was hot enough that the sensation of moisture was pleasant.

'Phalesia will always be my favorite city, but we have nothing to compare with the natural beauty you have here.'

'Always, lady?' Dion asked with a grin.

'Well, perhaps I could come to love Xanthos also.' She smiled.

'It's very different from Phalesia. No voting. No Assembly of Consuls. How do you feel about the citizens having no say?'

'Is that how it is with you?' she asked with a twinkle in her eye. 'The citizens have no say?'

He laughed. 'Fair point. We have guilds and temples, merchants and landowners. All make themselves heard, one way or another.'

'Yet you play no games and tell no lies,' she said. 'Democracy can be a dirty business.'

For a moment Dion remembered Aristocles, a man who fought bravely for what he believed in. 'But there is nobility also. Your father. I'm sure he's a good man.'

A darkness appeared in her eyes. 'He . . . Yes, of course he is. But he sometimes has to play along with the rest of them. Now,' she said, 'let's talk about something other than my father.'

'I have an idea.' Dion's eyes connected with hers and for a time neither of them spoke. His heart began to pound in his chest and his breath came short. He leaned toward her, coming in close, but giving her a chance to back away if she wanted to.

But Isobel smiled and tilted her head. Dion knew then that it was going to happen.

His lips pressed against hers. The kiss didn't last long before she broke it off and laughed. 'Is that what they call talking in Xanthos?'

'Sometimes there are better ways to communicate than with words.'

Her eyes were sparkling as she leaned in again. 'Then perhaps we should talk some more.'

⌐‾‾‾‾‾⌐

Isobel and her father, Philippos, walked together along Xanthos's sandy beach. The sound of the waves breaking on the shore covered their conversation. There was no chance of being overheard.

'I don't like these games,' Isobel said.

She glanced at her father, trying to read his expression. He could be quick to anger, and she'd known him to hold onto his wrath for an eternity. In public they were always the good-natured father and doting daughter, and her part was one she knew how to play well, but she sometimes wondered if he ever saw her as anything more than a means to achieve his ends.

Fortunately, he seemed to be keeping his good mood. 'Games, daughter? Dealing with people isn't a game . . . It's what life is all about. And you do it so well.'

'I like him, Father. And I think he likes me. Isn't that enough?'

'You have done well, Isobel. But your work is not yet finished.'

Isobel bit her lip. 'You're not listening. I'm not being false. Father, we actually enjoy being together. This isn't like with Lord Haemon. I don't want to do things just because you tell me to do them. It isn't necessary this time.'

Philippos's eyes narrowed. His voice was low, but it was swift and incisive. 'Following my instructions is exactly what you will do. The only reason you even have a chance of being queen is because I made it happen.'

'Be honest,' Isobel said bitterly. 'You aren't doing this for me. If people in Phalesia see that the king of Xanthos is taking an interest in your daughter, you'll be certain to become the next first consul.'

'Listen to me, girl, and listen well,' Philippos said. 'There are two different men I can give you to. Either of them will suit my purposes and boost my reputation. One is the young king of Xanthos. The other is Lord Haemon.'

Isobel clenched her jaw. Staring down at the sand, she fought to suppress a shudder. Lord Haemon leered at her, his eyes roving up and down her body every time he looked at her – and any woman her age. She'd hated it when he held her hand in his sweaty palm.

'At the moment,' Isobel's father continued, 'you are doing well with young Dion. But our visit will soon end, and this opportunity with it. You said you like him . . . It shouldn't be difficult for you. You must give yourself to him.'

Isobel winced. 'Father, is that necessary? He likes me and I like him too. I don't think he's ready . . .'

'Trust me.' Philippos gave a short laugh. 'Men are always ready. Tonight, my dear. At the banquet.'

Isobel hated him for what he was asking, despite knowing how high the stakes were for him.

She would not do it . . . Then something occurred to her.

She really did have feelings for Dion. For once in her life she wasn't pretending. If Dion found someone else, her father would marry her off to Lord Haemon.

Her father knew men's hearts or he would never have climbed so high in the Assembly of Consuls. She despised his cynicism, but every move he made was for a purpose.

And, more than anything, if the gods were kind, and she came to live in Xanthos as a queen, she would never have to take her father's orders again.

The banquet was in full swing. A lyre, tambourine, and flute player played festive melodies, the three musicians filling the Royal Palace's great hall with sound. The savory smells of roasting lamb and goat lingered; the attendees' bellies were already full and only the occasional drunken guest stumbled over to the fire pit to have the servants cut him more meat. Garishly dressed Xanthians gesticulated with their wine cups as they clustered in groups of anywhere from two to a dozen.

Glaukos and Philippos were a little apart from the rest, deep in discussion, while in the center of the banqueting hall, Dion sat on a bench covered in cushions with Isobel next to him, her body tilted to face him. If her previous clothing had been revealing, she now wore a scandalously low-cut chiton the color of gold, matching her necklace.

Dion lifted his cup to his mouth, but saw it was empty. As always, a steward refilled it before he'd managed to decide whether he wanted another.

Isobel laughed. 'Banquets aren't your thing, are they?'

'How did you guess?'

'The people who drink the most are either the ones who love the noise and the company, or the ones who use the wine to get through it. I'm getting to know you, Dion of Xanthos, son of Markos. You are definitely the latter.'

'Sorry,' Dion said. He hadn't meant to drink so much, but Isobel was right. It made him nervous to have Lord Philippos watching him with his daughter, and to be sitting in the middle of the hall, with people grinning and all eyes on him.

'Ignore them,' Isobel said. She put her fingertip under his chin and lifted his head. 'Look at me instead. So, what do you think?'

'About what?'

She chuckled. 'I was asking what you think of the law against slavery.'

'What I think of it?' He was surprised to hear himself slur. 'It was my idea.'

'Oh.' She leaned back, but then raised an eyebrow and gave him a smile. 'There is still slavery in Koulis, and certainly in Ilea.'

'We're trying to lead by example. It will end everywhere one day. Ilea will be the most resistant to change.'

'Have you met their king? They say he's terrifying, a big warrior, with an even bigger bodyguard who goes everywhere with him.'

Dion thought about the handover of Mercilles' wife and Jax's death. Despite the treaties and trade deals between Xanthos and Lamara, he hadn't seen Kargan since.

'I've met him. He's the man who captured Chloe.'

Isobel looked crestfallen at the mention of Chloe. Dion picked up his goblet and cursed his tongue as he tilted the cup back and drank a large gulp. The evening wasn't going the way he'd wanted it to. Being on display was causing him to say and do all the wrong things. His head was starting to swim. He was making a fool of himself. He regretted the drink immediately.

'I think I need to retire.'

A look of disappointment crossed Isobel's face. Dion stood up, but suddenly sat back down again and put a hand to his forehead. Glancing at his uncle, Dion saw him smiling slightly and shaking his head.

'I'm sorry . . .' Dion put his hands at his sides, planting the palms on the bench to steady himself. 'Perhaps we could get some fresh air?'

'Of course. Let me help you,' Isobel said.

Already mortified, he knew he would be regretting his behavior in the morning when he had no choice but to let her help him stand. He was the king, and a multitude of eyes were on him as he was forced to lean on her to leave the banqueting hall. Weaving around stools, he felt a surge of relief when the cacophony of the music grew more distant.

He wondered how Philippos felt about his daughter helping him, but then he was forced to concentrate on placing one foot in front of the other. With an effort of will, he glanced back into the hall and saw Glaukos and Philippos watching them depart, both looking pleased with themselves.

'Perhaps your balcony upstairs?' Isobel suggested.

'Good idea.' Dion nodded and immediately headed toward the steps that led up to his bedchamber. Unlike the Orange Terrace, the balcony would be far from prying eyes.

Taking the steps slowly, one at a time, Isobel helped him climb up to the palace's highest floor. She smiled as she led him by the hand, and as he gazed at her he suddenly remembered the feel of her lips. She truly was beautiful. He almost fell when he lifted his leg and found that the floor had leveled, and again when he tried to fend her away and stumble along the hallway, but she was always there to catch him.

'Sorry,' he kept saying.

'Stop saying that, Dion.'

He finally made it to the doorway of his bedchamber and then leaned against the wall, blinking and licking his lips. Taking a deep breath, he forced himself to walk in a straight line, heading for the balcony, but then something struck his legs and he realized it was his bed a moment before collapsing onto the soft mattress. With a groan he rolled over and forced himself to sit up. He found himself laughing and shaking his head as Isobel sat beside him on the bed.

But when he saw her serious expression, Dion sobered. He met her eyes. Fortunately, the curtains in the bedchamber were open, letting in a stiff breeze, helping to clear the fog from his mind. 'I'm going to miss you,' he said. 'I know it hasn't been long . . .'

'Not as much as I will miss you,' she said softly.

Dion moved until he was sitting as close as he could to her. Holding one of her hands in his, he leaned his face toward hers. She moistened her lips. His face came closer and closer, his pulse racing as their mouths became mere inches apart. Blood roared in his ears when their bodies pressed together and he could feel her heart beating as fiercely as his own.

Every sensation became heightened as he kissed her. At the same time, he became less aware of where he was, or even his own name. He never wanted the kiss to end. He reached out his arms and pulled her into a tight embrace, supporting the back of her head, caressing the tresses of her golden hair.

Isobel suddenly broke the kiss, leaving him gasping, feeling like he'd just fought in a battle or swum to the bottom of the sea. But then she stood beside the bed. She removed the pin holding her golden garment wrapped around her body. The chiton fell to the ground, and she kicked it free. Dion's eyes widened.

Suddenly Isobel was naked on the bed and her lips were pressed to his. He again pulled her in close, his hands traveling over the smooth skin of her back, feeling the curve of her hips.

'This is what I want,' Isobel said. 'It's what you want too, isn't it?'

Chloe's face flashed in front of Dion's vision. But Chloe was dead, and had been for a long time. He knew that she would want him to be happy.

He rolled them both over so that his face was above hers. Staring into her eyes, he reached out to move a lock of hair away from her face.

Dion then bent his head down and kissed Isobel again.

16

Eiric's gaze traveled the length of the defensive embankment. It was little more than a wall, waist-high, hastily formed by piling rocks one on top of the other. Half a mile long and curved, it blocked any access to the Blackwell Mines on the upper slopes, for on all other sides, steep cliffs plummeted to the green lowlands below.

Every few feet a silver-haired eldran stood behind the embankment, warily watching the thick forest at the base of the hillside. The humans' camp was just inside the trees, and despite the fact that it had been days since an assault, the soldiers of Tanus could come at any time.

Eiric turned around and looked up at the mines. Wide, deep holes, they gaped in the hillside as if the earth had laid a trap to swallow whoever entered. His eyes narrowed. He had no interest in the mines; the Tanusians were welcome to the metallic ores found within. But the trees around him did care when the humans slashed and burned for no other reason than to lug their precious ore to the road more efficiently. This was his homeland. He could feel a connection with Sindara in his blood and in his bones. As king, the plant and animal life communed with him. He knew the way the humans saw the situation, but this wasn't a border dispute, to be resolved by negotiating over some lines on a map. The miners, loggers, and soldiers of Tanus didn't belong here.

'This is ridiculous,' a deep voice said on Eiric's left-hand side. 'The humans think we're afraid to attack them. King Eiric, our hesitation is causing more suffering than if we acted decisively and drove them out once and for all.'

Eiric glanced at the man who'd spoken. Short but stocky for an eldran, Caleb had a broad, muscular torso and thick arms and shoulders. He was younger than Eiric, but had never shirked from danger or failed to support his king when there was dissent. Of the men and women who'd once served Triton, he was Eiric's most loyal ally. And he was magically powerful. In battle, he was a force to be reckoned with.

'Caleb, your king has already spoken,' Dalton said. 'If we assaulted their camp and slaughtered them in numbers, they would return in force. Tanus would call on the rest of Galea, and they wouldn't stop until we'd been driven from Sindara. We've all learned the lesson from long ago. We must tread a careful line.'

Standing on Eiric's other side, Dalton was always cautious, but like Caleb he was steadfast – even when he disagreed with what Eiric was doing. He was so old his hair was almost white, and he had wrinkled skin like parchment.

'You both know my reasons,' Eiric replied. Taller than both of his companions, he was slim but broad-shouldered, with golden eyes and skin so pale it was nearly translucent. Towering over them, he looked at each man in turn. 'I wish to avoid loss of life. On both sides. If I could have captured the mines without killing their soldiers, I would have. If we hold this place long enough, in time their will to rush this blockade and throw their lives away will fade.'

'But we are far more powerful,' Caleb protested.

'Yes, and if they become afraid of us, eventually they will even the odds,' Eiric said. 'We can rush their camp and destroy them. Tactically we can win the fight. But strategically we will lose the war.'

'King Eiric, I still maintain that there is another option,' Dalton said, his ancient voice thin and reedy. 'We can talk. Our friends in Xanthos can broker—'

'Friends?' Caleb's lip curled. 'Humans were never our friends.'

'The king of Xanthos is half eldran.'

'That's enough from both of you.' Eiric glared at his two companions. 'We will stand our ground. If they try to take our position, we will fend them off. But we will aim to kill as few of them as possible. Caleb, I'm looking at you to control some of the firebrands among—'

'They're coming,' Dalton said softly.

Soldiers with the brown cloaks of Tanus on their shoulders were leaving the trees, row after row of hoplites marching forward and then coming to a halt. Sling and javelin throwers formed up on both sides of the main host, while archers brought up the rear. An officer with a brown-crested helmet of horse hair rode a black stallion along the front of his force. He pointed his spear up at the mines. The soldiers began to slap their spears against their shields, creating a threatening rumble that rolled up the hillside to the eldren watching from behind the blockade.

Eiric and Dalton exchanged glances. 'There must be a thousand men down there,' Dalton said.

Eiric again looked along the length of the embankment. He had close to a hundred men and women ready to follow his lead. At present the eldren, slender figures with thin limbs and silver hair, appeared completely outclassed by their opponents. That would soon change.

'It's going to be difficult to keep the casualties low,' Eiric murmured.

'But we must try,' Dalton said.

A trumpet sounded. The soldiers began to run.

———

Hearing the trumpet, Gorlax nodded at the men around him. 'It's time.'

He had twenty men with him, all lightly armored, wearing leather breastplates, skirts of hide strips, and wooden spears strapped to their backs. Unwieldy swords had been left behind, but they were Tanus's elite, trained since birth in combat, their skills honed fighting wildren back in the days when they regularly preyed on their city's livestock and populace. Even without their usual equipment, they would succeed at the task the general had set them.

Gorlax tilted his head back, gazing up the cliff. He and his men had already planned their route. It looked sheer, but Tanus was a city surrounded by mountains, and they all had years of experience climbing similar faces. It was a difficult ascent, but not impossible.

'Remember,' Gorlax addressed his men. 'When you're climbing, you're on your own. Never scale below another man. When you reach the summit, scout the area and form a defensive perimeter until all of us are up. If you're slow, we won't wait for you, and if you can't make it up, we'll see you back at the camp. Understood?'

'Yes, sir,' the soldiers murmured.

'Once we've assembled up top, our plan is to stay hidden as we come at them from the rear. We'll pass the mines. Then, while the shapeshifters are distracted fighting the main force, we single out their king. You've all seen him. He's bigger by far than any of them. They're like animals. Wolves. When the alpha male is dead, they'll lose their cohesion. We have one goal only. To destroy the eldran king. Any questions?'

Gorlax met the eyes of each man in turn, before giving a sharp nod.

'For Tanus and the queen,' he growled.

'For Tanus and the queen!'

Gorlax was the first to walk to the base of the cliff, his men fanning out around him as he began his ascent.

———

Arrows filled the air, arcing before the sharp iron heads dragged them down. A multitude of shafts descended on the stone wall. Death rained on the eldren, who stood grimly, staring up at the sky.

But then mist clouded the entire length of the embankment. Winged creatures flew out to the left and right. When the arrows plummeted down, they sank harmlessly into the dirt or bounced off the wall.

Furies and dragons wheeled like birds, swooping down from above. Descending on the front ranks, they took dozens of men by surprise, enclosing arms, clawed forelimbs, or wide jaws around screaming soldiers and flying up again, before dropping the soldiers on their comrades. As the archers nocked new arrows and retrained their aim, the winged creatures descended again, but this time they landed in a thin line in front of the embankment. Thoughts flashed from one to another, coordinated by Eiric. Together they changed shape once more. Now a row of roaring ogres and bellowing giants stood to face the charging host.

With shattering force, the two groups collided.

Twice the height of any soldier, the ogres swatted spears aside and plucked up armored men to throw them sailing back the way they'd come. Head and shoulders taller than the ogres, the giants swept hoplites away in groups of three and four. The blows were strong enough to break limbs and knock men unconscious. The fear the eldren inspired caused more than one human to turn around and flee.

One golden-eyed giant, bigger than any other, fended off a spear, but the soldier was determined and dodged to the side, trying to bring the point up under his chin.

Eiric weaved his head to evade the next blow and reached forward to grab his opponent by the leg. Straightening, he leaned back and threw the man into two more of his fellows, sending the group into a flailing heap. An arrow stung his flank, but he brushed it away, glancing down at the small triangular wound it left behind.

Another stocky giant ahead of him – Caleb – was throwing himself deep into the enemy ranks, his arm wrapped around a human that he clutched to his chest, using the man as a shield. His free arm held a club the size of a small tree trunk. Careful to follow Eiric's orders, he was smashing the soldiers' legs, leaving broken bones and howls of agony in his wake.

Eiric reached down and swatted another group of hoplites out of the way. Glancing to his right, he saw Dalton, an old ogre with an enlarged jaw and wispy white hair, struggling against three swordsmen who were trying to encircle him.

You need help?

I'm fine. I can do this without hurting them.

Dalton snatched at one man and then the other, his meaty fingers closing over empty air as his opponents dodged out of the way. One of the swordsmen, younger than his two companions but possessing his share of bravery, jumped on top of the stone wall and then tried to leap onto Dalton's back.

But Dalton snatched him out of the air. He held his wriggling captive by both arms, four feet above the ground, his legs scrabbling uselessly, face white as a sheet. The ogre displayed him and snarled. The soldiers exchanged glances and backed away, desperate to save their friend.

Dalton then set the young man gently down and let him go.

Stunned, he rushed over to his comrades. They took him by the arms and without a word, they ran from the battle.

Dalton looked at Eiric. *See?*

Well done.

Turning his attention back to the battle, Eiric was tall enough to easily scan over the heads of so many men, and knew immediately that the attack was faltering. The combined strength of the eldren was simply too much for the humans.

Eiric, look out!

Eiric whirled. He saw Dalton moving, intercepting a group of twenty soldiers pouring over the embankment to attack from behind. With surprising skill, the newcomers leaped over the wall with just one hand on the top, short stabbing spears held in the other. Their eyes were on Eiric as they charged. They didn't see Dalton coming.

He barreled into them, heedless of their bristling weapons. But these were a different breed of soldiers than the ones they'd been fighting. Whirling, moving with incredible agility, first one and then another stuck his spear into Dalton's torso. Dalton roared with pain, still trying to swat them away without hurting them. Another spear stabbed into his back.

Dalton! Eiric cried. *Caleb, I need your help!*

Bellowing with rage, Eiric suddenly found that he could no longer think. Throwing himself into the fray, he was filled only with the desire to save his friend.

He bunched his fists and swatted the face of the first man who reached him, killing him in an instant. The next warrior – perhaps the leader, for he was the only one wearing insignia – scored Eiric's thigh with the point of his spear, but Eiric clasped his hand around the man's throat and squeezed until his spine snapped.

Then Caleb joined the fight, his huge club pounding at soldier after soldier. An inner voice screamed at Eiric as he tore the humans in half and stamped down on their torsos. But all he could think about was his friend, the first of Triton's group to support him, now on his back and staring up at the sky.

The clearing was tranquil, high in the misty tablelands, with evergreens on all sides and a carpet of lush grass. Liana, a slight eldran with flowing silver hair, green eyes, and a heart-shaped face, moved through the resting eldren, filling gourds from an earthenware jug and taking water to those of the wounded who were unable to walk.

Lifting the jug, she saw that it was empty, but then an older eldran entered the glade with a heavy ewer held in each hand.

'Zachary,' Liana said. Setting the jug down, she hurried over and took one of the ewers from him, grunting as she struggled with its weight. 'You shouldn't strain yourself.'

'Are you saying I'm too old to help?' he asked, his eyes twinkling.

Zachary was growing old. There were threads of white in his silver, shoulder-length hair, and in the thin eyebrows arched over his brown eyes flecked with gold. His face was narrow and his features were sharp, almost gaunt, with a crescent-shaped scar on his left cheek. But his back was straight, and he was tall enough to tower over her. His eyes were still the warmest and wisest she had ever known.

'Of course not,' Liana said.

'We are the same, you and I. We both chose not to fight. But even if we disagree with Eiric's actions, our values dictate that we must do our part to help.'

Liana smiled at Zachary, and together they refilled the smaller jugs. When their work was finished, she stretched as she walked to the edge of the clearing to gaze at the low mountains close to the edge of Sindara. It was safer for the wounded here, far from the relentless fighting. The energy of their homeland aided their recuperation and they weren't exposed to the elements. From her position she could see a hint of the gaping holes that were the mines' entrances. She couldn't hide the worry from her face.

'I'm sure he is safe,' Zachary said, coming to stand beside her.

'He is the king, and we both know that they'll do everything they can to kill or capture him.'

'Eiric is strong. He always was, even as a boy.' Zachary placed a hand on her shoulder and then squeezed. 'I'd best go and see to the wounded.'

He left Liana to her thoughts.

Liana and Eiric were now lovers, but with all the trouble at the mines, they hadn't yet spoken of marriage. Theirs was a tumultuous relationship, filled with passion and declarations of love, but also the occasional bitter argument that meant they sometimes wouldn't speak for days afterwards. She was angry at him for thinking that action was always needed when sometimes words could accomplish more. He accused her of always doubting him. But she couldn't back down, not when his actions placed him in harm's way.

As she turned away from the mountains, she caught movement out of the corner of her eye. A tall, broad-shouldered figure was stumbling through the trees, approaching from the far side of the clearing. She felt a familiar tightness in her chest as she recognized Eiric's face. But then she frowned. His silhouette was strange.

He was carrying something, and whatever it was, it was heavy. His burden required both his arms.

Liana began to run.

She left the wounded behind, crossing the clearing and plunging once more into the trees. When she reached Eiric, she gasped.

He was carrying Dalton, a man who was one of the oldest of their number, and had been instrumental in uniting the group from the Waste with those from the Wilds. Liana saw at least three gaping wounds in Dalton's chest, along with a tear stretching from just below his shoulder to his hip. Both Eiric and Dalton were covered in blood. Dalton was groaning.

'What happened? Eiric? Let me help.'

But when she tried to help him with his burden, he shook his head, despite his obvious exhaustion. He continued to walk slowly, every footstep labored as he headed toward the clearing.

Liana looked for Zachary. 'Zachary? Zachary!'

Zachary came quickly, helping them lower Dalton to the ground. Liana continued to ask Eiric questions, but he was in shock; she'd seen this look before: eldren who were close to each other could speak without sound and sense each other's presence; when they lost a loved one, the pain could be enough to turn them wild. As Zachary tended Dalton's wounds, Eiric sank to his knees.

'They surprised us,' Eiric said softly. 'I should have thought of it.'

'Are you hurt?' Liana asked, swiftly checking him over.

'No.' He shook his head. 'We pushed them back. Dalton . . .' His voice broke. 'Will he live?'

After seeing that Eiric had little more than scrapes and bruises, Liana helped Zachary to wash Dalton's wounds with the life-giving water of Sindara. As soon as the clear liquid trickled into the savage holes in his body, Dalton moaned with relief. His color slowly returned, and he closed his eyes as his ragged breathing became more even. Treating each wound in turn, Liana clasped the edges of skin together while Zachary stitched them closed with deer gut.

Finally Zachary took his focus away from his task to speak to Eiric. 'He will live, but it was a close thing. If the wounds had been any deeper . . .'

Eiric let out a sigh of relief.

'What happened?' Liana asked.

Eiric's golden eyes met hers. 'What happened? He was hurt because he was trying to save my life and at the same time stop the humans without killing them. Then . . .' He suddenly looked ashamed. 'Then I turned on them. Caleb and I . . . We tore them apart.'

'You've set yourself an impossible task. Perhaps . . .' Liana tensed; she could never be sure how he would react. 'Perhaps we should give the people of Tanus back their mine . . .'

His golden eyes flashed. 'It is inside *our* territory.'

'Yes, it is.' She frowned at him, taking a deep breath and lifting her chin. 'But we abandoned Sindara for hundreds of years. You can't blame the humans for expanding during a period in which we didn't live here. Surely we could come to some arrangement?'

'Arrangement? They are humans. They will never give up their gold and silver. This is our land. It was always ours. They have to understand that.'

'But you and Dion—'

'Don't mention his name.'

Liana's mouth tightened. 'But how can there be peace if we don't talk? Surely we could at least talk to Dion? Those soldiers aren't his.'

'Dion sent soldiers to the mine. They were prepared to fight us.' He scowled. 'And to think I once called him a friend.'

'His soldiers retreated when you made it clear you would attack. You don't know his side of things.'

'Enough about Dion. He is no friend to us.'

Eiric tried to rise, but Liana grabbed hold of his hand, forcing him to face her. 'Just because you are the king, does not mean I can't disagree with you.' He tried to jerk his wrist away, but she held him fast. 'You've been listening too much to those who once followed Triton. I know you're trying to be strong, but being forceful and having strength of character are two different things.'

He finally tore his arm free and stormed out of the clearing. Liana was worried; the fighting had brought out Eiric's darker side.

'He does love you,' Zachary said. 'He's just confused right now. Don't give up on him.'

'I won't,' Liana said sadly.

17

Shielding her eyes from the blazing sun, her other hand on the tiller as she peered ahead, Chloe felt sudden relief: she knew the city she was approaching. It wasn't Phalesia, but at least it was somewhere she recognized.

Despite using the wind to cut her journey down to days, she didn't know how to navigate by the stars, and had been forced to hop from isle to isle, following barren coasts. Then a storm blew her off course, confusing her further, and now, rather than the swift journey to Phalesia she'd planned, she had found herself at the Sarsican city of Myana.

Her father had taken her to Myana only once, when she was a girl, but she recognized the hilltop temple overlooking the city below, and the wide mouth of the Silver River that split Myana down the middle and emptied out in the harbor, which was full of boats of all shapes and sizes, from huge biremes to tiny fishing boats, all bobbing alongside a network of wooden docks.

When she reached the piers, wary of the other boats approaching and departing, she allowed the sail to go slack, remembering the things Dion had shown her as she guided the raiders' small vessel. Dropping the sail completely, she picked an empty berth and steered her boat toward it, but then realized too late that she still had far too much speed. With a smack, the boat ran hard against the wooden dock, jolting her forward out of her seat, but fortunately no harm was done.

Hearing the noise, a boy ran toward her, grinning at her embarrassment as he tossed her a rope to fasten the boat's bow to the quay.

'How long?' he asked, bold despite being just seven or eight years old. 'One day is two coppers.'

The raiders' boat contained a pouch filled with small currency and Chloe handed him four coins, although she didn't plan on staying long in Myana. He checked each coin over in turn and then nodded.

'Welcome to Myana.'

Chloe gathered her few possessions and her staff, then left the boat behind, moving from one walkway to another until she reached solid ground. Finally away from the docks, she paused as she tried to get her bearings. Her plan was to find someone who might sail her to Xanthos or Phalesia in return for the boat itself as payment.

She took a deep breath. Her vision of crumpled bodies in the Temple of Aeris in Phalesia, and of her sister Sophia, still and unmoving, had stayed with her all voyage. The Oracle had said it would come to pass, no matter what she did. But Liana had once told Chloe that she should act as if there were no prophecy, to never feel like her destiny was already written. She had to make it back home.

She scanned the area, wondering how to begin.

The quayside stank of fish and seaweed, which formed piles that steamed in the sun. Fishermen sat on stools, chatting while they mended nets. Dozens of gulls cried out to each other as they fought for the occasional morsel. Newly arrived traders, puffed up with self-importance, headed directly for the Silver River Market, scribes and porters in tow.

Hearing stern voices, she turned to see a heavyset man accosting each group of merchants in turn, weaving on his feet, his face covered by a thick black beard. The merchants wrinkled their noses as one after another turned him away. He wore a ragged tunic and his feet were bare, but despite being unable to afford sandals, the sword on his hip was sheathed in a well-crafted scabbard. Lurching from one trader to the next, he hiccupped and pleaded for work.

'Guard? Need a guard?' He tried to grip the arm of an old, dark-skinned merchant, but the merchant's lip curled in distaste as he shook himself free and ploughed on without responding.

'Anyone? Guard?'

The drunk saw that he'd run out of targets to approach and glanced in Chloe's direction. Immediately she turned her back and began to walk away from the harbor. There would be inns and taverns on the broad main avenue. She could feel the drunk's dark eyes on her as she left him behind.

She tried not to look back over her shoulder, and finally she rounded a corner and breathed more freely. It shouldn't take her long to find some sailors who could help her. A stout boat in return for helping her get home should be an attractive proposition . . .

Amos couldn't believe his eyes.

He could have sworn, in front of all the gods, that he had just seen Chloe. But Chloe was dead. Transfixed, he watched her walking away: a slim, dark-haired woman in a plain white chiton, heading determinedly for the inns frequented by the city's sailors, traders, and laborers. He shook himself. There were many in Myana who might match Chloe's description. His mind was playing tricks on him.

He turned back to the docks, but sighed when he couldn't see any more new arrivals. Scratching under his arms, he pondered. He could return to the harbor later in the afternoon, or he could see if there was any work in the drinking houses. At least if there wasn't work in the taverns he could pass the time more pleasantly, out of the sun, and then come back tomorrow. Yes, there was no point returning to the harbor in the afternoon. Tomorrow would be better. He'd find work eventually.

He looked down at himself, trying not to think about how low he'd fallen. Once, he had been captain of Phalesia's city guard, the commander of hundreds of strong soldiers. He'd led his homeland's defense against Ilea's attack and been hailed as a hero. When Aristocles needed help, it was Amos he always turned to. Now he was nothing, a nobody.

Amos scanned the area again. No one wanted to hire him. But he needed money. He licked his lips. Already he could taste it, smooth, sweet wine, flowing down his throat, lighting a fire in his belly.

He glanced up at the sun. It was after midday, definitely time for a cup. One of the drinking houses might have visiting merchants. He'd be using his time effectively.

Well, perhaps it wasn't quite midday, but any time was a good time for a drink.

———

Chloe left another tavern, shaking her head in disgust. The raucous shouts, guffaws, and singing of the sailors followed her until she left the place behind. As with the previous drinking house, the sailors she'd spoken to all had work and were using their time on leave to drink their wages dry.

She wondered where she should try next. She had to get to Phalesia, and if she hadn't had any success by the time the night was over she might have to try sailing herself. But she'd been lucky to find Myana. If she tried to go on alone, with little sailing skill or knowledge of navigation, she might never make it to the journey's end.

As she walked, staff in hand, the shadows in the streets were becoming long and tapered as heat left the day. Finally she spied one more tavern, smaller than the others. Around the corner from the avenue, on a narrow side street, she was in a disreputable part of town, not far from the Silver River Market. It was now completely dark and the light of oil lamps beckoned wayfarers inside, where warbling music and men's raised voices merged into a cacophony.

She hesitated and then entered.

The smell assaulted her. The ramshackle interior was dirty, with sticky floors and the stench of sweat and stale wine overpowering. Groups of men sat on stools around low tables, talking loudly and calling for wine from the bustling proprietor. A musician played a lyre in the corner, brow furrowed as he concentrated on his instrument to the exclusion of all else.

Taking a deep breath, Chloe approached one of the tables, where a wiry, sun-tanned sailor sat with a brawny companion. It was only when she raised her voice to be heard above the din that they looked up.

'I'm looking for someone who knows how to sail to Phalesia.'

The brawny man grinned at his wiry companion. 'What do you think, Taimos? Told you we'd find you work if we came here.'

'I can sail,' the wiry man said, looking up at her with heavy-lidded eyes. 'What's the job, beautiful?'

Chloe immediately knew that she didn't want to travel alone with him. He was thin and balding, with a grimy tunic and several days' stubble on his chin. And he was leering at her, eyes traveling slowly down her body.

'No matter,' she said, looking to the next table.

'Hey!' The brawny man scowled. 'You said you had a job for my friend. Let's hear it, woman.'

He was twice her size, with muscled arms and a red face. His necklace was made of iron links, the medallion bearing the impression of a blacksmith's anvil. He glared at her from under a patched felt cap.

She pretended not to hear him, taking her staff and moving away.

But then the blacksmith grabbed hold of her arm, gripping tightly. 'You deaf or something? I'm talking to you, girl.'

Chloe whirled to face him. Before she knew what she was doing, she'd cleared her mind. Her hand went to the top of her staff and a wind blew through the room, a gust strong enough to tear the cap from his head. The silver twist crowning the staff flared with white light and then subsided.

The entire tavern fell silent. Voices stilled and the music faltered. All eyes were suddenly on her.

'Let me go,' she said. 'Now.'

But the blacksmith was undeterred and maintained his hold. 'What are you?' He glanced at her staff. 'Some kind of witch?'

Chloe's heart skipped a beat when a man from the next table slowly stood up. But rather than face her, he turned to the brawny blacksmith, and she realized when she saw the thick black beard that he was the drunk from the docks.

'The lady told you to let her go. I suggest you do as she says.' He spoke in a low, ominous voice. It was somehow familiar, but his speech was slightly slurred, blurring the words together.

'Who are you, then? And what's it to you?'

The blacksmith shoved Chloe so hard that she stumbled back against another table. He began to stand.

The bearded man moved into action.

He calmly reached out to take the blacksmith by the back of the head and slammed him forward so that his face smashed against the table. The smith's wiry companion shot to his feet, but then he stepped back, eyes wide, when the bearded man drew his sword. Chloe stared at it. The workmanship was as fine as anything she'd seen. On the wide blade, near the hilt, was an embossed emblem: the eagle of Phalesia.

'Here now, we don't want any trouble.' The wiry sailor spoke with a trembling voice, arms spread.

'Good.' The bearded man turned to scan the room, and then murmured for Chloe's ears. 'I suggest we leave.'

He let her exit first, his dark eyes sweeping the room, daring anyone to challenge him. Chloe quickly left the tavern, relieved to be outside. A moment later the bearded man followed her, and with a quick wave of his hand, he led the way, walking with long strides, away from the dark street and back to the safety of the broad avenue. As they left the shadows, the moonlight cast pale rays on his back. He suddenly stopped in the middle of the street and then turned to face her.

Chloe's mouth dropped open.

He'd put on weight, but the height and frame and the posture were all the same. If it weren't for the beard, she would have recognized him immediately. His eyes were dark and penetrating, and his face was creased with crags and wrinkles.

'Amos? Amos! I can't believe it's you!'

Amos stared at her as if looking at a ghost. She was surprised to see his eyes becoming moist, then brimming with tears. All of a sudden he took two unsteady steps toward her and pulled her into a tight embrace. He started to mumble, sobbing the entire time.

'I thought you were dead,' he said. 'I'm sorry. I'm so sorry.'

'Shh,' Chloe said, holding him in her arms. 'It's all right.'

After his display at the tavern, she now found herself consoling him as he cried. She wrinkled her nose. He smelled of wine and sweat. He stank as if he hadn't bathed in a year.

'Shh,' she whispered. She repeated the same words, again and again. 'It's all right, Amos. It's all right.'

18

Chloe and Amos headed back to the harbor, walking in silence. When they reached the docks, they stood together, watching the moon's reflection on the water and the boats knocking against the wooden piers. Glancing at the taller man beside her, Chloe saw that he'd regained his composure.

'Where have you been?' he asked.

'I've been gone for a long time, I know,' she said. 'I was sick. I was taken to Athos to recover. Then, I've been . . . learning.'

He looked at the staff in her hand. 'I saw.' He hesitated. 'Listen, there's something you need to know. About . . . About your father.'

'I know.'

'Yes, but there's more. I know they say he died—'

'Nilus killed him. That's what you were about to say, isn't it?'

Amos's mouth worked soundlessly; he was truly stunned. 'But no one knows the truth.'

'The magi at Athos told me.'

'Ah . . .' He wiped a hand over his face and let out a mighty sigh. 'If you could know, Chloe, how it feels, not only to be exiled from your home, but to be the only one to carry a terrible secret. If you could know how it feels to experience just two emotions: guilt, the worst guilt imaginable, and an overpowering desire for revenge.' He was shaking, struggling to control himself. 'And then . . . to have someone else know the truth.' Again his eyes were glistening; he turned his head and wiped them.

'The magi at Athos taught me some of their magic . . . Amos, I want to confront Nilus. And Sophia needs me. That's why I'm here. I know that Nilus and three other consuls murdered my father.' Her mouth tightened. 'But that's all I know. What happened?'

'I left him. Your father.' He coughed, his voice quavering. 'When we returned to Phalesia I thought we were safe, and I left him. He asked me to find you, and I wasn't there to protect him. After all we went through together, when he needed me most, I wasn't there.'

'Amos, listen to me. I wasn't there for him either, and I've cried myself to sleep more than once. You can't blame yourself.'

'Nilus told everyone that your father's heart failed. The first I knew about it was when I saw a procession of priests carrying a body covered in cloth through the streets, the very night we returned. I'd just been speaking with him!' He bit his lip. 'I was stunned . . . Too shocked to do more than stare. Your father was always a strong man.'

'He was,' she murmured.

'Then the next night, one of my men, Patros, came to me. He told me the truth and said he was scared out of his mind, because the only other soldier to witness what happened was murdered in the street, and he didn't think it was thieves who did it. I couldn't believe it. Nilus, of all people! But I was determined to do something.' His eyes were unfocused as he relived the events. 'I was taking Patros to meet some of your father's friends, but Nilus's men found us first. I barely escaped with my life. Patros was killed. I fled Phalesia and I haven't been back since.'

Amos reached into a pocket and took out a small flask that sloshed. Removing the stopper, he put it to his lips and drank deeply.

'I wasn't there for him,' he said. 'Your sister was away and everyone thought you were dead. Now . . . Now Nilus surrounds himself with soldiers, always jumping at noises in the night. I thought if I could save up enough silver I could do something . . . Though I don't know what exactly, so I came here and started working as a guard.'

He looked ruefully at the flask and began to raise it, but Chloe's hand closed over his.

'Enough drinking,' she said. 'I need you, Amos. I need you strong. Did you think of saying anything to Dion?'

'What could he do? Denounce the first consul of Phalesia? Dion's a foreign king, and I have no proof.'

'What about Sophia . . . Do you know where she is? Does she know the truth?'

He shook his head. 'Your father was interred long before she came home. She's working as a novice priestess, last I heard.' He turned to face her. 'So what happens now?'

'I have a boat, but I don't know the way to Phalesia.'

He smiled wryly. 'You've come to the wrong man if you're after a sailor. But I can trade your boat in return for passage on one of the larger galleys. And then?'

'I think my sister is in danger. I have to find her. That's my first priority.'

'Nilus won't be happy to see you. Or me.'

'That's why you're going to keep your sword sharp.' She met his eyes. 'I need you to be sharp, too. Can you do that for me?'

'Yes, Chloe.' He smiled. 'I can't tell you how happy I am to see you. I'll get us passage, this very night, and I'll sort myself out. I promise.'

Chloe cursed as she passed yet another tavern and found Amos sprawled outside with half his body in the gutter. She looked up at the sun blazing high in the sky, then crouched by his side.

'Get up!' She slapped his cheeks. 'Amos! Get up!' She shook his shoulders until first one bleary eye and then the other opened. He groaned and raised himself before breaking into a coughing fit. Wiping his eyes, he sat with shoulders slumped and looked up at her.

'What time is it?'

'Mid-morning. You said the captain would depart at noon. I've been looking for you for hours!'

Amos sat dejectedly, breathing hard as he tried to summon the energy to stand. He reached into his tunic pocket, taking out the flask, but Chloe kicked it out of his hands, sending it skittering down the street. Gripping him under the armpits, she yanked him until he was standing. He put a hand to his head as he weaved from side to side.

'Get moving.' Chloe pushed and prodded until he took his first steps. She didn't relent until he was managing a brisk pace.

'Which boat is it?' she asked when they reached the harbor. 'It had better still be here.'

Amos looked worried as he shielded his eyes to scan the docks. Finally he pointed. 'That one.' He swore. 'It looks like they're getting ready to depart.'

'Run!' Chloe cried.

Pulling him along behind her, she sprinted toward the galley, waving and shouting. Half a dozen oarsmen were at the ready and the vessel was filled with barrels, sacks, and crates. The stern-faced captain glared at them.

'Get in!' he bellowed, pointing at the interior of his ship. 'Quickly now or we'll miss the tide. Another moment longer and you were going to have to find another way to Xanthos, deal or no deal.'

Chloe and Amos tumbled into the galley up near the bow, and a moment later the crew pushed off and oars thrust out from the sides. Chloe found a place to sit and cleared space for Amos. She breathed a sigh of relief, feeling the wind fresh in her face as the rowers maneuvered the vessel toward the harbor mouth. Turning to Amos, she saw that he'd turned green. Waves lifted them up and down. He met her eyes and swallowed.

'Amos. Are we going to Xanthos?' Chloe asked.

'We have to,' Amos said, giving a hiccup. 'Ships from Myana to Phalesia always stop in Xanthos.'

Chloe put out a hand. 'Give me your knife.' He looked worried as he handed it over, but she tested the edge, nodded, and handed it straight back to him. 'Something to take your mind off things. Shave your beard.'

'But the boat—'

'—is moving, I know. You're a warrior. Warriors should have a steady hand. It will take us several days to get to Xanthos. By the time we get there, you're going to be the Amos I know and love. Understood?'

He nodded slowly, his face turning even greener as he leaned out over the gunwale and dipped the knife in the water before starting to scrape the blade against his face.

19

Dion inhaled; the soft breeze was fresh and fragrant, carrying scents of thyme and lavender. He and Glaukos were climbing marble steps, passing manicured gardens and side paths leading to sumptuous villas. High overhead a perfectly blue sky promised fair weather, while the rays of the golden sun warmed the bare skin of his arms. Phalesia was always beautiful in the spring.

The steward climbing ahead of them, wearing a navy-blue tunic embroidered with gold, turned and smiled. 'We're nearly there. Not much farther, King, Lord.'

A pair of soldiers brought up the rear, also wearing navy and yellow: nephews of Lord Philippos, if Dion remembered correctly. Despite their youth, the two men looked at ease with their weapons.

'He didn't mention what the urgency was?' Dion murmured to his uncle.

'Philippos is a canny man. He wouldn't ask you to come all the way to Phalesia and visit his home if he didn't have something of importance to discuss.'

'If it's about this election . . .' Dion knew he had a thousand matters to attend to at home. 'I have no desire to get caught up in Phalesian politics.'

'You hosted him in Xanthos. Perhaps he is simply returning the favor.' A smile tugged at the corners of Glaukos's mouth.

Dion's brow furrowed. He was excited to be seeing Isobel again, but he was also worried that she might have told her father about their night of passion. He didn't regret it, but he knew that Lord Philippos wouldn't be pleased that they'd been together outside marriage. They'd only known each other for a few days.

Glaukos glanced across at him and saw his expression. 'Dion, I was jesting. He knows kings aren't asked to dinner like merchants and consuls. All will be clear soon.'

The steward came to a halt, indicating a side path as he bowed. 'Right this way.' He allowed Dion and Glaukos to enter first.

The wide path was paved with marble and framed by stunted evergreens, the trees carefully trimmed into the shapes of lean pyramids. Dion saw a villa at the end of the path: a grand, single-storied residence hidden from the lower city by a section of gardens and a final barrier of poplars. A sudden gust rustled the trees, making them sway from side to side.

Lord Philippos stood in front of his home with his servants arrayed behind him. As Dion approached, they all bowed as one, from the youngest, a girl in the costume of a cook's helper, to the oldest, a stooped manservant with thinning hair. Dion returned the bow and smiled, making the cook's helper blush as she grabbed hold of the girl next to her and they giggled together.

'King Dion.' Philippos stepped forward and gave a small bow before clasping Dion's hand. He then turned to Dion's uncle. 'Lord Glaukos . . . It is a pleasure to have you both in Phalesia, and a great honor to welcome you to my home.'

Philippos smiled broadly, opening his arms in a gesture of welcome. He was dressed in a white tunic fastened with a navy cord, contrasting with Dion's crimson tunic belted with gold. His dark hair was cut shorter than when he and Dion last met, but was still oiled. The eyes above his patrician nose were as sharp as ever.

'I was surprised and pleased by your invitation,' Dion said, choosing his words carefully. 'Fortunately, though matters in Xanthos are busy as always, I was able to make the journey, although by necessity I will be returning home tomorrow.'

'Of course. I understand completely.'

Dion looked around. 'I was expecting to see your daughter here. How is she?'

'Isobel is preparing herself, but will join us soon. You know how women are.'

'We do indeed,' Glaukos said with a smile. 'We look forward to her company.'

'Now, please. Come. Let me show you inside.'

The servants dispersed while Dion and his uncle fell in behind Philippos. They passed through a colonnaded terrace with grape vines trailing through the wooden beams above and found themselves in an expansive reception room with views of the gardens. Philippos indicated a cluster of low sofas and the three men sat, settling the folds of their tunics. Servants brought watered wine, olives, hard cheese, and flat bread.

Dion finally broke the silence. 'So, Lord Philippos, how goes the election? Have you secured the votes you need?'

Philippos shrugged as he took a dainty sip of wine from a silver goblet. 'A few influential lords are holding out. Lord Nilus has reigned over a period of peace in Phalesia, and although the treaty with Ilea was the work of Aristocles – may Aldus guard his soul – many credit Nilus with the result.' He set down his cup and then met Dion's eyes. 'How do you regard Lord Nilus, King?'

Dion was careful with his words. 'He has a swift mind, and makes a fair bargain. I've never found reason to say anything against him.'

'Hmm . . .' Philippos scratched his sharp chin. He hesitated, before leaning forward. 'King, I must confess that I've been dissembling. I asked you here for one reason alone, and it has nothing to do with politics. My daughter is in her sitting room, which is at the end of that hallway. Isobel is waiting for you. She . . . She has something to tell you.'

Perplexed, Dion glanced at his uncle. Glaukos raised an eyebrow, while Philippos stood and gave another small bow, before placing his hand over his heart.

'Please, King Dion. I apologize for the theatrics, but my daughter insisted, and she is someone I can never say no to. Please?' His eyes drifted toward the hallway.

Dion frowned and left his seat. Wondering what in the names of all the gods was going on, he left the reception and soon found himself walking down the hallway alone, feeling the two older men watching his back. Thoughts whirled through his mind. He remembered the fool he'd made of himself at the banquet, and worse still, the way he'd accosted Isobel in his bedchamber. Philippos hadn't appeared unfriendly at all – quite the opposite. Feeling his heart hammering in his chest, he took a turn at the end of the corridor to find a curtain of thick blue linen.

He reached for the fabric and then decided to clear his throat. 'Lady Isobel?'

Her soft voice replied immediately. 'King Dion. Please, come in.'

Dion pushed aside the curtain and entered the sitting room, seeing tall mirrors surrounded by stools and side tables, in a chamber crowded with statues and bright-colored flowers in vases. The air smelled perfumed; after growing up in a male-dominated household, it felt strange to be entering a room so strongly feminine.

Seeing Isobel sitting on a wooden sofa, facing the doorway, Dion stopped in his tracks. Her golden hair was brushed long and straight, glowing in the crisp afternoon sun that poured through the window, and her eyes matched the blue jewel in a brooch pinned to her coral-colored chiton. She still wore the medallion with the dolphin, dangling from her slender neck. She looked beautiful.

She didn't stand, and her chest was heaving as she looked up at him, each breath pressing her breasts against the material, making him wonder if they would stay constrained, as low-cut as her chiton was. She moistened her lips.

'Please.' She made space for him on the sofa, even though there were several stools and benches in the room. 'Sit beside me?'

He glanced back at the curtain. 'I am not sure if your father . . .'

Her smile lit up her face. 'My father won't mind, truly.'

Feeling caught up in a tide of events not of his making, wondering what she was about to tell him, Dion sat next to her, so close he was aware of her body's warmth and scent as she turned to face him.

He was surprised when she took his hand.

'Dion. I need to talk to you about what happened on the night of the banquet.'

He drew a deep breath and nodded. 'I don't know what I can say besides I'm sorry . . . I drank too much wine. I'm sorry and . . . thank you for . . . helping me to bed.'

She squeezed his hand as her lips formed a pout. 'You are jesting. You must be. Surely you remember?' She took his hand and pressed it against her breast. 'You don't remember this?' Her expression was mischievous. 'I remember every moment of it.'

He felt his face redden. 'I remember . . .'

'I am with child.'

His eyes widened and he started to cough. 'You're . . . ?' His eyes were burning as he fought to catch his breath. 'Did you just say . . . ?'

'The child is yours.'

Dion pulled away. Putting a hand to his temple, he suddenly realized he'd climbed to his feet and was standing beside the sofa. 'You're certain?'

She gave a little nod, still smiling, but with a small crease in her forehead. She was now biting her lip, looking concerned.

His head spinning, he sat down again. He stared at her flat belly, as if trying to see a change in her.

'I'm not showing yet.' She blushed.

'I . . .'

It was only then that the full import of what she had told him sank in. He was going to be a father. Filled with a sense of awe and wonder, he reached down and put a hand against Isobel's stomach. She let him, still searching his face.

'We are going to have a child together, King.'

Dion suddenly grinned and then gulped. He grinned again. He wiped a hand over his face and realized his heart was pounding like a drum. He felt like he'd been holding his breath underwater for an eternity and was only now gasping for air at the surface.

The beautiful young woman next to him took his hands again. 'Well?' she asked.

'Your father . . . Does he . . . ?'

'He knows.'

Seeing through a shimmering haze, Dion blinked moisture from his eyes. He was the youngest child and his father had always been distant, preferring Nikolas's company. His father had never seemed to realize that surely every child had something to offer.

He knew he could do better.

Warmth and affection flooded through him. He met Isobel's concerned gaze and squeezed her hands back.

'We should be married,' he said. 'I mean, that's if . . . ?'

She smiled. 'I would love to be your queen.'

Dion's arm reached around her back. He was reluctant to squeeze her too tightly, but she pulled him close as they kissed. She tasted sweet and her body felt soft, so that before his senses left him he pushed her away, gasping as he stood, pulling her up with him.

'I'm going to have a son,' he murmured, shaking his head with disbelief.

'Or a daughter.'

'Or a daughter.' He laughed. 'But I know he's going to be a boy.'

Dion felt so seized with emotion that he didn't know what he was supposed to do. 'Isobel, what's . . . What's the protocol in this situation?'

'Well, the wedding will have to be very soon.'

Realization dawned. 'Yes. Yes, you're right.' His sluggish thoughts finally came into focus. 'Your father. I have to ask his permission to marry you.'

'Dion, you're a king. And like I said, he knows.'

He shook his head. 'He must think I'm terrible.'

'Trust me, he doesn't. Come. Let's go and see him together.'

She led a dazed Dion from the sitting room and down the hallway. As he walked, Dion felt as if his body didn't belong to him. His mind was so active that he wasn't sure he was walking properly; he felt like a puppet on strings.

Philippos and Glaukos both stood as Dion and Isobel entered the reception. From their knowing expressions, Dion realized immediately that Philippos and Glaukos were well aware of the nature of the conversation he and Isobel had just had. But the thought didn't rankle in the slightest; he didn't care at all.

'Lord Philippos,' Dion said. He nearly stumbled over the words. 'I would like your permission to marry your daughter.'

Philippos grinned broadly. 'And you have it. Of course you do.'

The two older men cheered. Philippos and his daughter embraced, while Dion's uncle gave him a hearty hug.

'I'm going to be a father,' Dion said.

'You certainly are, my boy.' Glaukos beamed.

Then the young king of Xanthos and the next first consul of Phalesia were clapping each other on the back. Someone handed Dion a goblet, and he swallowed a gulp of wine without tasting it.

Philippos put his arm around his daughter and squeezed her. 'Now. We have a wedding to plan!'

143

Glaukos spoke up. 'My lord, I hope I don't speak out of turn, but we must call a priestess from the Temple of Aeris. I'm sure you understand that for the future of Xanthos, Isobel's health is now of paramount importance.'

'Of course, of course.' Philippos saw his daughter's worried face and spoke tenderly. 'There is nothing to be afraid of, daughter. You shall have the best care there is. After all, you are bearing the heir to a throne.'

'The last day of spring,' Glaukos said, scratching his chin thoughtfully and nodding. 'For the wedding, before the lady begins to show her new state. Sire?' He raised his voice. 'Dion?'

Still stunned, Dion turned when he heard his name and smiled. 'Of course, Uncle. The last day of spring is fine with me.'

Philippos lifted his cup. 'To new family.'

Dion grinned and held his goblet high. 'To new family.'

20

Sophia followed High Priestess Marina as they climbed up to the villa of Lord Philippos, the older woman walking with stately steps, looking solemn in her official robe. Trailing after her, Sophia carried a satchel filled with polished metal implements and packets of powders and herbs.

They were almost at their destination, and Priestess Marina, a tall, olive-skinned woman with a topknot, turned and looked her up and down. 'Hold your back straighter, Sophia,' she said sternly. 'You wanted to come, and I know you have the skill, but you must also look the part.'

Approaching thirteen years old, a slender dark-haired girl in a white novice's robe with blue trim, Sophia nodded and tried to look more priestess-like. But she knew Marina well enough to understand that the rebuke was more a display of the high priestess's own nervousness than anything else. Their task was one of the most important imaginable: a future queen was pregnant.

And Dion was the father!

Sophia was excited for him and had begged the high priestess to let her attend. Everyone knew that Dion had been in love with her older sister Chloe. But then Chloe had left Phalesia to find their father and her body was discovered on the road to Tanus four weeks later, beaten beyond all recognition, with only her clothing and necklace to tell anyone who she was.

Dion was as bereft as she was. After his coronation, despite his lack of a wife or heir, he'd been too grief-stricken to find another love. Knowing his pain, the pain of loss that she felt herself, Sophia hoped that marriage to Isobel, and the birth of his child, would bring him happiness.

Like Sophia, Dion had no parents to shelter him and support him. Like her, he'd lost his only sibling.

As always, thinking about Chloe made her sad. And then she felt guilt when her thoughts inevitably turned to Nikolas, the man who was clearly to blame for the darkness that had plagued Sophia's life. Everyone had believed her when she'd told them he'd simply collapsed in front of her. She'd then traveled by ship back to Phalesia . . . where it seemed as if her father's death was divine punishment for her crime.

She hadn't even been present at his funeral and was forced to cry over her father's tomb. They said Aristocles' heart failed him, but his heart was always strong. Nilus started acting strange around her, avoiding her rather than consoling her. Amos vanished. Finally, with no home to return to, and no family to support her, she had made a vow to devote herself to the goddess Aeris.

Lost in thought and unnoticed, she bowed when she needed to as they arrived at Lord Philippos's villa and the priestess asked to see Isobel. While the high priestess and the lord spoke, Sophia looked for Dion and saw him outside, touring the gardens with his gray-haired uncle. He was smiling broadly as he said something, waving his arms with enthusiasm.

Soon Sophia was following High Priestess Marina down a hallway, entering a sitting room at the back of the villa. As the high priestess greeted Isobel and seated herself, Sophia was careful to stand behind and to the side, holding the satchel, ready to serve if needed.

She'd seen Isobel before, of course – all the novices thought she was the most beautiful woman in Phalesia – but they'd never actually spoken. Now that she knew Isobel was going to be Dion's wife, she found herself inspecting her with interest. She was undoubtedly attractive, slim as a willow, with long blonde hair and bright blue eyes.

Isobel was tense, twisting her fingers in her lap as the high priestess matter-of-factly probed the soon-to-be queen about her health.

'When was your last cycle?' In these circumstances, the high priestess tended not to use titles.

'Six . . . Six weeks ago,' Isobel said haltingly. She dropped her eyes.

'And when were you and the king together?'

'Nearly . . . four weeks ago.'

'When did you notice that you had missed your cycle?'

'It should have come ten days ago.'

'Have you experienced any morning sickness?'

Isobel nodded.

'And how do you feel generally? Would you say you are in good health?'

'I'm a little tired.' She gave a slight smile. 'But we were all up late last night, and I've been working hard to help my father with the election. Is . . . Is everything all right?'

High Priestess Marina gave Isobel a series of examinations, and then finally broke out in a warm smile. 'Everything is as it should be, and both you and your future husband are young and strong. Come to me if you notice any change in your health, but otherwise, I will see you in a month.'

'What's going to happen to my body?'

'Nothing that isn't natural, my dear.' The high priestess stood. 'The time will pass swifter than you think. Before you know it, you are going to be a mother.'

Isobel let out a sigh of relief. She looked up at Sophia, and Sophia couldn't help herself returning her bright smile.

——————

'The priestess is leaving now. We can go back inside the villa,' Lord Philippos said.

Dion nodded and began to follow him, but then with surprise he saw the novice following in the priestess's footsteps.

'Sophia!' he called, hurrying over.

The imposing priestess bowed at Dion, her hands clasped together, buried in the folds of her robe. 'May the goddess be with you, King.'

'High Priestess,' he said with a nod and a smile.

She glanced at Sophia. 'I will leave you two to talk.'

A moment later they were alone and Dion was smiling down at Sophia. Her hair was longer than he remembered, and after the deaths of her father and sister, there was now a darkness in her eyes that hadn't been there before.

'Sophia, how are you? I haven't seen you in a long time.'

Dion's heart reached out to her. She'd lost everyone she held dear. He wondered if she was happy.

'I'm well enough,' she said. She blushed. 'King Dion.'

'It's just the two of us here,' he said with a laugh. 'I'm so glad it was you who came today. I know we have to keep it quiet until after the wedding, but'—he grinned—'it's exciting news.' He suddenly looked worried. 'Isobel . . . Is everything the way it should be?'

Sophia smiled at his discomfort. 'The high priestess said she's fine.'

'Good, good. Are you happy at the temple?' Dion asked, frowning. 'I can't imagine how hard things have been for you . . . after Chloe . . . and your father. And Sophia . . . I hope you don't blame yourself for Nikolas's death. Just remember, you've done nothing wrong.'

At the mention of Nikolas, Sophia looked down at the ground. 'The temple keeps me busy.'

'Listen, you know that I . . . You know that you can always come to live with me in Xanthos. Your father . . . He was always good to me.

He's the reason I made it back home. You and your family . . . You're . . . special to me.'

'Thank you, but no. Phalesia is my home.'

'If you ever need anything, anything at all, you only have to ask.'

For some reason Sophia looked as if she was carrying the weight of the world on her shoulders. But then she suddenly hugged Dion, her head buried in his chest, before pushing herself away.

'I'd best be going,' she said. 'I'm happy for you.'

21

Nilus, first consul of Phalesia, was at his villa, hosting his closest allies. The loftiest in the city, Nilus's residence crowned a hill close to the agora, and the view from the terrace was unrivaled among all the homes in the city. His home was elegant and understated, with two stories – one for the lord and his family and a downstairs level for the servants – and flowering plants framing both sides of the winding path that led to the streets below. It had significance in the minds of the people he ruled.

He'd always loved this villa . . . had desired it for himself. He'd spent many evenings here as a guest before it finally became his.

It had once belonged to Aristocles. But Aristocles was dead, and now Nilus occupied his home.

A plump, round-faced man, he had a short crop of neatly trimmed gray hair on his crown and wore a white tunic and a belt that matched his heavy gold necklace. He knew he was supposed to be slimming down, and he also knew that after his guests left, his wife would be nagging him, but he was anxious, and when he was anxious he ate and drank compulsively.

'Slow down, First Consul,' Consul Harod said. A big man with a gray beard, he reached out and tapped the side of the goblet in Nilus's hand.

Nilus scowled at him and tilted the cup back, taking a large swallow of sweet Sarsican red wine.

'Lord Harod has a point. The people do like a good-looking candidate,' Consul Anneas said. A haughty, athletic lord with fair hair who claimed that exercise sharpened the mind, he raised an eyebrow.

Consul Leon, a shorter and plumper man even than Nilus, pulled his seat forward. 'Ignore them, First Consul. Life is to be lived.' He picked up a bunch of grapes and lifted them high, biting them off the stem one by one.

The pleasure Nilus usually felt at hearing his title on other men's lips was tainted by the guilty secret he shared with these men. By habit, he glanced at the doorway, checking to see that his guards were posted and at attention. *Two on the inside. Two on the terrace. A further pair at the bottom of the steps.*

Nilus turned to glare at Anneas. 'I don't think I'm going to be making any sudden changes in my weight in time for the election.'

Anneas shrugged. 'It is never too late to start.'

Nilus took another gulp and then smashed down the goblet. 'Philippos is handsome, with a beautiful daughter, whereas I have no children. You all know it – now that Isobel is marrying the king of Xanthos, I am almost certain to lose the election.'

The idea filled him with panic. As first consul he could station guards where he pleased, but what about when he could no longer command the city's soldiers?

Nilus swept his gaze over his companions while he waited for someone to speak, finally reaching forward and slapping a sausage into some bread.

Seated across from him, Leon ate a series of sea urchins, one after the other, speaking with his mouth full. 'You're missing out, Anneas. These cost two silver pieces each.'

Nilus's scowl deepened. How would he afford to host these banquets? His friends would desert him. His guards would leave.

'Don't worry, First Consul,' Anneas said, looking down his long nose. 'Philippos's proposals don't meet the approval of everyone. He plans to institute a land tax and to extend the moratorium on slavery. Both are unpopular with the nobles.'

'Like you, eh, Anneas?' gray-bearded Harod said. 'Not everyone owns a thousand acres.'

Anneas spread his hands. 'How do you like paying wages to slaves?'

Leon shrugged. 'There will always be another election,' he said. 'And then another. And another.'

'Have you never heard of something called mortality?' Anneas snorted.

'We are not here to talk about other elections,' Nilus snapped. 'We're here to talk about *this* election.' The three consuls all leaned back, eyes wide as he brought silence to the room. 'My father always said that once a loser, always a loser.'

'A wise man, your father,' Harod said, nodding sagely.

'Shame about the son,' Leon quipped.

'You are a fool. Do you realize that?' Harod glared at the little man.

'Enough!' Anneas growled at them. He turned back to Nilus. 'Surely Philippos has a weakness? What about his daughter? I hear she was so eager to become queen that she threw herself at young Dion.'

'Bah,' Nilus said, reaching for some more hard cheese.

'First Consul?'

A new voice interrupted Nilus just as he filled his mouth and began chewing. Swallowing quickly, he turned to see Eudora, one of his younger and more attractive servants, hovering uncertainly. A slender woman with auburn hair and wide hips, she unfortunately wasn't as good in bed as she was to look at.

He grimaced as he gulped down the brittle cheese. If he hadn't had guests, he would have taken her to task; he could have choked.

'It is late, and I need to go to my mother. May I leave?'

'I remember,' Nilus said. 'Go.' He nodded at the door and the soldiers made way for her.

He reached for more cheese and frowned.

There had to be something he could do . . .

———

'Tastes awful,' the old woman muttered, talking around a mouthful of mush.

Eudora hovered anxiously, wringing her hands as she watched Sophia attend to her mother. 'Do as she says, Mother.'

'Chew it slowly, and then take a sip of the medicine to wash it down,' Sophia instructed.

The old woman on the stool nodded, grimacing as she chewed the bitter herbs. Kneeling on the cold stone floor, Sophia began to work at the old woman's fingers and hands. The old woman closed her eyes with relief, tears forming at their corners as Sophia tended to her arthritic joints.

'The medicine,' Sophia said with a smile, nodding at the wooden cup. Eudora came forward and lifted the cup to her mother's lips.

'Will it get any better?' Eudora asked.

'No.' Sophia shook her head. 'But if I come once a week, she can live with it.' She smiled up at her elderly patient. 'That's better, isn't it, Tharis?'

'Thank you, priestess,' Tharis murmured.

'Now,' Sophia said to Eudora as she kneaded the woman's hands and rubbed each knuckle in turn. She glanced at the auburn-haired maidservant. 'Did Nilus mention my father again?'

'No, he was only talking about Philippos. Lord Nilus was complaining that he is going to lose the election.'

Sophia frowned. 'Think carefully. Are you certain my father's name never came up?'

'I am certain, priestess. I promise. It was just the one time.'

Sophia's hands were growing tired, but she continued rubbing and squeezing nonetheless. 'And remind me what Nilus said again.'

'He said to one of the consuls—'

'Which consul?'

'Consul Carolas.'

Sophia nodded. 'Go on.'

'He said to Consul Carolas: "Be careful with your loyalties, or you'll suffer Aristocles' fate."'

Sophia pondered as she tended to Eudora's mother. Nilus had been cold to her ever since her father's death. He'd never offered her his sympathy, and if he saw her in the city, he would ignore her and turn away, swiftly walking in the opposite direction. She'd managed to force a confrontation once, asking him whether her father had said anything before his heart gave out. Nilus had stammered something about Aristocles being emotional about returning home. The man who was one of her father's closest friends now spent all his time with the lords Anneas, Leon, and Harod, consuls Sophia knew had been her father's enemies.

Nilus had mentioned her father's name in a threat to another consul. Sophia was determined to know the truth. If Nilus did have anything to do with her father's death, she vowed to herself that she would do something about it.

'Keep listening, Eudora. If he mentions my father . . . the slightest thing, I want to know.'

'I will, priestess. I promise.'

Sophia rose to her feet and began to gather her things. 'I'll leave more medicine with you, and I'll return in a week.'

22

At the harbor of Xanthos, where the headlands at each end of the curved shoreline protected his growing fleet, Dion conducted his weekly tour of the shipyards with Roxana.

He usually had an eye for detail, asking her question after question, probing the state of everything he could think of, from the supplies of oak, pine, and hemp to the disposition of the men. He regularly patted the sides of ships and explored interiors, rubbed sailcloth between his fingers, and ate from the mess to check the quality of the food. But today he was enjoying standing on the beach and having an overview, simply taking in all he'd accomplished.

For today was different; he felt that he was seeing the world through new eyes. He would soon have a babe, gurgling in his arms as he pointed out his mighty warships and merchant vessels. The babe would become a child, the child would grow, and he would have someone to share his passion for the sea with, to pass his knowledge down to. A son or daughter, tottering by his side and then walking, growing, standing tall, and making him proud.

'The work goes well,' Roxana grunted. 'We'll have six serviceable triremes by summer.'

Dion nodded absently.

Roxana raised an eyebrow. 'Am I boring you, sire?'

'No, sorry.' Dion smiled as he swept his gaze over the harbor. He saw an older fisherman with a youth who could only be his son, struggling together to get their net into their boat. The father patted his boy on the back when their task was accomplished.

Roxana's gruff voice brought Dion out of his reverie. 'She's really got you by the heartstrings, hasn't she?'

'It's not just her, it's . . .'

Dion clamped his words down. No one could know that she was with child until after the wedding, or the child's legitimacy would be brought into question. The only people who knew besides Dion and Isobel were Glaukos, Philippos, the high priestess, and Sophia.

'She's very beautiful, and I'm excited to be married,' Dion said lamely.

'And she's far away in Phalesia, and you can't wait to take her to your bed.' Roxana smiled and gripped his arm. 'I'm happy for you, Dion.'

He grinned as she slapped him on the back. 'Sorry if I'm distracted. You were saying?'

'It's nothing that can't wait.' Roxana gazed at the horizon. 'Have you heard from Fort Liberty lately?'

'I'm sure Cob is fine.'

She harrumphed. 'Of course he is. I was merely asking about the men.'

Now it was Dion's turn to smile. 'Roxana, can I ask you something?'

'You're the king, and you're asking me if you can ask me a question?'

'When did you last take some time off?'

'Eh?'

'Time away from ships,' he said. 'Just a short stint. Why don't you take the *Calypso*, sail to Fort Liberty, and surprise Cob? He'd be happy to see you.'

Roxana's eyebrows shot up. 'The *Calypso*?' She shook her head vigorously. 'No, I couldn't. She's your personal—'

'She's a pleasure to sail, and don't tell me you haven't had your eye on her. Tell Cob I asked him to show you the view from the cliffs. I'm thinking of installing a lookout and I want your opinion.'

'Well'—she tilted her head, frowning—'as long as it's important.'

'It is.' Dion fought to keep mirth from his expression. 'I'll keep an eye on things here.'

'Sire!'

Turning, Dion saw a steward hurrying over from the direction of the palace, getting sand on his sandals as he approached. 'Lord Finn . . . He's asked to see you. He said it cannot wait.'

'Some matter of trade, no doubt.' Dion clasped Roxana's shoulder. 'Give Cobrim my best.'

'Well?'

Finn jumped as Dion found him in the banqueting hall, not far from the Flower Terrace, a place where colorful blooms were tended with more care than anywhere else in Xanthos. Dion's mother and father had met their end there, and the fragrant flowers dispelled the dark memories that clung to the terrace like foul odors from the grave.

Finn's long hair was brushed and parted in the middle and he wore an orange tunic fastened with a bright-blue sash that hugged his slender frame. Standing over a door-sized slab of wood, he turned, blocking Dion's view, and his expression was deadly serious.

'Finn?' Dion frowned. 'What is it?'

'Dion . . . Do you remember when we returned from Malakai? You asked me to find anything I could about ancient Aleuthea: relics, statues, anything.'

'And?' Dion felt worry sink into his gut.

'All manner of dross came my way, and I was thinking of asking you if I could call off the search.'

'Go on.'

'And then this arrived.' Finn nodded at the wooden panel, but he was still obstructing it with his body. 'One of my agents found it in the Oracle's temple in Myana. Well . . . found it . . . stole it?' He shrugged. 'Be careful with it. It takes eons for solid teak to decay, but it's still delicate.'

'It's authentic?'

'The glossy red color comes from Aleuthean Crimson, an indigenous dye. It is genuine . . . I'd stake my life on it . . .'

'Finn,' Dion said in a low voice. 'Let me see it.'

Finn stood aside and Dion looked down.

It was an ancient panel painting, the artwork covering the entire piece of framed timber. It had faded, but the colors were still vibrant, the lines between the shapes distinct.

Finn crouched by the painting and brushed his fingers across the surface. 'It was formed by skilled hands; a master craftsman made it. See the finish? It feels smooth. It's been glossed with a transparent lacquer to preserve the paint.'

Dion was too engrossed to reply.

The painting depicted a stormy sky filled with dragons, hundreds of them, some massive and in the foreground, others wheeling in the distance. Wings like bats, thin as a ship's sails and just as big, flashed in a radiant sun as the creatures soared. Each set of wings curved and met at a lithe, reptilian body, covered in diamond-shaped scales. Powerful forelimbs gave way to sharp, finger-sized claws, outstretched and ready to rend and tear. Hind legs were stronger still: thick and muscular, tucked in under the body. Huge, wedge-shaped heads with sweeping protrusions behind them tapered to vicious jaws. Some of the dragons' jaws were parted, revealing rows of sharp teeth.

But these weren't the dragons that Dion was used to.

The dragons in the painting, rather than being silver, as all eldren were when they changed, or black, as Dion knew he became, were uniformly blood-red. Their scales were the color of fire, or of bright arterial blood.

'I don't understand it,' Dion murmured. He knelt and examined the painting, glancing at Finn. 'These dragons are red. Why?'

'I thought you might have the answer.'

'Me?' Dion shook his head. 'No. Perhaps Zachary might be able to explain it . . .'

'Do you know what that is?' Finn pointed out a glowing arch in the background of the painting, standing tall and proud on a hill. A small robed figure near the arch held a staff, appearing to be half the height of the strange artifact beside him. It wasn't a stone arch; it was rounded, and all of one piece.

'I have no idea.'

Dion continued to stare at the painting. 'This is troubling. They don't look like they're supposed to be threatening. It's almost as if they're being . . . glorified.'

'What does it mean?' Finn asked, perplexed. 'See the staff? Like the woman you saw in the palace.'

Dion met Finn's worried gaze. 'Is this the power Palemon came back for?'

'What do we do?'

'Keep searching. I don't care how much you have to pay, if you find anything else like this, bring it to me.'

Dion stared at the painting for a time longer before flicking a glance at Finn. 'Well?' He jerked his chin at the exit.

Finn left Dion muttering as he examined the painting.

'Red dragons. An arch . . .'

It had been a week since Sophia's last visit, and she was again at Eudora's mother's house. Nilus never released Eudora from her duties until late in the evening, and Sophia stifled a yawn as she crushed herbs and pounded at powders with a mortar and pestle.

She helped Tharis drink her medicine and rubbed the old woman's hands, feeling her own shoulders ache, but knowing she was bringing relief. Finally she heard footsteps and Eudora entered the small house.

'I am sorry for being late, priestess. Lord Nilus was hosting another group of consuls.' The pretty but careworn servant looked exhausted.

'It's fine,' Sophia said without pausing. 'She's improving. Aren't you, Tharis?'

'It is better.' The old woman nodded.

'Thank you, priestess,' Eudora said. She watched Sophia for a time. 'I have some news. Something unusual happened two days ago.'

Sophia looked up sharply. 'Something to do with my father?'

'No . . . It was something else. A strange man visited Lord Nilus.'

'Strange?' Sophia asked. 'In what way?'

'A hunchback. Is that what it's called?' Eudora bent forward, ducking her head into her shoulders and stooping.

Sophia frowned. 'I understand what you mean. Go on.'

'He wore odd clothing: trousers and a tunic with buttons down the front. He was pale, with dark hair and thick eyebrows. He spoke with an accent I have never heard before.'

'A foreigner?' Sophia wondered what business he had with the first consul, but then her father had occasionally met with representatives from Tanus or Sarsica. 'That's not strange in itself. What did they discuss?'

'He arrived late at night and asked to see Lord Nilus. He then said something to him, and suddenly Lord Nilus asked everyone to leave the villa, even the servants. We had to wait out on the terrace while they spoke. When his visitor left, Nilus seemed pleased.' Eudora shrugged. 'It was probably nothing.'

'Probably,' Sophia mused. 'See what you can overhear. I'll return next week.'

She didn't want to read too much into it. But then again, anything that made Nilus pleased could be something to be worried about.

23

With just one week remaining until his wedding, Dion knew he should be focusing on the rituals and festivities, and the presentation of his new queen to his people, but instead all he could think about was the painting.

It was late at night, and he again stood in the banqueting hall, crouched in front of the wooden panel, staring at the dragons. He examined the distant glowing arch. The descendants of Aleuthea had returned and claimed Malakai, which was close to the site of the sunken city. What did it all portend?

'Dion.'

He glanced up to see his tall, gray-haired uncle approaching. He was surprised to hear himself addressed by his first name, something Glaukos did only when he was being gravely serious.

When he saw Glaukos's expression, Dion straightened, immediately concerned. His uncle's face was as white as a sheet. In all the time he'd known him, Dion had never seen him look so disconcerted.

'Dion . . .' Glaukos said again. His mouth worked soundlessly.

'Uncle?' Dion rushed to his side. 'What is it?'

'You have a visitor. Out . . . Outside . . . On the Orange Terrace.' He shook his head with apparent disbelief. 'You . . . need to go.'

Dion felt his heart beat out of time at his uncle's reaction. 'Who is it?'

'I'm . . . I'm sorry, lad. I'm sorry things had to turn out this way.'

Now truly alarmed, Dion left the banqueting hall and reached the Orange Terrace via the throne room. Though it was late, the fruit on the trees was bright, lit up by the flaming torches on tall poles. As always, the ocean breeze carried the smell of citrus, rustling the branches, with the backdrop of waves crashing on the shore forming a staccato rhythm.

He walked quickly, following the winding path past the stone table and continuing toward the rail facing the sea.

He came to a sudden halt.

It was a cloudy night, but he could see a woman dressed in a white chiton, standing and facing the sea. The wind was blowing her dark hair around her face and ruffling her clothing against her slender figure.

He knew his imagination was deceiving him. In a moment she would turn around and she would look nothing like the woman he thought she was.

She moved slightly, her face now in profile. Strong sensation, like pain mixed with grief, gripped a cold hand around Dion's stomach. It couldn't be her. Her name formed on Dion's lips, but he couldn't say it out loud; there was no way this was the same woman, for she was long dead. His heart threatened to leap out of his chest. Blood roared in his ears. He put a hand out, supporting himself on one of the orange trees.

She turned around to face him.

'Dion,' she said with a smile.

'Chloe?'

She moved a little closer, and as the flickering light from the terrace caught her face, it no longer felt like he was staring at an apparition. It was her. She had the same almond-shaped eyes, triangular face, and wide mouth with ruby-red lips, the same sharp nose and flowing dark hair. She was real, flesh and blood. She was standing in front of him, as beautiful as ever, just a couple of paces away. He had dreamed about her, had nightmares about her death. He met her brown eyes and looked into them, and he forgot all about the sounds of the sea and the ocean breeze.

He took a step toward her. 'Is it you?'

She came closer, moisture brimming in her eyes.

He took another step, and then he was suddenly moving. He wrapped his arms around her, pulling her close. Their lips pressed together and he lost all sense of where he was, only knowing that the woman he loved was alive. The kiss was urgent and strong. It went on forever. As he clutched her to his chest, she kissed him back just as fiercely. He felt her tears on his face, and realized that he was crying as well. His heart pounding, he used every sense to tell himself she was real, inhaling deeply, holding her as tightly as he could.

'Chloe.'

'Dion,' she breathed, her chest rising and falling, her warm body pressed tightly against his.

Finally he looked into her face again.

'How?' He knew his voice was shaking, and he tried to control it, but failed.

'It's a long story, but I promise, I'll share every detail.'

Dion realized he was holding both her hands. His vision was shimmering, so that he had to blink to clear it.

'King Dion,' a male voice interrupted, and Dion reluctantly released Chloe's hands to see a familiar figure standing a polite distance away. Clean-shaven, but with weathered, craggy skin, he was stocky and dressed in a leather breastplate, skirt of leather strips, and sandals. Dion recognized him immediately, despite the fact that he'd put on some weight.

Dion gathered himself, calming his breath, although his heart was still racing.

'Amos,' he said warmly. He walked forward and they embraced. 'I haven't seen you since . . .' His eyes flicked to Chloe.

'Since Lord Aristocles' death,' Amos said. 'It has been a long time, I know. I've been away.'

Amos's eyes were a little bleary, but his bearing was steady. The former captain of Phalesia's guard glanced from face to face. 'I know you two have a lot to catch up on.' He gave Chloe the same inquiring look he'd once given Aristocles. 'Chloe, if it suits you, I'll return to the palace later?'

'Amos,' Dion protested. 'You can't leave. Go inside and find any of the stewards. Tell them I said to prepare rooms for you and Chloe. Have you eaten? Would you like some wine?'

'Wine . . .' Amos licked his lips. 'No wine.' He shook his head firmly. 'But I'll take water and food. Thank you.'

Giving a small bow, Amos headed inside, leaving Chloe and Dion standing alone together on the terrace.

He stared into her eyes. He looked down at her hand. She reached toward him, but then he suddenly remembered; seeing Chloe had driven out all knowledge of Isobel and his child.

'Chloe . . .' He had to explain. 'I thought you were dead.'

'So did Amos, and everyone else, it seems. A man . . . He left that body on the road. He wanted everyone to think I was dead.' She hesitated. 'But why didn't the eldren tell you I was alive? Perhaps Zachary, or Liana . . .'

Dion shook his head. 'I haven't spoken with any of the eldren in a long time.' He told her about the Blackwell Mines. 'Now Eiric thinks I betrayed him. I sent a messenger to invite the eldren to the'—he realized he'd been about to say 'to the wedding' and quickly recovered—'to invite them to Xanthos. But I don't expect to see them.'

Chloe was surprised. 'But you and Eiric were friends.'

'No longer. The eldren are sequestered in their homeland, spurning contact with humans once again.' He wiped a hand over his face. 'I have so much to talk to you about.'

He reached out and took her hand, standing close. He was aware of her warm body next to him. He couldn't help contrasting her with Isobel. Isobel was attractive, bold, and sensual. But Chloe was more than beautiful; she was brave and intelligent, dedicated and somehow . . . real. He knew her family and she knew his. He'd sailed with her and fought with her, slept by her side and faced armies with her. The eldran part of him had known he loved her, and needed to protect her, forcing him to change his shape, before he'd even known it himself.

But that was all in the past now. He was going to be a father, and Isobel would be his wife.

'Chloe . . . When we saw each other last . . . I was confused. You and my brother were betrothed . . . I felt I had to choose between being eldran or human, and Nikolas made me think I'd never be welcome in Xanthos again. But then I met some people, and they helped me realize that it was possible to be accepted. Your father . . . He invited me back with him . . . Then Nikolas died . . . I became king . . .' He hesitated. 'I was devastated when they told me you were dead.'

'What are you trying to tell me?'

'I . . .' he stammered. 'I'm . . . I'm getting married.'

'Married?' She drew back, stunned. 'Who is she?'

'Isobel, daughter of Lord Philippos. She's from Phalesia.'

'Philippos . . . the consul?' Chloe was struggling to hold back tears.

'Yes.'

She yanked her hand free, turning away.

'I'm sorry,' Dion said. 'I thought you were dead.'

'Is she pretty?'

'I suppose she is,' he said slowly and then gave a slight smile. 'But she's nothing like you.'

She took a deep breath and then faced him again. Her eyes were red and her jaw tight; her posture was rigid.

'May I ask you for a favor, King Dion?'

'Chloe . . . please . . . You of all people are never allowed to call me that. Of course. Anything.'

'I need to get to Phalesia.'

'How soon?'

'As quickly as possible.'

'The tide turns in four hours. I'll have a fast boat take you, and you'll arrive with the dawn. You can sleep here until then.'

'Thank you,' she said formally. 'I think I'll rest now. I don't expect to see you before I leave.'

'Chloe, please . . .'

Dion's eyes followed her as she walked inside.

———

Despite the sumptuous quarters she'd been given and the softest bed she'd had in months to sleep on, Chloe was wide awake.

She tossed and turned, thinking about Dion and hating the way she'd left things. Of course she wanted him to be happy. He'd no doubt known Isobel for a long time, and loved her deeply. He was a king, and a king needed a queen. Isobel's father was an important landowner. Though Chloe didn't remember anything about Lord Philippos's daughter, she knew Dion well enough to know that he wouldn't have agreed to marry her unless they shared a deep connection.

She tried her best not to be jealous, but thinking of him with another woman was gnawing at her, making it impossible for her to sleep. Finally she came to a decision. She didn't know when she would see him again. She wanted to know about his new love. She couldn't leave things like this between them.

Thunder rumbled in the distance, heralding a storm. She rolled out of bed and, wearing a thin linen shift, padded on bare feet out into the hallway, continuing on to the king's bedchamber. She saw light peeking under the heavy curtains and peeled the cloth aside. Listening for the sounds of heavy breathing, she entered, peering ahead. But disappointment sank into her chest when she saw that the bedchamber was empty.

She glanced around with sudden curiosity. His personal quarters revealed so much about him. A burning oil lamp, rumpled linen, and empty bed immediately told her that, like her, he hadn't been able to sleep. The heavy bureau standing against the wall was covered with valuable ceramics and golden statues, but it was all shoved to the side to give space for the model sailing boat someone had probably carved for him as a gift. His discarded clothing was bunched in the corner, making her smile; this was a palace that needed a woman's guiding hand.

But her smile slowly fell. The Isobel she imagined was as captivating as the goddess Edra, and would be sharing this bed with the man she loved.

She turned to depart, knowing she was violating his privacy, but then she saw movement out of the corner of her eye. Dion was bare-chested, wearing just a loose pair of trousers. He was standing on his bedroom balcony, high above the ground, and staring out into the night.

Chloe held her breath, starting for the exit when she heard his voice.

'Chloe?'

She blushed as she turned to face him. With his flaxen hair, square jaw, and lightly stubbled chin, he was undeniably handsome. But it was his eyes that made her melt whenever he looked at her, particularly the way he was looking at her now. Her gaze drifted down his body. The ridges of his abdomen were clearly visible. He wasn't tall, but he was several inches taller than her, and his shoulders were broad, his arms strong.

'Can't sleep either?' he asked. He gave her a tender smile. 'Come, join me out here.'

She crossed the room, and soon they were standing together on the balcony as they looked out at the distant storm on the horizon.

'I am happy for you,' Chloe said. 'It just came as a shock . . . Will you . . . ?' She swallowed. 'I want you to tell me about her. How did you meet? How long have you known each other?'

'We met just over a month ago,' he said. 'My uncle introduced us, and we spent a few days together. The next time I saw her, we agreed to be married.'

Chloe's eyes narrowed. 'And you love her?'

'There's something you need to know.' He hesitated, turning to meet her eyes. 'Isobel is with child.'

Realization dawned.

'It's a secret of course,' he said. 'And it will remain one. We were . . . together just once.'

'You're . . . ? Oh, Dion.' She embraced him, but when she pulled away she knew that her eyes were glistening. 'You're going to be married, and a father. I can't tell you how happy I am for you.'

He reached out to wipe a tear from the corner of her eye. 'Now, tell me your story. You've changed. There's something different about you.'

The wind was cool, and Chloe shivered.

'You're cold,' he said. Without another word, he came closer and put an arm around her, standing so that half his bare chest was pressed to her back, with their heads close together.

As the clouds parted and revealed a crescent moon, Chloe told Dion everything – about Vikram and her awakening, about the rebirth of Sindara and her trials at Athos.

'The Oracle said I would have a chance to end a grave threat. But'—she turned her head so she could look at his face—'I didn't learn everything the magi had to teach. For now, I just want to see my sister. I had a terrible vision when I was at Athos.'

His gentle brown eyes were concerned. 'What vision?'

'A scene of blood and death . . . In the temple . . .' She took a deep breath, shaking her head. 'It could be nothing.'

'That's why you're so anxious to get to Phalesia,' he said softly.

She nodded.

They were both silent for a time, bodies close together, taking warmth from each other. She remembered the time they'd kissed, swimming in the pool, out in the Wilds. As her pulse began to race, she realized her chest was heaving. She knew that if he tried to kiss her she would have to turn him away, but she didn't know if she would have the strength.

'Chloe . . . I know we said that we can be friends.' He sighed. 'But when I'm married, everything is going to change. We will never be able to share a moment like this again.'

She turned in his arms, reaching up to stroke his cheek. He was too honor-bound to do more than hold her, she knew then.

'The Oracle . . . You said she helped Marrix destroy Aleuthea because of an artifact?' he asked.

She nodded.

'There's something I have to show you.'

He led Chloe by the hand, taking her to the banqueting hall and showing her the painting.

'It's Aleuthean. Do you know what it means?'

Chloe sat on the floor in front of it and Dion sat beside her. She furrowed her brow as she examined the painting.

'Do you see the magus on the hill, standing near the glowing arch? He's holding a wind staff, like mine—'

'Yours?' Dion interrupted.

169

She nodded absently. 'There are four powers, linked to the four metals. Some magi are better at controlling particular materia than others.'

'What about the dragons?'

She shook her head, perplexed. 'I don't know what the red color means. But the artifact . . .' She pointed to the glowing arch. 'Perhaps this is it.'

24

Sophia lifted the ewer when the high priestess nodded to her.

Deep in the inner sanctum of the Temple of Aeris, Isobel was on her knees, hunched over a basin. The future queen of Xanthos was wearing a crimson chiton and her gold necklace glowed in the candlelight. It was deepest night and the temple was deserted, for these rituals were sacred, and with just five days until the wedding, the blessings of all the gods and goddesses must be asked for and obtained.

A circle of six young acolytes, girls new to the temple, stood facing Isobel, all holding candles. Lord Philippos, clad in a white tunic, hovered near his daughter with his hands clasped behind his back, watching the high priestess, ready to be called upon. The scent of sandalwood and lavender oil dominated the area, which was sectioned off from the main temple by a framework of latticed screens.

Taking the ewer from Sophia, the high priestess lifted it above the basin and poured the holy water over Isobel's head.

'We pray for Aeris to bless your body, mind, and soul.'

'The goddess hears our prayers,' the acolytes said in unison.

'Isobel, daughter of Philippos, son of Paolos, I invoke the goddess Aeris's blessings upon you,' High Priestess Marina intoned. 'I invoke the goddess's blessings for health and vitality, for the strong children you will bear, for the wisdom you will share with your husband.'

The high priestess, tall and commanding in her ceremonial robe of pale blue trimmed with gold, turned and nodded at Isobel's father.

'Lord Philippos. Approach your daughter.'

Lord Philippos took a deep breath and stepped forward to play his part. His penetrating eyes were uncharacteristically wide and uncertain.

'Philippos, son of Paolos, the goddess wishes to know that you give your daughter freely to King Dion of Xanthos.'

Philippos nodded. 'I do.'

Sophia reached for a towel and dried Isobel's hair.

'The goddess acknowledges the bond between father and daughter. Isobel, your mother in heaven gives her blessing.'

Sophia was close enough to Isobel to hear her breath catch at the mention of her mother.

'Philippos,' the high priestess instructed. 'Take this incense. Circle your daughter three times and repeat after me.'

As Philippos reached for the clay pot holding the stick of smoking incense, Sophia heard low male voices, echoing throughout the cavernous temple.

She frowned. Whoever it was, they should know better than to disturb a holy ritual in the temple's inner sanctum. Why hadn't the men of the city guard turned them away? Perhaps something urgent required Philippos's attention? But what could be so important?

The gruff murmurs became louder. Boot heels rang out on the stone. Sophia was puzzled, and then worried; whoever these men were, their speech was accented and unfamiliar.

Leaving the high priestess holding the incense, Philippos turned and peered through the latticed screen. The high priestess cleared her throat, lifting the incense pointedly for Isobel's father to take.

The shuffles and footsteps broke the stillness of the night, despite the fact that the men approaching were obviously trying to stay quiet. Someone coughed. Metal clanged against metal. Isobel climbed to her feet, and the high priestess turned also. Sophia exchanged frightened glances with Isobel.

Sophia began to discern silhouettes. Initially they were dark shadows, but then they became clearer. Pale-faced men in black cloaks were creeping steadily forward, surrounding the inner sanctum.

'Father?' Isobel said in a tight voice.

Sophia glanced at High Priestess Marina, but even she looked afraid. The strangers were encircling the area, blocking off every exit. Terror stabbed into Sophia's chest when she saw that the cloaked men were holding drawn swords.

'Who goes there?' Lord Philippos called out.

Panic struck Sophia like a nail through the heart. Where were the guards?

A short, solitary figure walked up to the screen. His back was bent and his shoulders were oddly high. Bushy, black hair crowned his scalp, and his eyes were dark and fierce. Glaring at the people on the other side, he lifted his leg and smashed his boot against the lattice.

The entire screen came crashing down with a resounding clatter of falling wood.

Isobel screamed.

⌣

Kyphos first checked that his men had blocked every exit before kicking down the screen. He swiftly scanned the people on the other side, instantly dismissing the circle of young acolytes, and the high priestess and her assistant. His gaze alighted on the king of Xanthos's blonde-haired bride, an attractive, slender woman in a crimson garment. She was clutching the well-dressed lord who was the only male present, and he knew she must be Isobel.

Kyphos nodded in satisfaction. It was just as the man Nilus had said he would arrange: there were no guards, and the area around the temple was deserted at this time of night.

He glanced at his men. Swords drawn, they hugged the shadows, waiting for his command. He once more appraised the priestess, her assistant, the young bride, and her father. Staring out at him, their eyes were wide with horror. The six acolytes looked anxious and confused. Isobel was trembling with fear as she clutched her father's arm, while the olive-skinned high priestess's chest heaved; she looked as if she knew what was coming. Her assistant, a dark-haired girl of twelve or thirteen, had a defiant expression, but her eyes were afraid.

The consul in the white tunic swallowed. He finally broke the silence. 'Who are you? What do you want?'

Kyphos's boots crunched down on the fallen lattice as he approached Isobel and her father. He brought a yelp out of the six acolytes when he glared at them.

'Go,' he grunted. 'Get out.'

Shrieking, the young girls all fled, and Kyphos called out to his men. 'Let them pass!'

Soon the acolytes were gone, and Kyphos continued to advance, staring at each of the four remaining people in turn. Two of his warriors joined him, swords held out in front of them. Lord Philippos whirled, turning to check every exit, but they were all blocked. His face was white when he touched his hip, realizing there was no sword by his side. 'Guards!' he cried. He shouted at the top of his lungs. 'Guards!'

There were just a few oil lamps burning, casting wan light on the area. Kyphos reached Isobel, bringing his face further into the light, while the two flanking swordsmen spread out at his sides.

The lord stepped in front of his daughter, protecting her. 'Who are you? What do you want?' His voice was shaking.

Kyphos remembered the bargain he'd made with the man Nilus. 'Philippos, I presume?'

'Yes.' Lord Philippos took a step forward, pressing his daughter even farther behind him. 'What do you want with m—?'

Kyphos turned and nodded at one of his companions, who stepped forward and without a word ran the lord through.

The point entered just below Philippos's sternum, the warrior grunting as he pushed the hilt with both hands, shoving the blade hard through the initial resistance until the weapon slid in more easily and finally emerged from the lord's back. Philippos's eyes shot wide open. His face twisted in agony as he gasped. He clutched at the blade, heedless of the razor-sharp edge.

'Father!' Isobel screamed.

The swordsman grunted again as he pulled on the hilt. Red blood poured from the wound in the blade's wake, staining the nobleman's white tunic. Philippos stared down at his chest and then staggered forward. He fell to one knee and coughed. Crimson liquid spattered from his lips and then he tilted, staring up at the ceiling. He fell backward, hands pressed around the wound in his chest.

Isobel gasped. She crumpled, falling to her knees before her father's corpse. There was sudden movement as the dark-haired girl, ignoring Kyphos and the two swordsmen, rushed to the nobleman's side. She pressed down on the gash in Philippos's chest, despite the fact that the man's unblinking eyes announced his departure from life. Realizing her efforts were futile, the novice stared up at Kyphos, her hands red with blood and her narrowed eyes accusing.

'Spill no more blood!' The high priestess spread her arms and spoke in a powerful voice. 'The goddess sees all!'

Kyphos hesitated. The girl glaring up at him from Philippos's side was young, an innocent. The high priestess was unimportant to his purpose. Nilus had said he needed to kill everyone; he'd insisted that Kyphos leave no witnesses. But Kyphos couldn't bring himself to kill two priestesses in their own temple.

'Then stay out of our way,' he snapped. He turned to his men, pointing at Isobel. 'Take her.'

'No! No!' Isobel cried, staring at her dead father as the two swordsmen hauled her to her feet.

Lunging forward, the high priestess grabbed one of the warriors and tried to hold him back. The warrior snarled and tossed her away, shoving her with terrible force. The woman's head struck the solid stone of the rear wall hard enough to leave a red mark before she slid to the floor.

The dark-haired girl cried out and launched herself at the other warrior. With a start Kyphos saw that she had a ewer in her hand, and, showing surprising strength, she lifted it high and shattered it against the back of the man's head. He roared in pain and responded instantly, smashing her across the face with the hilt of his sword.

Isobel broke away and ran for freedom, only to be met by one of Kyphos's men. The black-cloaked warrior wrapped his arms around her while she kicked and screamed.

Nearby, the injured swordsman stood over the fallen girl, his face red and chest heaving. He kicked her hard and then lifted his sword.

'That's enough,' Kyphos ordered. 'Leave her. We have what we came for.'

The swordsman glared at him, but Kyphos was undeterred as he met the man's stare. 'You heard me.' He nodded in the direction of the sea. 'It's time to go.'

The warrior nodded, but he kicked the girl once more in the head before they regrouped to take their struggling captive away.

Kyphos waved an arm and with a glare commanded his men to silence, but there was no quieting the writhing, moaning young woman and the soldiers' grunts as they hauled her down the steps leading from the temple to the agora. Fortunately the area was devoid of people, and he kept them moving with speed as they crossed the paved square and reached the sloped embankment that loomed over the shore.

He glanced back at the city, checking in all directions, motioning for his men to descend the diagonal stairway, before following them down. He was the last to leave the steps, his boots crunching on the pebbled stones of the beach. Small waves crashed on the shore. A stiff breeze whistled, covering the sound of Isobel's muffled cries.

Walking down to the sea, Kyphos peered into the darkness and finally saw a small sailing boat pulled up, half in and half out of the water. He gathered his group and led them to the slender figure standing by the vessel.

'You have her?' Zara asked.

'We do.'

'I'll take her from here. You know what to—'

'It was my plan,' Kyphos growled. 'Yes, sorceress. I know what happens next.'

Kyphos ordered his men to board the boat and get it moving. Soon it was drifting away, leaving him standing alone on the shore, watching as the sail caught the wind, until eventually it was gone from sight.

25

The rising sun filled the sky with pink and pale gold as the sleek galley approached the pebbled shore. Chloe was finally home.

She took in the sights of her homeland. She lifted her eyes to the high summit of the Temple of Aldus, remembering the battle to save Phalesia from the Ilean invasion, and then her gaze traveled down the steps carved into the cliff to see the white stones of the beach below the embankment. She'd walked with her father on that shore. Her homecoming was tinged with sadness.

The central agora was empty so early in the day, but she continued to scan right to the lyceum, library, and the temples of Aeris and Edra. The sight of the Temple of Aeris made her stomach clench with worry. The galley's bow had barely scraped against the pebbles before she'd jumped ashore, landing lightly on her feet.

She headed directly for the diagonal stairway leading up the sloped bastion and began to climb, taking the steps two at a time. Behind her, Amos grunted as he hurried to catch up. Cresting the stairway, she immediately headed for the Temple of Aeris, cutting a straight path through the agora.

She could feel her heart pounding. The sounds of the waking city were distant, barely heard. She swiftly climbed the wide marble steps and took the path that would lead her to the columned entrance to the temple. As the grand structure filled her vision, she stopped in her tracks.

Amos finally drew up beside her, panting. 'By the gods,' he said under his breath.

Dozens of armored soldiers wearing the blue cloaks of Phalesia surrounded the area. There were so many of them.

Far too many for a normal day.

The blood drained from Chloe's face. She turned to Amos. 'Sophia.'

She ran up the path to the temple, ignoring everything around her as she rushed into the entrance. Sweeping past consuls in white tunics and curious city folk being held back by the soldiers, she felt a hand grasp hold of her arm, but pulled herself free. Seeing that one of the latticed screens separating the inner sanctum was smashed, she hurried forward as two guards tried to stop her.

The Phalesian soldiers' mouths dropped open when they saw her face. Hearing Amos shout, they looked past her shoulder, eyes widening when they saw the man hurrying to keep up with her. Unimpeded, Chloe rushed into the inner sanctum.

She saw priests and priestesses, and blood in pools on the stone floor. Braziers, ewers, and a large basin had all been shoved to the side to clear the area.

She immediately saw her sister.

Sophia was on a bed pallet on her back, close to the center, lying motionless with her eyes closed. The girl's face was a mass of bruises; her left eye was mostly closed, and there was a terrible red mark on her temple. Nearby a priest of Aldus leaned over the sprawled-out corpse of a well-dressed man with dark hair, performing last rites. A priestess of Aeris was doing the same for the tall, olive-skinned high priestess, Marina.

For a moment Chloe was too stunned to move. Then with a gasp she rushed over and knelt at Sophia's side. Remembering her vision, she prayed for her sister's chest to move. Part of her was screaming that this wasn't happening.

It wasn't the same as her vision, for what she'd seen in the white fire must have been mere moments after whatever attack had taken place. She was here. This was happening. Sophia had been moved to a pallet. *Because she's dead, or because she's not in immediate danger? Please. Please, let her breathe.*

Chloe took her sister's small hand and squeezed it. She leaned over Sophia's mouth and listened for breath.

'Chloe,' Amos said.

She looked at him with horrified eyes and followed his gaze to see him looking at Sophia's chest. She bit her lip. At first Chloe doubted herself when she saw her sister's novice's robe stir. She stared intently, praying for it to be true. Then she saw her sister's breast rise and fall.

There was movement, she realized. Her sister was alive.

Tears streamed down her cheeks as she held Sophia's hand.

———

Sophia groaned as she opened her eyes. Through blurred vision she could see a high stone roof overhead, glossy and white, reflecting the daylight. She blinked and suddenly tasted bile at the back of her throat as her stomach churned. She rolled and heaved. Someone held a bowl as she emptied the contents of her stomach. Afterwards, a gentle hand wiped her mouth with a cloth.

She pushed the bowl away. Her ears were ringing. Her head throbbed with every beat of her heart. She gingerly put a hand to her head and moaned when a burst of agony struck like a stabbing dagger. But she was a healer, and she needed to know the extent of her injuries. Undeterred, she continued to press her face, feeling lower down and wincing at the bruises on her cheek. Her lip was swollen and painful to touch. Despite the fact that the Temple of Aeris was shadowed, the light was so strong that she was forced to close her eyes.

The ringing in her ears slowly died down and she was able to hear words, spoken in a soft, feminine voice. A familiar voice. She felt confused; she wondered if she was thinking clearly.

'Sophia . . .' The voice sounded wretched. 'Oh, Sophia.'

With a gasp, Sophia suddenly remembered. She again saw the sword plunging into Philippos's chest. Isobel's struggles as the men took her away . . . The high priestess slamming against the wall . . . The hunchback who gave the orders.

'Isobel,' Sophia gasped.

'The men who took her are long gone,' a grim male voice said. Recollection penetrated through the haze of pain.

'Amos?'

'I'm here,' Amos said. 'No one's going to hurt you again. Not while I'm here.'

'We're both here,' the female voice said. Experienced hands began to dab at Sophia's face with a moist cloth.

Sophia felt as if she couldn't breathe. 'Chloe,' she whispered. 'Chloe?' She started to cry. 'It can't be you.'

'I'm so sorry. I came as quickly as I could.' She could hear tears through her sister's voice.

'I don't understand. You're alive?' Sophia briefly wondered if she was dreaming, but the pain told her this was real. She'd been alone for so long, with no one to turn to.

'I'm here, Sophia. How do you feel? Try not to move too much. You've taken some injuries to the head. I've cleaned the wounds, and I think you'll be all right, but you need to rest. Do you remember what happened?'

Sophia tried to think. She gained the impression that there were several people standing around her besides Amos and Chloe, listening to her words. 'Men came to the temple. They killed Philippos and took

Isobel.' She sucked in a sharp breath. 'High Priestess Marina? Is she all right?'

'She's dead,' Amos said. 'I'm sorry, Sophia.' He leaned in closer. 'These men. Do you remember what they looked like?'

Sophia would never forget the hunchback's dark eyes. As she fitted the pieces together, connecting Eudora's story with the events of the previous night, she gasped. 'Nilus! He was behind it.'

She forced her good eye open and stared up at her sister, seeing Chloe's concerned face hovering over her. It was true. Chloe was alive and kneeling beside her. *It really is her.*

Chloe and Amos exchanged glances.

'Nilus? How do you know?' Chloe asked.

'I've had someone watching him. Eudora, one of his servants. A few days ago she saw a hunchback with Nilus, and then last night a hunchback came to the temple and killed Philippos and took Isobel.'

'Nilus killed Father,' Chloe said.

Sophia looked up into her sister's eyes. 'I . . . I suspected . . . but . . .'

'It was Nilus and three others. Nilus held the blade himself.' Chloe turned to someone. 'Have you sent word to King Dion?'

'Yes, a fast messenger.'

'Send two more. By sea and by road.' Chloe then turned to Amos. 'In the meantime, Amos, do you still have friends among the soldiers?'

He nodded. 'A few.'

'Sophia, what was the servant's name? The one who saw Nilus with the man who killed Philippos?'

'Eudora.'

'Where can I find her?' Chloe's eyes narrowed. 'It's time to deal with Nilus once and for all.'

26

The Assembly of Consuls was in session at the lyceum. The men sitting on the raised tiers surrounding the central floor were shouting, angry and red-faced. As first consul, and – after Lord Philippos's murder – the man now certain to be re-elected, Nilus was speaking, but struggling to be heard over the din.

'Not only is this sacrilege,' he thundered from the speaking floor, despite the fact that half the seated men around him weren't listening, 'but it is also an outrage, an assault on our very institutions and the people we most hold dear. It is sacrilege. Sacrilege! Any attack on a consul is an attack on our entire Assembly. And the capture of Lady Isobel, well, that – that! – is an affront to all of our sons and daughters.'

Lord Philippos's supporters, on the opposite side of the gallery from Nilus's faction, shook their fists and cried out. 'Sit down!' an elderly consul shouted. 'You were no friend to Philippos. Who will challenge you now, Nilus the Sly?'

Ignoring him, Nilus pressed on. 'We must do what we can to aid the king of Xanthos. It is obvious that whoever these men were, they came to kidnap Isobel and her father got in the way.'

As another roar of outrage greeted Nilus's words, Chloe moved quickly through the crowd, heading down the long series of steps that doubled as seats to reach the floor. Men turned in surprise when she pushed through, but then fell silent, stunned when they recognized her.

The din faded. The youngest men were surprised to see a woman in the lyceum, but the rest were shocked beyond belief. They remembered seeing Chloe in this very building defending the eldren. But Chloe, daughter of Aristocles, was supposed to be dead.

Reaching the floor, empty except for Nilus, she raised her voice as she approached the portly first consul. She came to a halt in the center of the lyceum. Her eyes narrowed, staring at him directly. Rather than apprehension or fear, she felt only anger.

'I agree with you, *Uncle* Nilus,' she called out. 'Philippos did get in the way. Like my father, Aristocles, he was an obstacle to your ambition.'

'Chloe?' Nilus's mouth dropped open. His face was pale; for a moment he was at a loss for words. 'What are you doing here?' Regaining his composure, he frowned. 'We are in session – no women allowed!'

His allies raised their voices. 'Get her out!'

But the faction of consuls loyal to the late Lord Philippos stood up and cried, 'Let her speak!'

Chloe raised her hand. As the lyceum fell silent, the consuls sat down again, many leaning forward to hear what she was going to say. Having seen her father practice his speeches a thousand times, Chloe knew to speak clearly, turning and sweeping her eyes over the rows of staring men, so that everyone present could hear her words. 'I think that this time, on this day, the Assembly can make an exception.'

Now the common citizens on the higher tiers were calling out to allow Chloe to speak. Aristocles had served as first consul since before most of them had come of age. The appearance of his daughter, a woman once wed to Nikolas of Xanthos and long supposed dead, was something they wouldn't allow Nilus to simply dismiss.

As the shouts became a growing clamor, a panicked Nilus looked up, past the rows of faces. 'Guards!' But no guards came forward, and he glanced around, spreading his hands. 'Lord Aristocles' daughter is alive,' he said weakly. 'I suggest an adjournment . . .'

'There will be no adjournments!' Chloe thundered, and instantly the entire lyceum went silent. 'Philippos was not the first man to get in your way, *First Consul.* You murdered my father, Aristocles, elected leader of Phalesia, and I am here to make sure that everybody knows.'

'Utter nonsense.' Nilus peered at the upper tiers again. 'Guards!'

In unison, a dozen men in hooded cloaks, scattered around the chamber, rose to their feet. They threw back their hoods and opened their cloaks to reveal grim faces and leather armor. Each soldier placed a hand on the sword at his side.

Chloe deliberately rested her eyes on Amos, standing three tiers above the floor. Following her gaze, the consuls and citizens all gasped audibly as they saw his craggy face, somber eyes, and the blue cloak of Phalesia on his shoulders. Murmurs filled the lyceum as they recognized the former captain of the city guard, connecting his disappearance with the time of Aristocles' death.

'Two soldiers witnessed Nilus and three others kill my father,' Chloe called in a voice loud enough to be heard by everyone present. 'All four murderers wielded a knife. All four have blood on their hands.' She whirled and pointed. 'I name the three other killers as Consul Harod, Consul Leon, and Consul Anneas.'

'Preposterous!' gray-bearded Consul Harod cried.

Consul Anneas folded his arms and shook his head. 'The ravings of a mad woman.'

'I refuse to hear another word of this.' Consul Leon began to rise from his seat but a cloaked and hooded man behind him gripped his shoulders, pressing Leon back down and shaking his head.

'Before Nilus had them both murdered, one of the witnesses told Amos.' Chloe nodded in Amos's direction. 'You all know Amos. He is the man who led our defense against the Ilean invasion, a man who was always loyal to my father, and to this city and its democratic foundations.'

Chloe's face turned grim.

'But with my father dead, murdered by men sitting here today, and no one to believe him, Amos was forced into exile, still grieving for his lord and friend, knowing that he had been killed in cold blood, stabbed in the chest by consuls of this Assembly.'

Voices clamored, but Chloe lifted her arms, and when she spoke again they were listening.

'And now,' she said, 'regarding Lord Philippos.' Instantly the lyceum was quiet. She pointed. 'Eudora? Can you please stand?'

Seated beside Amos, Nilus's auburn-haired servant hesitantly stood and peeled the hood away from her head. She looked terrified, huddling close to the former captain.

'Lord Nilus,' Chloe said. 'I'm sure you recognize one of your servants, as will many of the consuls she has served.'

Chloe met Nilus's eyes directly. His complexion had gone gray; he was gnawing his lips and twining his fingers together.

'Eudora saw a man come to you, a hunchback with a foreign accent. You ordered your house evacuated while you and this man spoke.'

'And what of it?' Nilus said. 'I have many visitors.'

'You admit seeing him.' Chloe nodded. She made sure her next words could be heard by all. 'My sister Sophia, who was aiding the high priestess, saw the same hunchback confirm Lord Philippos's identity before having him killed.' She scanned the room. 'You all know the motive. Only with Lord Philippos dead could Nilus win the election.'

This time the cacophony was deafening. The men of Lord Philippos's faction roared and surged forward. Chloe was suddenly surrounded by men in white tunics on all sides, almost knocking her off her feet in the sudden tide. Cries and shouts filled the chamber as fists started flying. The floor became a sea of roaring men, old and young, snarling and grabbing hold of each other, rolling and grappling on the ground while the few consuls who'd kept their heads vainly cried out for order.

Chloe whirled, looking for Nilus, but she was shoved to the side and lost her balance until one of Amos's soldiers helped her regain her feet. She pushed through when she saw Nilus's balding head and finally grabbed the back of the man's tunic in desperation, but when he turned she realized he wasn't Nilus after all. She looked for Amos, but he was busy trying to restore calm.

Finally he bellowed, 'Order!'

He teamed up with his men and they pulled consuls apart from each other, tossing them back toward their seats until he had claimed the speaking floor.

'Order, order! All of you, by Aldus! Take your seats!'

Accustomed to commanding men on the field, his shout was like the roar of the god of justice himself. Fully armored, he paced the center of the floor.

'Back in your places!'

As Amos gradually restored a semblance of normality there was a new outcry around the tall, gray-bearded figure of Consul Harod. He was still seated, looking surprised, a knife protruding from his ribs. His unseeing eyes didn't blink as crimson blood bloomed on his tunic.

Nearby, Consul Anneas, a savage mark on his temple, was being restrained by one of Amos's men, who stood behind him with a muscled arm around his neck. Consul Leon writhed in the grip of another soldier and pointed at Anneas. 'It was his idea!' he yelped.

'And Nilus? Where is Nilus?' Amos demanded.

'He's gone, sir,' one of the soldiers called back.

'Go to his home. Search the city,' Amos barked. 'Find him!'

Cloaked soldiers ran from the lyceum. With the floor now empty except for Amos and Chloe, she again raised her voice. 'Does anyone here doubt what I am saying? Nilus murdered my father to become first consul. He then had Lord Philippos killed to hold on to power.'

She ran her eyes over the assembled citizens and consuls, who were looking uncertain as they realized the leadership of Phalesia had been thrown into disarray.

'Now, in the meantime, this leaves us without a candidate for the election,' Chloe said. 'I suggest you nominate new candidates. And despite the fact that women cannot vote – a foolish rule if ever I've heard of one – I have a proposal. I suggest that for the next election, you nominate someone whose loyalty cannot be questioned. We have all had enough of conspiracies and betrayal. I suggest you consider a non-politician who understands the city's needs and also knows the workings of the Assembly.'

Every set of eyes was suddenly on Amos, who stood in the center of the lyceum, looking both stern and commanding in his armor. Many of the consuls had been allies of Aristocles, and now they began to nod and murmur to each other, much to the surprise of Amos, who looked utterly speechless.

'I'll leave you to it,' Chloe said.

———

Later, back at the temple, Chloe was pleased to see her sister sit up on the pallet and reach for the water jug herself. Sophia's arm was a little unsteady as she poured water into her cup, but Chloe knew not to help her.

'The thing I don't understand,' Chloe said with a frown, 'is why you were in Nikolas's camp in the first place.'

Sophia looked uncomfortable. 'I thought that I could help the wounded, and maybe I could do something to stop the fighting. But then he died, and the fighting stopped anyway, so I came home.' She changed the subject. 'What are you going to do about your studies at Athos?'

'I don't know.'

'You might be the next oracle.'

'I don't want to be an oracle.'

'But if the visions keep coming . . .'

'Maybe they won't. I haven't had another since I saw you.' Sitting beside the pallet, Chloe reached out and stroked her sister's hair.

'But it came true.'

There was silence for a time.

'I can't believe Nilus escaped,' Sophia said.

'We'll find him. But at the moment Dion needs me.' Chloe looked in the direction of the harbor. 'I'm going to have to leave you again for a time, but I promise I'll be back.'

'Where are you going?'

'To find a ship. We have no idea who this hunchback was, or where he was going. Dion won't even know what's happened. Time is running out.'

'You heard Amos,' Sophia said. 'They'll be long gone.'

Chloe glanced at her staff, resting against the wall nearby. 'There's still a chance to catch them.'

27

It was late at night and, as he often did, Dion stood outside his bed-chamber, on the tallest balcony of his palace, looking out at the distant horizon. A stiff breeze blew a chill wind against his face and snaking clouds passed across the moon, interspersing the ocean with moonlight and shadow. Down below, he could see one of the guards standing outside the palace walls; he waved, but the man didn't wave back.

Leaning forward on the rail, his thoughts turned once again to Chloe and then to the woman he would soon marry. Chloe was alive, and he felt like a black hole in his heart had been replaced with sunlight. But he was having a child with Isobel. In time, he would come to love her. And the idea of having a son or daughter brought him more pleasure than he'd ever thought it would.

Lost in thought, he heard a throat clear behind him.

Dion whirled. A brawny man with a strangely stooped posture stood on the balcony, just a few feet away, regarding him with a cold stare.

Seeing the hunched shoulders and thick black hair, the dark eyes and grim expression, Dion was shocked to recognize Kyphos from his visit to Malakai. Like Dion, he was unarmed, but though shorter, the hunchback was by far the bigger man.

Dion's eyes narrowed. 'How did you get in here?' He swiftly turned and leaned forward over the balcony rail. 'Guard!' he called out.

'He can't hear you,' Kyphos said.

The clouds crossed over the moon and in the sudden light Dion saw that the guard was leaning awkwardly against the wall, his dead body propped up by his spear. The sight sent a chill down Dion's spine. He spun again to face the man who'd accosted him in his private quarters.

'Don't worry,' Kyphos growled. 'If I wanted you dead, you would be.'

'What do you want?'

Kyphos reached into a pocket and took out something long and golden, a piece of jewelry. He spread it on his meaty palm for Dion to see, displaying the length of delicate chain and the beautifully crafted dolphin, rotating it.

'We have your young bride. She tells me she is with child. Your child.'

Dion's heart beat out of time. 'If you harm her . . .'

'Listen carefully, Dion of Xanthos. You belong to King Palemon now. You and I . . . We are going to travel together. You are going to change your shape . . . and you are going to carry me to Malakai.'

Dion clenched his fists. A stone was plummeting through his chest, sinking heavily into his stomach. Rage and fear swamped him in equal parts. But he knew he couldn't fight the hunchback. He had to think about Isobel. Lifting his chin, he took a step forward, looming over Kyphos and staring him down. He pointedly touched the silver necklace at his throat. 'I cannot control my changing.'

Kyphos smiled. 'I am sure you can.'

The warrior from the frozen north suddenly rushed toward Dion and grabbed him. Pinned against the rail, Dion struggled to hold back his opponent's powerful arms, but found himself off-balance. The two men wrestled, but despite his frame, Kyphos's strength was overwhelming. The hunchback freed an arm to rip the silver necklace from Dion's neck and threw it over the balcony. It was a long drop. Seconds passed before Dion heard the tinkle of metal striking the ground.

Kyphos's nostrils flared as Dion tried to fend him off. Finally the hunchback gained the upper hand.

His face grim, Kyphos shoved Dion hard.

Dion found himself teetering backward uncontrollably. It was a drop of three stories – far enough to kill him if he struck his head on the paving stones. For a moment he wasn't sure if he would fall, but then Kyphos pushed him again.

A heartbeat later he was in the air. His limbs flailed as his body turned over and over. He could sense the ground coming up to smash his body and, without meaning to, he felt his body . . . changing.

His scream became a piercing animal cry. His body thickened and elongated, mist enveloping him from head to toe. He realized what had happened only when he swept his wings down at the ground in time to arrest his fall. Two more sweeps of his wings lifted what was now a black-scaled dragon high. He flew up until he was eye to eye with the hunchback on the balcony.

He parted his jaws and roared in Kyphos's face. But his enemy was undeterred.

Kyphos pointed out to sea. 'To Malakai. Understand? Or we'll cut your pretty bride's throat.'

Dion roared again, a cry of pure rage and frustration, the sound shattering the stillness of the night. The barking of dogs and shouts of alarm filled the air, waking the citizens of Xanthos from their slumber.

Kyphos met Dion's pale, almond-eyed stare and pointed again, out to sea.

The dragon snorted and lowered its head, and Kyphos climbed onto its back.

28

The lean galley pounded the waves. The sail pocketed the wind, sending the vessel leaping forward like a racehorse whipped at the gate. It was the same fast Xanthian ship that had carried Chloe to Phalesia, and she now stood in the very center of the vessel, legs apart, riding the motion of the sea.

Chloe's jaw was clenched tightly as she clutched the staff in her hand. The silver cone glowed fiercely, summoning strange forces. She was channeling the wind, gathering it and throwing it at the sail, using it to make the ship ride the sea so fast that the hull was skimming over the waves, leaping from one set to the next.

She drew on the inferno within her, feeding the flame, calling forth the silver fire and then releasing it through her body time and time again. Meanwhile, as the captain called them to greater efforts, the oarsmen were pulling at the sea, oars churning the water into foam, wide eyes on the woman in their midst.

'Remember, lads!' called the captain, a veteran sailor with a round, bright-red face. 'These raiders have captured a lady of Phalesia, the future wife of our king! Pull hard and you'll all be rewarded!' He crossed the deck to speak to the complement of twelve Phalesian hoplites, sourced at the last minute from Amos. 'Men, keep your spears and swords close. If we catch 'em, we can't allow harm to come to the lady. Our faith is in you.'

Chloe felt the encroaching grip of fatigue, but she used her anger and determination to keep going. The people they were trying to catch had killed Isobel's father in cold blood, as well as High Priestess Marina. They'd beaten Sophia, and almost killed her too. They now had the mother of Dion's unborn child, and the gods only knew what they intended to do with her. She forced herself to remember Dion's excitement about becoming a father. After experiencing terrible darkness in his life, he had a chance to become truly happy. Whoever these people were, they couldn't take that away from him.

She'd been sailing for two days now, and after her experiences at Athos, Chloe had become skilled at controlling the wind. The magi would be proud of her – if they ever forgave her for leaving. The glossy twist on her wind staff was showing only the slightest discoloration, and the color of the flame inside her was purest silver, with no taint to it at all. They'd long ago left Phalesia and then the island of Orius in their wake.

'Sail ho!' a youth standing at the bow called out.

The disciplined oarsmen continued to row, but everyone now tensed and looked to the captain. Some of the soldiers stood, unsteady on their feet as they shielded their eyes from the glare of the sun.

'What ship?'

'A small vessel,' the lookout replied. 'Single sail. We're gaining on them!'

Chloe called on more of the fire raging inside, feeling it surge, channeled into her hand and released through the staff. The mast creaked as the vessel picked up still more speed. She glanced behind her to see the helmsman change their course, and now when she peered ahead, along with the crew she saw a triangular sail. Soon she could make out figures on the deck.

They were warriors, pale-skinned men in strange garments, staring back at the approaching vessel. And seated in the middle of the mid-sized sailing boat was a blonde-haired woman wearing a crimson chiton.

A soldier sat on either side of her, and her eyes were wide with terror. Isobel!

The sleek galley was rapidly gaining on its quarry, but the sailing boat's speed was surprising. It changed course, and Chloe frowned as the movement of the sail revealed another woman, standing in the middle of the vessel. Chloe could only see her back, but she was raven-haired and slender, and wore a supple, figure-hugging garment the color of the deep blue sea.

Like Chloe, she was clutching a staff . . . A staff with a metal twist of silver on its top.

Chloe remembered what the magus at Athos had told her about Nisos and the magic he'd brought to Aleuthea.

The people who had taken Isobel used magic.

The distance between the two vessels closed to a hundred paces. The woman slowly turned, facing Chloe. Her cold eyes narrowed. The sorceress was beautiful, with high cheekbones and straight hair as dark as deepest night. But her face was like stone; there was no compassion in it at all.

The conical spiral on top of the woman's staff suddenly glowed fiercely and the sorceress's lips moved.

It happened in an instant. A wave rose up, growing larger and larger with every passing moment. Forming between the two vessels, charging like a raging beast directly toward the pursuing galley, it sucked up the ocean around it as the sorceress's magical wind gathered force. The wave grew to the height of the galley's mast, so immense that the oarsmen turned in their benches and cried out with fear.

Chloe had thought her abilities had been tested on the journey. She now realized that her true test was at hand.

Pushing past the transfixed crew, she raced to the front of the boat. Facing the looming wall of water, she lifted her staff high and cried out, drawing on more of the silver fire than she ever had before. She concentrated on the knowledge that in the open sea there was nothing to stop the wind for leagues; it was all around her, ready to be gathered and unleashed. Her skin prickled and her vision blurred as she unleashed the greatest force she'd ever controlled.

A second, challenging wave now formed in front of the Xanthian galley and grew in an instant, becoming so big that it matched the wave heading for the ship.

The two waves sped directly toward each other. If the sorceress's was victorious, the galley was doomed.

The great walls of water collided, just fifty paces ahead, and spray filled the sky, shooting in all directions. Chaotic wind ripped the spray apart, tossing it in strange spirals and directions the laws of nature would never allow. The sea became a churned-up mess of peaks and troughs. Unable to change its path, the galley sped straight into the raging water, the crewmen crying out in fear as the bow lifted nearly to the vertical before slamming into a deep valley and almost tipping over. Chloe fell to the boat's deck, gripping the gunwales on either side as water crashed over her head, soaking her through. She coughed, tasting salt, then wiped the stinging liquid from her eyes.

But the two waves were gone, and the galley's tumultuous movement finally began to subside.

'Onward!' the captain roared.

Chloe climbed back to her feet. Legs apart, staff in hand, she drew in a deep breath. Eye to eye with the cold stare of the sorceress, she summoned yet another wave, while her opponent simultaneously called forth her own.

The cone-shaped silver device at the top of Chloe's staff glowed before subsiding. At almost the exact same instant, the matching device on the sorceress's staff lit up brighter than the most luminous moon, almost blinding.

Drawing up the water around it, pushed forward by a powerful gust, Chloe's wave grew to the height of the last.

The sorceress's blue-tinged lips curved in a smile.

The gathering wind released from the woman's staff was so thick it was visible as streams of pale air. In an instant an opposing wave grew, a wall of water that became taller and taller, rising to a height bigger than Chloe had ever thought possible, nearly twice the height of the galley's mast. Chloe's own wave approached, but it was only half the size, and she held her breath as the two waves met head on.

The approaching wave rolled over Chloe's without pausing.

'Hold on!' the captain screamed.

The mountainous wave began to break, towering overhead before smashing down onto the galley. Suddenly air was replaced with water. Wood shattered as splinters went in all directions. Chloe's vision became filled with white foam as she felt herself plunging deep under the sea, limbs scrabbling and trying to pull her back to the surface while she was tossed back and forth in the currents. From underwater her vision cleared for an instant and she could see planks and swimming men everywhere. But downward force continued to push everything down, deeper and deeper.

Her chest heaved, lungs clawing at her throat and begging her to open her mouth. Pulling at the water with both arms, kicking furiously with her legs, finally she managed to make headway toward the surface. A plank swirled past her head, missing her skull by inches, and she dodged another as she fought the pain in her screaming chest.

Finally she burst free to the surface before another wave hit her, crashing down onto her head, knocking her under again. Gulping salt water, she coughed and tried to push her way to the top once more. For a long time she could only concentrate on keeping her head up and trying to eject liquid from her lungs, even as the surging sea swept her away.

Still clutching her staff, finally she was able to get her bearings as the peaks and troughs continued to toss her around. She could see crewmen in the distance and tried to swim toward them, but then yet another wave swept her away. She paddled over to one of the planks that were now the last remnants of the proud galley and pulled herself onto it. Holding on to the plank, resting her staff across it, she rode out the next, smaller wave.

When the sea finally calmed, she realized she was alone. The ship carrying Isobel to some unknown destination was a speck in the distance. There wasn't a crewman from her own galley to be seen. She called out, but no voice returned her calls.

The ocean was wide and featureless in all directions. She didn't even know where she was, or where the currents would take her.

She knew then that she would be lucky if she survived. When thirst and starvation sapped her strength, and she could no longer hold on to the floating plank, she would die.

29

Back in his normal form, Dion woke to a swift boot kicking him in the side. He rolled over and glared up at the man standing over him.

'Get up,' Kyphos grunted. 'We need to keep moving.'

With a scowl, Dion roused himself, and as the fog of sleep gave way to remembrance, despair sank into his gut. He was at a rough campsite on the top of a mile-high cliff. A sheer precipice nearby plummeted down to the Chasm. Across the void, the opposite cliff appeared hazy in the morning light. Birds wheeled in the sky, while far below, water rushed through the narrow gap, mingling the waters of the Maltherean and Aleuthean seas.

'Here,' Kyphos said in his gruff voice, tossing him a pouch. Dion glanced warily at his strangely muscular, stooped captor, before opening the pouch to see that it was filled with trail mix. 'Eat.'

Dion ate slowly as he watched the hunchback, who paced and stretched before turning and walking to the cliff edge to gaze down into the Chasm. With his enemy's back turned, Dion could easily rush forward to push him over the edge and kill him.

But he couldn't. Isobel needed him. His future child needed him. He had to find her.

'Finished?' Kyphos turned away from the precipice. 'We need to get moving if we want to reach Malakai today.'

Dion climbed to his feet. 'Where is Isobel? What is it you want me for so badly?'

'All will become clear, half-breed.' Kyphos looked up at the sun. 'Come, it's time to go.'

───╲╱───

The walled city with its tall tower approached at speed as Dion swept his black wings up and down. He'd been changed for hours and used his rage and sheer determination to fight the encroaching wildness. He was desperate to know that Isobel was safe and unharmed. If he forgot who he was, he wouldn't be able to help her.

Leaning forward, clutching the knobs behind Dion's neck and gripping his flanks with his knees, Kyphos bellowed a command. 'Down!'

Dion banked on the tip of a wing, turning sharply, making the hunchback cry out in alarm. He wheeled, swiftly losing height as he continued to turn in a wide circle. Down below he saw the yellow shore, the wooden pier, and fishing boats pulled up on the beach.

'In front of the city!' Kyphos barked. 'Near the harbor gates!'

Dion felt the sudden desire to roll over until he shook this irritating man-thing off his back, before flying away to hunt. He blinked his huge eyes, trying to focus his attention on the shore. Putting on more speed, he now plummeted toward the city, knowing he couldn't stay in this form much longer. He heard the rider on his back shout out with fear when he came to a sudden halt, beating his wings just a dozen feet above the ground.

Finally he landed in front of the city walls. His wings swept one last time as his four limbs touched down on the rocky ground. He shuddered at the weight of Kyphos on his back, anxious to return to his normal form. The fearful hunchback slid off and moved away.

Dion growled as he focused his attention. He had to concentrate to remind himself that he was a man, who walked on two legs and talked. With a sense of overwhelming relief, he felt the familiar sensation of changing as a mist rose and clouded him from head to tail.

The vapor shimmered and dispersed. Dion was revealed as he'd been when Kyphos came to him in his palace: a sandy-haired, athletic Galean man with pale brown eyes, wearing a thick white tunic. Hunched on the ground, he slowly climbed to his feet and looked around to get his bearings.

The tall walls of Malakai loomed over him. In front of the harbor gates, near the statue, a dozen soldiers stood in formation. Waiting at the front of the group, tugging on the braids of his beard, Palemon had his legs apart and his fingers hooked into the belt of his dark trousers.

'Follow me, king of Xanthos,' Kyphos growled.

Knowing he had little choice, Dion fell in beside the hunchback. As they approached, Palemon tossed something, a heavy metal hoop, to Kyphos, who caught it out of the air.

'Stop,' Kyphos instructed. 'Stand still.'

Kyphos held up an iron collar. Dion paled, unable to tear his eyes off it, seeing that it could be fastened by spearing an arrow-shaped rod through a hoop. He also saw that the connection worked in only one direction. The collar had a series of notches, enabling it to be fastened tighter, but never looser.

'I'm not putting that on.'

'But you must,' Kyphos said.

Dion shook his head, dread creeping up through his chest. 'There's no way to get it off.'

'A magus can do it,' Kyphos said. 'But at any rate, this isn't a discussion. We have your woman.' He paused to let his words sink in. 'Now crouch. Good. Don't move.'

Dion swallowed as Kyphos fixed the iron collar around his neck, fitting the arrow through the hoop and tightening it along the notches.

Feeling his throat become more and more constricted, he tried to keep his breathing slow and steady. The collar gave a final click and the hunchback nodded to himself. Dion reached up a hand to touch the metal now circling his throat. It was tight and made his skin crawl.

'There,' Kyphos said. 'Now come.'

Kyphos jerked his chin in the direction of the waiting soldiers and their king, and Dion had no choice but to follow him. The hunchback led him directly toward the dark-eyed ruler of Malakai.

'Kyphos,' Palemon said, reaching out to clasp the shorter man's shoulder. 'You have done well, my friend.' He then turned. 'And King Dion of Xanthos. This time we meet without pretense.'

'I want to see Isobel,' Dion said.

'His young bride,' Kyphos explained. 'She is also carrying his child. Zara is bringing her by ship.'

'Leverage indeed.' Palemon nodded. Taller than Dion, he towered over him. 'You will see your woman soon enough. For now, there is something I want you to do for me.' The imposing king's glare was unrelenting as he pointed at the ground. 'When we last met, I noticed that you didn't bow. Now, I want you to kneel.'

Dion lifted his chin, meeting Palemon's eyes, stare for stare. 'If that is why you brought me here, I will kneel when I see her safe and well. I will then return to my kingdom and gather my armies and those of my allies, before we grind you into the dust.'

Palemon glanced at one of his captains. Two soldiers left the group, circling around behind Dion, who continued to scowl at the taller man. Suddenly Dion felt crushing pain in the back of first one knee and then the other as they smashed his legs until he fell to the ground.

'That is better,' Palemon said. 'My blood is nobler than yours, half-breed. Never forget that.'

Sprawled on the ground, Dion gave no sign of pain as he tried to lift himself up, but then he felt a soldier's boot heel on his back, keeping him pressed on his stomach. Lifting his head, he saw a man in a gray robe come forward, carrying a staff with an iron claw on the top. Half of his face was melted, like wax held to a fire.

'Magus Tarik,' Palemon said. 'It appears we must await Zara's arrival before we can be sure of his cooperation. Put our captive in one of the cells below the Sky Tower. Post a guard on him at all times.'

The magus bowed. 'I will see it done, sire,' he said in a rasping, flinty voice.

'Welcome, King of Xanthos,' Palemon said. 'Welcome to Malakai.'

30

Dion paced his strange cell as all manner of thoughts rushed through his head. He thought about Isobel and wondered where she was, and if she was safe and unharmed. And back in Xanthos . . . his disappearance must have been noticed. What was his uncle doing? What could he do? Would he and Isobel ever leave Malakai alive?

Above all, what did Palemon want with him? He had gone to great lengths to capture Isobel. He clearly wanted Dion's cooperation with something. But what were they going to force him to do?

He had been alone now for a long time, and had been given hard bread and water, enough to last several days. The cage was big, large enough to house a crowd of prisoners, and aside from the iron collar around his neck he was free to roam. The iron bars on three sides – the gate and the shared walls between cells – were as thick as his wrists. The rear wall was solid stone.

When the sorcerer, Tarik, brought him here he'd seen that there were perhaps a dozen cells, arrayed in a long line, all empty. He was underground, beneath the immense tower, and could shout as loud as he wanted without any hope of being heard. There were two guards outside the main entrance at street level, armored soldiers with swords and large, powerful crossbows.

Until he had more information, he couldn't even begin to prepare an escape plan. He needed to know that Isobel was alive and well, and where she was being held prisoner. If he could remove his collar, nothing would then stop him from freeing her and escaping. But for now, he had to bide his time.

Gripping the bars on the gate and peering out into the darkness, lit only by the wan glow of an oil lamp, he frowned as he examined the far wall. There was writing on it, carved in haste, for the lettering was far from even. The symbols reminded him of the writing he'd seen decorating the exterior of the Ark of Revelation, but it was an utterly unfamiliar language and meant nothing to him at all.

His gaze continued to rove along the wall, until it stopped on something else inexplicable. There were several pegs in the wall, from which hung what appeared to be lengths of shining copper chain, each coiled up like a whip or a harness. In this place, where there was little to look at but bare walls and iron bars, the chains sent a shiver down his spine.

Unable to sit or stand still, he resumed pacing his cell as his worried thoughts turned to one topic after another. This place felt old and alien. He wondered if it was built by the ancient Aleutheans.

Hearing voices, he looked up.

Palemon entered with a woman at his side. Dion remembered Zara, the sorceress who had allowed him to go free. She carried a staff with a glowing circle of gold on the top, filling the shadowed chamber with light. The disfigured magus, Tarik, followed behind them. And then, supported between them, two soldiers dragged a slumped, bound woman.

Dion rushed forward, gripping the bars. 'Isobel!'

She lifted her head, looking harrowed. Her crimson chiton was torn and travel-stained, her blonde hair in disarray. The sight of her made him want to scream, or roar with rage. Kyphos hadn't been lying. If Dion didn't do what they asked, they would kill her.

'Dion, what's happening?' Isobel said hoarsely. 'Why are they doing this?'

'Isobel, listen to me. I'm going to get you out of here. I'll find a way. How is . . .' He recalled that Kyphos knew. 'How is the child?'

Isobel started to cry. Dion grabbed at the collar around his neck, pulling it hard, making the iron cut into the skin of his throat, wanting nothing more than to rip it off and change his shape.

'They killed Father.' She spoke in between sobs. 'Please, Dion . . . I don't want to die.'

Dion drew in a sharp breath. He glared at Palemon. 'Be strong, Isobel. I promise you I'll do everything in my power to get you home—'

'Enough.' Palemon cut the air with his hand. Approaching the bars, he scowled at Dion. 'As you can see, your young bride is alive. Do as we say and she won't be harmed. Zara, perhaps a demonstration.'

Standing beside Palemon, Zara turned and nodded at the scar-faced magus. Lifting his staff, Tarik touched the iron claw to the bare skin of Isobel's arm, before glancing at Dion to make sure he was watching.

'No—!' Dion gripped the bars.

Tarik's eyes narrowed and the iron claw flared up brightly. The metal glowed like a red-hot poker, and Isobel screamed, writhing in the grip of the soldiers as she tried to pull away. Her skin sizzled and the smell of burning flesh wrenched at Dion's guts, making him feel sick. Wisps of smoke rose where the iron made contact with her arm.

'Stop!' Dion shouted. 'Stop it!'

'That will do,' Palemon said.

Tarik lifted the iron claw away from Isobel's arm, revealing a hand-sized, blistered patch of skin. Isobel continued sobbing; if she hadn't been supported by her guards, she would have collapsed.

Palemon nodded at the soldiers. 'Take her away.'

Dion called out to her, but she didn't respond to any of his cries. Then she was gone.

'Where are you taking her?' he demanded.

'We will keep her safe and we won't harm her further,' Palemon said. 'Provided you do as we ask.'

Looking through the bars at the tall king from across the sea, Dion knew that it was coming now. They were going to tell him why they'd gone to such lengths to capture Isobel and bend him to their will. What would it be? Would they ask him to betray his people, his friends?

'What do you want?' Dion asked through gritted teeth.

Palemon tugged on the braids of his beard. 'Most of all, as you know, we want ships.'

Dion met Palemon's dark eyes. 'You must know that no matter what you do to us, Xanthos would never give up its fleet. Whatever your plans are, they won't succeed.'

'I thought as much,' Palemon said, nodding. 'But as for our plans, you don't even know the half of it. Sorceress?'

'We first need to test the most basic element of our theory,' Zara mused. 'We need to know that he won't turn wild.' She considered for a time and then looked directly at Dion. 'We need you to change into dragon form.'

Dion blinked, confused. A moment later Tarik threw the bolt and hauled the gate open before entering the cage. Dion looked warily at the magus, knowing he had to be as strong as he'd asked Isobel to be.

Tarik put his fingers on the clasp holding the collar shut and Dion felt a flash of heat on his neck before the collar slid open. The magus then took the collar with him and left the cell, closing the gate once again.

'Well?' Palemon's eyes narrowed. 'You heard the sorceress. Change.'

Dion realized he had no choice. 'For how long?'

'Until we say.' The sorceress stepped forward, the light from her staff shining on her pale face. 'If you cannot change, you are of no use to us.'

It was difficult, but Dion drew on his wild emotions of frustration, fear, and rage, to bring on the animal side within. He imagined himself as a winged creature and then came the familiar sensation of shifting.

Mist filled the cell, thickening until it coated him like a blanket of cloud, elongating and changing shape. The mist flickered like the shimmer of heat rising from the earth on a hot day, and suddenly dispersed.

Then he knew it was done.

Now a black-scaled dragon, Dion raised his angular, wedge-shaped head. He folded his wings, shook his long body, and snarled.

For a moment, all three onlookers drew back, putting distance between themselves and the bars. Then they exchanged glances and approached once more.

'Why black?' Palemon asked. 'I thought they were silver.'

'He is a half-breed,' Zara said.

Tarik smiled as he appraised Dion, the expression making his melted face look sinister. 'His mixed blood certainly hasn't affected his size.'

Hefting the collar, the gray-robed magus opened the gate once more and entered. He approached, even as Dion growled, filling the near-silence with a low, rasping rumble. A shiver of pain shook Dion from nose to tail as he felt the magus clamp the iron collar around his neck. Fastening the arrow through the hoop, Tarik tightened it to one of the first notches.

'Now what?' Palemon asked as Tarik left the cell and closed the gate behind him. 'How long must we wait?'

'One day,' Zara replied. 'If he becomes wild, it will happen within a day. We'll return tomorrow.'

For the first time, Dion realized that the feelings of encroaching wildness were gone. But with the collar around his neck, he couldn't change his shape.

He was trapped in the form of a dragon.

31

Palemon could barely contain himself as he walked down the stone-walled corridor. He'd slept little the previous night, too filled with anticipation, and now he glanced at Zara as she struggled to keep up with his long strides.

'Sire, slow down,' Zara said. 'We don't know what we're going to find.'

But he ignored her, passing the door that had once sealed the underground chamber from the world and approaching the long row of cages. Coming to a halt outside the barred gate of the third in the line, he peered in. The oil lamp had run out of fuel, and it was so dark he could barely see the shadowy outline of the beast within. He was forced to wait for Zara to arrive before the cage's occupant became clear.

Finally the sorceress approached and her staff lit up the area. Palemon saw that the black dragon inside the cell was looking out at him with a steadfast expression. A low growl came from deep within its broad chest as the thin, sweeping wings folded in to its back and then spread out again. The black scales and sharp teeth made it seem like a thing out of a nightmare.

For the first time, he truly appreciated how invincible a warrior on dragon back would be in battle. Riding his powerful steed, he could command the sky, and strike an opposing force from above, or even circle behind. The tough hide was strong enough to stop all but the luckiest arrow. The claws on the dragon's forelimbs could rip a man's head from his shoulders or tear a full-grown horse into pieces.

Palemon tried to remind himself that he was not looking at a dragon but at a man in dragon form. He finally gave up. He was looking at a weapon, a weapon that would soon be his to control.

'Well?' Palemon asked. 'Is it wild? How will we know?'

Zara walked up to the bars and spoke softly. 'We are going to gouge out Isobel's eyes before shoving a spear into her belly.'

The dragon rushed the gate, snarling and roaring as it slammed into the bars, making the slender sorceress drop her staff and jump back. Crouching to pick it up, she smiled as she turned.

'He is still in there. This is good, sire. Very good. We now know that when collared, they cannot shift from one shape to another. We also know that when collared, they don't become wild. It is time.'

Zara walked to the wall, near the Aleuthean script, and lifted the closest of the copper chains. She hoisted it high, examining every link, checking the strange symbols at the connecting points. Nodding in satisfaction, she then returned to the gate.

'Remember what we can do to your woman and the child she carries,' she said to the creature inside the cage.

Without asking for help, she threw the bolt and hauled the gate open. Palemon admired her bravery as she stepped forward, narrowing the space between her and the dragon until she was five paces away, then three. Soon she was within range of its claws and then beside its head. Zara reached out and stroked the dragon's face.

'Never forget,' she said to the black dragon, her voice so low that Palemon could only just hear her. 'Never forget what we can do.'

The dragon remained subdued as she demonstrated her power over the creature, but it wasn't true dominance, and the hatred was clear in the dragon's huge, almond-shaped eyes, narrowed with anger, and in the rumbling breath stirring at the back of its throat.

Zara now lifted the copper chain and followed the contours of the black dragon's face, reaching past the protuberances at the back of its head, and feeling behind the skull to reach for the collar.

Palemon decided to enter the cell, eager to witness what would happen next. 'How do you know what to do?'

'It appears to be simple enough.' Zara demonstrated was she was doing, despite the creature's jaws being close enough to bite through her slender waist in a single snap. 'See?' She held up the midpoint of the length of chain. 'This hooks onto the collar. We are left with two chains fastened to the connection point, like reins.'

'Let me,' Palemon said.

The dragon whimpered as he stepped forward, taking the chain from her hands. As Zara had said, there were actually two sections of metal links, both joined to a connecting hoop in the middle. The central clasp was engraved with tiny symbols. The device was surprisingly light.

With anticipation, Palemon leaned over the dragon's head, his height enabling him to reach forward to take the collar. He levered open the connecting hoop and in one swift movement fastened the chains to the collar.

He gasped.

'What is it? Sire?' Zara gripped his arm, concerned.

Palemon waved her away. A pulsing rhythm connected the chain in his hand to the thoughts of the creature it was shackled to. The experience was visceral, understood in the same way that sound doesn't need to be explained to a child. With the reins in his hand, he had a magical bond with the black dragon. He could feel what it felt: he knew that it was thirsty, and afraid, and ashamed at its own loss of autonomy. Palemon knew, without a doubt, that it was now bound to his will.

He smiled.

'Move,' he said to the sorceress. 'Step back. Open the gate – wide.'

Zara exited the cell and opened the gate as far as possible, anxious but also curious.

'Down,' Palemon said to the dragon.

A thrill coursed through him as the dragon dipped, bending a foreleg. Placing a foot on the limb, Palemon grunted as he shifted his weight to grab hold of one of the ridges behind the creature's head. He pulled his body up and then settled himself astride its mighty back, feeling the power of the creature under him.

'Forward,' Palemon commanded.

He held the reins tightly, one in each hand, as the dragon lumbered through the open gate until it had left the cell. He then turned it to face the wide passage.

'Sire . . .' Zara said. 'Perhaps—'

'Forward!' Palemon roared.

Feeling his desires instantly communicated through the magical chain, the dragon began to bound, racing ahead down the corridor, all four limbs carrying it along as fast as a galloping horse.

Abandoning the wide-eyed sorceress, Palemon and his black steed left the cells in a heartbeat and climbed the sloped passage. On his command the creature turned to enter the paved floor of the tower's central shaft and then the wings spread wide, easily accommodated in the shaft's wide diameter. Each beat of its wings propelled Palemon higher and higher as he climbed to the summit, until he shot out of the tower and the dragon took wing on the open sky.

⌣

The ground below passed by in a blur as the powerful black dragon sped forward, climbing higher and higher, until the creature and its rider were soaring above the clouds. Gazing down, Palemon saw the city shrink until it became the size of a dinner plate. He swiftly left behind the walled settlement of stone nestled against the shore of the deep blue sea, the connection point between the lands of the southern desert and the world.

'Faster!' Palemon commanded. The wings beat down furiously and the wind now whistled past the king's face so quickly that his eyes watered and he could hear nothing besides the roar of air shrieking in his ears. With a start he wondered how the dragon could hear him and then he made a sudden realization.

Higher. He projected the command mentally rather than speaking it aloud. The copper reins quivered in his hands and the dragon climbed, obeying his will. In turn he could feel something of the dragon's thoughts. He could sense frustration and weariness, and profound violation, but Palemon didn't care; his steed was his to command.

The afternoon sun was setting in the west and he put it at his back, leaving Malakai far behind as he sped through the sky, heading east until he saw an immense lake in the distance on his right. Remembering the maps he'd seen, he knew that this was Lake Tara, an important freshwater lake, fed by a snaking waterway of rapids and waterfalls from the deep interior of the southern continent. He was flying so fast that soon Lake Tara was behind him, rather than ahead.

Teeth gritted, so high up that to fall would mean death in the smallest part of an instant, Palemon nonetheless felt soaring exhilaration as he continued onward. He cared nothing for the growing fatigue of the creature beneath him; when he returned he would feed it and let it rest. For now, he planned to revel in his newfound power and freedom.

The terrain below was far greener than Imakale, and he knew he was in Shadria, a dominion of the Ilean Empire and a region that had revolted in the past, but was now firmly in the grip of King Kargan in Lamara. Continuing onward, he then saw a long coastline, perpendicular to the path of his flight. The stretch of water he was looking at was the Shadrian Passage, the wide waterway that separated Shadria from Ilea and divided the Salesian continent neatly in two.

He ordered the dragon to fly lower as something caught his eye.

The city of Verai, capital of Shadria, was larger and far more sprawling than Malakai. It grew from a hazy collection of manmade structures to a thriving metropolis of ziggurats and temples, with perfectly formed canals surrounded by markets and houses, and palm groves seeming to fill every vacant space. Palemon saw a great curved harbor opening up onto the Shadrian Passage, and then he noticed something that made him frown. He ordered the dragon to fly toward it.

He was now low enough that there was little chance his winged steed would be mistaken for a bird, but his thoughts were far from the reaction in Verai as a dragon swooped overhead. He'd seen something worth investigating. Circling over the bustling city, slowly descending, he peered down as the slanted rays of the setting sun cast a reddish glow on the land below and the shoreline of the harbor came sharply into view.

Palemon scanned the long beach, where dozens upon dozens of landing barges rested side by side. Workers and crews scurried about, apparently preparing the vessels for departure. His intuition told him that only something momentous would cause so many landing craft to make preparations at once.

A worker dropped the barrel he was carrying and pointed up. Soon everyone was staring up at the dragon, transfixed at the sight of this magnificent black-winged creature soaring just a few hundred feet above.

Back up! Palemon ordered. *Take me across the passage.*

He felt pressure push him down into his seat as the dragon's wings pounded the air, climbing the sky until it was flying just below the pillow-like clouds. Leaving Verai behind, Palemon watched the ripples of ocean waves speeding past. It took time to cross the water, and he could sense the dragon flagging, its thoughts becoming filled with despair and exhaustion, but he ordered it on regardless.

A new stretch of barren coastline took form: the land of Ilea. Palemon was approaching the far side of the Shadrian Passage. Hugging the shore was a dark mass, like a congregation of ants.

Take me closer.

Palemon kept his distance as he soared overhead, but he knew without a doubt that he was looking at an army. Ilean orange-and-yellow banners snapped in the breeze; the colors were everywhere, and the army encampment was immense. Lean galleys bobbed on the waves, ready to carry the commanders' orders to Verai. Several men paced the rocky shoreline, making plans and gazing to the west expectantly. The landing barges would come any day.

And Palemon knew what the Ilean king, Kargan, wanted. He wanted to regain the city that Palemon had claimed as his own.

That's enough, Palemon commanded. *Back to Malakai.*

32

Chloe struggled to hold onto the plank, wondering how much time had passed, wondering when her strength would give out.

Tossed in the relentless motion of the open sea, she kept her head down so that her dark hair could ward off the worst of the sun's rays. She wanted to lick her lips, but her tongue was so swollen that it filled her mouth like a lump of dry wood. A throbbing headache pounded at her temples. She felt both nauseated and starved.

She was drifting, and to try to kick in one direction or another would serve no purpose other than to exhaust her. Now and then she lifted her head and scanned the horizon, but it was never anything but empty. The ocean was vast, and there was next to no chance that a passing ship would pick her up. She was beginning to believe that this was it; this was how her life was going to end.

She thought about the life she'd led, once filled with so much love and hope. Her greatest regret was clear. Liana was right: the moment her father had suggested marriage to Nikolas, she should have told him no. She should have gone to the Wilds and helped Dion come to terms with who he was. Together, they could have been happy.

She hadn't sought out magic; the power had found her. She'd always wanted to be a healer and maybe even a leader, someone who showed the world that women could make a difference just like men. Yet when she'd been betrothed to Nikolas, and promised the life of leadership and prestige she'd thought she always wanted, she'd known that it wasn't enough. Meeting Dion had opened her heart to love.

Bitterness filled her as she drifted. Her father. Dion. The gods took everyone she loved away from her. And now they were going to take her life.

Squinting against the bright sun, she looked at the wrist-thick length of polished wood tangled in her arms. It was increasing the difficulty of holding onto the plank, and she stared at it for some time before realizing that it was her staff. As she grew weaker, she decided to let it go. It wasn't much effort to release it, and soon she was watching it drift away.

Her eyes were still on the floating staff as it rose and fell on the waves, when she heard a piercing shriek.

She lifted her head and recoiled. A dragon flew toward her. With another loud cry it saw her and swooped down. Lithe and lean, with glossy scales of shining silver and wings tucked in close to its body, it was ready to snatch her out of the sea and devour her.

Fear jolted her into action. Chloe looked for her staff, but it had drifted a stone's throw away. The dragon plummeted, soon close enough for her to make out the grass-green color of its narrowed eyes and see the curved teeth in its reptilian jaws, large enough to swallow her in a single mouthful. It reached out with grasping claws, but Chloe ducked under them and it rose back into the sky, preparing to descend for another strike.

Forced to choose, she let go of the plank and used her last reserves of strength to swim. She paddled frantically and reached out for her staff but her hand splashed on nothing. Kicking hard, groaning with effort and exhaustion, she tried again, and this time her fingers closed around it.

She looked for the dragon, scanning the sky in terror. It was turning in a tight circle, screeching as it plunged down to meet her.

Then she remembered.

There were no more wildren.

The dragon flew down to her, but this time slowed its speed, wings beating at the sea while it hovered. Chloe looked into the angular eyes. This time, when she saw their grass-green color, she understood. She gave a short sob. She knew this dragon. She'd flown on its back before.

The dragon lowered itself as much as it could, struggling to keep its wings above the surface. A wave lifted Chloe up as the huge creature leaned one forelimb into the water, and with a surge of effort she grabbed hold, close to the knee, before a second wave carried her still higher, and with a sudden burst that made her weak muscles scream, she pulled herself up.

The dragon tilted further, dangerously close to the water. Grunting, Chloe lunged, reaching out and grabbing hold of one of the knobs behind its head. She cried out as she expended her last energy to pull herself onto the dragon's back.

Then, with her legs on either side of the creature's flanks, darkness overcame her and her head fell down onto the leathery skin of its back.

Chloe jolted awake when she felt the dragon make contact with the ground. Blinking as she looked around her, she saw that she was on a tiny, uninhabited island, little more than a rocky hill and a white beach with a few scraggly trees on the far side. The dragon turned its head, and she knew she was being asked to get off. She slipped down from its leathery back, falling to the sand.

She was so weak that she sprawled on the ground. Her lips were as dry as parchment. Nausea made her stomach churn. Her skull was pounding with a regular tempo. Lifting her head, she managed to see mist dispersing as the dragon changed its shape.

The mist revealed Liana in the dragon's place.

'Can you stand?' Liana said as she rushed to Chloe's side. The eldran crouched and lifted Chloe under the armpits, hauling her to her feet.

Chloe nodded weakly at her friend, her tongue too swollen to talk.

Liana looked the same as ever: a pretty eldran with a heart-shaped face, slight of build, with shoulder-length silver hair and pale-green eyes. Wearing a deerskin tunic and no shoes on her feet, she looked like an eldran in every way. Perhaps she seemed older, her bearing somehow more mature, and there was a shadow in her eyes, but it might simply have been concern for Chloe.

'Shh,' Liana soothed. 'I know this place. There's a spring. Just a little farther. You can do it.'

Liana helped her over the uneven terrain, taking her in the direction of the small grove of trees. Just past the nearest tree, at the base of a flat rock, was a small pool of water, fed from somewhere underneath. Chloe collapsed onto the ground, her face mere inches from the pool. She cupped her hands and reached out. The feel of the cool water against her skin was one of the most pleasant sensations she'd ever felt.

The wetness only served to highlight how dry her mouth was; she couldn't even lick her lips as she lifted her hands, moaning as the first touch of blessed liquid moistened her tongue. She missed getting most of it into her mouth, but a small trickle touched the back of her throat and she reached out again and brought more water to her lips, her tongue finally able to move. The next time, she slurped at her hands, gulping down mouthful after mouthful. Her headache faded away in an instant. Sensation came back to her lips. Her tongue no longer felt twice its normal size. Her thoughts became focused on more than her thirst, and she began to take stock of where she was.

'Small sips,' Liana said.

Chloe wanted to drink the entire pool to the bottom, but she was a healer and knew the wisdom of the eldran's words. Forcing herself to turn away from the pool, she sat up and met her friend's eyes.

'How?' she croaked. Clearing her throat, she tried again, speaking more firmly the second time. 'How did you . . . ?'

Sitting beside her, Liana looked sad. 'Today is the last day of spring.'

'I don't . . . ?'

'It's the day of Dion's wedding. Eiric didn't want me to go, but I went anyway. And then . . . when I arrived in Xanthos . . . I discovered Dion had vanished, and his bride was captured in Phalesia. They said you'd gone after them. The short, bald man—'

'Cob,' Chloe said.

'Yes, that was his name. He said that he thought the people to blame were in Malakai. I left to see what I could learn, and then I found the wreckage of a ship near some sailors making camp on a beach. They told me you'd been lost at sea.' She put her hand against Chloe's forehead. 'And then I found you.'

Chloe regarded the young eldran at her side. She hadn't seen Liana since the reclaiming of Sindara, and she had changed. Gone was the uncertainty. Liana had blossomed into a confident young woman.

'Chloe . . . I didn't know everyone thought you were dead. I last saw you with Zachary. I thought you'd decided to return to your home, and then . . . the fighting started . . .'

'It's all right,' Chloe said. 'I understand.'

Chloe cupped her hands and drank more water, feeling strength return with every mouthful.

'How is Eiric?'

'He is who he is.' Liana looked down at the ground.

'Is there something between you?'

Liana sighed. 'I don't know. I love him, and I know he loves me, but every time I get close to him something happens to push us apart. He's so consumed with being a leader that he forgets a king can also be gentle. Triton was unyielding, so Eiric thinks he has to be too. Zachary . . . Even though Eiric is his son, he tells me I shouldn't accept him as he is, not until he's found his way.'

'Wise as ever. How is Zachary?'

'Old,' Liana said with a smile. 'He spends a lot of time alone.' She raised an eyebrow. 'So what should we do now? Isobel is long gone. We don't know what these men wanted with her, or Dion.' She glanced at Chloe. 'They were going to be married today. It must be hard for you.'

Staring into the pool, it was some time before Chloe replied. 'I was jealous,' she said with a shrug. 'Of course I was. I still am. But I have to help them.'

'Then I'm going to help you.'

'Can you fly?'

'I need to rest, and so do you, but the answer is yes.'

'Then we'll rest. And then we'll go to Malakai.'

33

'How big was this army you saw?' Kyphos asked.

'Too big,' Palemon grunted, pacing the length of the throne room, his brow furrowed in concentration. 'Kargan has moved swiftly. The barges were ready to depart. They'll cross the Shadrian Passage and bring the army across. Then the Ileans will be heading our way.' Palemon looked out to sea, wondering what his next move should be. 'These relics of Nisos the Archmagus work as they should. We have six sets of copper chains, but only one dragon, a dragon that won't eat and grows weaker by the day.' He pounded a fist into his palm. 'I can feel it. We're so close! Power. We need power. We need to seize the initiative if we are ever going to get the ships we need.'

When Kyphos didn't reply, Palemon turned away from the window, glancing at the stocky warrior, who was gnawing at his lip.

'You have something to say, Kyphos?' Palemon walked over and stared down at him. 'Out with it.'

'Sire, while you and the sorceress have been busy in the Sky Tower, I've been spending time in the city. There is . . . something I've been meaning to show you. The solution to our problem might be closer than you think.'

'How so?'

'Come, let me show you. You can make your mind up for yourself.'

Kyphos led Palemon out of the palace and through the city streets. As the two men strode side by side, walking quickly, Palemon occasionally glanced at his right hand man but stayed silent. Together they followed the broad avenue that led to the harbor before turning into a side street that took them to the city's main market square.

The market was bustling. Stall after stall lined the square's perimeter, where people in colorful linen tunics and desert dwellers in loose burnooses browsed the goods on offer. A central fountain spilled water from the mouth of a dolphin into a marble basin, and aromas of grilling meat wafted over from some of the food vendors. Palemon cast Kyphos an inquisitive look, but the hunchback was grim-faced and close-mouthed as he crossed the square. Anyone who saw the imposing king, unmistakable by his gray-streaked braided beard, and the stooped frame of the man who walked at his side, blanched and moved swiftly out of the way.

Kyphos came to a halt in front of a stall, unremarkable compared to any of the others on both sides, where a dark-haired young woman was selling fruit and vegetables.

'Watch,' Kyphos said.

The woman handed an old priest in a faded yellow robe a heavy cluster of grapes. Placing the grapes in his basket, he handed out a copper coin, but the woman shook her head.

'You can pay my husband,' the young woman said with a smile and a nod to the man at her side, who was taking coins and balancing them on a scale before offering change.

'Well?' Palemon asked. 'What am I here to see?'

'Look at her,' Kyphos murmured.

Palemon frowned and watched the busy market stall. The woman had pale skin and black hair that was streaked with silver despite her youth. She had a lithe, willowy build, with slim arms and a slender neck, and was pretty, in a delicate, elfin fashion, but it was her eyes that were both strange and captivating. One orb had an iris of emerald green, while the other was light brown.

'She never takes the money herself,' Kyphos said.

Palemon saw a necklace at the woman's neck, a thin copper chain holding a round medallion. The medallion had a sheaf of wheat embossed in the center.

'You think . . . ?' Palemon started. 'But she's wearing a necklace.'

'The king of Xanthos wore a necklace also. And the metal might not be pure.'

Palemon contrasted the young woman with her husband. A few years older, he had a square face and a brawny build, with short dark hair and a manner of open friendliness with the customers. Faces like his were everywhere, whereas the woman unquestionably stood out from the other people in the market.

'She isn't the first I've seen with strange eyes or silver-streaked hair, but she bears the marks stronger than any other.' Kyphos turned to Palemon. 'The queen of Xanthos was a pure-blooded eldran and no one knew, not even her own family. After the fall of Aleuthea, people have become lax in their vigilance.' He lowered his voice. 'Sire. There are eldren in the population.'

Palemon tugged on the braids of his beard, thinking for a moment, before he came to a conclusion and pushed through the crowd to approach the stall. As citizens turned to face him, indignant glares became expressions of fear when they saw the broad-shouldered king with the dark, penetrating eyes – the strange new ruler of their city. Reaching the front, he lifted his chin and stared at the woman eye to eye. He was tall, and she was just as tall as he was.

Looking slightly panicked, she wrung her hands behind the table of wares. 'King . . .' The young fruit seller cast a frightened look at her husband.

Palemon turned to Kyphos, who had followed him but looked as if he had no idea what his king was going to do next. 'Give me a silver coin.'

Looking perplexed, Kyphos handed one over.

Palemon reached out to the woman. 'Take this coin.'

'If you want to buy . . .'

'Take it!' Palemon barked.

'My husband . . .'

'I said take it, girl.' Glaring at her, staring unblinkingly into her odd-colored eyes, Palemon thrust his hand at her, matching her uncertainty with an unbending will of iron.

Reaching into his open palm, the young woman hesitantly took the silver coin. She held it for the briefest instant before her nose wrinkled and she set the coin down on the table.

'Good enough for me,' Palemon said.

'I don't understand.' The young woman bit her lip, evidently wondering if she was receiving a gift or an obligation.

Palemon glanced at the husband, evaluating him along with the wife, and decided the man wouldn't present any trouble. Inclining his head at Kyphos, he walked a short distance away while the perplexed woman stared at his departing back.

'She may be, or she may not be,' Palemon said. 'But here is what you are going to do. Seize her, seize her parents. If she has eldran blood, then one of her parents will too. There is no point in questioning them; it's likely that they don't even know. Kill the husband if he gets in the way—'

Kyphos frowned. 'And if there are children?'

'Children?' Palemon scowled. 'Use your own judgment.'

He looked back, seeing that the stall was now deserted, the crowd hurrying away as if it was tainted by his visit. The young woman and her husband were still watching with wide eyes.

'Listen to me, Kyphos. I want you to round up anyone in the city with odd-colored eyes. Hair is easily changed, but the eyes don't lie. Start immediately. Root them all out. I'm going to speak with Zara. Do not fail me in this. Understood?'

Kyphos hesitated and then nodded. 'Understood, sire.'

Palemon strode away, leaving Kyphos alone in the market, watching the frightened woman.

Two days later, Palemon stood on the stone ledge that circled the top of the cylindrical Sky Tower, just below the summit.

With Zara's help, he now understood its purpose.

He gazed down at the ground far below and imagined the sensation of falling. The height was great enough that the plunge would easily kill a man, breaking his body, shattering his skull on the paved stones at the tower's base.

Lifting his head, he looked across the gap to the far side. Standing on the same ledge and facing him were seven captives, four men and three women, each with a soldier standing beside them. The soldiers held poles with metal clasps gripping their captives' throats. Some of the people Kyphos's search had unearthed were old and others young. They all had eyes open wide with terror, wailing and moaning in a way that made Palemon wish he'd thought of gagging them. At the end of the row of captives, first in the line, was the pretty young woman from the market. Streams of tears poured down her face as her lips moved in prayer.

The Sky Tower was the same as it always was – wide enough to easily accommodate the biggest dragon, with a stairway leading down from the stone platform, curling around the edge of the inner wall – except for one change. Just below the ledge, iron chain, strong but easily removed, now stretched across the gap, connected from one hook to another, forming a net over the hole.

Becoming impatient, Palemon finally saw the slender figure of Zara, as always clad in her figure-hugging dress, climbing up the stairway. Stopping just below the ledge, she looked everything over before nodding.

'We are ready, sire,' she called.

Palemon nodded back to her. He then met the eyes of the soldier at the end of the row. 'Do it.'

The soldier holding the sobbing young fruit seller took a deep breath and used his pole to force his captive to the edge of the platform, guiding her by her collared neck. Gasping and choking, with both hands trying to pry the metal clasp from her throat, she tried to resist, but the soldier was strong and determined, and he forced her to the very edge, until her toes were over the drop. His mouth tightening, the soldier then moved quickly.

He pushed a lever to open the collar around the woman's neck. In the same instant, he shoved her with the pole, prodding her sharply between her shoulder blades.

She screamed and tumbled off the edge, falling through the wide holes in the net of iron chain while Palemon leaned forward to peer down and witness the inevitable outcome. He waited for the thud of her body as she struck hard stone. He was expecting it so much that he had his teeth gritted: he didn't actually want her to die; that wasn't his objective. Her limbs clawed at the air as she fell with her back to the ground, staring wide-eyed up at him.

Suddenly Palemon gasped.

She vanished in a heartbeat. A cloud of white mist obscured her body, filling the entire bottom half of the shaft. The mist flickered, like sheet lightning in a storm.

There was no thud of her body breaking on the flagstones. Instead, he heard the snapping sound of wings.

A mighty winged creature flew up out of the cloud, wings beating the last shreds of white into nothingness. The dragon screamed, an ear-splitting shriek that must have been heard all over the city. It launched itself upward, heading directly for the open sky above and the promise of freedom. With odd-colored eyes, a narrow head that reminded him of a snake, and wings like a bat, its color was somewhere between silver and black and it was about half the size of the dragon that was the king of Xanthos, still penned below the tower.

The dragon shrieked again when it struck the net of iron chain, trying in vain to fly through and make its escape. But now it was too big to get through the holes. Every onlooker watched wide-eyed as the creature crashed against one wall and then the other before it began to tire.

Weakened by its struggles, the wings began to beat more slowly as the charcoal-gray dragon realized there was no chance of escape. It lost height, knocking against the wall once more before falling to the ground. Palemon gazed down from above, leaning over the ledge to see. He watched the slaves assembled at the bottom run forward and throw more lengths of iron chain over the beast, standing around it in a circle, grunting as they held it down. The scar-faced magus, Tarik, then came forward and clamped an iron collar around its neck. Soldiers stood by with heavy crossbows, keeping a wary eye on the monster in their midst. Tarik then fastened a set of copper reins to the collar.

Immediately the dragon settled.

Palemon felt a thrill of satisfaction as the magus led the creature away by the reins. He glanced across at Zara, and she smiled triumphantly.

'Next!' Palemon called.

The next captive was a middle-aged man with black, wiry hair cut close to his scalp and darting eyes that were a pale shade of green. Moaning with fear, the man struggled against the soldier behind him, but with a collar around his neck and a dagger pressed to his side, he was soon pushed forward. The soldier levered the collar open and kicked him in the back with a booted heel.

The captive's scream echoed in the hollow tower as he fell through a hole in the iron net and struck the ground seconds later. With a sharp crack, he was changed from a living, breathing human into a motionless heap. The slaves dragged the body away, leaving a bright-red smear on the stone.

'Next!' Palemon called again.

The next captive looked as if she thought she was living in a nightmare and would surely soon wake, barely struggling as she was released and pushed through the net. Palemon watched intently as the old woman cried out, her limbs flailing as he waited for her to hit the hard stone.

But his breath caught as he saw the cloud of pale mist. A flying creature burst out of the ether, a monster that resembled the woman, but with jaws enlarged and bat-like wings sprouting from her shoulder blades.

The woman had eldran blood, but she was no dragon. This one was a fury.

Palemon glanced at Zara and shook his head.

Zara issued orders down to the soldiers. A moment later two crossbows twanged in quick succession. The fury shrieked as the bolts struck home, and plummeted to the ground, writhing and twitching before the slice of a blade silenced the creature, pumping its lifeblood over the stone. The fury's corpse was dragged away.

Palemon called out yet again. 'Next!'

34

Dion's eyes were thin slits, breath rumbling in his chest as he watched yet another dragon herded into a cell. Confused ramblings washed over him, feelings of terror and bewilderment crashing through his mind. For a time, he believed they were his own thoughts, but then he realized they were coming from the new occupants of the other cells.

Why did they do this to me?

Can anyone hear me? I think I can hear you. Please, someone talk to me.

No, no, no, no . . .

She's dead. And now . . . this . . . I truly hope she's in a better place.

Please, Helios, help me.

The flood of terror eventually subsided, then faded altogether.

He was still exhausted from his flight all the way to the far side of the Shadrian Passage. Palemon had urged speed, and the enthrallment of the chains gave Dion no choice but to obey.

And now he was starving, intentionally taking neither food nor water.

Eventually his eyes closed. Time passed as he slept.

———

He lifted his head as two sorcerers, both carrying staffs, approached the gate to his cell. One of them was short and had savage burn marks on his face. He remembered his name: Tarik. The other was also a magus, a tall, lean man in a gray robe.

'The king wants six of them ready to depart,' Tarik was saying.

'This one isn't eating.' The lean man stopped outside Dion's cell, rubbing his chin as he looked through the bars. 'It's weak.'

The pair regarded him for a time.

'We have others now to take its place,' the scar-faced magus finally said. 'We already have more dragons than chains.' He nodded as he made a decision. 'Take its chains; we'll use them on another.'

The lean sorcerer threw the bolt and opened the creaking iron gate. Some property of the magical shackles meant that Dion was unable to do anything as he watched the magus come in close and begin to unfasten them.

But then the chains were gone.

He was still frozen into this form, but he could no longer be controlled with a thought. His eyes narrowed as he watched the magus beside him, gathering the chains in his arms. He wanted more than anything to open his jaws and bite the man in two. Instead, he lowered his head to the ground and glared at the two sorcerers. He glanced at the hunk of cooked goat meat in the corner of the cell. He was hungry, but he had to trust that his plan would work; if they wanted to talk to him they would have to let him change back to his normal form.

Taking the copper chains, the lean sorcerer walked over to inspect the uneaten food. A moment later Tarik entered the cell and spoke to his companion. 'Why do you think he isn't eating?'

The sorcerer shrugged. 'Nothing wrong with the food. The others all ate.'

Tarik approached, examining Dion from nose to tail, walking along the length of his body. 'This one was the first. We need to find out what's wrong . . . if he's refusing to eat or unable to.' He scratched the melted-looking tissue on his face. 'I'm going to take his collar off so he can change.' He crouched, scowling as he stared into Dion's eyes. 'Don't forget what we can do to your woman.'

The magus put a hand to his collar, accompanied by a sudden burst of heat.

But then the collar was gone.

The sense of relief was stronger than anything Dion had experienced before. With barely a conscious effort, he felt the sensation of changing, and then he was lying face down in front of the two watchers. He realized he was gasping.

He was clad in the same tunic he'd been wearing when Kyphos came to his palace, but the material was ragged and crusted with dirt. His body felt like another garment, something worn rather than part of his being. Tears leaked from the corners of his eyes as he sucked in deep breaths. The more time he was spending in another form, the more he was becoming like a domesticated animal.

'Well?' Tarik asked, collar held in one hand, staff clutched in the other. 'What is it? Is it the food? Do you want it raw?'

Dion rolled over and sat up, head spinning. He finally licked his lips and managed to speak. 'I want to see her.'

'His woman,' Tarik snorted, raising an eyebrow at the other magus. He turned to Dion again, frowning down at him. 'Here is what you are going to do. You are going to change back again, and then you are going to eat.'

'No.' Dion slowly shook his head. 'I won't.'

With a growl of irritation, Tarik handed the iron collar to his companion. He then took his staff in both hands and stepped forward. Tilting the staff, he brought the iron claw hovering near Dion's abdomen. 'Don't test my patience, half-breed. We can force you to change.'

Dion looked from side to side, taking in the other dragons, all penned in cages like animals at a slaughterhouse. He remembered the thoughts of fear and confusion his eldran senses had picked up.

'These others didn't even know they had eldran blood. They weren't in control of it.' Dion's lips thinned. 'I am. Push me off a cliff, or whatever it is you do. I'll only die.'

Tarik snarled. He pressed the iron claw against Dion's side. The black metal at the end of his weapon glowed.

Dion screamed. The pain was agonizing, a sensation of fierce burning, as if his skin was being peeled away in slabs and his insides ripped out. He smelled his own sizzling flesh as the pain went on and on. He was only able to writhe and gasp until the magus finally pulled his staff away.

The pain eased, but it didn't let up, leaving Dion twitching on the ground. 'I won't change,' he whispered.

'Wait here,' Tarik said to his companion. 'Keep an eye on him.'

———

Dion felt something hard prodding him in the burned skin of his abdomen and his eyes shot wide open. He put a hand to his forehead, waiting for the pain to subside, swallowing to prevent his stomach from retching and causing him even more agony.

The lean sorcerer moved to prod him again, but he shuffled away. His wary eyes on the gray-robed magus sharing the cage with him, he forced himself to stand.

The sorcerer jerked his chin in the direction of the iron gate. At the same instant, Dion heard a quiet, feminine voice, familiar but quavering.

'Dion?'

Despite the pain he was in, he rushed to the iron gate, gripping hold of the bars and peering out. When he saw her standing on the other side, he drew in a sharp breath.

Isobel had lost weight, and there were dark, heavy shadows under her blue eyes. Her once-lustrous blonde hair was matted, and the expression on her pretty face was wretched. Thin and sallow, she barely filled her plain linen tunic. She looked anything but the way a healthy woman should.

'I . . . I wanted to see you,' Dion stammered.

'What have they done to you?' she whispered.

'Here she is then,' Tarik said, standing beside Isobel with his staff in hand. 'Now change your shape and eat your food. If we don't see you eating, we'll kill her right now, in front of you.'

'How are you?' Dion looked firmly into Isobel's eyes. 'Have they hurt you?'

She hung her head and started to cry. 'I want to go home.'

'That's enough,' Tarik spat. 'Did you hear me? If you want her to live, do as I command.'

Shoulders slumped, Dion glanced at the sorcerer sharing the cell with him and nodded. 'Don't hurt her,' he said. 'I'll change.'

He stood back from the bars, his eyes on Isobel the entire time. He hoped that she could be strong, for just a little longer, for both her sake and their unborn child's. His plan was desperate, he knew, but it was all they had. He was without a collar. There were two sorcerers, but no soldiers. Isobel needed him.

Dion's heart began to race, hammering at his chest with powerful blows. Sweat broke out on his forehead as he closed his eyes.

His brow furrowed as he imagined a new form. Finally letting his wild fury run free, he clenched his fists at his sides and began to feel the change coming over him.

But rather than a winged creature, he summoned indomitable strength.

Visualizing a powerful torso and limbs strong enough to crush a man with a single blow, he knew that in the thickening cloud, they wouldn't know until it was too late, and he had to make every moment count.

He felt his body growing in size. He cried out, the sound becoming deeper as his chest swelled. His shout became a roar and he opened his eyes, legs apart and arms raised above his head.

Dion had changed into a giant.

Thrusting head and shoulders above the mist, he roared, his gnarled head brushing against the ceiling as he looked down at the tiny sorcerer sharing his cage. With a single powerful blow, he swatted the gray-robed sorcerer to the side, sending him crashing into the bars with enough force to break his bones.

A strong kick smashed the bolt holding the gate fastened and he tore it wide open. Dion stormed out of the cage, heading directly for Tarik. Eyes wide with shock, the scar-faced magus lifted his staff, but Dion's fist punched into his torso, sending him flying through the air before he struck the wall, crumpling instantly.

Isobel stood frozen with terror, gazing up at him. He knew how he looked – hideous, terrifying, three times her height – but he tried to communicate compassion with his eyes as he bent down and picked her up in his arms like a child.

Then he started to run.

Knowing he had just this one chance, every thought focused on getting Isobel away from this terrible place, he rushed out of the chamber and into the wide, high-ceilinged corridor. He sprinted hard, powerful legs carrying him forward faster than a man could run. Exhaustion tried to slow him, starvation sapped his will, but he bellowed and pushed the sensations away. He needed to make it to the open streets. He had no other plan.

Lumbering through the corridor, he followed the sloping path and then the curve of the tower's wall. Finally he saw the broad archway and bright sunlight. Beyond, tantalizingly in reach, was the city.

Still carrying Isobel in his arms, he ran for the archway, startling two soldiers with crossbows standing outside. He barreled into them, knocking both men sprawling to the ground, before setting Isobel down.

He headed back to the nearest soldier, who gazed up in horror at the giant towering over him with both fists clenched above his head. Bringing down his arms, Dion caved in the man's chest, the armor of steel links offering no protection. He took two steps to reach the other guard and stamped down with his leg, once, twice, finally letting his rage swamp all other emotions.

Sweeping his eyes over the area, he realized he'd made it; he had escaped the tower and was standing in the streets. In all directions city folk were fleeing in terror, but he ignored them. He rushed back to Isobel. Now he needed to become a dragon, and he prayed she would know what to do and leap onto his back.

Something sharp and painful kicked into his thigh.

Whirling, he saw that two more soldiers had rushed from the tower, both with crossbows in their hands. Dion lumbered toward them, but his injured leg failed him and agony shivered through his body as he fell to one knee. A moment later the second crossbow thrummed, sending a flash of black iron through the air before a powerful blow punched into the left side of his abdomen.

Glancing down, he saw two thick black shafts protruding from his body. Compared with his size, they were like harpoons embedded in the hide of a whale, but the pain was crippling. He reached down and grabbed the shaft in his leg, gasping as he pulled. He felt it tear, and then he plucked it out, tossing it away and reaching for the shaft in his lower chest. With a sharp grunt, he dealt with it like the other, ripping it from his abdomen and throwing the iron bolt to the ground.

Pain now mingled with fatigue. Panting, he stood, before falling to his knees again. He involuntarily felt his shape slipping away from him.

No. Hold on. You have to hold on.

Panic filled him. The soldiers had fired their crossbows; he still had some time. The priority was to get Isobel free.

He distantly heard the sound of swords being drawn, but he ignored the soldiers as he tried to drag himself back toward Isobel. His chest heaved as his face screwed up. He now tried to imagine himself as a flying creature. The sky was his element. He had wings that would carry Isobel to safety.

But when he felt himself changing, he knew he didn't have the strength. His size grew smaller, his body withdrawing into itself, collapsing like a wineskin with a hole in it. As gray mist clouded his vision, despair sank into his gut.

He'd planned to fly away with Isobel. But now he was on the ground, returned to his normal shape. He looked up to meet her eyes.

'Go,' he said.

Her wide, frightened eyes cast him a final plaintive look, before she turned and started to run.

But Isobel took no more than three steps before Dion heard a twang.

A metal bolt darted through the air. Strong enough to pierce a dragon's hide, it speared her in the very center of her back. As it struck it made a sound like a fist punching a pillow, knocking her forward before sending her falling face down onto the stone.

Shocked, uncomprehending, Dion traced the bolt's flight back to the source: a soldier had reloaded. The string of his crossbow still thrummed. His expression was surprised.

As a voice screamed in Dion's head that this wasn't happening, he started to crawl toward Isobel. He panted as he dragged himself along the ground, eyes burning, so stunned that he felt numb. His vision was blurred when he finally reached her.

He heard a rush of footsteps. Suddenly he felt a sword point pressed into his back.

'Soldier, stop! Don't kill him.' He heard Tarik's rasping voice.

Dion ignored the sword as he turned Isobel over and stared into her face.

The breath rattled in her chest. 'I . . . I . . .'

Her lifeblood pooled underneath her, and her eyes glazed as she shuddered.

He would never know what she was trying to say.

35

In a man-sized cell, somewhere far from all hope, Dion lay on the ground and shivered. An iron collar once more enclosed his neck, tight enough to hurt. His ragged tunic did nothing to ward off the chill, for the cell was dark and damp, and never saw natural light. But it wasn't the cold that hovered over him like a shadow.

He again saw the thick iron crossbow bolt, far too powerful for Isobel's slender frame, plunging between her shoulder blades. He imagined how she'd felt, terrified, far from home, vainly trying to flee, before agonizing pain ripped through her insides. He again saw her quivering and shuddering as she tried to speak and then took her last breath. She was dead. The child she'd carried was dead with her.

Once, Dion had dreamed that he would have a son or daughter, with a name, and a unique personality, and perhaps Isobel's beauty. He would watch his child grow, nurturing his or her talents, imparting wisdom where he could. He would keep his child safe; for what was the most important role for a parent, if not to protect sons and daughters from danger?

Trembling on the ground, he looked up when he heard a voice.

A middle-aged woman was standing over him. She was dark-haired and slender, with delicate features, and wore a flowing chiton of pale-blue silk and a golden necklace. Her eyes were concerned as she crouched at his side.

'My son.'

'Mother?'

'Your struggles are nearly over,' she said. Kneeling beside him, she smoothed back his hair. 'Let the darkness come.'

'It hurts,' he said, and he knew he wasn't talking about the wounds on his body.

'I know,' she soothed. 'Now you understand, don't you? Why I hid what I was, even from your father. They'll never see us the way they see each other. We'll always be feared or used. Never treated as equals.'

'I'm not an eldran . . .' Dion murmured.

'But you're not human either, Dion.'

He closed his eyes and then opened them again when he heard another voice. His mother, Thea, was gone. In her place was an older, broad-shouldered man wearing a tunic that left one shoulder bare. His white hair was curly and he had a wispy beard. He had a slight limp as he paced the cell.

'If I'd known what you were,' he growled, 'I would have disowned you the day you were born. And now you're the king.' He sneered, waving his hands in disgust. 'Look at you, boy! Some king you are. You thought you could do it better than your brother? Well, you thought wrong.'

'I tried, Father.'

'You tried.' Dion's father scowled. 'I've been watching you your whole life. From what I can see, all you've done is fail.'

Dion put his hands over his eyes, holding them there while he drew in a long, shuddering gasp of air. He waited, and when he finally slowed his breath and the pounding of his heart, he heard only silence. He took his hands away and looked up.

There was another man standing over him. Tall and brawny, a younger version of Dion's father, he had a barrel chest, thick black hair, and a matching beard covering his face. Where Dion's father had been

240

scathing, his older brother Nikolas gazed down on him with sadness in his eyes.

'I cast you out because you are not human. You understand that, don't you? I loved you, Dion. Why did you have to be some kind of . . . monster? You hurt everyone around you.'

'I am who I am,' Dion protested weakly.

'Exactly. And that has always been your problem.'

Shaking his head from side to side, the vision began to slowly fade away.

'Nikolas . . . Don't go,' Dion pleaded.

But his older brother had disappeared. And now Dion found himself looking at a stooped, stocky figure peering at him through the bars of his small cell.

The hunchback turned and barked at someone out of sight. 'You. Yes, you! Get over here.'

'What is it, Kyphos?' An older warrior with a bald patch on his crown approached, wiping at his eyes and stifling a yawn.

'Look at him. He's at death's door!'

The old soldier's eyes flickered disdainfully at Dion for a moment before he shrugged. 'He's a prisoner.'

'Don't you realize, you fool? He's a king! He's a valuable hostage. Go, quickly. Find someone to tend his wounds. And get some food and water. Go!'

Casting a dark expression at Dion, the old soldier muttered to himself as he hurried away.

Dion blinked as he looked up at Kyphos. He shivered again, still lying on his side, arms clenched around himself.

'I never wanted her killed,' Kyphos sighed, his shaggy eyebrows closing together over surprisingly sorrowful eyes. 'But what is done is done. I'm sure you are wondering what is to become of you. You were important to us once. You may be important again.'

'Nikolas . . .' Dion whispered.

Shaking his head, Kyphos walked away.

———⌣———

'This was your fault.'

Resting on the floor, with his back against the wall, Dion looked up sharply. Palemon stood outside the tiny cell, gazing down at him through the bars. He stood with legs apart, dressed for battle, with a chain shirt over his black trousers and the hilt of an immense sword poking up from behind his shoulder.

Dion climbed slowly to his feet, pleased that in the days since Kyphos's visit he was now able to stand and at least look his enemy directly in the eye. 'My fault?' he said softly. 'As surely as night follows day, her death can be squarely laid at your feet.' His voice strengthened. 'You killed her father. You brought her here, against her will. You got what you wanted from me, and all she wanted was to go home. Instead, when she ran, you put an iron bolt into her back.'

Dion's eyes burned, but he didn't wipe them, instead meeting Palemon's stare directly.

'One day, you will learn your place,' Palemon growled. 'And one day you will realize that it was your own actions that led to your woman's death. Then, when you do, you will kneel before me.'

For a time the two men stared grimly at each other, until a clatter of footsteps echoed from the stone walls and a new voice broke the silence.

'Sire,' Kyphos said, his voice urgent. 'Zara and the others are ready. It's time.'

'I leave you to your thoughts,' Palemon said to Dion. Kyphos cast a glance in Dion's direction, before Palemon followed the hunchback away.

As soon as they'd left, Dion gasped and immediately slid down the wall until he was once more on the ground. Standing for so long had taken a toll on his body. It would take him time to regain his strength.

He looked down at the hard stone floor, pondering. Palemon was right. He did have some thinking to do.

He remembered Isobel's smile, and the way she'd boldly leaped into the cold pool at the waterfall. She'd been so nervous and excited to be carrying his child. But instead of being tended by the priestesses and being given warmth and love, instead of experiencing the joy of being a new mother, she'd suffered pain and horror, before her life was taken away from her.

Of course Dion blamed himself for failing her. He had replayed his attempted escape through his mind again and again, thinking about how events could have played out differently.

But there was one thing he knew above all. It was that if Isobel's death was anyone's fault, it was Palemon's.

And if he wanted revenge, he would need to be patient.

———

Palemon clutched the reins in his left hand, feeling the dragon beneath him utterly under his control. This steed wasn't as powerful as his last, but it was still the biggest of the group, a charcoal-colored dragon with wings that stretched out for dozens of feet at both sides – the young woman from the market was bent to his will. With every mental command, the living weapon underneath him responded instantly.

High in the sky, wearing armor of steel links, Palemon flew at the apex of a wedge of six riders. Glancing over his shoulder, he checked on the other five dragons, all mounted by sorcerers, nodding when he saw that every one of them held his or her fire staff, ready to unleash their power. He pointed with his sword and veered, and the rest of the formation followed suit. Just behind him, Zara sat upon a smaller jet-black dragon, flying close enough for Palemon to see the flash of her white teeth as she smiled.

It was deepest night and difficult to read the terrain, but he could make out the strip of black water that could only be the Shadrian Passage. The group of six was approaching Verai, the city's lights glittering like a jewel.

Palemon ordered his dragon to descend, and those behind him followed suit. Swooping over the Shadrian Passage, he led his magi toward the city by following the coast, slightly out to sea to avoid detection. Half a mile below, fishing boats and rocky coves vanished behind them; the group of dragons was traveling at speed. The number of vessels increased as they flew over storehouses, and then finally Palemon saw the wide curve of Verai's harbor, a stretch of sandy shore a mile or two ahead, enclosed at both ends by fingers of stone.

He breathed a sigh of relief when he saw that the landing barges were still there, although they appeared to be ready to leave at a moment's notice. The wide, slow-moving, flat-bottomed vessels would only be able to make the crossing to Ilea on a day with perfectly still weather.

He raised his sword and cried out.

The vessels were drawn up on the shore, side by side, becoming larger as the dragons descended. There were dozens of barges, and Palemon needed to destroy all of them. Distant cries of terrified men filled the air as people on the shore stared up at the sky.

The wedge of dragons now broke formation as every rider selected a target. Crimson fire lit up at the ends of the sorcerers' staffs. Each dragon circled over its chosen vessel and then swooped.

Balls of flame began to rain down on the barges.

Speeding through the air, the orbs of fire rolled over and over before striking the barges' polished timbers in showers of sparks. Flame licked the decks in the wake of every salvo. The dragon riders swept over the nearest vessels and then flew up, choosing their next targets before descending once again.

More coiled flames shot from iron claws. An inferno soon raged below, following the harbor's arc, as ship after ship was set aflame.

Palemon ordered his dragon to slow and hovered just above a barge's deck, touching his sword to the rolled-up sailcloth horizontal to the mast. Bringing on his fury and channeling to his sword – the weapon he'd brought across the sea, once carried by Palemon the First – he felt savage triumph as the steel began to glow and then flame ignited the sailcloth. He climbed into the sky again, directing the dragon to fly on to the next ship.

He ignited three more and then ascended to a lofty height, watching as his magi rained their power onto the landing craft. They all knew not to leave a single vessel untouched, and he nodded in satisfaction, looking on as ship after ship blazed, checking along the line, scanning to see if any were missed. When Zara came to join him, he raised his sword again and the riders once more brought their dragons into a wedge formation.

Palemon smiled. The Ilean king, Kargan, may have powerful armies, but if he couldn't transport them across the Shadrian Passage, he would never be able to attack Malakai by land.

Kargan would have no choice. He was a former naval commander. Ilea's fleet was the largest in the world. He would come by sea.

And Palemon needed a fleet of his own.

He lifted his glowing sword and pointed back in the direction of Malakai.

36

Kargan, King of Kings, ruler of the Ilean Empire, paced the terrace outside his audience chamber, occasionally glancing out at the harbor, other times glaring at the towering man who stood with his hands hooked into his trousers, his broad face expressionless as always.

'This is taking far too long,' Kargan said. He swept his arms to indicate the sky, where just a handful of clouds drifted in the breeze. 'Surely this is fair enough weather?'

'The Shadrian Passage is windy,' Javid said. 'The general must choose his time, and make the crossing with care, or you will lose ships and, more importantly, men.'

'I would gladly lose a barge or two if it meant we recaptured Malakai swiftly.' Kargan's eyes narrowed. 'The treasury is running low. My soldiers get paid by the day. Do I need to explain the situation further?'

'You think General Rhian is being overcautious?' Javid asked.

Kargan scratched his beard. 'It's possible. Perhaps I should have given command to Dhuma. He showed leadership in bringing so many men home.' He finally made a decision. 'Time is running out. Come with me.'

Kargan left the terrace and strode back into the audience chamber, with Javid following close on his heels. As always, ever since Malakai's capture, Kargan scowled when he saw the tapestry with the map of the seven cities of the Ilean Empire. Passing the throne, he leveled his gaze on one of the palace guards standing with his spear held in front of his chest.

'You,' Kargan ordered. 'Go and find me a messenger.'

The guard bowed. 'At once, Great King.'

Kargan impatiently paced the length of the throne room while he waited. He glanced at Javid, wondering if his adviser and bodyguard was curious about what he was about to do, but the man's expression was too inscrutable to know.

'Great King?' The messenger finally entered. A lanky youth with a neatly trimmed beard, he had the long legs and muscled flanks of a runner, and would be as capable on horseback as he was on foot.

Kargan faced the messenger, glowering at him, but inwardly pleased when he saw that the youth's gaze remained steady. 'I want you to make all haste to General Rhian, or failing him, Captain Dhuma.' He raised an eyebrow. 'You know where they are?'

'With the army. On the shores of the Shadrian Passage.'

'Good lad. Tell them that unless there's a storm to end all storms, they are to cross the passage with all haste. Tell them I understand it's best to have fair weather, but every day they wait is costing the treasury too much money. Understood?'

'Of course, Great King. When should I leave?'

'Immediately!' Kargan barked.

'Great King,' Kargan heard Javid say softly, the words meant for his ears alone.

Kargan rounded on Javid. But then he saw that Javid was looking at the arched entrance to the audience chamber. Following Javid's gaze, Kargan's eyes opened wide.

A palace guard was leading an older man into the room. With weathered skin and sharp features, the newcomer clutched his helmet under his arm and wore a captain's insignia over his well-worn leather armor. He bowed when he entered, and Kargan frowned when he saw heavy shadows under his eyes; he looked like he hadn't slept in days.

'Dhuma?' Kargan asked incredulously. 'What in the names of all the gods are you doing here?'

'King of Kings . . .' Dhuma hesitated. 'I came personally to bring important news.'

'Leave us.' Kargan swept his chin at the messenger. 'Ignore what you heard.'

The youth ran out of the room, leaving Kargan facing Dhuma. Kargan raised an eyebrow expectantly.

'News?' Kargan growled. 'You crossed the passage? General Rhian is ill? Well, what is it?'

'The barges . . . They're all gone. Every last ship . . . burned to ash.'

Kargan felt heat come to his face. 'Burned? By whom?'

Dhuma swallowed but stood fast. 'While the barges were still in Verai, there was a raid. People . . . People on the backs of dragons. They set them all on fire.'

'Is this some kind of joke?' Kargan spluttered. 'Were you there yourself?'

'No, Great King. But I brought witnesses. They say there was a man leading the raid. He was tall, and carried a glowing sword, and had a braided beard. It is clear that this must be the same warrior I saw kill your cousin on the walls of Malakai. Even many of my men now know the name Palemon. There were six of them, all on the backs of dragons. The five who rode behind Palemon were fire-wielding sorcerers.'

'Ridiculous,' Kargan snorted.

To Kargan's surprise, rather than continue to keep his distance, Javid came forward to stand beside him and Dhuma. Normally, joining them would have been a serious breach of protocol, but Dhuma was obviously too fatigued and worried to care.

'Lord Kargan, you should take this seriously.' Javid frowned. 'When I was a child,' he said in the irritating lecturing tone he sometimes used, 'my mother told me stories about Aleuthea. There were always dragons involved – dragons, giants, and serpents. We have all heard that the Aleutheans killed the eldren and destroyed their homeland, but have you ever wondered why?' Javid spread his hands. 'From a small island nation, they were powerful enough to dominate the rest of the world. We must face the truth. It appears that this Palemon may be who he says he is.'

'Tell me, Javid, what did the stories say about fire-wielding sorcerers?' Kargan growled. 'And about a man with a glowing sword?'

'The Aleutheans possessed magic. Wizards with staffs appear in all of our myths. Sometimes they help the heroes in the stories, providing guidance and prophecy; other times they terrorize a village or a town, and it is the hero who must defeat the sorcerer to reclaim the princess.'

Kargan shook his head. He turned back to Dhuma. 'You say there were six of them?'

Dhuma nodded.

'Just six. No matter how powerful they are, we can deal with six. And we were unprepared for an attack from the sky. We may have lost our barges, but we have a powerful fleet here in Lamara.'

Kargan began to pace again as he pondered.

'Dhuma, I'm ordering the army home,' he said. 'We won't attempt to cross the Shadrian Passage again. We have to put them down, and quickly. No land crossings. We need to assault Malakai directly.'

'You have my agreement,' Dhuma said.

Kargan punched his fist into his palm. 'This time we'll travel over water. I'll lead the fleet personally, through the Chasm and into the Aleuthean Sea. We'll embark from Lamara, warships in the lead, filled with archers. We'll bring the infantry in a second wave.'

'I'll talk to the captains,' Dhuma said. 'Some of them have experience fighting wildren.'

'Good, good.' Kargan clenched his jaw. 'Send a fast messenger to General Rhian. Tell him to make all speed for Lamara. By the time the army returns, I'll have every bireme ready to depart. We'll soon end this once and for all.'

37

Chloe gazed up at the tall, circular tower, wondering what its purpose was. She glanced at Liana, walking beside her. There was a tightness around her friend's eyes: Liana was anxious, echoing Chloe's own mood. They were both strangers here, and if Malakai was truly where they'd taken Dion and Isobel, then they were in a city ruled by people whose intentions were clearly hostile.

Together they took in the sights of a city that was dirty and grand, dilapidated and beautiful. Many of the walls were crumbling, made of rust-colored mud brick, but others were well made and clad with venous marble, smooth to the touch and glistening in the midday sun. Sagging shop fronts in market squares faced proud statues that would impress the master craftsmen of Phalesia. The streets were filled with a greater variety of people than anywhere she'd been except Lamara: desert clansmen wrapped in cloth, dark-skinned traders with small armies of personal guards, swarthy slaves carrying nobles in covered litters, and commoners in bright-colored tunics.

Chloe was glad that the streets generally followed a simple grid. She could pretend to walk with purpose; she didn't want her and Liana to be singled out as foreigners. She still carried her staff, but she'd removed the silver device from the top, keeping it in her satchel, and now the staff simply looked like a traveler's walking stick.

Despite the wide variety of people in Malakai, she was worried about Liana. Again she glanced at her friend. Dressed in a dusty, plain chiton the same gray color as the paved avenue, the slight eldran had dyed her shoulder-length hair red with henna, as she'd once done to disguise herself in Phalesia. But like Chloe, Liana wasn't wearing a necklace, and glancing at the passing city folk, Chloe could see that this singled them out.

'Which way?' Liana murmured.

Chloe scanned ahead, deciding to travel where the city appeared to be denser. 'Right.'

'What are we looking for?'

'We need necklaces. Have you seen? Not a soul without one.'

They turned into a broad avenue with wide gates at the far end revealing the distant sea; this road appeared to lead to the harbor, with rows and rows of tightly packed structures on both sides, enclosed by the looming walls. Markets lined both sides of the boulevard, and seeing a row of craft stalls, Chloe moved to the side of the street and paused at the junction to a side alley. She unfastened the belt holding her chiton and slid out three silver coins from the inside fold.

'Hold these?'

Liana shook her head. 'I can't.'

'Sorry.' Chloe smiled, and instead kept the coins in her palm as she tied the belt around her garment once more. Touching Liana's arm, she then approached the stalls.

She inspected the wares, moving along from one vendor to the next, leaving the tiny statues of gods and goddesses behind and ignoring the hawkers' pleas until finally she saw the glint of jewelry. Coming to a table where necklaces hung from a vertical board with rows of little pegs, she began to scan the display.

'All the finest quality.' The vendor was an older man with graying hair and an imperious manner. 'Pure copper.' He waved a hand over another section. 'Also pure silver. You are interested in gold? I can show you gold also.'

Chloe glanced at Liana before addressing the vendor. 'Do you have any bronze?'

The vendor frowned. 'No bronze. By decree, the necklace must be pure.'

Chloe raised an inquiring eyebrow at her friend and Liana gave a slight nod. Running her eyes over the display, Chloe pointed out two copper necklaces, with matching circular medallions displaying the cross and double loop of Aeris. 'How much for these two?'

'For two beautiful women such as yourselves, a special price. Two Ilean drachmas or three Shadrian dinari.'

'This is all I have.' Chloe handed over a Phalesian silver eagle, making sure he didn't see she had more.

'May I?' The old vendor indicated the scale on his table and Chloe nodded. He weighed the coin and examined the imprint of the eagle. 'Foreign coins. Phalesian, yes? I have seen these before. You have come a long way, yes?'

Chloe lifted her chin without replying, fixing him with a stare. 'Is it enough?'

The vendor hesitated, but then finally nodded. 'The silver is good. Two of these coins.'

'I told you I have just the one.' Chloe held out her hand. 'Give me back my coin. There are other markets.'

He suddenly spread his arms and smiled. 'A lucky day. The most special of prices for the two beautiful ladies. May the good King Palemon bless you both.'

He handed Chloe the necklaces. 'Thank you,' she said, turning away. But then, with a start of realization, her brow furrowed as she glanced back at him. 'Did you just say Palemon?'

He looked slightly worried. 'Palemon is king of Malakai. He is a good king. A gracious king. He liberated us from Ilea.'

'Is that truly his name?'

The old vendor looked from side to side and lowered his voice. 'He has returned. He is said to be the descendant of Aleuthea.' His gaze drifted to the tall tower that dominated the city, as if linking it to the new king.

'That tower. What is it?'

'It is the Sky Tower. In deepest night, winged creatures, dragons, fly out at the king's bidding. My sister saw them herself.'

'Dragons?' Liana asked.

The vendor suddenly glanced past Chloe's shoulder and sealed his lips. Turning his back to them, he began to busy himself around his stall.

Turning around, Chloe saw a group of four warriors moving down the avenue, heading in the direction of the harbor. Their skin was far paler than the locals, and two had thick beards. But strangest of all, they wore armor of metal links. She remembered the painting Dion had shown her. Dragons . . . Armored soldiers . . . Already she was thinking they'd come to the right place. The warriors paid no attention to the locals, and the city folk looked away, pretending not to see them as they strode down the street.

Chloe waited until they'd passed and then led Liana away from the market. Lifting a necklace, she faced her friend and hesitated.

'Do it,' Liana said. 'I can't put it on myself, and I won't be able to change. But I can bear it.'

Liana lowered her neck and Chloe fastened the necklace around the eldran's throat. She then gathered her own long, dark hair at the back, before clasping the second copper necklace around her neck.

Feeling out of her depth, but knowing that Dion and Isobel both needed her, she lifted the medallion. She gripped the symbol of Aeris tightly.

'Come on,' she said to Liana. 'Let's find somewhere to spend the night.'

———

Finally, as they approached the denser heart of the city, Chloe and Liana began to see the symbols of beds carved on wooden boards above doorways.

'I don't like this place,' Liana said.

'Nor do I,' said Chloe. 'But it will take us time to get our bearings. If they're in this city, someone will know.'

She chose a guesthouse with a better-maintained sign and cleaner doorstep than some of the others. Peeling the curtained doorway to the side, she entered the dark interior, Liana following close behind.

The interior was larger than she'd expected. She looked around, seeing a rectangular room with half a dozen stools surrounding a carpet. Stairs at the back most likely led up to the guest rooms. Catching movement through a doorway, she saw a fat, olive-skinned woman, her body wrapped in a voluminous chiton pinned in several places.

'Hello?' Chloe called out.

At the sound of Chloe's voice, the middle-aged woman entered, smiling and setting down the basket of linen in her arms. She had a friendly expression and several wobbling chins, and wore her hair pulled tightly back from her forehead, tied in a bun.

'We're looking for a room.'

'Of course, please, sit, sit.' The plump woman indicated a pair of stools. 'Can I get you tea?' Without waiting for answer, she called over her shoulder. 'Goran! Bring tea!'

'Coming!' a male voice called back.

'So.' She clapped her hands together. 'Two rooms?'

'Just one room,' Chloe said. 'With two beds.'

'For how long?'

'We'll begin with three days and then we'll see.'

'Three days . . . Three days . . .' she mused, before calling behind her again. 'Goran! Where's that tea?'

'I said I'm coming!'

'Where are you from?' She rubbed her chin, pondering. 'I can't place your accents.'

'From Myana,' Chloe said.

'The Sarsican capital? By Helios, that's a long way away. Travel by ship, did you? What brings you to Malakai'—her brow creased slightly—'all alone?'

'We're both merchant's daughters,' Chloe said. 'Traveling with our fathers. I'm Chloe, this is Liana.' She couldn't see any harm in using their real names; no one knew them in Malakai. 'We've had enough of sleeping aboard, so we convinced our fathers to let us stay in the city while they conduct their business.' She smiled. 'They'll be checking up on us now and then.'

'I'm glad to hear it.' The plump woman harrumphed.

She appraised them for a time, looking at Chloe and then studying Liana. She peered into Liana's face, her eyes widening slightly, and then a man entered with a tray bearing two cups of steaming tea.

Goran was the woman's opposite: skinny and elegantly dressed, with thinning hair and a sharp nose. He cast a quick glance at his new guests, but kept his head down, obviously subservient, patiently holding out the tray.

'My husband always takes his time,' the woman said with a smile and a shrug. 'Here you go.' She passed a cup of tea to each of them. 'Now, my name is Madam Tomkin. May I ask how you plan to pay?'

Chloe handed Madam Tomkin one of her Phalesian silver eagles. Moving to stand in the light, the woman examined the coin.

'Yes, this will do fine. Fine, fine.' The plump woman hesitated. 'Listen, I don't mean to speak out of turn, but the city can be a dangerous place these days, especially for foreigners.' She nodded at Chloe. 'You'll fit in all right.' She then looked meaningfully at Liana. 'But your friend might want to stay in her room.'

Chloe and Liana exchanged glances. 'Thank you,' Chloe said. 'We'll take your advice.'

'Glad to hear it.' Madam Tomkin brightened. 'Now, make yourselves at home. My house is yours. Take your time. Finish your tea. My husband will then show you your room.'

38

Kyphos entered the audience chamber to find Palemon brooding and staring out the window, hands clasped behind his back as he pondered the empty blue canvas of the sea.

'Sire.'

'Eh?' Palemon spoke without taking his eyes off the horizon. 'What is it?'

'I have something for you.'

Kyphos turned and nodded at the pair of soldiers. Between them they held a lean young man with flaxen hair and brown eyes. Washed and clean-shaven, with his hair neatly combed, he wore a plain white tunic and sandals. Despite the iron collar around his neck, neither his hands nor feet were bound.

'I present to you . . . the king of Xanthos.'

Palemon frowned as the soldiers and their captive approached. 'Why is he here?'

Kyphos nodded at the soldiers, and they released their captive. Dion took a deep breath and walked slowly, laboriously, toward the tall, bearded king. He stopped in front of Palemon, chest heaving.

He then sank to his knees and bowed his head. 'I kneel before you,' he said hoarsely.

'Why isn't he with the others below the tower?'

'He has a message for you,' Kyphos said.

'Let me serve you,' Dion murmured, still kneeling and staring down at the ground.

Kyphos walked up to place a hand on the top of Dion's head. 'I'm sure you realize, sire, that he is still valuable to us. Not only as a hostage, but also for the knowledge he has.' He met his king's eyes. 'We already have more dragons than copper chains to control them.'

Palemon tugged on the braids of his beard. 'It seems you finally know your place,' he said, walking forward and towering over Dion. 'But how can you serve me?'

'I know about the eldren and their king.' Dion coughed, obviously struggling to talk. 'I know about Ilea and the forces they can muster. If I help you get what it is you want, perhaps you will leave my people in peace.'

Palemon pondered for a time. 'Tell me what you know about the eldren.'

'They are at war with Xanthos and Tanus. Their king, Triton, is a cruel and powerful ruler. He has one eye and is easily the most powerful of his race.'

Palemon's eyebrows went up. 'And how many ships are there in your fleet – vessels large and sound enough to make an ocean crossing?'

'Nine biremes,' Dion said. 'One trireme – the ship that you saw yourself. The other large fleets are controlled by Kargan of Ilea and Lord Lothar of Koulis. Sarsica and Phalesia are among the smaller naval powers.'

Palemon looked out to sea, as if seeing the ships he needed arrayed along the horizon. He nodded to himself. 'You have done well, Kyphos, but we shall see how useful he continues to be. Also, I don't know if I like him with so much freedom. Have him chained in this room.'

Kyphos nodded at the soldiers. Coming forward, they lifted Dion to his feet and shuffled him to a place against the wall, several feet from the throne, before sitting him back down again.

'Guard him here,' Kyphos instructed one of them. 'You,' he said to the other. 'See to the king's wishes.'

'And fetch Zara,' Palemon said. 'We have plans to make.'

⁓

Dion hung his head, motionless and slumped, while a brawny smith and his assistant pounded an iron hoop into the solid stone of the wall. Palemon's soldiers then came forward and fastened a chain to the circle of iron, before connecting the chain to the manacles around his wrists. His legs remained unbound, but the chain wasn't even long enough for him to stand.

He knew he had to gather his strength. He must learn about his enemy.

He had to bide his time if he wanted to have his revenge.

Keeping his head down, eyes on the floor, he gingerly leaned his back against the wall as he heard Palemon address a newcomer. 'Zara, finally. We need to talk.'

'Why is he here?'

'He is here to serve me in whatever capacity I wish. Now'—from the shifting of Palemon's voice, Dion knew he was pacing around the chamber—'we have six dragons, but it is not enough. We must have more. Many more.'

'We have only six sets of copper chains. I am sorry, sire, but despite my attempts, I cannot unravel the mystery of their construction. Archmagus Nisos was far more skilled than we are today.'

There was silence for a time, before Palemon finally spoke in a low voice. 'I have an idea,' he said slowly.

'Sire?' Kyphos asked.

'Just yesterday I took one of the dragons out to sea. I have now flown over the sunken city.'

Zara sounded puzzled. 'And?'

'The locals have long known where to find the Great Tower of Aleuthea. It is far larger even than the tower in Malakai. It was simple enough to find, buried in the sea below one of the Lost Souls, an isle called Widow's Peak.'

'You think what we need might be there?' Zara asked. 'Preserved, after all this time?'

'The vault under the Sky Tower was perfectly sealed.'

Kyphos snorted. 'Apologies, sire. But are you saying we should dive to the Aleuthean tower, swim down, and somehow retrieve more chains?'

Dion lifted his head.

'No, that isn't what I'm proposing,' Palemon said. 'Zara . . . You and your sorcerers . . . I have seen you perform powerful feats of magic . . .'

'What are you suggesting, sire?' Zara asked, her mouth tightening.

Palemon had turned his full attention on her, his eyes lit up with fire. 'You can summon a strong enough wind to turn a calm sea into a towering wave. I can only imagine what you and your magi can do working together.'

'What is he saying?' Kyphos raised an eyebrow at Zara.

Zara's lips thinned. 'He is suggesting that my sorcerers and I might be able to expose the ancient city.'

Dion fought the urge to gasp.

'Sorceress,' Palemon said. 'Malakai is just an outpost. Yes, it was the nearest city to Aleuthea, but it pales in comparison to the glory of our ancient homeland. Think of all we might discover. I am certain we would find more chains, but Archmagus Nisos built many artifacts. We might even find this arch.'

'Arch?' Kyphos asked.

'There is a message,' Palemon said, 'written on the wall of the chamber below the Sky Tower. The Arch of Nisos . . . Something to do with dragons.' He shrugged. 'That is all we know.'

'It would be dangerous,' Zara said.

'But how?' Kyphos raised an eyebrow. 'Tell me, sorceress: how do you intend to expose the city?'

'Wind,' Zara said. 'I believe it's possible.' She turned back to the king. 'I'm surprised I didn't think of it myself.'

'We have bought some time, by destroying the barges,' Palemon said. 'But soon Kargan of Ilea will be leading a fleet to our shores. Work on this problem. You will have my full support. Whatever you need: gold, silver, copper, or iron. Slaves. Anything. The Ileans will be back. Kyphos will help you in any way you require.'

39

Chloe put her head to the window and looked out, once again gazing at the tall, circular Sky Tower. It was early morning and the rose-colored rays of the rising sun glowed on its stone exterior.

Dragons, flying out in the night. Something told her the old market vendor hadn't just been telling tales.

'So what now?' Liana asked.

'Now, we learn what we can about the city. Dion is important, and if he or Isobel are here, someone will know about it. We—'

Chloe was interrupted by the sound of gentle knocking on the door.

'Ladies?' It was Madam Tomkin's voice. 'I've brought you tea.'

Chloe swiftly crossed the room to stand beside the door. 'Thank you, Madam Tomkin, but we don't want anything.' She glanced at Liana, checking that the eldran had her necklace on.

'The cups are hot,' Madam Tomkin said, her voice quavering. 'Can't you open the door?'

Chloe was about to reply when the door burst inward, throwing her against the wall. Soldiers clad in chain armor rushed into the chamber. Sent sprawling, she fell to her knees.

'Nobody move!'

Strangely accented voices barked commands. Liana cried out, and Chloe saw a bearded soldier pressing her friend's face down onto her bed. The soldier lifted something – an iron collar – and fitted the circle of black metal around Liana's neck as she struggled against his grip.

Another soldier loomed over Chloe, glaring down at her, daring her to move. She tried to stand, but he pressed on her shoulders, shaking his head.

A short man in a gray robe entered.

With close-cropped black hair, he carried a staff with an iron claw fixed to the top and had an imperious manner, obviously in charge. But most striking was his disfigured face: two thirds of it was burned, leaving ripples of pale scar tissue. With a curl to his lip, he glanced at Chloe, peering into her eyes, before looking away dismissively and roving his gaze over the room.

A sorcerer, Chloe realized.

The magus's eyes alighted for a moment on Chloe's staff, leaning against the wall, but fortunately it was still without its silver device, and he continued to scan the room. He finally nodded to himself and approached Liana, still hunched over the bed with her face pinned to the linen.

'Let me see her,' he said in a rasping voice.

The soldier rolled Liana over, the eldran's chest heaving as she stared at the approaching magus with wide-eyed fear. The sorcerer peered into Liana's grass-green eyes and appraised her from head to toe, taking in her pale skin, delicate features, and henna-dyed hair.

'Almost certainly,' he said. He glanced at Chloe. 'The other is human. She means nothing. But this one . . .' He reached down to Liana's delicate throat, below the iron collar, lifting her necklace between two fingers, before yanking it hard enough to break it. He tossed the necklace onto the floor. 'She may not realize it, but I will be surprised if she doesn't have eldran blood.'

'Leave her alone,' Chloe said. 'She doesn't know what you're talking about.'

'Most likely she doesn't.' He smiled. 'But the eyes don't lie, and soon we will know without the slightest doubt.' He nodded to the soldier holding Liana. 'You have your orders.'

'Yes, Magus Tarik.'

The soldier twisted Liana's arms painfully behind her back, and with the collar pressed tightly against the skin of her throat, she gasped as he forced her to move. Chloe felt the cold grip of fear on her heart as Liana cast a terrified look in her direction, knowing that there was nothing she could do. She heard Liana being manhandled down the stairs before the man guarding her finally moved away, but he was immediately replaced by the sorcerer.

He looked down at her. 'Be careful about the company you keep. You will not be seeing her again.'

Staff in hand, the magus left the bedchamber, heading back down the stairs as the soldiers dragged Liana out into the street.

Slowly climbing to her feet, for a long moment Chloe felt frozen into place, taking in the empty room. It had all happened so quickly. Her senses were still reeling.

Then she set her jaw and moved into action.

She grabbed her satchel and staff, before racing out of the room, passing a terrified-looking Madam Tomkin on the landing as she ran down the stairs after them. Reaching the ground floor, she saw Madam Tomkin's skinny husband, Goran, staring in the direction of the departing soldiers.

When he saw Chloe, he only shrugged. 'She had the look, and I don't want any trouble.'

Knowing she needed to find out where they were taking Liana, Chloe sped from the guesthouse and scanned the busy street. It only took her a moment to spy the crowds all giving a wide berth to the spectacle of Liana being forced down the street, struggling in the grip of the soldiers. Chloe began to run as she tried to catch up, but they were moving swiftly. She almost lost them when they turned into a side street, but she sprinted as fast as she could, seeing them turn again before becoming obscured by a crowd.

She'd almost caught up to them when the magus turned back, his eyes scanning. Wondering if Chloe, red-faced and panting, had something to do with what was happening just ahead, people in the crowd began to stare at her.

The sorcerer was about to spot her when she felt a hand grip her upper arm. A rough pull jerked her out of the crowd and into a sheltered doorway.

A short, stocky older man with a completely bald head looked up at her and put his finger to his lips. 'Chloe,' he said. 'You need to come with me. We'll find a way to help your friend, and perhaps you can help us save the king.'

The bald man led Chloe a short distance to a large tavern and drinking house. It had three stories and dozens of balconies on the upper floors. The lower level, open to the street, had enough seating for a hundred, but only a few people huddled on the stools, leaning on the tables, conversing and drinking tea.

'It's called The Trader's Rest,' he said. 'Our rooms are above. You have lodgings?'

'I did, but I'm not going back.'

His wary gaze checked in both directions before he nodded. 'We'll get you settled here.'

He continued to scan the room as he led Chloe past empty tables to a quiet corner, but even she could see that no one was paying them any attention. When they'd reached the back of the room, he offered her a seat at a table a little away from the rest and asked for tea when a boy came round to take their order.

'My name is Cob. I'm a friend of—'

'Cob?' Chloe gasped with relief. 'Dion told me about you. I know who you are.'

'I don't need to ask, do I? You're here for the same reason I am.'

Chloe opened her mouth, but then snapped it closed as the boy approached with their tea. Finally she answered, speaking in a low tone. 'Where are they taking Liana?'

'Your friend?' His round face screwed up. 'Is she an eldran?' Chloe nodded and Cob scratched the stubble on his chin. 'Dion's mentioned her. What happened?'

'They wanted her . . . We'd only just got here . . . The innkeeper gave us away.' Chloe's expression darkened when she remembered what the sorcerer, Tarik, had said. 'It's like they're rounding up anyone who might have eldran blood.'

Cob spread his hands. 'We haven't been here long, and I can't hazard a guess what they want with her. But we'll find out.'

'How did you know what I looked like?'

'I saw you once before. At the harbor in Phalesia, around the time that Ilean warship first arrived. You were yelling at us to stay clear of it.' He grinned. 'I feel like I know you, lass. Sailing is a lonely business. I've heard him talk about you many, many times.'

Chloe glanced down at the table and felt her face redden. She changed the subject. 'What have you learned so far? Is Dion here?'

'He's here. At least, he was recently.'

She looked up sharply. 'How do you know?'

His face turned grim. 'I have some news, and I'm afraid it isn't good. Isobel is dead.'

Chloe put a hand to her mouth.

'They killed her in the street . . . We spoke to people who saw it. An arrow took her right between the shoulder blades. Seems Dion was trying to rescue her at the time.' Cob rubbed at his eyes and glanced away. 'So the bride of our king is dead, along with his unborn child.' He cocked his head. 'You knew, didn't you?'

Chloe nodded, not trusting herself to speak as tears welled in her eyes.

'If he's still alive – and I have to tell myself he is – he'll be a broken man.'

'You mentioned others. Who's with you?'

'We couldn't risk more than a couple of us. Dion's uncle thinks there'll be a ransom attempt, but he hasn't met Palemon. We're the Free Men, and our king is not free. There's me, and there's Finn.'

'Finn? Where is he?'

Cob scowled. 'Getting himself into trouble.'

———

Finn entered the throne room grandly, swirling his crimson cloak as he turned to face the king. He gave a majestic bow, culminating in a flourish. Palemon appeared unimpressed, but Finn allowed not the slightest sign of his rising trepidation to show. He could do this.

'So you are a historian?' Palemon asked.

'A chronicler, King Palemon. Famed throughout the Maltherean Sea. My name is Fustalonious and—'

'What kind of a name is that?' Tall and imposing, standing in front of the ebony throne, Palemon's expression was puzzled.

'Er . . .' Finn thought furiously, his pulse racing. He swirled his cloak once again to gain a few moments. 'Great King, it is the name that will bring your glory to the world. I, Fustalonious of Lyre, have come halfway across the world to chronicle your return . . . The return of the King of Kings, descendant of Aleuthea, ruler of the world.'

Finn gave another bow. He struggled not to look away from the king, at the slumped man chained to the wall a few paces from the throne. Part of him wanted to cry out Dion's name, but he had to act his part if he wanted to help his friend.

When Palemon didn't reply, Finn pressed on. The king's face was emotionless, giving away nothing. Finn knew he had to hide his fear.

'I will give anything to be able to document your past, present, and future, Great King. Telling your tale will be its own reward. Aleuthea sank beneath the waves and your people were never seen again, but behold, here you are!'

'We aren't all here,' Palemon growled. 'I brought but one tenth of my people with me. I left many behind. Too many.'

'And I want to see you aid their return also. I will help you, Great King, in any way I can.'

'You are familiar with the noble families of the Maltherean?'

'Of course!' Finn's face lit up. 'I can name every member of the council of five in Koulis. There's Lord Tavin, Lord Bradlock, Lord Zarmos . . .'

'Enough,' Palemon said, cutting the air with his hand. Finn breathed an inward sigh of relief. He'd been naming sailors from the Free Men, and was worried he'd slip up and name Tanny the Sour or Redknuckle.

'So, chronicler, you will know, then, who this is behind me?'

Palemon watched Finn's face intently while he peered at Dion, as if trying to match features in his memory. 'By the gods, is that Dion, king of Xanthos? Son of Markos and brother of Nikolas?'

Palemon tugged on the braids of his beard. 'It is.' He pondered for a moment. 'So it appears you are who you say you are. Chronicler, I intend to claim the entire Realm of the Three Seas for my own. This record you want to transcribe . . . Will it help me achieve this?'

Finn put certainty into his voice, adding a touch of indignation: Fustalonious was a man who took himself very seriously. 'Undoubtedly. I can hold my head high and tell you with certainty. Of course! I will write my chronicle – with you, Great King, tall and magnificent, with a braided beard and the biggest sword the world has ever seen, as the central figure. All will know of your power and presence. Mothers will tell their children, and men will regale each other with tales of your exploits. Your name will be known across the land.'

Palemon tilted his head, considering as he slowly looked Finn up and down. He saw before him a slight, reedy man, with fine features, long hair, and thick eyelashes. He carried no weapon, and nor did he look like the kind of man who knew how to use one. But his hair was fashionably cut, and his fine crimson cloak was made of thick silk dyed with the most expensive of pigments.

'You may return tomorrow,' the king said finally. 'But let it be known, chronicler, that I will have scribes read your account back to me, and if I'm displeased . . .'

Finn bowed. 'You will not be, Great King.'

'And I have just one rule.'

'Of course, anything—'

'Keep your fluttering mouth shut. For a man who claims to listen and record, you talk far too much.'

40

Liana was terrified. She was standing on a stone ledge, and a soldier was forcing her to the edge. Staring down into the tower's shaft, through the wide gaps between the iron chain that formed a net, she saw the hard stone floor far below. Barely able to breathe, she swallowed when she saw the crimson blood stains at the bottom.

She tried to reach out to someone, anyone, but the collar around her neck interfered with her abilities. She pictured Eiric's face, but when she attempted to touch his mind, her senses hit a wall.

She screamed as the soldier pushed her from behind.

At the same instant, she felt the collar around her neck open. For a few seconds she tottered, arms waving wildly.

Eiric! Help me! she cried out with her mind.

But then the soldier gave her a second hard shove and she fell down into the deep central shaft of the tower.

She plummeted through the net of iron chain in an instant. The encircling stone wall passed by in a blur. As her limbs clawed at the air, her body tumbling, the ground rushed up at her.

Just a moment before, she'd seen a slave girl's head shatter on the stone. Utterly terrified, wailing in fear, staring up at the sky and watching the circle of blue sky grow smaller and smaller, she was unable to prevent her instinctive response.

She imagined halting her flight, growing wings that would prevent her fall. With every fiber of her being focused on fleeing this terrible place, the shift was dramatic and instantaneous.

Suddenly she felt the familiar sensation of changing, her body elongating and wild thoughts overwhelming all others. A gray cloud whitened her vision. Relief flooded through her, as just before striking the ground, she became a dragon.

Her powerful wings beat away the last shreds of mist. A few sweeps arrested her motion as she rolled. She stared up at the circle of blue sky overhead, thoughts confused, filled only with a desire to escape. She put on as much speed as she could, climbing the shaft again.

With a shudder she crashed painfully into the net.

Shrieking and wheeling, she hit the wall and then craned her neck downward to see slaves in ragged tunics calling out to each other, watching her intently.

In their hands were lengths of iron chain, some slender as whips, others thick and heavy. Desperate to get away from them, she flew up to strike the net again. With nowhere to go, she slammed hard against the stone wall, scratching at it with her forelimbs, biting and snapping in vain.

Something grabbed hold of her leg. The grip of iron was painful, making her shudder at the touch of cold metal.

Screeching, she peered down and saw a chain wrapped around her hind leg. The chain went taut as three slaves pulled in unison, hauling her toward them. Now spiraling out of control, she crashed into the opposite wall while still more slaves worked together to bring her to the ground.

A moment later she struck the blood-streaked floor, sending the slaves scattering. Braver souls ran forward, throwing iron netting over her, pinning her down. She snapped at anyone who came near, reaching out with her claws, even as she became tangled. Glaring at her enemies, she promised to disembowel the first who dared to come close.

The circling slaves hung back, wide eyes filled with terror, torn between the threat of not following their orders and the danger posed by the silver-scaled dragon in the center of the tower's floor.

Two men in gray robes pushed through.

As Liana glared at them darkly, a rumbling growl began deep in her chest and exited through the gaps in her sharp teeth. She immediately recognized the short man with the burned face who had captured her. His companion, a bearded older man, raised a staff with a golden disc on its summit and suddenly she was blinded.

She snapped and writhed, lunging in all directions, but before her vision could clear, a heavy iron collar went around her neck, and she heard a click as it was swiftly fastened tight enough to constrict her breathing. For a brief moment she was stunned. The encroaching wildness that came from being in another form had vanished, as had the ability to change back to her normal shape.

Panicked, as the stars darting across her vision subsided and her sight returned, she lunged at a scrawny slave nearby. A swipe from her claw sent the man flying through the air until he crashed against the wall. Her tail lashed out, whipping another slave across the neck.

Moving with surprising dexterity, the robed man with the melted face came around her other side and fixed strange reins of shining copper to the collar.

Liana went still. She was suddenly transfixed, unable to move. There was a connection between her and the scar-faced sorcerer. She could sense his satisfaction at dominating her will. In turn, she felt violated, knowing he was aware of her every thought.

'A fierce one,' said the bearded sorcerer who had called the blinding light. 'The biggest we've had yet. And look at her color. Bright silver. You don't think . . . Magus Tarik, is her blood pure?'

'How would I know?' Tarik's voice rasped. He turned and barked at the slaves. 'Clear this place up. It's a mess.'

He then took the copper chains and led Liana away.

———   ———

'I was right there looking at him,' Finn said.

'How is he?' Chloe asked, leaning forward on the table. They were alone in a corner of The Trader's Rest, and she was anxious to hear every word.

'Bad.' Finn winced. 'I'm sorry, but he's not in a good way.'

'How bad?'

'I couldn't look at him too closely, but he's been hurt. He's chained to the wall, and just . . . sits there, staring at the ground like he's lost all hope. He must have known who I was, but when I tried to catch his eye, he didn't even glance at me.'

Cob coughed and looked away. Chloe put her head in her hands. She told herself she had to be strong.

'At least we know where he is,' she said hoarsely, forcing the words out. 'We can do something now to free him. What about Liana? Did you find anything out about where they might have taken her?'

'I'm sorry,' Finn said with a sigh, shrugging. 'I didn't even know about her until now.'

'A man at the market said something about dragons flying in the night,' Chloe continued. 'He said they come out of the tower. Does that mean anything to you?'

'The Sky Tower . . . That's where Isobel was killed,' Cob said. 'There's always a guard outside the door.'

'Do you think Liana's there?'

'I don't know,' Finn said. He put vague hope into his voice. 'I might find out more tomorrow.'

'By the gods, what's happening in this world?' Cob rubbed his hand over his face. 'Princess . . .'

'I'm not a princess anymore.'

'Chloe . . . I'm going to be frank with you: Finn and I . . . We're out of our depth. We're going to need you to find out whatever it is that's going on here.'

'I'll try.' She was silent for a time, before she looked up sharply. 'I want to see him.'

Finn shook his head. 'I don't think that's poss—'

'I said I want to see him. You managed to.'

'It's too dangerous,' Finn protested.

Chloe lifted her chin. 'Tell me exactly what you saw, and what was said. I'll find a way to make it work.'

Cob gave a wry chuckle. 'You're exactly the way Dion always said you were.'

Finn frowned, but Chloe continued to stare directly into his eyes. Finally he started to talk.

41

Chloe watched, amazed, as a transformation came over Finn before he'd even reached the palace. Suddenly he was walking with long strides, despite the fact that he wasn't a tall man. He lifted his chin and put a disdainful, self-important expression on his face. Remembering her part, Chloe scurried after him, head down and shoulders slightly hunched. She furrowed her brow, trying to make herself appear obsequious, and slightly worried, which wasn't difficult at all given the circumstances.

Her heart was racing. Even if all went well, she would soon be face to face with the people who'd killed Isobel. She would see Dion, and if she was lucky, speak to him. It already weighed down on her to think of the pain he must have endured. She was frightened at the thought of seeing it written across his face.

Finn slowed to allow her to catch up. 'Do you have any acting experience?' he asked under his breath. He threw up his hands. 'Of course you don't. Why did I ever agree to this?'

'I can read and write.' Chloe frowned. 'We won't be caught.'

She held a roll of papyrus in one hand and clutched a satchel over her shoulder. The satchel and papyrus had both cost a fortune, but Finn insisted on procuring only the best.

'That remains to be seen,' Finn muttered. He glanced ahead, before meeting her eyes. 'We're almost there. Remember, you are my scribe and I am your master. I will act accordingly, and I expect you to do the same. Follow behind me at all times, and keep your head down. Write what I tell you to write. Never question. Speak as little as possible. Understood?'

'Yes.' Chloe scowled. 'I understand.'

'Good. This is no game, Chloe.'

Finn increased his stride once more, forcing Chloe to walk with quick steps to keep up with him as she followed from a distance. They were now skirting a long fence of iron spikes, and soon came to an open set of gates, where half a dozen pale-skinned warriors stood guard.

Making a dramatic entrance, Finn didn't slow in the slightest as he swirled his cloak and imperiously swept through with nothing more than a slight nod. 'Fustalonious, king's chronicler,' he called without slowing, as if far too busy to give them more than an instant of his time.

'Let him through.' The guards stood aside to let them past, but as they crossed a central courtyard Chloe saw another pair of guards standing at the base of a set of steps. These two were watching them intently as they approached.

Finn gave a broad smile, coming to a halt. 'I am Fustalonious, king's chronicler'—he bowed—'and this is my scribe.' When Finn nodded at her, Chloe kept her eyes on the ground.

As the guards examined them both, Chloe struggled to keep her composure. If she appeared frightened, or attracted their curiosity, their plan would fail, and she and Finn would most likely be killed.

'The king is expecting you,' the older of the two guards said in a deep baritone.

'Come, scribe,' Finn ordered.

Chloe followed close behind as he climbed the steps and then walked along a stone passage with soft mats of dyed wool underfoot. Light beckoned ahead and then she saw that they were approaching an expansive throne room.

Finn entered grandly. Chloe trailed after him, but she couldn't help herself.

Her eyes immediately went to Dion.

He was slumped against the rear wall with an iron collar around his neck and his hands behind his back. There were manacles around his wrists, connected by a chain to a metal hoop embedded in the wall. His sharp jaw was clean-shaven, his flaxen hair was oiled, and his tunic was clean – but his downcast face was pained; she could see that at a glance. She felt a surge of emotion, wanting nothing more than to rush to his side, but she tore her eyes away.

Her gaze then moved to the tall king standing at one of the windows and staring out to sea.

Palemon was everything Finn had said he was: tall and regal, with flowing dark hair streaked with gray, and a long beard fashioned into braids. He wore a bleached leather vest, black trousers, and high boots. When he turned to acknowledge Finn's entry, his eyes were narrowed and penetrating, his strong jaw fixed with determination.

Chloe's hands felt clammy and sweat broke out on her brow. She was suddenly extremely grateful for Finn's presence, for his confidence and habit of drawing attention.

'Great King,' Finn said, walking with his head held high to the center of the room. 'I hope this day finds you well.' He gave a complicated bow, twirling his cloak, and then glared at Chloe.

Shaking herself, Chloe scurried to stand just behind Finn before sinking to her knees and putting her head on the floor. She wondered if she was doing it right: the customs of the south were novel to say the least, and she only had her memories of the sun king's court in Ilea to go by. Glancing at Finn, she saw him jerk his chin for her to get up, and climbed to her feet, although she kept her eyes fixed firmly on the floor.

'Who is this?' Palemon's voice was like his appearance: bold, commanding, solid. His accent had the same clipped inflections as the men who'd taken Liana.

'She is my scribe, Great King,' Finn said.

Palemon's gaze flickered to Chloe. 'A female scribe?'

'The city is short on scribes,' Finn said with a smile and a shrug.

Palemon's eyes lingered on her for an instant before dismissing her.

'Once again,' Finn continued, 'I thank you for allowing me to chronicle your rise to greatness. I am sure you have many matters to attend to, and so I will keep these visits short. Please, continue doing what you were doing before I arrived. May I begin by taking note of your description?'

'Whatever you think best.' Palemon turned back to the window, staring out to sea, in the direction of the Lost Souls, the peaked islands that marked the sunken city of Aleuthea.

'Close to seven feet tall,' Finn said softly, 'with eyes like coal – eyes that can penetrate a man's flesh to peer into his soul. Scribe?'

With a start, Chloe remembered what she was supposed to be doing. She swiftly unrolled the papyrus, looking around for somewhere to work before finally seating herself on the floor. She took two small clay pots out of her satchel and set them down on the ground, the first containing water, the second pigment. Taking a reed, she dipped it in water and then rubbed it over the powdered coal.

She wrote as Finn elaborated, describing his subject's virtues. Her hand moved furiously, and Chloe silently thanked her father, Aristocles, for insisting that she study at the temple.

Palemon suddenly turned. 'The king of Xanthos tells me that recently wildren roamed the seas, the land, and the skies, but that this is no more. Tell me, chronicler, is this true?'

Chloe fumbled, making a mistake in her work. As soon as she heard that Dion had given Palemon information, she couldn't stop herself from staring at him. But he made no sign at all, still sitting slumped and dejected, staring at the ground. Her heart reached out to him as she thought about how hard it must be for him to give Palemon the knowledge he wanted without betraying the people he loved.

'Yes, Great King,' Finn said. 'The eldran king, Eiric, blew the horn, and—'

'What name did you just say?' Palemon's eyes flashed. He glanced at Dion, and then rounded on Finn. 'Did you just say *Eiric*?' He marched over to Dion and put his fingers under his captive's chin, lifting Dion's head. 'This one told me his name was Triton.'

'Triton is correct, Great King,' Finn said hurriedly. 'He has one eye, and leads with a strong hand—'

Palemon let Dion's head fall as he turned again to Finn. 'Then why did you say Eiric?'

Chloe knew Finn well enough to see the tightness in his eyes. Even so, his manner was still poised and confident, despite the danger they were in.

'Eiric is the Ilean name for him,' Finn said. 'In their ancient language, it means "He with One-Eye . . ."'

Chloe had a sudden realization, accompanied by a faint stirring of hope. Dion was lying to Palemon. The fact that he was filling his enemy's head with nonsense told her that perhaps he wasn't as broken as he appeared to be.

'Hmm . . .' Palemon began to pace the length of the room, evidently thinking about the eldren and their king.

'Great King.' Finn licked his lips.

'What is it?'

'Today I will set the scene, taking note of physical descriptions and principal actors, and tomorrow we will begin on the detailed story of your exile and return.' Finn paused. 'But there is one thing I would like to see first. The great sword that you wielded when you conquered the city. Perhaps we could fetch it? And on the way you could tell me about the land you came from. My scribe can remain here and take note of this impressive audience chamber, with its throne and royal captive.'

Palemon glanced at Chloe. He waved a hand.

'Scribe.' Finn nodded at her. 'Make sure to capture the full magnificence of the throne.' He then turned to Palemon. 'Now, King Palemon. What was it like? This land across the sea?'

'It was cold,' Palemon said. 'I did not realize how cold it was until I came to these lands . . .'

Palemon and Finn walked out of the room together, their voices drifting away.

Knowing that the time had come, Chloe's chest began heaving nearly as fast as the tempo of her heart. She collected her materials and quickly shuffled over to Dion until she was sitting beside him.

'Dion,' she whispered. 'It's me.'

Close up, the suffering was written across his face. Her eyes burning, she saw him through blurred vision as she waited for a reaction. Finn had said he was a broken man, but even that description hadn't come close to what she was seeing now. She prayed for some sign that he was still in there, somewhere.

'Please, Dion. It's Chloe.' She blinked and a tear fell from her eye, trickling down her cheek. 'Please . . . Dion, look up.'

Suddenly he spoke in an undertone, growling with surprising vehemence. 'I know it's you. Leave. Get out while you can.'

'We're here to help you.'

'I can't be helped.' He lifted his head to look up, and now the expression on his face was pure malice. 'I'm waiting for my opportunity, and then I'm going to kill him.'

'Dion, listen to me. You can't. You'll be throwing your life away.'

'My life is gone already. They killed her in front of me. They took all I had.'

The low murmur of Finn's conversation with Palemon suddenly returned, becoming louder. Chloe's breath caught. As soon as the two men entered the room, she realized it was too late to leave Dion's side. With a shaking hand she dipped her stylus and started making marks on the parchment, pretending to be taking note of her surroundings, including the chained-up man beside her.

But then there was a new sound of approaching footsteps and she heard a strong, female voice.

'Sire,' the woman called, her speech as sharp as a knife, telling Chloe that she was someone who had no qualms about interrupting her king. 'I need to speak with you. Alone.'

'This is Zara,' Palemon said to Finn. 'I am sure you will have no problem taking note of her appearance.'

Chloe glanced up and her eyes shot wide open.

The cold-faced sorceress she'd faced on the Maltherean Sea stood barely a dozen paces away. The woman was exactly as she'd been when they'd faced each other in a contest of wind: straight, midnight-black hair, high cheekbones, brilliant blue eyes, and skin like stone. If she saw Chloe's face . . . the deception would be over.

'Who is this, sitting there with the half-breed?' The sorceress's eyes narrowed when she saw Chloe. Chloe kept her head down, like a lowly scribe should, allowing her long, dark hair to fall around her face.

Finn's voice sparkled with forced jocularity. 'She is my scribe, and documenting the physical features of your captive — eye color, hair color . . . I'm sure you understand. However, I am here to chronicle, not to impede. Scribe, you are finished. Come.'

The sorceress glared, but Chloe continued to keep her head down and back to the woman. She collected her possessions and then hurriedly followed Finn out of the chamber.

⌣

'Well?' Palemon raised an eyebrow, but Zara waited until the fool and his scribe had departed before she spoke.

'I have news, sire. It is as we predicted. A great fleet is embarking from Lamara. King Kargan leads personally.'

Palemon looked out at the sea. 'So, sorceress, the moment presents itself, our crisis and opportunity. Everything hangs in the balance. You are certain you can expose the sunken city?'

'Not all of it, of course, but from Cape Cush I believe we can hold the sea at bay while we explore the vault beneath the Great Tower of Aleuthea.'

'Hmm.' Palemon rubbed his eyes; his sleep had been even worse lately, visions of his people in Necropolis making him cry out in the night. 'Let us say for a moment that we are successful – if we are not, then nothing will help us. Let us say that we find dozens of magical chains. How would you suggest we capture so many eldren? It has been a long time since a half-breed turned up in the city.'

'A carefully planned raid. We take the dragons we have to Sindara, arriving in the dead of night. We collar and capture as many as we can before returning and chaining them.'

Palemon shook his head. 'There's so much that can go wrong.'

'There is no other way.'

'How far is Cape Cush?'

'With soldiers and slaves . . .' Zara replied. 'No more than a few days' travel.'

'This Arch of Nisos? You still have no idea what it might do?' Palemon asked.

'None.'

His scowled, but he finally nodded. 'Six dragons are not enough to achieve our goals. If we can get more chains from Aleuthea then we can bend more beasts to our will. Your magi are ready?'

'They are, sire. All we need is the order.'

'Then tell Kyphos to prepare for our departure.'

42

The day after visiting the palace, Chloe sat in a corner of The Trader's Rest, staring into the dregs of her tea. She heard a voice call her name and looked up to see Cob approaching. He glanced around before seating himself opposite her.

'Where have you been?' Chloe asked.

'Exploring. Talking to people. Learning. Aren't you supposed to be with Finn?'

Chloe explained what had happened, telling Cob about Dion's quest for revenge and her almost being seen by the sorceress. 'And so Finn thinks it best I don't go back with him.'

'He has the right of it,' Cob said. 'He's there now? At the palace?'

Chloe nodded. 'He's hired a real scribe. He'll simply say that he finally found a man.'

'Fair enough.' Cob sighed. 'So the poor lad's not as broken as he appears.'

'He's vengeful,' she said. 'I'm worried that he'll do something that will get him killed.'

Cob rubbed at the wrinkles on his forehead before sighing again. 'Chained as he is, I can't see a way to free him. You think Palemon would ransom him?'

'Not for gold. For ships, maybe.'

He shook his head. 'Dion would die rather than give up the fleet he's built.'

'I know,' Chloe said sadly.

'Listen,' Cob said. 'While you and Finn have been busy . . . I think I might know where your friend is.'

Chloe looked up sharply.

'People talk,' Cob said with a shrug. 'They're keeping dragons in that tower, somewhere in a vault underneath. Meanwhile anyone with odd-colored eyes gets rounded up and is never seen again. When you put the two together . . .'

Finn entered the tavern. Scanning the room, he finally saw Cob and Chloe and hurried over. 'I have news.'

'Is it Dion?' Chloe asked. 'Is he all right?'

'Just as you last saw him. Didn't meet my eyes, not once.'

'What is it?' Cob asked.

'They're planning some kind of magic, something big,' Finn said. 'Parting the sea, they called it. There's a promontory a few days' march from here – Cape Cush . . . Cob and I saw it from the *Liberty* when we last came to Malakai. It's the closest point between the mainland and the Lost Souls. Everyone's going there. They're assembling slaves and almost all their soldiers on the shore.'

Chloe lifted her head. 'This could be our chance. While they're away, we can—'

'No such luck, I'm afraid.' Finn interrupted. 'Palemon wants me there, and he's bringing Dion too.'

There was silence for a time as they pondered. Chloe again remembered the Oracle's words, a suggestion of danger, a fork in the road, rather than prophecy. *If unchallenged, they will gain the power of artifacts better left at the bottom of the sea.*

'I have an idea,' she said slowly. 'The sorcerers plan to part the sea. We all know the reason why. There is something they want in the sunken city. Something important.' She met Cob and Finn's eyes. 'We can't let them have it.'

'But how can we—' Cob began.

'There's only one way I can think of them going about it.' In response to their puzzled expressions, Chloe explained. 'The four materia – gold, silver, copper, and iron – each correspond to a power. Gold can bring light. Silver can harness the wind. Copper can manipulate sound. Iron can project fire.' She paused. 'Only one power would allow them to part the sea. They are going to use the wind.'

Cob and Finn exchanged glances.

Chloe continued, 'We've worked out that they brought perhaps a dozen sorcerers with them from the place they left. Have you seen any in the streets lately? My guess is they are all busy working on the spell. Something that powerful is going to require their combined strength. But,' she said slowly, 'wind is dangerous and unpredictable. The magic is easily disrupted.'

'What are you saying?' Finn asked.

'I think I can break the spell.'

Cob frowned, while Finn looked merely puzzled.

'Think about it,' Chloe said. 'The sea parts, exposing the city. They enter.' She clapped her hands together, making Cob jump. 'The sea rushes back in.'

The old sailor's brow furrowed. 'We'd kill them all. It would be chaos.'

'And in that chaos we could free Dion.'

'How?' Finn asked.

'With Liana's help.' She held out both her hands, and first Cob, and then Finn, clasped her palm. 'And with yours.'

———

It was just after dawn, a time when only a few early risers walked the streets. Chloe forced down her fear as she followed Finn to the gaping maw of the archway at the base of the Sky Tower. This time, she wasn't pretending to be a scribe. She clutched her reassembled staff in one hand, the silver spiral just above her clenched fingers. This time, she was ready to fight.

Chloe's mouth tightened. Her friend was somewhere under the tower. Liana had come to Chloe's aid when she'd been drifting on the Maltherean Sea.

Now Liana needed her.

Two soldiers stood guard outside, both holding huge crossbows, the weapons cocked and ready. Pale-skinned men from across the sea, they were clad in armor of metal links and wore two-handed swords in sheaths strapped to their backs. The scars on their hands and their cold-eyed stares made it clear that these were men who weren't afraid of fighting.

As she and Finn approached the guards, Chloe saw something on the ground that almost made her stop and stare. It was a faint, reddish-brown smear, staining the paved stones of the road. Chloe swallowed, remembering how Isobel had met her end. With an effort she kept walking.

Wearing his expensive crimson cloak, Finn strode up to the closest soldier, a young man with a bristling black beard, and looked him straight in the eye.

'I am Fustalonious, king's chronicler, here on the orders of King Palemon.'

The two soldiers lifted their crossbows and exchanged glances.

'Let us in,' Chloe said firmly.

'Who are you?' The bearded soldier asked Chloe. He glanced at her staff, seeing the silver twist at the top. His frown deepened. 'You are not from—'

Chloe pointed her staff at the guard and released her power. In an instant the silver device flared up with white light and a blast of air struck him in the center of his chest. His eyes shot wide open as he flew back and slammed against the tower wall. With a sound like the crack of a whip, his back broke before he crumpled.

The next soldier fumbled for the lever of his crossbow as she turned to him. Chloe brought forth a second surge of inner fire, feeling it flow through her body, channeled into the silver. She leveled her staff and wind punched into his chest, throwing him back against the stone, his feet several inches above the ground as his face became filled with terror.

Chloe's eyes narrowed as she thought about the smear of Isobel's blood on the ground. She walked forward, still holding the staff pointed at the soldier, with the constant surge of silver flame cascading through her mind, scattering her thoughts but leaving her anger intact. She summoned more of the white fire, her staff glowing fiercely as she moved it from low to high, sending the man sliding up the tower wall until he was high above the ground. His eyes were wild as he shook his head from side to side.

Only then did she break contact with her power. The soldier plummeted to the earth, striking hard enough to kill him.

She hurried to the open entrance of the tower. Reaching the dead guard, she crouched and drew his dagger from the scabbard at his belt.

Finn was looking at Chloe with wide eyes.

'Take this.' She handed him the dagger. 'Come on.'

With Chloe in the lead, they plunged inside and followed a broad corridor. Passing a second, inner archway, Chloe glanced at the tower's interior shaft, devoid of people, but with dried blood smeared on the paving stones. Exchanging glances with Finn, she kept moving. The floor began to slope downward, and it was some time before they came to an immense door that perfectly filled the stone tunnel, made of what appeared to be gold.

Chloe noticed the symbols around the golden door. Similar symbols decorated the device at the top of her staff.

The golden door was open, and now Finn's heavy breathing betrayed his fear. Dagger held out in front of him, he followed just behind her as they entered another corridor, taking them deep beneath the tower.

Entering a cavernous chamber, first Chloe, and then Finn, came to a halt.

Flickering torches lit up walls of stone and a row of iron cages. Chloe smelled the sickening stench of caged animals. Written on one wall was jagged lettering in a language she couldn't understand.

A dark figure lunged out of the shadows.

A soldier ran at them, swinging his sword. Remembering the teachings of her bodyguard, Tomarys, Chloe weaved to the side and thrust out her staff at ankle height. The guard tripped and lost his footing, falling face forward on the stone. Finn crouched and grunted as he made a swift movement with the dagger. The guard went still.

For a time there was silence as they both scanned the area for more enemies. As her eyes adjusted to the dim light, Chloe lifted her staff when she saw a figure in the corner, but then lowered it. The wretch was an elderly slave, huddled with his hands above his face. He was cowering near a long water trough and a series of buckets.

'Keep an eye on him,' she said to Finn.

She moved to the row of cages, taking her first good look at their occupants. She drew in a sharp breath.

Ten of the twelve cells had creatures inside them, wretched-looking dragons with breath rumbling in their chests and shivering wings. Their heads were all raised: they were watching her and Finn with intent, almond-shaped eyes. She approached the nearest cage and the creature inside suddenly lunged at the bars, stopping short just before crashing into the black iron, snarling and making her leap back.

Warily continuing her assessment, traveling along the row, she saw that the dragons' colors ranged from jet-black to dark silver. Some of them had strange copper chains fastened to their collars.

Finally she stopped.

The lean, silver-scaled dragon was the largest of them all and the only one of its color. Lifting her head, Liana looked out at Chloe with pain-filled eyes the shade of green grass.

'Chloe,' Finn hissed. 'I can hear shouts. Be quick.'

Chloe swiftly threw the bolt and pulled the gate open to enter the cage. Her brow furrowed as she approached Liana and examined the red metal chains fastened to the collar around her neck. Magical symbols decorated the connecting clasp between the two lengths, and they were draped on either side of Liana's flanks like reins. As the shouts become louder and Chloe heard the clatter of footsteps, she clasped a length of copper and her eyes went wide.

The bond with Liana was real and immediate. In an instant Chloe knew that the Aleutheans' magic gave her the power to dominate her friend utterly. It was a feeling of both intimacy and violation. She could sense Liana's mingled fear and hope. It made her feel sick.

'Chloe!' Finn cried.

Reaching over Liana's neck, Chloe found the central joint and unclasped it, tossing the strange reins to the ground. But when she looked at the collar, she realized that the stout iron only fastened in one direction, like a barbed arrow. There was no apparent way to remove it.

She began to feel panic. How did they remove the collars? She knew there must be a way. As Liana began to stamp at the ground, Chloe furiously examined the collar, but could see no way of opening it.

'Chloe!' Finn called.

Biting her lip, she thought about the magus who'd captured Liana. He'd carried a staff with an iron claw: a fire staff. She thought about what she knew of the crafting of iron, which was little, but she knew that heat could make iron expand. In this case, the heat would have to be extreme, and it would have to be perfectly focused, or the wearer of the collar would die.

Finally Chloe cast her mind back to her time with Vikram. The magi at Athos hadn't taught her the use of iron, but she knew that anger could feed the flame inside. But it was dangerous. If she got it wrong, the magic could cause Chloe to burst into flame.

She thrust the thought to the side. She needed anger, not fear, but anger was easy to come by. These people had captured her friend and enslaved her, keeping her in a cage like an animal.

Closing her eyes, Chloe put her hand around the iron hoop and fed the fire inside her mind.

She drew on her anger, at the same time imagining a fire without light, without wind, without sound. It was as black as coal and filled her from head to toe with heat. Her skin prickled, the sensation strongest where her fingers gripped the iron. The fastening felt warm in her hands and then searing hot. The dragon whimpered, and Chloe gasped as she felt an explosion of flame inside her. Heat came to her cheeks, but then suddenly the collar fell open.

Chloe threw the circle of black iron to the ground. As Finn shouted at her to hurry and men's shouts grew louder, she knew there was only one way for them to escape. 'Liana, can you stay in this form, for just a little longer?'

The dragon gave Chloe a surprisingly determined expression. Without warning, the silver dragon hurtled past Chloe toward the open door of the cage and spun in a tight turn, forelegs scratching at the ground, wings crackling like a sail catching the wind.

Chloe ran out of the cage. She saw Finn standing guard, peering into the corridor. 'Finn!'

Hoisting her staff, Chloe pulled herself up onto the dragon's back as Finn rushed over, awkwardly climbing on behind her. The silver dragon put her head down and started to run.

Immediately four running soldiers came into view. Chloe held on tightly with one hand and pointed her staff up the tunnel. She fed the fire inside and felt the power of the materia rush to the surface and travel into the metal spiral. She drew on every reserve, even as exhaustion threatened to crush her and pain spiked through her temples. With a cry she sent a burst of wind through the tunnel powerful enough to blow them tumbling out of sight.

Liana gathered speed as they climbed the tunnel, and then Chloe saw bright light. They raced through the archway leading to the vertical shaft and Liana's wings opened up. A piercing shriek of joy bounced off the walls as they flew up and out of the tower, heading in the direction of the rising sun.

'Well,' Finn called. 'I suppose that's the end of Fustalonious.'

43

Dion stumbled, the whipcord tied to his collar pulling tight. The sudden tension pressed the iron band against his skin, choking him before he managed to keep moving and create some slack.

His hands were tied behind his back with tough leather. He knew that if he fell, he wouldn't be able to prevent his head striking the ground. Hauling him by the whipcord, the camel moaned in irritation. The wide-bellied, long-legged beast had no trouble navigating the uneven terrain, forcing him to jog to keep up. Nestled in a huge, curved saddle just behind the animal's hump, Palemon rode the camel comfortably, his eyes fixed straight ahead.

In the distance, heat rose from the ground in shimmering waves, while high above, the sky was devoid of clouds, promising that the blazing sun would only grow fiercer as it rose to dominate the sky. The air smelled of sweat and animals. All around, camels grumbled and donkeys hawed. Warriors from the frozen north were red-faced in their chain mail but never made a sound of complaint. A sharp crack came from the direction of the baggage train: somewhere a porter's shoulders had been sliced by the lick of the slave master's whip.

It was an immense column leaving behind the city of Malakai, heading for Cape Cush and the treasures they hoped to find beneath the sea. The king led from the front, towing Dion like an animal being taken to market, while behind them walked several gray-robed sorcerers and scores of Palemon's soldiers. Not far from the king, Zara and Kyphos were both riding camels of their own.

Panting as he tried to moisten his parched lips, Dion distracted himself by thinking about the days ahead, and Zara's plan to unearth the relics of Aleuthea. He wondered whether he would be able to take advantage of the situation to kill the man he'd sworn he would destroy. Much of his submissiveness and halting speech was pretense, but he knew that he was far from at his strongest. Nonetheless, if the chance came, he would seize it without question. He would take Palemon's life, even if it cost him his own.

With little to do but ponder, his mind turned to Chloe and Finn. He hadn't seen Cob, but he knew the old man would be with them. Finn's ruse was over: Palemon was convinced that Fustalonious of Lyre – as he still believed Finn to be – had worked his way into the king's favor solely to free the dragons. The tall king had raged about his chronicler's deception, while Dion had fought to keep a smile from his face. He was glad that Chloe and Finn were now far away.

He coughed in the dust. The cord fastened to his collar jerked tight again as he struggled to keep moving.

———

Finn crouched behind a gnarled tree and peered from his hilltop perch, gazing in the direction of the shore. He watched as the cloud of dust finally revealed the shapes of men and animals. As expected, the column was traveling in the direction of Cape Cush, a promontory jutting out from the coast, with smooth rock vanishing into the sea below.

He lifted his gaze and saw Widow's Peak, one of the largest of the Lost Souls, and the closest to shore. He then looked back at the collection of soldiers and slaves traveling from Malakai. They'd finally arrived. He needed to hurry back to let the others know.

He turned, preparing to leave his concealment, when he suddenly heard a piercing shriek, immediately followed by the sound of flapping wings.

He ducked as a charcoal-colored dragon flew overhead. Tilting his head back, he saw the huge flying creature's underbelly and the sun shining through the thin wings, revealing bones and pulsing veins. The strong hind legs were tucked up under its body and its tapered head darted about as it sped past.

Finn saw the armored rider, reins of copper in his hands, sweep his eyes over the terrain before he performed a tight turn. He climbed the sky and hovered while his mount's powerful wings swept up and down with slow, leisurely movements.

The rider continued to scan the area, and Finn held his breath. He leaned into the scant protection of the desiccated tree, wishing it had some leaves. He hunched his head into his shoulders. He realized he had his eyes squeezed tightly shut.

The dragon shrieked again. Finn heard a snap as its wings caught the air. He counted the seconds, huddled to the trunk, waiting for a thump as the dragon's legs struck the ground.

Another animal cry sounded, but this time it was further away. Opening his eyes, Finn risked looking up. The twin arcs of dragon wings were becoming distant; it was climbing the sky and heading back toward the cape. He now saw several other winged silhouettes circling over the column like birds of prey eyeing a carcass. The riders all wore Aleuthean chain mail, glinting in the sun, and carried long, sharp spears.

Judging his moment carefully, he waited until the group had begun to settle in at the cape before breaking cover and running back to the hidden cove.

Finn found the others near the shore, resting in the shade of a rocky overhang. Chloe sat cross-legged on the sand, her eyes closed, breathing slowly in and out. Nearby, the slender eldran, Liana, still appeared harrowed, with shadows under her eyes and sallow skin, but she now looked better than she had in days.

'What are you doing?' Finn asked Chloe.

She opened her eyes. 'Meditating. You've seen them?'

'They're here,' he said.

'I sensed dragons,' Liana said. She glanced up at him, and he saw that her grass-green eyes were surprisingly steely. 'You weren't seen?'

'It was a close call. One of them . . .' Finn saw Liana's eyes narrow, and decided to cut his explanation short. 'No, I wasn't seen.'

'Then it's almost time,' Liana said.

'You're sure you're up to this?' Chloe asked her.

'You know what they did to me. Dion will have experienced far worse. I'll do whatever it takes to free him.'

'Liana is ready,' Finn said. 'And so am I.'

'But still no sign of Cob,' Chloe said. 'If I can break the spell, Liana can help me rescue Dion. But there's a good chance we'll both be weak, and without a boat . . .'

Finn rubbed his chin. He was more worried than he liked to admit. While they freed Liana, Cob's task had been to go back for the boat he and Finn had sailed to Malakai. 'He should have returned with the *Calypso* by now.'

'You said it was hidden? Could he be having difficulty finding it?'

'Cob?' Finn shook his head. 'No. The old man never forgets a thing. He must have run into trouble.' He gazed into the distance. 'I'm going to have to search for him.'

'I agree,' Chloe said. She spoke firmly. 'This doesn't change the plan. Liana and I will go to Widow's Peak. We will be overlooking the Great

Tower when they part the sea. If I can disrupt the spell, we'll be safely away from the water.' Her eyes narrowed. 'I plan to destroy as many of their soldiers and sorcerers as I can. I might even be able to take out Palemon himself.'

'But if I can't find Cob . . .'

'You have to. Find him. Find the *Calypso*. You can do this, Finn. We're counting on you.'

44

The sun climbed the sky. Gentle waves lapped the rocky shore. It was a pleasant day, with a sea breeze cooling bodies made hot by the long march and the rays of the radiant sun.

Palemon watched from his seat on a tall wooden throne, placed for his use not far from the water's edge, as Zara and her sorcerers made preparations for their magic.

He gazed out over the sea, looking at the distant shard: Widow's Peak. He thought about the city Zara's spell would reveal. The home of his forefathers.

Aleuthea. The greatest city the world had ever known.

A dozen generations may have lived in Necropolis, but long before that, Palemon's ancestors grew their island metropolis into the most powerful nation in the Realm of the Three Seas. They built the Library of Kantos, the Temple of the Magi, the Royal Palace, and the Tomb of Caphri. At the Coliseum, slaves from all over the Realm fought each other in bloody bouts before crowds of fifty thousand. Archmagus Nisos created great wonders: the golden disc and copper bell at the summit of the Lighthouse, the copper chains, and this mysterious arch.

Back in Necropolis, the magi had always told tales of Aleuthea, and there were written accords brought with the exiles from before the fall, but since his return, Palemon now knew far more about his ancestors. He knew that they enslaved the eldren and kept dragons in a vault below the Great Tower in Aleuthea, a structure that Zara said was visible through the sea, in the deep water below Widow's Peak.

Feeling anxiety and excitement in equal measure, he gripped the arms of his throne and watched as Kyphos got the slaves and soldiers into order while Zara assembled her magi just above the water's edge. His breath quickened as six sorcerers, some old, some young, but all skilled at commanding the wind, stood in a line facing the water. Overhead, swooping dragons circled at the height of the lowest clouds.

Soon all was ready.

Palemon glanced at the king of Xanthos, sitting on the hard rock beside the throne with shoulders hunched and head bowed between his knees. These so-called kings had no idea what real power was. They were soon going to find out.

Palemon scowled when he saw that Dion was barely aware of what was happening. He wanted him to see this. Feeling growing irritation, he clicked his fingers at a slave, who shuffled over, his head bowed in deference as he brought him a skin of water. Palemon took the skin and immediately tossed it at Dion's feet.

But he frowned when the king of Xanthos didn't move, merely looking up at him with a pained expression, lifting his wrists to show that they were bound with tough leather. Palemon drew the dagger at his belt and leaned down to whip the blade through the bindings. Immediately Dion reached down and picked up the skin, pulling out the stopper and drinking greedily.

'Watch, King of Xanthos,' Palemon said. 'One day, if the gods smile on you, it might be you writing this history.'

Dion ignored him, gulping mouthful after mouthful of water.

'Sire.' Zara approached. 'We are ready.'

Palemon drew in a long breath, savoring the moment, more tense and eager than he'd ever been before. 'What will I be able to see from here?'

'The Great Tower is our objective. I expect the structure to follow a similar configuration to the tower in Malakai, although its diameter is of course significantly larger.'

'Will we see the Royal Palace?'

Zara hesitated. 'No, sire. I am afraid it is much further out to sea. Our magic will not reveal it. But you may see the Lighthouse from here.'

Palemon closed his eyes and drew in another deep lungful of air before opening them again. He clutched the arms of the chair, his knuckles white. Finally he nodded at Zara. 'Begin.'

Zara walked to the front of the row of six magi facing Widow's Peak. She entered the sea, the breeze blowing her hair around her face as she stood with her ankles in the water and raised her staff high.

Everyone on the shore fell silent. Even the dragons cleared the skies, retreating from the open sea and the region of the Lost Souls.

Zara's staff began to glow.

For a moment nothing happened, but then, looking overhead, Palemon saw the clouds all moving, as if tugged in strange directions. They weren't following the same path: some scattered up the coast, some inland, others out to sea. But they were all moving away from the sorceress's staff.

A strong wind began to blow.

The six magi then lifted their staffs. Silver fire lit up every conical swirl at the tip of every pole. Palemon felt the hair rise on the back of his neck as the gusts of wind gathered pace.

Zara stepped forward until the water was at the depth of her calves. She lifted her staff still higher and cried out. The magi behind her then entered the shallows and began an eerie humming chant.

The sky was now entirely devoid of clouds. From slave to soldier to sorcerer, wind was blowing hair wildly and whipping clothing against bodies. Gripping the throne's arms so tightly that the wood creaked, Palemon leaned forward. He glanced down at the king of Xanthos and saw that he'd been looking up at Palemon, rather than at the sea.

'Watch,' Palemon said, his voice only just audible above the wind.

Zara now tilted her staff, lowering the tip inch by inch until it was horizontal, and then she was bringing the glowing silver cone down to the water. Palemon watched as a wave formed in front of her. It grew from nothing to become a towering crest as big as those he'd seen on the open ocean while sailing from Necropolis. The wave sucked up the water around it, becoming taller and fuller, drawing away from the sea bed underneath. It was growing by the instant, swelling into a towering wall, suddenly fifty feet high.

One moment Zara was calf deep in the water, the next she was standing on open ground.

Three of the sorcerers behind Zara peeled to the left, the other three to the right. Those on the left lowered their staffs and pushed the water to the left, while those on the right did the same in the other direction.

Zara now started to walk forward. Her hand danced around the silver cone at the top of her staff, and occasionally her high-pitched cry could be heard above the howling. The waves now grew to the size of mountains, looming cliffs of water a hundred feet in height . . . then two hundred.

The sorcerers continued forward. The wind flattened Zara's dress against her body and pulled at her long hair. The group descended, losing height, soon hundreds of paces from shore. When they were a mile out, on both sides of a cleared sea bottom, blue walls rose up as the magi held the sea at bay. Fish leaped from the slick walls of water to plop onto the sand that had been covered by ocean a moment ago.

Crabs skittered. Seaweed hugged the hulk of a fishing boat that sank long ago.

Palemon thanked the gods for the gift of the sorceress. No one else had her skill, or her ambition. Who else would be bold enough to attempt something like this?

With each step Zara and her brethren took, the walls of water on either side of them grew, until they were so tall that Palemon could no longer judge their height. Blood was roaring in his ears; he was flushed with excitement, and he had yet to see the ancient city.

The magi were now far from shore. When they were a quarter of the distance to Widow's Peak, two sorcerers, one on either side, stopped to hold the wall of ocean while the others continued.

There was now a pathway along the downward slope of the sea bed. Zara continued and eventually another pair of magi stopped and put their backs to each other as they faced the tall waves.

Unable to sit any longer, Palemon rose from his chair and stood with his fists bunched at his sides. In the distance, he could see the small figure of Zara walking down the ocean bed. On the narrow pathway, near one of the standing sorcerers, a sleek shark as big as Palemon himself writhed on the ground, mouth gaping as the thin slits of its gills sucked at the air. A school of baitfish shot out of the liquid wall, in the open air for a moment before plunging into the wall opposite. Three magi on either side of the path now held the sea at bay. Past Widow's Peak, a waterfall tumbled and foamed like the pale eruption of a volcano.

Zara was no longer walking; she was climbing a gentle slope. Ahead of her, water continued to recede from the terrain. Leaving behind the last pair of magi, she raised her staff and a blinding white light rolled out in a concussive wave.

Finally the sea parted to reveal the lost city of Aleuthea.

Every man and woman at the cape watched with mouths open as they looked upon a place that hadn't been seen in three hundred years. What was recently a mysterious sea was now a city filled with majestic structures of stone, all covered in dripping ocean growth. The city was lopsided; when it collapsed it fell at an angle. The worst damage must be on the far side, obscured by Widow's Peak, for what Palemon could see was surprisingly well ordered, although it was like a painting that had been ripped to shreds and then haphazardly put back together. Long jagged cracks had torn avenues in half; steps looked like something from a madman's dream; statues had fallen and tumbled down the hill.

Widow's Peak was now a mountain, spearing the sky between the two walls of water. Towering sheets of liquid, pushed back by magic alone, had peeled away from the Great Tower and were pent in place as if held back by the arms of the sea god.

The Great Tower was mostly intact, although a section of the top half had crumbled away. On lower ground was an even taller tower, tilted alarmingly but revealed in all its glory: the Lighthouse. Both were small in Palemon's vision but unmistakable. He felt a thrill course through him.

Palemon glanced at Kyphos, who was staring open-mouthed at the result of Zara's spell.

'Kyphos,' Palemon called over the wind.

Kyphos shook himself. He waved an arm and cried out, ordering the soldiers and slaves to head for the ancient city. Leading from the front, he became the first of a long line of people, all following the path between the high walls of parted sea to head for Aleuthea.

Palemon knew the danger, and couldn't help wondering how long the spell could last.

But despite agreeing to stay behind, he wished he were going with them.

From a rocky hollow on Widow's Peak, a hiding place that faced the mainland, Chloe and Liana suddenly found themselves looking down on the remains of a city. In an instant their island became a sharp peak overlooking the dripping structures. Their location gave them the perfect vantage to watch the breathtaking power of the sorcerers.

On either side of the path to the cape, impossibly tall waves loomed as if frozen in time. The crests curled inward again and again, only to be thrown back by the wind before repeating the cycle.

'How long can they hold back the sea?' Liana asked, raising her voice to be heard above the howling wind.

'I don't know.' Chloe shook her head. She saw one of the six sorcerers stationed to maintain the spell moving, and then realized that the silver spiral at the end of his staff had crumbled away almost to nothing. The radiant light faded, but he was ready, and reached into a satchel to pull out another device and fix it to the end of his staff. A moment later a silver glow shone from the new spiral. 'It can't last forever.'

'Look, here they come.' A thin line of slaves and soldiers now walked along the path that had recently been ocean bed. Liana cast an anxious glance in Chloe's direction. 'You can break this spell?'

'I . . . I think so.' She nodded decisively. 'I can.'

Chloe could feel the magic coursing through the air. The fire inside her welled up; with so much wind around her, she knew she wouldn't have any difficulty summoning her power.

'When?' Liana asked.

'Finn said Palemon would be watching from the shore. Dion will be with him. Just be ready.'

Chloe watched the long column of armored soldiers as they herded the ragged slaves up the slope and then through the city, weaving around fallen blocks of stone and climbing slippery steps, always heading toward the tall tower below.

She knew that if she could break the spell she needed to catch as many as possible when the sea rushed back. If the water enveloped them when they were burdened with the artifacts they'd come for, there would be no chance they could ever be recovered again.

Zara was down there, and the hunchback, Kyphos. She could see them both clearly. The raven-haired sorceress was the first to reach the tower.

45

Puffing and panting, far from the events at Cape Cush, Finn followed the shore as he rounded a tall headland. Leaping from rock to rock, scrambling across a gully where the sea surged below, he finally climbed a crest and on the opposite side saw the familiar cove.

He cursed.

They'd thought the *Calypso* would be safe on this small sandy beach obscured by rock on all sides; even the approach from the sea was partly hidden. But neither Cob nor the *Calypso* was anywhere to be seen.

He climbed down to the beach and then paused, hands on his hips as he bent from the waist, chest heaving as he regained his breath.

He scanned the area. The sand had been broken up by the footprints of many men. A long gouge, unmistakably made by the *Calypso*'s keel, led directly to the water.

He decided to climb higher to gain a vantage.

It took him a long time, slipping and scrabbling at the rock, scrambling on all fours, but finally he reached the top of the headland and gazed up and down the coast. He was too far from Cape Cush to see what was happening, but there was an eerie feel to the air, and he saw clouds moving, telling him the great spell was underway. He had to hurry. His friends needed him.

Turning, he shielded his eyes, gazing in the other direction, away from the cape and further up the coast. The headland gave way to a long beach, and as he squinted, he realized he could see a cluster of dark shapes. A thin stream of smoke rose from a fire. *Some kind of camp. That lump could be a boat . . .*

He began to scrabble down, ignoring the stitch in his side.

———

Finn approached the camp boldly, chin held high, despite being unarmed.

The desert clansmen were in the throes of a festivity.

At least a dozen men were seated around the fire, clapping and singing. Farther away, a tribesman wrapped in loose cloth was urinating against the cliff. The sand was soft underfoot and made a fine bed for those who'd already drunk their fill of fermented mare's milk, sleeping and snoring in the sun.

As he neared, Finn glanced past the camp to the sailboat pulled up high on the beach. The *Calypso* looked whole and undamaged. It was a valuable vessel, sleek and beautiful. These men weren't going to give it up lightly.

Nor would they give up their captive.

Finn's eyes were now on Cob. The old man was circling the fire, dancing a strange jig to the raucous calls of the clansmen.

Cob's shoulders were slumped as he stumbled around the narrow patch of sand between the fire and the onlookers. He kicked a burning log, wincing as he hopped on one foot for a few steps. His round face was bruised; he looked exhausted. He was barely able to dance from foot to foot, but every time he slowed someone shot an arrow into the sand at his feet and he wearily lifted his head to keep moving.

The music came from a man resting against a log and playing a warbling melody on a flute. Beside him, a companion flicked a rhythm on a drum held between his knees. A wineskin passed from one clansman to another. Clapping in time to the music, the revelers were singing some strange tribal tune, chanting with guttural voices and swaying from side to side. Someone occasionally let out a yip.

Finn scanned the group and saw that there was one clansman who wasn't singing. He had a hooked nose and a neatly trimmed beard, and unlike the others he sat on a carpet. Rather than drinking from the skin, he held a silver goblet that he sipped from sparingly.

Finn put a scowl on his face and walked through a gap between two of the seated men. He stood beside the fire and faced the man leaning back on the carpet.

The singing came to a halt. The clapping stopped. Cob sank to his knees, panting.

Finn ignored the mutters and stares and brought his eyebrows close together as he met the headman's gaze directly. He slowly lifted an arm to point at Cob.

'That man,' he said, 'is a thief.'

The headman shrugged, picking at his hooked nose. 'He stole from you. We stole from him.'

'No,' Finn said, shaking his head. He put an expression of indignant anger on his face, although deep within he was utterly terrified that he was going to get both himself and Cob killed. 'He didn't steal from me. He stole from the king. That vessel over there is the king's boat. And I am here to get it back.'

'King?' The headman ceased picking his nose and leaned forward, raising an eyebrow. 'Which king?'

Finn nodded in the direction of Cape Cush. 'The great King Palemon. Look at that boat. You think it belongs to an old dwarf?' He sneered in Cob's direction. 'It is the king's personal craft. He cares about it more than his favorite concubine. It is his joy, the one great love of his life. It gives him more pleasure than anything else in this world. And he wants it back.'

The headman looked at the *Calypso* and then at Finn. He licked his lips.

'Janko,' one of the onlookers said, 'we saw the army—'

'Silence,' the headman interrupted. He considered for a time. 'The king sent you to find it? Alone?'

'No,' Finn said, lowering his voice. His eyes drifted to the nearby cliff, high above the beach. 'Not alone.' He stopped talking, knowing that it was more powerful to let the headman come to his own conclusions.

'The king . . .' The headman began to look nervous. 'He won't punish us . . . ?'

'That depends on one thing,' Finn said. 'If I can give him the thief who took his beloved vessel.' He pointed at Cob. 'Alive.'

The headman's brow furrowed as he pondered. Finn turned his expression of disdain into a glare.

The headman suddenly climbed to his feet, spreading his arms and smiling. 'Of course the king may have it back. We were merely safekeeping it for him. Tell him that Janko of Negara is his loyal servant.'

'I will, Janko of Negara,' Finn said. 'Now someone bind him up for me. And get this boat launched. I'll sail it to the cape myself.'

Janko clicked his fingers, and his men leaped to do his bidding. Finn's heart was racing, but he kept his expression slightly irritated, watching with arms folded until the *Calypso* was being dragged to the water. He followed as they launched the vessel, throwing Cob, tied and bound, up front.

Only then did he nod to the headman and enter the shallows himself. He climbed aboard as the clansmen gave the boat a push and then they exited the water, watching from the shore.

Feeling the eyes of the desert men on him, Finn whispered urgently. 'How do I sail it?'

'Unwrap the ties around the sail,' Cob said hoarsely. 'Loosen that rope there, on the cleat.'

Finn followed Cob's instructions, knowing that the tribesmen were still standing on the beach and the waves were threatening to push the *Calypso* back to shore.

'Now pull on the rope to hoist the sail,' Cob wheezed. 'Harder! Quickly now! Good. Tie it up again.'

Finn leaped from one task to another, trying to appear calm rather than frantic with haste.

'Now take the tiller and keep us angled out to sea,' Cob instructed.

The sail crackled, stretching as it pocketed the wind, and Finn let out a sigh of relief as he finally left the watchers behind. As soon as they were out in deep water he found a knife and sliced through Cob's bonds.

'Now,' Cob growled, sitting up and rubbing his wrists. 'Not a word of this. To anyone. Ever.'

'Of course,' Finn said seriously. 'But I have to say, where did you learn to dance with such grace—?'

Cob lunged forward, and the boat tilted dangerously as Finn leaped out of the way.

46

His gaze fixed on the Great Tower, which loomed over the ancient city like a grave marker, Kyphos walked on the slippery paving stones, leading the thin line of soldiers and slaves from the front. He climbed step after broken step and passed through a stone arch, seaweed draping from it like a curtain, still standing despite all its years underwater.

Following an ancient road, the hunchback looked around himself in wonder. He saw stout houses and gutters on the sides of the streets, larger temples, and even a grand edifice of four stories.

A final set of wide steps led up to the tower.

A stout cylinder, it was as tall as the Sky Tower in Malakai but far wider, made of immense bands of fitted stones one on top of the other. It was discolored from its time under the sea, and a wide gouge was broken from its summit, but it was so similar to the tower in Malakai that its purpose was unmistakable.

Long ago, the inhabitants of this city had forced eldren into dragon form and caged them underneath this tower. When called to battle, the dragon riders of Aleuthea had poured forth in multitudes from the open top. Able to fly from one end of the Realm to the other, nothing had stood in their way.

Raising his head as he climbed the steps, Kyphos saw Zara standing outside the tower's entrance, staff in hand, looking out at the walls of water on either side. Now that the spell was established, only the six magi on the path to the cape were needed to maintain it.

'Sorceress!' he called out. She ignored him as she entered the arched opening at the base of the tower and vanished inside.

'Come on!' Kyphos called to his men, hurrying now.

He finally reached the top of the broken steps and checked behind him to see that the soldiers and slaves were still on their way. Calling out to the sorceress, he peeled aside the draping lengths of ocean growth and plunged into the darkness of the tower.

It took some time for his eyes to adjust, but soon he saw that the layout was similar to the tower in Malakai. Cocking his head, he heard Zara's footsteps further down the wide corridor. He headed after her, following a passage filled with creepers and weeds, shells and flopping fish. Fully aware that he didn't belong here, a place so recently underwater, he continued past the opening that led to the tower's central shaft and followed the sloping floor down.

He found Zara standing outside a sealed metal door of solid gold.

The sorceress muttered to herself as she brushed aside debris to reveal symbols where a handle would normally be. Closing her eyes, she pressed her fingertips to the gold and concentrated.

The symbols glowed with a sudden, fierce fire. They lit up in an instant and then the light slowly began to fade.

With a heavy creaking sound, the door swung open.

The floor beyond was dry.

Zara lifted her staff and pointed the silver device into the darkness beyond. A strong breath of air blew past Kyphos's back, gusting into the deep vault underneath the tower, refreshing the interior.

Kyphos heard the sound of boots on the stone floor and glanced behind him to see the first of the soldiers arriving. The man was wary, but looked relieved when he saw Kyphos standing with the sorceress. More men appeared behind him, brave warriors from Necropolis, who'd faced orcas and white bears, and assaulted the city of Malakai and won.

Looking ahead once more, Kyphos cursed. Zara had already gone through the door. With only the fading light of the symbols to see by, he could just make out the faintest outline of her silhouette.

'There may be danger,' Kyphos called back to the soldiers. 'Wait a moment before following.' He then hurried after the sorceress, the soldiers behind him exchanging glances.

Up ahead, Kyphos saw Zara raise her hand. A golden ring on her finger lit up with a radiant glow, providing enough light to see. As he hurried to catch up with her, Kyphos expected to come to a chamber like the one in Malakai, but was surprised to find himself standing with the sorceress in a long corridor. A series of wide passages, perpendicular to the central corridor, headed out on both sides.

'What is this place?' Kyphos asked.

Zara cast him an impenetrable look, continuing her exploration. He followed her into the first of the side passages and immediately saw cages flanking the corridor, stretching all the way to the end, until the passage terminated in a blank stone wall. Within each cage was a skeleton. Every one of them had a gaping hole in its skull.

'What did you say, sorceress?' Kyphos asked when he heard her mutter under her breath and noticed that she was scowling.

'No chains,' she said.

'The dragons . . . Why were they killed?'

Zara shrugged and they left the passage, moving into the next. Soon they'd confirmed that all the others were the same.

'So many,' Kyphos said. 'They must have had scores of dragons.'

Zara nodded absently. 'A hundred or more. Come. We can't dally.'

She walked briskly to the end of the long corridor and then stopped, lifting her hand to cast light ahead.

Peering over her shoulder, Kyphos saw that they were now at the top of a set of stairs leading downward.

Without another word Zara descended, moving so quickly that Kyphos, with his shorter stride, struggled to keep up. At the base of the stairs they found another golden door, and the sorceress hurried to put her fingers to the symbols, closing her eyes and then making a short grunt.

The golden door swung soundlessly open.

As if triggered by its opening, sudden light poured from behind the door. It was as bright as daylight, and for a moment Kyphos was blinded. He blinked and gradually his sight adjusted.

Zara entered, and Kyphos heard her gasp. He followed, and they both took in the immense hall they now found themselves in.

Orbs of solid gold glowed brightly, fixed to the wall at regular intervals. They revealed a magnificent vault, a gigantic store room, filled with magical items.

Kyphos and Zara walked along a central aisle, passing copper chains in multitudes, hanging from row after row of racks. Sun staffs with devices of gold, assembled on stands, filled an entire section. Wind staffs occupied another stretch, with resonance staffs and fire staffs precisely arranged in order. Along with the staffs were other weapons: swords, spears, and lances.

But then Zara's footsteps increased as they passed through a gap between the racks and stands. She had her eye on something at the far end of the cavernous store room. Hurrying after her, Kyphos saw that she had fixed her gaze on an arch.

Given its own space apart from the other artifacts, it was big enough to dominate the far wall. Twelve feet high and eight feet wide, it was fashioned from metal, braided from four strands, each a different hue. Kyphos and Zara exchanged glances, then approached the arch in awe, no longer hurrying, their eyes on the mysterious relic. They stopped in front of it, and the hunchback realized that the thick strands that made up the braids were the yellow of gold, white of silver, red of copper, and black of iron. The arch stood on its two feet, supported by circular pedestals.

Kyphos heard mutters and gasps and glanced back to see that the soldiers had entered the chamber and were looking around, taking in the artifacts with wide eyes. He suddenly remembered that they didn't have long.

'The chains,' he called. There were dozens and dozens of them. 'Each of you, take command of a group of slaves. Get them all. Quickly now!'

'No!' Zara countermanded, glaring at Kyphos, daring him to disagree. 'The arch.' She reached out a hand and touched it gingerly, obviously fascinated as she examined it up close. 'Take this first.'

47

From her shelter on Widow's Peak, Chloe saw that the slaves and the soldiers who commanded them were exiting the tower. This time the slaves were burdened.

A dozen bare-chested men struggled with an immense arch, obviously heavy. Even the soldiers lent a hand, navigating the best path through the shattered streets of the ruined city, helping them with its bulk as they climbed over the rubble. Following behind were more porters carrying lengths of chain over their shoulders, chains that glinted red in the bright sunlight.

Chloe remembered the painting Dion had shown her in his palace. The sky had been filled with dragons, their scales the color of blood. The copper chains and the arch were linked somehow. She didn't know what the arch did, but it couldn't be anything good.

'Chloe?' Liana's wide eyes betrayed her anxiety.

More artifacts came from the tower, carried in the arms of the slaves: weapons, staffs, metal chests, even pieces of armor. The last of them left the structure even as the burly men with the arch exited the city and began to cross the pathway between the towering walls of water, heading for the higher ground at the cape.

Chloe nodded. It was time. If she could break the spell, here and now, the wind would become a storm. The waves would break. Chaos would ensue. The slaves were lightly clothed, but the armored warriors would sink to the bottom in their chain shirts. Zara and the hunchback were from a land of ice. They wouldn't be able to swim.

With so many soldiers and slaves below, there would only be a few people left at the cape. No one would understand what was happening. Taking advantage of the confusion, she and Liana would seize Dion from his captors before anyone could react.

Feeling the howling wind around her, brushing cold fingers against her skin, Chloe left the sheltered area to stand on the steep hillside. She raised her staff. The six magi still held the sea at bay, silver spirals glowing fiercely as the towering waves surged above them.

She had to act quickly if she wanted to obliterate Palemon's soldiers and sorcerers, and sweep away the artifacts from the ancient city. She fed the flame, feeling the fire rise up until it surged inside her body, threatening to engulf her if she didn't set it free.

'Chloe!' Liana's scream was piercing, cutting through her concentration.

Chloe whirled to see a dragon with a gray-robed magus on its back descending from above. As the dragon's flight followed the slope of the mountain, heading directly for them, the creature parted its jaws and the sorcerer narrowed his dark eyes. He was short, with close-cropped hair, two thirds of his face disfigured by a savage burn mark. His right hand held a staff crowned with an iron claw; his left hand clutched the chains of red metal connected to the dragon's collar.

Chloe recognized him in an instant. He was Tarik, the sorcerer who'd taken Liana at the guesthouse.

Liana paled. 'The dragon. It can sense me.' She thought for a moment and came to a decision. 'I'll lead them away.'

'But—'

Liana was already moving, her gaze fixed on her approaching enemy as mist enveloped her. The gray smoke shimmered and then as a silver-scaled dragon she burst out of the cloud, flying directly at her opponent. She ducked underneath the coal-colored dragon and bit hard under its belly. She then flew directly away from the peak as the sorcerer turned his mount and chased after her.

Chloe looked back at the slaves carrying the arch.

She lifted her staff again, her brow furrowed with concentration, and prepared to summon her power.

It was time to break the spell.

———————

Dion was biding his time, waiting for the right moment to strike. He glanced sidelong at Palemon, who was watching the procession of ancient artifacts from the lost city below.

Dion's arms and legs had been freed, but he was still collared. He remained slumped on the ground beside Palemon's makeshift throne, presenting himself as weak and pitiful, never a source of threat. There were no soldiers in the area, but Palemon carried a dagger at his side, and Dion knew that the tall king from across the sea was the far superior warrior. He needed to find the right moment to seize a weapon and then take his revenge. The opportunity would come.

Palemon was pacing in front of the tall chair, watching as the first of his men climbed down from the ancient city. Dion frowned as he saw that a dozen labored to carry something broad and heavy, glistening in the bright sunlight. Palemon stopped, waiting with fists clenched as they struggled with its weight, laboring along the path through the parted sea.

'The Arch of Nisos,' Palemon murmured. 'She found it.'

Unable to tear his eyes away, Dion saw that behind the arch a long line of warriors and slaves bearing loads of all shapes and sizes trailed down from the tower. He shook himself. He couldn't worry about magic. His quest was for revenge, and would no doubt see him killed, but he had to have faith that others like Chloe would do what was needed and save their homelands from the growing threat of these people from the frozen north.

Rage boiled up inside him as he thought about all that Palemon had done, and planned to do in the future. Scores of innocents had been killed in the tower in Malakai, murdered when their bodies broke at the bottom of the shaft. Others had been trapped in a strange, alien shape. Isobel, a vibrant young woman with child, had been slaughtered as she tried to flee. Dion had been collared, beaten, starved, and forced to kneel to a man he despised.

Palemon glanced down at him. 'This city will live again. My glorious ancestors—'

'Their time is done,' Dion said, unable to stop himself. 'Your ancestors are all dead. As you and your people will soon be.'

Palemon gave a wry chuckle. 'It appears that you have some bark left in you. You think this is your era? A time when a half-breed is king, slaves are freed, and weak soldiers battle each other?'

'And you – you believe you are strong?' Dion replied. 'You don't even have the courage to enter your city.'

Palemon gazed out at the remains of Aleuthea, the city that the warriors of Necropolis, Zara and her sorcerers, and Kyphos the hunchback had all seen up close. A city he might never see again.

His mouth tightened. He grabbed Dion around the iron collar, hauling him to his feet. 'Come, King of Xanthos. Let me prove to you, once and for all, what makes my blood nobler than yours.'

———

With Cob and Finn gone and Liana battling the sorcerer Tarik, Chloe's plan was falling apart, but there was still a chance of destroying Palemon's forces and the artifacts he'd come for. Everything now came down to her.

Her gaze took in the long line of slaves and soldiers. She knew what Dion would want her to do.

The wind was so fierce that it made her eyes sting as she lifted her chin, fixing her gaze on the two towering walls of water, so impossibly high above the cleared pathway on the ocean bed.

She took a deep breath and began to summon her magic. She could feel it inside her, begging her to free it. Silver flame darted up to fill her vision with white.

She drew on the fire until she was holding onto as much as she could, feeling it writhe and twist. With a shout she released it, throwing a strong gust down the path between the twin walls of water. Again she summoned her power, feeling the wind that was holding the sea at bay drawn to her staff. Once more she pointed her staff and released a torrent of air.

She could sense the spell unraveling, like threads plucked from a tapestry. The howling wind became even more intense; now its direction was chaotic.

Pain built up in her head, but she ignored it, drawing almost more of her power than she could handle, preparing to rip the magic to shreds.

She stopped. Her heart beat out of time.

Two figures were walking in the opposite direction to the slaves, following the pathway in the parted sea as they headed toward the sunken city. Already they were in the area of danger. One was Palemon, tall and imposing, with dark clothing and gray-streaked hair.

The man following behind was Dion.

Chloe suddenly remembered the Oracle's words.

You will have an opportunity to destroy our ancient enemy and end a great threat.

Chloe knew without a doubt that this was the opportunity the Oracle had foreseen. If she could break the spell, she would destroy almost every one of the descendants of Aleuthea. She would kill their king. Zara and Kyphos, whom she hadn't seen leave the tower, would surely die. The artifacts would be washed away, never to be seen again.

The soldiers would drown in their heavy armor. The sorcerers would fall to magic of their own making.

She was faced with a choice. Finish breaking the spell and abandon Dion to his fate, or try to save him and let the artifacts make it to shore.

Her staff was still leveled down the pathway between the waves, and without warning her power burst free, torn from her body, sending another blast of air down the corridor. She had drawn so much that she was unable to hold onto it, and she sensed still more threads of Zara's magic being torn.

As the wind tore at her hair and clothing, panic filled her. Dion, the man she loved, was directly in harm's way. She realized she might not have a choice at all. She had already started to unravel the spell, and soon it would break completely.

48

Leaving behind the procession of people carrying heavy metallic artifacts, Palemon walked with long strides, impatiently glancing over his
shoulder, lip curling in scorn as Dion lagged behind.

Dion's struggles were only partly pretense; he was weary from the
journey to Cape Cush and weary of life.

He decided that he was going to make his move now.

He tried to keep up with the king as they climbed the buckled
streets. Sea life was everywhere, coating the buildings and the ground,
making the scene look strange and unreal, reminding him that the spell
of the sorcerers was the only thing preventing them from drowning. He
glanced at a sorcerer as they passed. The man's face was white, his teeth
gritted as he maintained the spell. Legs apart as he held his staff high,
he looked like he was fighting a battle and losing. The wind was savage,
becoming fiercer with every passing moment.

'See all we built?' Palemon spread his arms.

'All I see is death,' Dion panted. 'Look at your feet.'

Palemon glanced down and saw a grinning skull, just a few inches
from the broken road. He scowled at Dion and then nodded back in the
direction of the cape. Following his gaze, Dion saw that the arch had
made it to safety. 'I look forward to showing you what we are capable of.'

Soon they were passing the remains of bigger buildings. The king
reached the wide marble steps leading to the tower and began to climb.

When Palemon paused to gaze around him, Dion was able to sidle closer, his eyes on the dagger on Palemon's hip.

But then he tripped on the crooked steps and felt a burst of pain in his thigh as his injured leg gave way. He stumbled and fell down, bracing himself with his hands. The tall king strode over and again yanked him to his feet by the collar.

Dion's hand reached for the hilt of Palemon's dagger.

But even as he focused his thoughts on the struggle to come, knowing he would need every ounce of his strength to kill his enemy, he saw a change come over the king from the frozen north.

Palemon's head jerked as he caught movement higher up. Following his gaze, Dion's eyes opened wide. He released his grip on the dagger's hilt.

Chloe was running down the steps, heading toward them with a staff in her hand. Wind tossed her dark hair around her face, revealing her expression of fierce determination, brown eyes blazing, jaw set, cheeks as tight as a drum. She wasn't hiding or hesitating; she was approaching with speed.

Palemon frowned as she neared. 'I know all of my people. Who are—?'

Chloe lowered her staff and pointed it at the king. The silver glowed a split second before a blast of concussive air struck Palemon in the center of his chest. His face showed shock as he flew backward, his body sailing down the marble steps until his back struck a stone the size of a table and the breath shot out of his chest.

Chloe rushed to Dion's side, closing her eyes and clasping a hand around his iron collar. Sudden heat flared against his skin before the metal fell to the stone.

'Come on!' she cried, taking him by the hand and pulling him in the direction of Widow's Peak.

'No,' Dion said, shaking his head.

'Dion, we have to run! The spell is breaking!'

'I have to kill him!'

Piercing shrieks sounded above. Chloe and Dion both looked up.

Five dragons plunged down from the sky. Their wings swept furiously as they fought the growing chaos of the wind. Narrowed, glaring eyes were fixed on Dion and Chloe, and their claws were extended, jaws parted and ready to snap. Whip-like tails trailed behind them as the creatures descended. The spear-carrying warriors astride them were coming to the protection of their king.

Dion glanced one last time at Palemon and cried out in frustration. Palemon had to die.

But Chloe needed him more. And now, for the first time since Kyphos had found him at his palace in Xanthos, there was nothing stopping Dion from being able to fight.

He sprinted up the marble steps, gaining height, shifting his shape even as he moved. He had no difficulty bringing on the sensations of wild ferocity, imagining his hands growing to ten times their size, feeling his body stretching and changing, his legs pushing his torso into the sky, head and shoulders becoming enlarged and grotesque. As the magical wind shredded the mist into nothingness, Dion lunged up, bunching his gigantic hands into fists. As the first dragon came down, he dodged the snapping jaws and punched it hard in its wedge-shaped head.

Screaming in pain, the stricken creature tumbled, the rider almost losing his grip on the reins as it veered. When the next dragon came, Dion weaved and gripped it behind the head, shoulders straining as he threw it, sending it flying through the air until it struck the ruins of a stone house, shattering the structure to pieces, the building caving in on top of both the dragon and its screaming rider.

Panting, he looked up at the sky.

The first dragon he'd hit in the head had rejoined its fellows. There were now four of them, preparing to attack as one. Already feeling weak, Dion knew he couldn't defeat them all.

He heard Chloe call his name.

'Run!' she cried.

———〜———

'Sorceress!' Kyphos grabbed Zara by the upper arm. Again she shook him off. She was hunched over a magically sealed chest, trying to decipher the spell holding it closed. Ignoring him completely, she muttered to herself and traced symbols with her fingertips. 'Zara!' he cried. 'We've taken all we can. We have to leave!'

The chest suddenly snapped open, and with a sound of triumph Zara peered inside. Leaning over her, Kyphos saw two heavy tomes, one beside the other, both several inches thick.

'They're too heavy!' Kyphos urged. 'We're the only ones here. We have to get out of the city!'

The sorceress reached inside and grabbed the first of the heavy volumes, struggling with it as she gave it to Kyphos's unwilling hands. He hefted its weight, knowing that even he would struggle to carry it.

Zara reached inside once more, but Kyphos grabbed her and stared directly into her face; this time he didn't relent. 'You are not listening to me. Surely you realize we're in danger?'

She suddenly looked around as if waking from a dream. The blood drained from her face. 'The spell. Something's happening.' She looked at the book still in the chest.

'Leave it,' Kyphos hissed. 'I'll take this for you, but there is no way you can carry the other.'

She hesitated, but then nodded. 'You speak sense. Come on.'

Clutching the tome to his chest, Kyphos now followed as Zara led the way, and together they ran out of the vault, but it wasn't until they came to the level of the cages and heard the howling wind that they both started sprinting. They dashed along the long passageway and through the golden door until they came to the sloping corridor and finally burst free of the tower.

The wind felt as if it was coming from all directions, first pushing them one way, then the other. Moving against it was difficult, but at least the towering waves on both sides were still holding. Sea spray filled the air, shrouding the city below in gusts of salt water.

'We need to get to safety!' Kyphos called above the wind, struggling to carry his burden.

They rushed down the steps, but then Zara made a cry of surprise. Following her gaze, Kyphos saw a figure in dark clothing near a large block of stone, trying to rise to his feet against the pressure of the gusts. 'The king!' Kyphos cried.

He threw himself against the flurries of air that felt like solid punches, reaching the king's side and setting the book down. The king was panting, eyes half-closed as he tried to stand.

'Sire, what happened?'

'Woman with a wind staff,' Palemon gasped.

Turning, Kyphos scanned the area, looking up toward Widow's Peak but seeing nothing. He now looked down into the city, and his eyes widened when for a moment the spray cleared. Fighting the fierce gale, dragons were swooping at the buildings. The creatures snapped at something hidden in the structures.

'The dragons will do what they need to,' Kyphos said. 'Zara, help me with the king.'

Working together, they lifted him up, one on either side of him. Kyphos suddenly felt a sharp pinch on his arm and saw Zara pointing at the tome on the step. Scowling, he bent and picked it up, struggling to help his king and hold the heavy book to his chest.

'Come on,' Kyphos grunted.

Feeling resistance, Kyphos glanced at Zara. She had stopped in her tracks, and was looking out at the towering waves. Her face was completely white. 'We're too late,' she said. 'Someone is breaking the spell.'

49

Chloe and Dion were hiding in a broken structure, a bath house, with rows of sunken pits and the occasional mosaic still visible in patches on the grimy tiled walls.

Chloe glanced at Dion, now in his normal form. He looked awful. His eyes were bleary and red, and an ugly blue bruise circled his neck. It seemed impossible that moments ago he'd been a towering giant.

She peered through a crack in the wall and saw a dragon craning its neck to peer into the window of a house across the road. The spear-carrying warrior on its back scanned in all directions. A shriek sounded somewhere above, sending a chill running down Chloe's spine.

The dragons were searching the area. It wouldn't be long before she and Dion were found.

'If you have any ideas, now's the time,' Dion said.

'I can tear the spell apart. Break it completely.' Chloe cast Dion a frightened look. 'But we're in the direct path—'

'Palemon is still in the city,' he interrupted. 'Do it.'

'But . . .' She trailed off.

He came to stand beside her. He took her hands, his piercing, soft-brown eyes full of intelligence and compassion. 'Trust me. I'll protect you.'

Taking strength from him, she nodded.

Staff in hand, she headed to the half-collapsed doorway, poking her head out to scan the immediate area. For the moment, the dragons' attention was elsewhere.

Chloe rushed out of the bath house, and now she was exposed. She sprinted to the center of the wide avenue made of stone, surrounded by ancient buildings of Aleuthea. Lifting her staff, she drew in a deep breath.

Even louder than the fierce wind, she heard piercing animal cries of triumph as her enemies spotted her. A moment later a sinuous shape of charcoal gray plummeted down from the sky, gold-flecked eyes glaring with malice. The soldier on the creature's back hefted his spear, leveling the sharp point at her.

She forced herself to ignore them as she raised her staff, closed her eyes, and cleared her thoughts of everything except the feel of the wind. She sensed the fire at the bottom of the well surge up, and she fed it still more, seizing as much power as she could and then sparking the flame again.

The snap of fluttering wings was suddenly broken by a thunderous bellow and then a thud followed by a crack. It was a struggle for her to keep her eyes closed. She stood in the middle of chaos, the raging wind trying to push her body in all directions. She ignored the grunts of a giant and the shrieks of the dragons he was fighting. A great shattering crash of stone sounded nearby, but she remained steadfast.

When she opened her eyes, everything was washed with silver.

She lifted the staff still higher, pulling all of the power from the fire inside her into her body, feeling it drawn to the metal device. The silver glowed so brightly that she couldn't see anything else. All she was aware of was a thick, pulsing cord of white energy, pouring into the staff.

With a sharp cry, she severed the connection. Chloe unleashed her power.

She felt it roar through her body, making her stand up on the tips of her toes as she shuddered. The silver faded from her vision, but now she could actually see the wind gathering pace around her, drawn toward her staff and converging, forming a tornado. With another cry, she pointed the staff and sent the whirlwind through the path between the walls of water, ripping through the opposing magic and tearing it to shreds.

As the fiery glow of silver flared up and then began to fade, she saw the dragons screeching as they fled into the sky. On both sides the walls of water were breaking, forming crests that collapsed in slow motion.

'Take my hand!' she heard Dion bellow.

With a roar louder than any thunder, the towering waves broke.

Hiding above a cloud, Liana waited for the scar-faced magus and his dragon to appear below her. In the brief moment of respite, she tried not to think about Chloe and Dion, wondering if they were safe. She knew she needed to focus on her own struggle.

She remembered being held down on the guesthouse bed while Tarik loomed over her. She again saw herself falling into the deep tower shaft, terrified beyond belief, forced to change her form, only to be brought down by the cold touch of iron.

But nothing was worse than the violation she'd experienced when the scar-faced sorcerer had connected his mind to hers with copper chain. He'd been able to feel what she felt, and to command her with a thought. She was no longer herself; she was his.

Killing the sorcerer would eradicate just a small amount of evil from the world, but it was hers to destroy.

Finally, gazing down, she saw her enemy appear, flying in a circle below the cloud, searching for her.

Staying silent, she descended from above, claws outstretched, her eyes narrowed as she flew directly at the magus on the dragon's back. Tarik saw her at the last instant and attempted a tight turn, and although she missed him, she managed to grab the dragon with her claws. She soon found herself locked in a deadly embrace, with each dragon snapping at the other's soft underbelly.

She screamed in pain when her enemy's sharp teeth gouged a furrow in her neck. The tear was dangerously deep, and already one of her eyes was half-closed from their previous encounters. She craned her long neck, trying to keep it out of the way of the dragon's jaws, at the same time trying to snap at either Tarik or a place where his mount's gray scales were already torn. The magus sent a ball of flame at Liana's head and she ducked, feeling fire scorch her back.

She shook her head in an attempt to clear the fog of agony. If she wanted to defeat her opponents, she would have to use abilities they could never match.

As soon as the thought occurred to her, she began to change her shape, and soon the shifting sensation came over her. Now, still in the air, she was a giant, with a thick torso and protruding jaw, but also a woman's build. Far larger and heavier, she continued to grapple her winged foe, holding the dragon fast. Her enemy struggled, but she held on, her jaw set tightly. She squeezed, trying to break any bones she could. Her stomach was in her mouth; they were falling with speed. She looked down to see the sea rushing up at her.

With a mighty smack, they struck water, and the dragon shrieked as its wings thrashed at the sea. Still Liana gripped with all her strength, and now they were sinking. Her lungs screamed at her as the depth grew and the color of the sea became darker, carrying scant light from the surface to the depths. Her chest heaved, but still she held fast. She saw Tarik trying to untangle himself, but his wrist was caught in the copper chains.

Liana felt darkness come over her, along with a terrible feeling of weariness. She saw the magus on the dragon's back writhe, his eyes wide with shock. He gave one last shudder, mouth gaping like a fish, and then went still.

The dragon continued to thrash, but it was deep enough now to simply let it go. Watching it drift away, Liana continued to plummet into the ocean depths. She closed her eyes as her limbs relaxed and she sank down, deeper into the sea.

But then she suddenly opened them.

Above her, she could just make out the fluttering silhouette of the winged dragon; it was still twitching. Liana arrested her sinking motion, kicking with her legs, but a giant's shape wasn't made to have command of the ocean.

She told herself that the sea was her element. She was longing to swim to the surface with her elongated body, thrusting at the water with her tail.

The change came over her.

Now a powerful serpent, she rushed for the surface. Swimming past the dying dragon, she had one final look at the motionless body of Tarik, still astride the drowning creature in the midst of its death throes.

Then Liana left them both behind.

Standing on the steps outside the Great Tower, Kyphos saw the dark-haired woman lift her staff and realized she must be the woman the king had mentioned. Then a bright light flared and suddenly it was impossible to see. Kyphos blinked as the light gradually faded. Wondering what was happening, he looked wide-eyed at the sorceress on Palemon's other side.

'We're too late,' Zara said again.

Kyphos watched in horror as the towering walls of water began to break. The waves closest to the shore of Cape Cush collapsed first, roaring with a thunder more powerful than any storm. Blue seawater became white foam, churning and roiling, surging over itself, pounding the ocean bed, making the cleared pathway vanish in an instant.

As the spell tore apart and the waves collapsed, the sorcerers below disappeared in the blink of an eye. Down in the city, the dark-haired woman with the staff and the king of Xanthos were enveloped in an instant.

'To high ground!' Kyphos cried. 'The tower!'

Palemon groaned as they got him moving. Kyphos risked a quick glance over his shoulder and saw the sea rushing in their direction, flooding the city's streets and rising quickly. Palemon saw the threat and forced his body into a run, the three of them now sprinting for the tower's entrance. They dashed through the arch and found the second entrance that led to the vertical shaft. Immediately they started to climb the slippery steps cut into the wall.

Even as they sped up the stairway, waves pounded at the tower from the outside, shaking the structure to its foundations. Just below their footsteps, the frothing water was now rushing up as fast as they could run. Zara and the king helped each other over the rubble at the top. Soon they were at the highest point of the tower, staring out at the surging ocean. Wind was screaming, pushing and pulling in all directions.

First Kyphos, then the others looked up into the sky.

The spell still had some power in it. A wave twice the tower's height was speeding toward them, on the verge of breaking.

'We're dead men,' Palemon said.

But then, looking still higher, Zara lifted her hand and waved. Following her gaze, Kyphos saw that the dragons had already seen them and were swooping down. As the wave surged forward, the broad backs of three winged creatures reached their level. Palemon leaped off first, the rider catching him deftly before immediately flying away. Zara went next, and then it was Kyphos's turn.

He jumped across, almost sliding off the dragon's leathery back but grabbing hold of the man in front at the last moment.

He hoped Zara appreciated the efforts he'd made to keep hold of her precious book.

50

Cob scoured the sea, tightening the sail to send the *Calypso* leaping over the wild waves. The hull smacked against the water, making his teeth jolt together. Time and time again the vessel's bow threatened to plunge under the sea when it dipped into a hollow. His arm was tight and sore, the tiller shuddering in his hand.

'Faster!' Finn called back to him.

'I'm doing all I can! In this wind, you're lucky I'm keeping us heading in the same direction!'

Appearing from nowhere, a wave was suddenly coming at the boat from behind, which made no sense at all. Water crashed over the stern, swamping the interior and soaking Cob to the skin. Another wave struck them from the port side, tilting the boat precariously before it righted itself. A series of smaller waves rocked the vessel to and fro.

'Do something useful and start bailing!' Cob bellowed.

'Look!' Finn pointed.

Closer to Widow's Peak the sea was more than frenzied, filled with towering waves and spinning tornadoes, mountains of foam and gusting wind.

'What in the names of all the gods is happening out there?' Finn cried.

'How should I know?'

Cob held the tiller with a white-knuckled grip, angling the *Calypso* directly toward Widow's Peak and the worst of the ocean's fury. A powerful geyser of foam rose up to momentarily envelop the sharp peak of rock before falling back down again. The *Calypso* was a tough vessel, but she'd already been nearly swamped, and they had yet to approach the isle.

'What now?' Finn's eyes were wide with fear.

'We follow the plan,' Cob said grimly. 'We sail for the peak.'

If they'd been in dangerous seas before, a mile from the isle they realized that what they'd experienced was nothing in comparison to what they felt now. Cob had sailed his entire life, but at least the storms he'd survived followed rules.

He took them in one direction then another, doing everything he could to face the waves as the boat climbed one face and then tumbled into the next. He prayed to Silex, his heart hammering in his chest. The onslaught was terrifying. The *Calypso* heeled to the side as a squall slammed into the sail, threatening to capsize the small vessel. Finn bailed constantly, his face as white as a sheet. Fighting the unpredictable wind and navigating the waves that came from all directions, Cob's arm ached so much that he had to focus all his concentration on holding fast. The boat was half-full of water, and if another wave rushed in, they would sink.

But then, all of a sudden, the *Calypso* steadied. The wind gradually died down and the waves subsided. Little by little, the ocean reached a new equilibrium, becoming level, a normal sea once again. While Finn continued bailing, Cob was able to wipe his eyes and gaze ahead. He saw the rocky isle of Widow's Peak growing larger in his vision.

He nervously exchanged glances with Finn. Below the surface, the city of Aleuthea was underwater once more. Cob's chest tightened as they came within hailing distance of Widow's Peak.

'Please,' he muttered. 'Dion . . . Chloe . . . Where are you?'

Cob was now circling the isle, but the steep slopes showed not the slightest sign of life.

Then Finn stood, grabbing hold of the mast to steady himself. He cried out and pointed. Cob saw movement in the water and pushed the tiller sharply, taking them toward what appeared to be a person swimming. No, two people.

One was a young man, his hair plastered to his crown, gasping for breath. Dion was treading water. He held Chloe in his arms, her eyes closed as he struggled to keep her head high.

Cob lashed the tiller in place and leaped across the boat to lower the sail, slowing the vessel down. The first to come abreast, Finn grabbed hold of Chloe as Dion held her up. Cob then took hold of Dion's outstretched arm, hauling him until he and Chloe were both sprawled out in the pooled water in the floor of the boat.

'Liana?' Cob asked.

Panting and wheezing, Dion lifted his head, staring at Chloe anxiously until she coughed, ejecting a stream of water. He then pulled himself to his feet and gripped the mast.

'Lad, take it easy,' Cob protested.

Dion's sodden tunic was ragged and torn. He had a circle of bruises around his neck, along with red scratches on his face and body.

But he gazed toward the horizon and shook his head. 'Liana. Take us out to sea,' he said hoarsely. 'I can sense her.'

Cob drew alongside another of the Lost Souls, a low island far out to sea, distant enough from the events at Cape Cush that the waves were gentle, and the wind blew as it should. He exchanged a worried glance with Finn as he dropped the sail, allowing the *Calypso* to coast to the rocky shore until it struck with a gentle nudge.

Liana was sprawled on her stomach. She wasn't moving.

Dion leaped out of the boat before anyone could stop him, stumbling and almost falling but righting himself. Rushing to the slight young eldran, he crouched at her side and put his ear against her mouth. 'She's breathing,' he called back. His jaw set tightly, he lifted her up in his arms. 'Finn, be ready. I'll pass her over.'

Despite Cob's position at the helm, when Finn settled her, he didn't need to be a healer to know she was in trouble. One of her eyes was half-closed and both were bruised, with dark pits surrounding them. The back of her head was scorched and there was a gash on one of her arms that seeped crimson blood.

More worrying still, she didn't make a sound as they rested her in the bottom beside Chloe.

'Will they be all right?' Finn asked Dion.

Dion's face was grave. 'They have to be.' His gaze took in everyone on the boat, first Chloe and Liana, then Finn, and finally Cob. 'You all came for me. I won't forget it.'

Cob harrumphed. 'Where to, lad?'

Dion glanced back in the direction of Malakai. His eyes rested there for a long time before he looked forward once more.

'Home,' he said. 'Sail for home.'

'And if we're followed?'

'Then I'll do what I can to hold them off.'

Cob shook his head, seeing that Dion was barely holding himself together. But he steered them away from the Lost Souls, and prayed to the gods that the skies would remain clear.

51

Two days' sailing from the Lost Souls, somewhere on the edge of the Aleuthean Sea, Dion, king of Xanthos, stood on a sandy beach, staring out at the blue expanse and thinking. Despite his exhaustion, he was up before dawn, and the water was calm, with barely a breeze to ruffle his flaxen hair. He gazed out at the horizon for long enough to watch the purple sky become pink, and then a slender piece of light crested the edge of the world. The occasional cloud glowed red as the sun burst into existence, its morning rays angled to the sea, shimmering on the surface.

He inhaled, breathing in fresh air, exhaling slowly, bringing calm to his senses after the recent chaos and despair. But despite the sight of the *Calypso* nearby, the vessel that would soon take him home, he was still shaken.

He couldn't stop thinking about the things these people from across the sea had done. Unprovoked, they had stolen Isobel, the woman carrying his child. They'd used him as their test subject, putting a collar on him and enslaving him with copper chains.

His nostrils flared as he felt rage rising up to the surface. He remembered the iron crossbow bolt plunging between Isobel's shoulder blades. He reminded himself of the terror in her eyes as she'd died, trying to tell him something with her last breath before her lungs filled with fluid.

In the end, Chloe had saved him, but she'd been forced to delay breaking the spell, and the artifacts of ancient Aleuthea had made it to shore. At least Palemon and his two minions were dead, swept into oblivion. He now needed to destroy the sorcerers and soldiers who'd survived. He would need to make alliances, with men like Kargan, ruler of the Ilean Empire. They both had reason to eradicate the nation of Aleuthea once and for all.

As he seethed, he sensed someone coming up to stand beside him. Forcing calm, he spoke without turning. 'How are you feeling, Liana?'

'You can sense me?'

'I've accepted who I am. I will never wear a necklace, or a collar, again.'

'That makes two of us. But be careful, Dion. I could feel your anger even as I approached.'

He changed the subject. 'How is Chloe?'

'Still exhausted. I think it's more than almost drowning. The magic is catching up to her. She keeps mumbling something about the wind.'

Dion turned and met Liana's eyes. 'Should I be worried?'

'Did she tell you that she left Athos before it was safe for her to do so? She wanted to find her sister, but also to find you. You know that she loves—'

Liana looked away as she abruptly stopped speaking. Dion's skin tingled. He shielded his eyes, staring out to sea.

He glanced at Liana. 'Can you sense . . . ?'

She nodded.

They appeared in the dawn sky, distant enough to look like a flock of birds, but growing far too large, far too quickly. Wings swept up and down, arcing on both sides of the sinuous bodies they were connected to. The wings were thin as parchment, large as a big ship's sails. The rising sun shimmered off their scales, glinting like bright light shining from steel.

Dion watched as a dozen silver-scaled dragons came into view.

Their formation was tight, swooping down with discipline and speed. As their features became clear, Dion took in their small but muscular forelimbs and powerful hind legs, their arched necks and angular heads, with protuberances swept back from their skulls, creating a series of knobs almost like a frill.

They were all big, the size of Dion or Liana when changed, but Dion's mouth dropped open as he saw that they were led from the front by an immense dragon with a wingspan twice the length of any other. If he hadn't recognized the lead dragon's irises, the color of molten gold, and sensed his indomitable will, he would never have known who he was, for Dion had seen him before in dragon form but never like this.

Suddenly he could hear them, the crackle and snap of their wings as they swept at the air, and then they were descending to the beach. One by one, they shifted form even as they made contact with the ground, and now Dion was looking at Eiric, along with an assembled group of twelve tall, angry eldren.

Eiric had changed, he could see at a glance. He was as lean as ever, with sharp features and skin as white as snow, contrasting with his golden eyes. But he now had a powerful, regal presence and wore a crown of twisted laurel leaves on his head, although he was clad in the same deerskin clothing as his companions.

Eiric only had eyes for Liana.

He'd barely changed his form before he was rushing toward her, ignoring everything else. Breathing heavily, his face revealing ragged emotion, his eyes widened as he inspected the bruises on her face. He took her hand and held it up, examining the bandage on her arm.

'My love . . . I felt your pain from a world away,' he said softly. 'Liana, tell me. Who did this to you?'

When Liana lowered her head, Eiric turned his golden eyes on Dion, his expression of rage naked and raw, but Dion met his gaze firmly.

'We should not be fighting each other,' Dion said, regarding the man who had once been his friend. 'You and I, we were once close. We need to stand together as we did before. For our enemy – our true enemy – did things to Liana, and to me, that must be avenged.'

'Who are these people?' Eiric said in a low, urgent voice.

'They are the descendants of Aleuthea.'

Eiric looked at his brethren. 'Dalton, Caleb, all of you . . . Wait here.' He turned back to Dion. 'You and I, Dion, King of Xanthos . . . It appears we need to talk.'

He then reached out to stroke Liana's face.

'I will be back soon, my love. We are going to repay these people for everything they did to you.'

'They chained her, collared her?'

Dion nodded.

Eiric's fists were clenched at his sides. 'We won't leave a single one of them alive. At least this king is dead.'

'It was all Chloe . . .' Dion shook his head. 'She was incredible. Tore their magic apart. I've never seen anything like it.'

'So, Dion . . . Where does this leave things between you and me?'

'I tried talking to you—'

'You deployed your soldiers against us.'

'I had to,' Dion said. 'I'm half-eldran, but I'm the ruler of a human kingdom, and Queen Zanthe of Tanus is our ally.' He tried to keep the ire out of his voice. 'You didn't even reach out to me before you attacked the mines.'

'What else was I to do?' Eiric scowled. 'It's our territory. You humans will never give up your quest for metal.'

'Look at it from Zanthe's point of view,' Dion said. 'Tanus started working the mines when Cinder Fen was a dangerous place. The people of Tanus know that if they lose the mines, they will become poorer. Without a harbor, Tanus has few resources. Zanthe has the popular support of her citizens. Even if she wanted to, even if I begged her, she couldn't agree to let you have them.'

'You are telling me nothing I don't already know. And you wonder why we fight?'

'Eiric . . .' Dion said slowly. 'Have you ever thought of buying them from her?'

Eiric's fierce expression shifted to a puzzled frown.

'Sindara has a wealth of gemstones. You once gave me a pouch yourself, and I remember you saying that they're easily found, if you know where to look.'

'She would accept that?' Eiric asked.

'If you gave her a settlement, it would allow her to save face, and she would be able to lavish the proceeds on her people. You might even be able to establish regular trade, benefiting you both. Tell me, were you ever in danger of losing any of your skirmishes? Were the soldiers of Tanus a serious threat?'

'No. Not at all.'

'The price might not be as high as you think.'

Eiric looked away, scratching his sharp chin pensively. He finally sighed, turning back to face Dion. 'I'm sorry, Dion. I should have come to you.'

'I'll help to restore peace between Sindara and Tanus. But for now . . .' Dion's face became grim. 'We have an enemy to face.'

'We may have an ally,' Eiric said. 'On our way here, we saw a mighty fleet. Thirty or more ships flying orange-and-yellow flags were sailing toward the Aleuthean Sea.'

Dion looked up sharply. 'Kargan. He's trying to take back Malakai.'

'Does he know what he will be facing?'

'He may be aware, or he may not. Either way, I'm sure he could use our help.' Dion put out his hand. 'You and I, King Eiric. Shall we fight together?'

'My friend,' Eiric said, clasping his palm. 'I think we shall.'

———

Dion was crouched next to Chloe, holding her hand. Lying on a blanket on the sand, she was mumbling in her sleep.

'The wind,' she whispered. Her face looked pained as she twitched. When she shuddered and her voice grew louder, he finally decided to shake her.

'Chloe. Chloe!'

She opened her eyes. Her irises were entirely black. But then she blinked, and in an instant they were again a soft shade of brown.

'Dion?' Her face was pale as she looked up at him. 'I was having a terrible dream.'

His heart reached out to her. Despite this magic that had cursed her, she'd left Athos behind to help her sister, and then she'd somehow made it all the way to Malakai to rescue him. She'd saved him from himself, for he knew that even if he'd managed to seize Palemon's dagger, he would surely have been killed. She'd pushed herself beyond endurance, and now she was paying the price.

'I know,' he said. 'You kept saying something about the wind.'

Chloe's brow creased as she turned away. She was so beautiful, it hurt him to look at her. He wanted to take her in his arms, but instead he simply held her hand.

'I've come to tell you something,' Dion said. 'Eiric is here. He's brought with him some of the most powerful warriors of Sindara. And Kargan is on his way to Malakai with a fleet.'

Chloe glanced up sharply. 'You're leaving?'

'I have to help.'

'I'm going with you.'

'No.' He shook his head. 'I want you and Liana to take care of each other, and for you both to look after Cob and Finn.'

'If this is about vengeance—'

'It's about more than that. It's about the things they uncovered from the sunken city. It's about magic we don't understand. We have to stop them before they become unstoppable.'

She was silent for a time. 'When will I see you again?'

'I'll find you,' he said. 'I promise.'

'Dion . . . Be careful.'

He nodded. 'I will.'

52

Zara was in the central shaft of the Sky Tower in Malakai. Standing near the middle of the blood-stained floor, she watched as the slaves carefully tilted the metal arch until it was standing tall on its disc-shaped feet.

She then approached the strange artifact built by Nisos the Archmagus.

The rays of the midday sun shone down from above, glinting off the braided metal. Small symbols of magic decorated its surface, so many that she couldn't hazard a guess as to their purpose. Whatever the arch was, it was powerful, fashioned from all the four materia: gold, silver, copper, and iron.

'But what does it do?' she murmured to herself.

Walking around it, examining it as she pondered, she bit her lip, brow furrowed in concentration. *Why an arch? The shape must be related to its purpose. What can be done with an arch?*

She glanced at the magus beside her, a rangy man with a neat beard. He shrugged. 'I defer to your wisdom, sorceress.'

Zara scowled.

She'd read the ancient tome that she'd recovered from the vault, but her poor knowledge of Old Aleuthean made the reading difficult, and the book covered many topics. She desperately wished now that she'd taken the second volume, which she suspected covered the arch in more

James Maxwell

detail, but what was done was done. Anything she learned would have to be through experimentation.

'Perhaps more time with the tome?' the magus ventured.

'I've learned all I can,' Zara muttered. She spoke for herself as much as her companion as she circled the Arch of Nisos, while the sorcerer and the slaves all hung back. 'Whatever it does, it must be something remarkable, for it would have taken a long time to gather so much precious metal. Nisos built it as an older man, late in Aleuthea's history. The war with the eldren was won many years before, and the last of the dragons had died in captivity.'

She rubbed her chin, circling slowly around the object of her attention.

'Without dragons,' she said, 'it was difficult for the ancient Aleutheans to maintain their empire. Whatever the arch's purpose, it was intended to solve this problem.'

She stopped circling and now faced it. Stepping forward, she examined it more closely, running her fingers over the metal. She finally narrowed her gaze at the angular symbol at the apex, far larger than any other.

'Slave!' she called to a scrawny lad with a scar below his eye. 'Come here so I can climb onto your back.'

The slave apprehensively came forward and crouched on the ground, moving until he was on his hands and knees. Climbing onto his back, Zara stretched until she was resting her fingertips on the angular symbol at the arch's highest point.

Closing her eyes, in the same way that she'd opened the sealed gates and the magically locked chest, she tried to link the symbol with gold, then silver, then copper, and finally iron. Nothing happened. She sighed and opened her eyes.

Then she had an idea.

Fingers still pressed to the symbol, she closed her eyes again. But rather than a single materia, she summoned the power inside her with

344

a mixed flame, despite the danger of channeling more than one materia at once.

The fire of her magic surged up, suddenly drawn out of her like her lifeblood was pumping out onto the sand. So much was sucked out that she felt weak, and had to fight to keep her knees from buckling.

Hearing gasps from the people around her, she finally severed the connection and opened her eyes. She stumbled off the slave's back and gazed up at the arch as the youth climbed to his feet. Zara felt a thrill of satisfaction.

The relic of Nisos had been activated. The entire arch was glowing and pulsing, radiant with the colors of the sun and moon, fire, and shadow. It fairly hummed with power, shimmering like a rainbow of molten metal.

Zara stepped back. She smiled and waited.

Slowly her smile faded. Nothing else happened.

The arch was functional; she could see that much. She frowned, returning to the first basic question she'd asked herself. *Why an arch?*

'You.' She nodded at the young slave. 'Walk through it.'

The youth stood frozen on the spot, staring at the glowing arch and then at Zara. She frowned and walked slowly toward him, her finger lifted. The youth's face turned pale, terror showing the whites in his eyes. Though she didn't hold a weapon, he backed away from her.

'Do I need to ask you again?' she hissed.

The youth gulped and looked at the relic, before returning his gaze to Zara and then nodding. He walked hesitantly toward it, glancing over his shoulder, as his fear of the unknown fought his fear of her.

Finally the youth reached the Arch of Nisos and stood in front of it. Taking a deep breath, he walked through.

White light dazzled Zara, blinding her.

Far away, in the land of Sindara, a pool at the bottom of an immense basin glowed with a gentle green light. Beside the pool, a lawn of lush grass interspersed with young willows and elms stretched from the basin's limestone walls to the water's edge, almost encircling it. Bees buzzed over the grass, searching for flowers to pollinate. Sparrows flitted about with apparent indecision. It was a pleasant place, filled with the magic of life.

An onlooker would have seen the pool gradually shift in color. From the shade of emerald, the glow from within its depths suddenly changed to yellow. The yellow deepened and became fiery orange.

Finally the pool was searing red, the color of blood.

But only the rustling trees and the birds that suddenly took flight were present to witness the transformation.

The pool's color then shifted back to green.

———

In a deep cave on the island of Athos, the Oracle sat and stared into a white fire, struggling to see the future, casting along the twisting paths of fate before attempting the next fork in the road, trying to find a path that would lead to the least death and destruction.

The pale flames flickered and danced, burning without tinder over the solid stone of the cavern floor. The fire was her link to the Source, the great jewel buried at the very end of the tunnels.

The Oracle's breath caught. Her eyes shot wide open.

The white fire in front of her flared up to twice its height. She backed away, keeping her distance.

The fire began to change color.

The Oracle shook her head as it shifted to orange and then an angry red. For a moment the flames cast iridescent crimson light throughout the cavern. Feeling the hairs stand up at the back of her neck, she realized she was holding her breath.

Finally the fire shrank and the light dimmed, changing hue, returning to its previous appearance.

Soon the fire was white once more.

'No,' the Oracle whispered. 'Not again.'

Zara blinked and her eyes slowly regained focus. The flash of blinding light left sparkles in her vision, dancing stars that disappeared one by one.

Just a moment before, the young slave with the scar under his eye had entered the arch. She looked for him, expecting him to emerge from the other side, but now all she could see was mist billowing around the gateway, a mist that gradually cleared.

She saw the flash of a reptilian tail.

Zara gasped. The billowing cloud cleared further and now there was a long, sinuous shape where she'd expected the youth to be.

Wings fluttered, blowing away the last shreds of vapor, revealing the creature in all its glory.

Zara's wide eyes traveled from one end to the other.

A spiked tail broadened as it reached two powerful hind legs. Thin, wide wings like canvas folded in and out, connected to the creature's broad back by a framework of bones, with skin stretched over them as taut as a drum. Muscles rippled in the shoulders, while under its belly two smaller forelimbs scratched sharp claws on the stone floor. In front of the shoulders, a slender, serpentine neck craned, supporting a head ten times bigger than that of a horse, with angular protrusions sweeping back from the brow and eyes as big as Zara's hand.

It was a dragon, chest heaving, looking back at Zara with a panicked expression, a thin scar under its eye. There was no mistaking what the arch had done.

Yet this dragon was different from any that Zara had seen before. The stories had always said that the eldren were silver scaled. The mixed-bloods she'd forced to change were sometimes the color of charcoal, other times a lighter gray.

This sinuous monster's scales were red, a deep shade of crimson. The color of bright arterial blood. It was deadly, but for the time being it was confused.

That could soon change.

Zara shook herself.

'Quick!' she barked at the magus with the neat beard. 'Get copper chains. Go!' She leveled a finger at the group of stunned slaves.

'And somebody find me the king!'

53

Dion, Eiric, and twelve of Eiric's most powerful warriors soared high in the open sky, searching for the fleet of Ilean warships. When they combined their forces with Kargan's, the fate of the people from across the sea would be sealed.

The ocean stretched on endlessly, the rows of waves rolling relentlessly forward below them.

You saw them in the Maltherean? Dion addressed Eiric.

Yes.

They might still be crossing through the Chasm, Dion said. *Let's head over there.*

Agreed.

Eiric passed the instruction to his fellows, and the fourteen dragons all wheeled. But then Dion suddenly sensed shock and awe from his companions, swamping him with emotion as he tried to filter it out. Wondering what had alerted the eldren, Dion's gaze swept over the sea, but he couldn't see anything.

Dion . . . The sky, Eiric said.

He looked higher, casting his vision in all directions, and then he saw them.

Dread sank into his chest, slowly turning to horror. He was stunned, unable to believe what he was seeing.

Distant, but so numerous that they filled an entire swathe of sky, well over a hundred dragons were flying in the direction of the Chasm. Traveling in close formation, each had a rider on its back, an armored soldier or a sorcerer with a staff.

How is this possible? Eiric asked. The eldran king's composure was truly shattered; he was as shocked as Dion was himself.

The scene was just like the painting. It could only be the Arch of Nisos. The descendants of Aleuthea had found it, and now they'd put it to use.

And as in the painting, all the dragons were fiery red. Their savage coloring, bright scarlet, contrasted with the eldren's silver scales and Dion's black.

Dion knew then that Palemon had accomplished the impossible. He'd secured the copper chains he needed, but more importantly, he now had the dragons to harness.

Eiric . . . They found an artifact in the ancient city. An arch. I . . . I don't understand it. But we're too late.

We have to get out of here, one of the other eldren said.

I know, Eiric replied. He turned, and the golden orbs of his eyes met Dion's. *But they have a purpose. We know what they plan to do.*

Kargan paced the deck of his flagship, the *Nexotardis*, and proudly took in the sight of the fleet around him. If Javid had once thought that he wasn't taking this Palemon seriously enough, well, he couldn't say that anymore. He'd spent a fortune and deployed the full might of Ilea, the most powerful naval force in the world. Bireme after bireme sailed ahead, oars churning the sea into foam, pulling in beside each other to form long rows.

Under the command of their skilled captains, the warships were forming up as soon as they passed through the narrow strait that divided the Maltherean and Aleuthean Seas. Flags communicated positions; helmsmen nudged vessels to keep them all in their place. With only the occasional signal to a wayward vessel, Kargan managed it all with a lifetime's experience behind him.

At the back of the armada, another eighty-foot-long bireme exited the steep-walled Chasm. It was a dangerous crossing, with towering cliffs on both sides, but Kargan hadn't lost a single ship. The first row of vessels drifted forward, clearing space for the newcomers. Crewmen shouted to one another, voices carried on the stiff ocean breeze.

'That's the last of them,' General Dhuma called from the other side of the ship. Dhuma had been instrumental in preparing the fleet's departure, and Kargan had finally restored the man's rank.

'Raise the flag,' Kargan ordered. 'We're now on the Aleuthean Sea, and we'll maintain battle formation from here on.'

Sails unfurled on every vessel and drums stirred the blood, the pounding beats sounding primal, sparking a memory from the days when men lived in caves. Leaving the Chasm far behind, miles soon separated the armada from the narrow passage and Kargan again paced the deck as his thirty-two biremes spread out to form two perfect lines. He squinted ahead into the setting sun.

'Messengers! Assemble!' Kargan bellowed. He headed up to the bow, nodding as he cast his eyes over the fleet, before turning to wait impatiently near the forked bench as the dozen young messengers gathered.

'Take these orders to the captains,' Kargan said. 'We'll head slowly to Malakai through the night. Keep the men rested; work them in shifts. We'll arrive with the dawn. My flag will signal the attack.'

He gazed ahead, to the row of sixteen warships that made up the first wave. Their decks were cleared for battle and they were burdened mainly by archers. The *Nexotardis* was at the midpoint of the second wave, where Kargan could watch every ship and issue adjustments if needed. The vessels at his flanks traveled far more slowly under the weight of all the heavily armored soldiers on board.

'The first wave,' he continued, indicating with a sweep of his hand, 'is to take the brunt of any attempts to strike the fleet itself, whether from the sea, land, or sky. When we arrive at the city, the captains are to engage with any enemies and peel to the sides, allowing our troops to disembark on the shore.'

Kargan glowered at the young messengers.

'Understood?'

The youths nodded. They'd all been trained to recall orders word for word, even to the point of Kargan's inflections and hand gestures.

'Our first objective is to control the harbor. Then, when we've unloaded the men, we'll storm the gates.' He glanced at Dhuma. 'I know Malakai. The gates facing the harbor aren't strong. Our iron ram will make short work—'

Kargan frowned when he was interrupted by a growing chorus of chatter. The murmurs became cries, and then he began to hear distant shouts of alarm. He turned and faced forward, shielding his eyes.

'What is it?' he muttered.

All around him, men were gazing at the sky. Finally, spread across the sunburned heavens, Kargan saw them. A great flock of birds hung just over the horizon, growing larger and larger with every passing moment. Their wings were spread in twin arcs, joined at the middle by a lean, muscled body. The wings were more like a bat's wings than a bird's . . .

Immediately he realized what they were.

The witnesses to the destruction of the barges at Verai had spoken of five dragons, or sometimes six. He had enough archers to deal with half a dozen dragons, and enough ships to cope with losses.

But this was . . . a hundred or more. He was staring at more dragons in one place than he'd ever thought possible.

He opened his mouth to order any man with a bow to draw his arrow, but for once his voice failed him. Wave after wave of scarlet dragons, dozens upon dozens of them, soared down from above, plunging to meet the lead warships. There were riders on the dragons' backs, he saw – soldiers in armor of chain. The pale-faced warriors held huge swords, spears, and axes in one hand while the other gripped metal reins as red as the beasts they commanded.

In an instant the sky was a confusion of flying monsters, separating further into groups of three and four, diving down onto the ships. Archers on the nearest warship in the forward line fired arrows that bounced harmlessly off the dragons' tough hides. Fixing his stunned eyes on the biggest of them all, Kargan saw its jaws bite down on a bowman, tearing him in half. Its rider, a tall warrior with long, gray-streaked hair swept past the file of archers, decapitating one man after another with his broadsword. Behind him, a stocky man with bushy eyebrows bent down from his own dragon to strike his axe into the crewmen who were trying to flee in terror.

Every ship in the first wave suddenly had half a dozen dragons snapping and tearing over it like scavengers on a corpse. On a distant bireme, a blinding silver light appeared at the end of a robed man's staff, accompanied by a powerful blast that threw a dozen crewmen into the water. An ear-splitting sound filled the air and everywhere archers' weapons fell out of their hands as they collapsed and clapped their hands over their ears. Seeing the tall warrior make another sweep, clearing the ship's deck with every blow of his sword, Kargan noticed his braided beard and face set in a mask of fierce determination, and then with a start he realized who he must be.

Palemon was more powerful than he'd ever imagined. This magic . . . He couldn't begin to comprehend it.

All along the warships of the forward line, brave soldiers who'd fought across the empire were throwing down their weapons and leaping over the sides of their vessels. The ships themselves were surprisingly intact; the dragons and their riders were targeting the crews, leaving the vessels undamaged.

Despite the efforts of the occasional Ilean soldier who managed to score a hit on a dragon's crimson hide, or archer who landed an arrow in an Aleuthean warrior's eye, the outcome of the assault was never in dispute. Soon the sixteen ships of the front line would be floating without crews, dead in the water. A crippled warship drifted away from its fellows, sail blazing, decks a flaming inferno. It looked as if one of Kargan's captains had sacrificed his vessel rather than let it fall into enemy hands.

And soon the dragon riders would turn their attention to the second wave of biremes.

Kargan swallowed. His face drained of color as he watched it all unfold. He was a man used to winning. He'd helped Solon gain his empire and then seized power against all odds after Solon's death.

Now he was going to lose his entire fleet.

'Turn us around!' he roared.

He felt a strong hand grip his upper arm. Whirling, he saw Javid, the huge man looming over him, staring into his face. 'There is no way to fight this. We have to abandon ship if we want any chance of survival.'

'No,' Kargan said. 'I cannot lose my fleet.'

'The decision has been made for you! We have to dive overboard—'

Javid's voice broke off as he looked into the water. Kargan followed his friend's eyes, staring down at the sea. An immense silver-scaled creature, long and serpentine, as wide as the ship but twice the length, was passing under the *Nexotardis*.

Something struck the bow, hard enough to make the entire vessel shudder from keel to mast. But rather than disappear, the pressure continued, and suddenly the *Nexotardis* was moving. The bireme tilted as a powerful force pushed against the vessel's end and it began to spin on its axis.

Kargan couldn't fathom what was happening. He stared down and saw the great silver leviathan, perpendicular to his warship, its head pressed against the bow as its tail thrashed at the sea, rotating the bireme until it was once again facing the Chasm.

Then he heard a voice calling his name.

Kargan turned to see a young man with flaxen hair and pale brown eyes approaching. Though he wasn't as tall as Kargan, he had an athletic build and carried himself with authority, despite the fact that he was wearing a ragged tunic and was soaked to the skin, dripping water on the deck as he walked. He looked familiar, but Kargan couldn't recall where he'd seen him before.

'King Kargan,' the young man said again. 'I am Dion of Xanthos. You cannot defeat them, but I can help you survive.'

Dion's gaze traveled to the ships flanking the *Nexotardis* on both sides, and Kargan now saw that nearly every bireme had a serpent rotating it to point back toward the entrance to the Maltherean Sea.

'The eldren are here to help you,' Dion said. He glanced at the forward line of biremes and the struggle taking place, and shook his head. 'I thought Palemon was dead, but it appears otherwise. He wants ships. And we both need at least some of your fleet to survive.'

Kargan hesitated, but then nodded. 'What do we do?'

'Signal your captains to row. We need your men to work harder than they ever have before.'

'And the enemy? Won't they just follow?'

'Leave them to us. Just get your ships moving. Head back to the Maltherean Sea.'

Without another word, Dion ran to the side of the vessel and leaped off, diving head first into the water.

'I suggest we do as he says,' Javid said.

Kargan shook himself. 'Run the flag for ramming speed! The serpents are here to help!'

Suddenly the pressure on the bow eased, and looking down into the water, Kargan saw a dark shadow passing beneath the ship. The *Nexotardis* was now facing the Chasm, while the other vessels in the row were in varying stages of turning toward their only hope of escape.

The sail went taut as it pocketed the wind. The drum began to pound below decks, immediately thundering at ramming speed. Oars pulled at the water, over a hundred rowers knowing that they had to match the rhythm of the drum if they ever wanted to see home again.

Finally the *Nexotardis* was moving, the first of the biremes to head back toward the Chasm. Two more warships followed after, and then another three. In a ragged column, they began to pick up speed. Soon each flat-bottomed ship was skimming over the water. The blades of the oars churned furiously, moving back and forth in the time it takes to draw a sharp breath. The wind picked up as Kargan clenched his fists at his sides, willing speed out of the crew of the *Nexotardis* and from every other ship he might be able to save. He crossed the deck and looked into the Chasm, with its narrow breadth and mile-high cliffs, then glanced back at the dragons swarming over half the fleet he'd brought from Lamara.

Their battle was nearly over. Most of the biremes were floating without crews to guide them. The occasional trio of dragons fought over one warship or another, but the majority were regrouping in the sky above, sunlight shining off their scarlet bodies.

The towering cliffs enveloped the fleeing biremes, casting them into shadow. The narrow defile that was the Chasm's entrance was now the only thing separating the two forces. With sheer rock walls on both sides, it was nonetheless wide enough for Kargan to see the scores of red dragons hovering in the air above the ships they'd captured, wings beating down, each rider bringing his mount beside another. The dozen surviving ships of Kargan's fleet sped as fast as they could for the waters of the Maltherean Sea. But they would never be able to move fast enough to escape.

Then something happened that made Kargan gasp.

At the end of the Chasm, the surface of the sea erupted at over a dozen places. For a moment everything was a confusion of spray and mist.

Then fourteen silver-scaled dragons climbed the sky, forming a line, blocking the Chasm's entrance. No, Kargan realized, thirteen silver dragons. One, in the middle of the group, was as black as night.

The red dragons and the eldren faced each other at the same height.

Kargan gripped the rail tightly.

Dion, Eiric, and twelve powerful dragons from Sindara flew higher until they were hovering in the sky. They were facing a force several times their number. Their enemies had warriors with sharp weapons, and sorcerers with staffs.

But the king of Xanthos and the king of the eldren were undaunted.

Across the void, Dion's gaze rested on one of the dragon riders, a tall warrior with gray-streaked hair and a braided beard. Somehow Palemon had escaped from the ancient city. If he chose to fight, Dion would do everything in his power to kill him.

Collared, unarmed, Dion had been no match for Palemon. But now he was a powerful dragon, with wings as black as night, far larger than the scarlet creature Palemon had enslaved to his will. Eiric was bigger still, the most immense dragon Dion had ever seen, and would strike terror into his enemies.

And Dion knew what it was that Palemon truly wanted.

As the two forces faced off, neither making the first move, Dion was well aware that every passing moment gave Kargan time to make his escape. He watched Palemon, seeing the copper chains in one hand, broadsword in the other. He remembered what it had felt like to be under the power of those chains.

Palemon, Dion projected his thoughts toward Palemon's dragon. *I know you can hear me.*

There was a slight delay, but then Palemon's menacing voice came back to him, relayed through the connection between dragons. *You will never win this fight.*

True. But know this. If you choose to fight, I will kill you. And more importantly for your people, the eldren with me will destroy the ships you've captured. What is it you truly want?

As time dragged out, the tension building, Dion waited for his enemy to make the first move.

———

'What are we waiting for, sire?' Zara cried. 'We should attack!'

Palemon's dragon, the same fiery color as the blood dripping from his sword, kept its place in the sky beside Zara's. There were more dragons behind and below him, dozens and dozens of them, each carrying an armored soldier or a skilled magus. The air was filled with the sound of beating wings.

Clutching the reins of copper in his left hand, Palemon shifted in his seat, rotating slowly, until he was gazing down at the vessels he'd seized from the Ileans. He counted them to himself. There were exactly a dozen seaworthy vessels. The crews had been plucked off their top decks like weeds from a garden, but the oarsmen, no doubt slaves to a man, would be cowering at their benches, ready to serve.

He glanced at Kyphos on his other side. 'Kyphos!'

'Sire?'

'How many ships do we need to rescue our people from Necropolis?'

'About a dozen, sire.'

'So we have what we need?'

Kyphos hesitated, scanning, and then nodded. 'I believe we do.'

Palemon narrowed his eyes at the eldren blocking the Chasm. He longed to take the battle to them, but there would be losses, and risk to the ships he'd captured. More than anything, he had to save the people he'd left behind in Necropolis.

'Then let's get these ships back to Malakai.' He raised his sword into the sky.

'But, sire—' Zara protested.

'You heard me, sorceress. Our people need us!' Palemon growled. 'Let our enemies lick their wounds. We are now unstoppable. Another day will come.'

He issued a command, and his dragon left the formation. A second command made the creature put on speed, and a moment later the rest of the red dragons fell in around him.

Palemon swooped down toward the sea. He flew over his new fleet, smiling in grim satisfaction.

54

Chloe climbed the familiar steps leading up to her father's villa. She couldn't believe how little had changed. Her favorite rose bush was blooming. A step was cracked that hadn't been before. There was a new statue on the side of the winding path, a life-sized pony carved out of a single block of white marble. She smiled. Sophia had always liked horses.

She gazed up at the villa as she neared. For a time it was occupied by Nilus, but now someone new was living at the home of Aristocles, who had been one of Phalesia's longest-serving first consuls, a man who lived on in memory if not in life.

Reaching the terrace, she stopped for a moment and looked around. The stone rail needed cleaning, but the paved floor was swept. The views of the city were still breathtaking, and she could clearly see the temples, the library, the lyceum, and the agora. The marble columns at the cliff-top Temple of Aldus made her remember the moment when she'd first discovered that Dion had eldran blood. Even the terrace itself carried memories: she'd experienced an earthquake that nearly killed her sister while standing in this very spot.

Finally Chloe dispelled the memories. She tore her eyes away from the view and walked toward the open doorway, leaning in as she peered inside. 'Hello?'

She heard a shriek that made her smile. Then suddenly her sister was running at her with arms open, grabbing hold of her tightly. 'You're back!'

'Of course.' Chloe returned Sophia's hug. 'I promised you I would be.'

Sophia looked well; her wounds had healed and she was no longer clad in a novice's uniform, instead wearing an embroidered silk chiton with a pale-blue ribbon in her hair, the color of the sky.

She dragged Chloe inside, leading her by the hand. A moment later a tall, broad-shouldered man with close-cropped curly hair and craggy skin appeared at the entrance to the kitchen, his hands dusty with flour. Amos looked abashed at his own palms as he quickly wiped them on his expensive silk tunic.

'Like a pair of twins,' he said, grinning and shaking his head.

'Uncle Amos! Chloe's twice my size,' Sophia protested.

'Perhaps not that different, Sophia. You're growing more quickly than you know. Chloe, please, come in, come in . . .' Amos looked anxious. 'You know I don't have to invite you in? This is your home too.' He glanced at his hands. 'We were making meal cakes,' he said, smiling apologetically. 'If I'd known you were coming . . .'

'I wanted to surprise you both,' Chloe said, returning his smile.

'Dion and Isobel?' Amos asked. Sophia bit her lip, facing Chloe as she waited for her to respond.

'Dion was well enough, last I saw him,' Chloe said, choosing her words carefully. 'In truth, I have a long story to tell.'

'Uncle Amos, can Chloe have her old room again?' Sophia asked.

'Of course she can.'

Despite Amos's protestations, Chloe wrapped her arms around him, ignoring all the flour. She then held him back to stare into his face. 'I almost forgot. Congratulations on your appointment, First Consul.'

'Please, don't call me that,' Amos said. He sobered as he looked around the reception. 'In this house, it's your father who will always be first consul.'

361

'I can feel him here too,' Chloe said sadly. 'I keep expecting him to come in and start waving his arms, ranting on about one vote or another.'

'Listen, Chloe . . .' Amos swore under his breath, shaking his head. 'I've never had a way with words . . .' He tried again. 'I always promised your father that I would look after his daughters, and it is a promise I will give my heart and soul to fulfill. If . . . If it's all right with you, I'll raise Sophia, and I'd like you to live here too.'

'Please, Chloe,' Sophia said.

A sudden surge of emotion struck Chloe without warning. She put a hand over her mouth, fighting the urge to cry.

'Chloe?' Sophia asked. 'Are you all right?'

She forced the words out. 'I'm fine.'

Chloe had been cursed with magic, but it was magic that enabled her to save Liana and Dion. After breaking the spell, her raging power had caught up with her, but on the way home, using the things she'd learned at Athos, meditating constantly, she'd managed to tame it once again.

For months she'd been trapped on Athos, but despite not finishing her training, she knew she'd done the right thing to leave to help the people she loved.

Now she had a home once again. She had people who cared for her. She had a homeland to defend.

'Chloe?' Sophia asked again.

She cleared her throat, steadying herself. 'I'm just glad to see you both so happy.'

'Listen, Chloe,' Amos said. 'You look like more than anything you need to rest. Have dinner with us, and when you're ready, you can tell us what happened.'

Chloe nodded.

With another smile, Amos returned to preparing the meal, and Chloe gazed around the reception, surprised that it looked the same as it always had. It was she who felt different.

'I like your ribbon,' she said to Sophia, who touched it with a self-conscious smile. Something occurred to Chloe, and she raised her voice so Amos could hear her. 'What about Nilus? Did you ever find him?'

'We're still looking,' Amos called back. 'But never fear, we'll find him, one way or another.'

Chloe was surprised when Sophia took her arm. Meeting her eyes intently, Sophia spoke in an undertone. 'When Zachary was here for Dion's wedding, I told him about Father, and he offered to help me find Nilus.'

Chloe wasn't surprised; Zachary and Aristocles had been close friends. She put a hand to her mouth. 'And?'

'We don't have to worry about Nilus anymore.'

Far away in Sarsica, in a region of vineyards and undulating landscape, another villa sat on a hill, overlooking the rows of carefully manicured plants trailing from one stake to another.

Parmella, a matronly servant – Nilus's only servant – checked on the living room, apprehension gnawing at her stomach. She watched her master, unseen and unnoticed. As he often did, Nilus was standing at the window, admiring the view as he drank wine from a golden goblet.

She knew him well enough to know that he was about to run out of wine. True to form, he set the cup down on the nearby table and lifted the earthenware jug, tilting the mouth toward the goblet.

'Parmella,' he called out, frowning when he saw that the jug was nearly empty. 'Parmella!'

'What is it, Lord?' Parmella came forward.

Nilus rapped the side of the jug with his fingertip. 'Get me more wine,' he said. 'Enough to last the evening.'

She nodded. 'Of course, Lord.'

Taking the jug, Parmella left the kitchen to trudge to the store room at the rear of the house. Meanwhile Nilus returned his gaze to the distant rows of grape vines and the slaves moving slowly from one to the next as they tended the stems.

Entering the store room, Parmella's chest was heaving as she set the jug down on a bench. She reminded herself that she was now a rich woman, able to enjoy an early retirement. Nilus was an exile, a traitor and murderer. Tension formed in her neck and shoulders as with shaking hands she reached up to a shelf.

The small wooden box was hidden behind the jars of olives and cheese. Parmella kept her ears pricked, listening intently for the sound of footsteps as she took the box and set it down beside the empty wine jug. It was tied with a blue ribbon, the color of the sky, and fastened with a dainty bow.

She knew she had to move swiftly now, but fear was causing her fingers to fumble with the ribbon. Finally she removed the lid. For a long moment she stared at the box's contents, transfixed by the sight of the black powder inside.

'Parmella!' Nilus called from the living room.

Blood roaring in her ears, Parmella picked up the box and tilted its contents into the wine jug. She tapped it against the jug's mouth, making sure all of the powder entered the vessel. She then put the lid on the box and slid it back into its hiding place on the shelf.

'Parmella!'

She took the jug to the barrel and filled it with wine. Red liquid splashed into the container, wetting her trembling hands as she struggled with something she'd done a thousand times. When the jug was full, she set it down on the bench and wiped her hands with a nearby rag.

She took the jug and returned to the reception. Nilus was still standing at the window. He scowled at her.

'What took you so long?'

Fortunately he wasn't the type to notice her drawn face.

'I'm sorry, Lord.'

He looked pointedly at his empty goblet, and Parmella fought to keep her hands steady as she filled it. Immediately he lifted the goblet and tilted it back, drinking a long swallow.

'Well?' He glared at her. 'You can go.'

'Yes, Lord.'

Parmella set down the jug and trudged away, but rather than leave the reception completely, she hung back near the hallway leading to the store room. She watched as Nilus contemplated his vineyards. As always, he drank quickly, muttering under his breath.

She didn't know whether she was afraid that it would happen, or that it wouldn't.

But then Nilus suddenly staggered. He put his goblet down on the table and raised a hand to his temple.

Parmella approached him once again. 'Is everything all right, Lord?'

He turned to face her, his expression suddenly stricken. He took great gulps of air. His face was steadily turning white.

'Wha—?'

His knees gave out from under him and he collapsed, sprawling on top of the table, knocking the empty goblet onto its side. He stared at Parmella as she came closer until she was standing over him. He toppled onto his back.

She knew she had made a promise. It was important that she said these next words.

'I am to give you a message,' she said. 'This is for Aristocles.'

Nilus twitched and shuddered as he looked up at her.

The name of his old friend was the last sound he ever heard.

55

It was late in the evening and Chloe stood at the top of the sloped embankment, staring out to sea. The full moon was just beginning to rise, casting a glistening silver shimmer on the water. She kept her ears carefully pricked. They had arranged to meet at this time.

She watched the breaking waves that hissed as they struck the white pebbled shore. The sound was soothing. The salty breeze tossed her dark hair around her face, but this wind was gentle, nothing like the winds she'd experienced before.

She smiled. The home of Aristocles would be a happy place once again, a place where the new first consul and his adoptive niece would get covered in flour making meal cakes and find strength and purpose from each other. Important consuls would throng to the villa for banquets and discussions. Amos would finally let go of his guilt at failing Aristocles. And if the shifting tides put Phalesia onto a war footing, there would be no better man to lead.

She cocked her head when she heard a sound.

It was the sound of sails catching the wind, or wings snapping in a final descent. She glanced up, but the sky was empty, and she wondered if she'd heard it at all. But then she whirled and her smile broadened.

Liana was walking toward her; they'd agreed to make this rendezvous. But she wasn't alone. With her were two other eldren, both tall and lean, although one was old, with a crescent scar on his cheek, and the other wore a crown of laurel leaves on his head.

'It is good to see you, dear one,' Zachary said.

'Zachary!' Chloe cried.

The first to reach her, he opened his arms and held her tight. Finally he released her, and she turned to embrace Liana. Then, despite Eiric's protests, Chloe even pulled him into a hug. She heard Liana laugh.

'Eiric,' Chloe said. She looked around. 'Is Dion with you?'

Eiric shook his head. 'He had to return to Xanthos.' His face turned grim. 'Palemon is alive. Dion must prepare his people for war.'

'Palemon's alive?' Chloe's stomach clenched at the news. But she also felt disappointment sink into her chest. Dion had other things on his mind than her.

Glancing at Liana, Chloe knew her friend could read her easily. 'You know that Dion needs time,' Liana said softly.

'Which brings us to our purpose here,' Eiric said. 'Dion said he can help us broker peace with the other nations. If we are to fight together, we will need alliances. But Dion has his own concerns with his kingdom.' He met her eyes. 'Chloe . . . Will you help us? Will you plead our case, and bring peace between humans and eldren, as you have done before?'

Sweeping her gaze over the group, Chloe saw Zachary, Liana, and Eiric all looking at her expectantly, filled with hope.

'War is coming,' Zachary said. 'Whether we want it to or not.'

'Please, Chloe?' Liana asked.

Chloe smiled. 'You are my friends. All of you. You don't even need to ask.'

Dion sat at a high table in his palace's banqueting hall, his uncle and adviser seated across from him. There were two others at the table: Finn, his master of coin, and Roxana, the commander of his fleet. Together they leaned over a map spread out on its surface.

'So Kargan made it back to Lamara,' Glaukos said.

'He did,' Dion said. 'We spoke before we parted, and we've pledged to join forces.'

'Poor man,' Roxana said. 'He lost half his fleet.'

'There is still plenty of fight left in him,' Dion said, shaking his head as he remembered Kargan's fury. He turned to Finn. 'What is the state of our finances?'

'Strong,' Finn said.

'And our fleet?' he asked Roxana.

'With Ilea's losses . . . ?' She spread her hands. 'We now possess the most powerful naval force in the world.'

'Dion . . .' Glaukos corrected himself. 'Sire . . . What of the eldren?'

'I'm certain we can broker peace between Sindara and Tanus.' Dion met his uncle's eyes. 'Eiric will fight with us.'

Glaukos's jaw was clenched. He looked at Dion's face, and Dion knew what he was seeing: bruises and scars, eyes filled with pain and darkness. 'We will wreak vengeance on them, lad, for what they did to you.'

Dion nodded. He'd learned something, ever since he'd first visited Malakai to discover Palemon's intentions. After inheriting a kingdom in turmoil, he'd been consumed with bringing peace to the Maltherean Sea. Nikolas had been eager to seek out battle. Dion had seen himself as different.

But there were times when peace wasn't possible. His nation's security was the very reason for developing alliances, wealth, and power.

'War is coming,' he said. 'We must be ready to face it.'

ACKNOWLEDGMENTS

My sincere gratitude to the team at 47North for being wonderful to work with at all stages of the publishing process, with particular thanks to my editor, Emilie, for tireless dedication and support.

Thanks go to Ian, for editorial insight and diligence, and to my amazing readers: Amanda, Juliet, Margaret, Nicole, Danielle, Vanessa, Amy, Hannah, Jessica, Harley, Lydia, Constance, Michelle, Shuh, Erin, Marie, Kimberley, and Kristin.

Thanks to all of you who have reached out to me and taken the time to post reviews of my books.

Finally thanks must go to my wife, Alicia. Your shining light banishes the deepest darkness. Your love inspires me every day.

ABOUT THE AUTHOR

James Maxwell grew up in the scenic Bay of Islands, New Zealand, and was educated in Australia. Devouring fantasy and science-fiction classics from an early age, his love for books translated to a passion for writing, which he began at the age of eleven.

Inspired by the natural beauty around him but also by a strong interest in history, he decided in his twenties to see the world. He relocated to London and then to Thailand, Mexico, Austria, and Malta, developing a lifelong obsession with travel. It was while living in Thailand that he seriously took up writing again, producing his first full-length novel, *Enchantress*, the first of four titles in his internationally bestselling Evermen Saga.

Copper Chain is the third novel in his highly anticipated new series, The Shifting Tides, following *Silver Road*.

When he isn't writing or traveling, James enjoys sailing, snowboarding, classical guitar, and French cooking.